Spellbinding Tales of
Terror and Romance
Signet Double Gothics:

The White Peacock
&
Shadow Over Grove House

More Gothics from SIGNET

The White Peacock
and
Shadow Over
Grove House

by Mary Linn Roby

A SIGNET BOOK

NEW AMERICAN LIBRARY

TIMES MIRROR

Originally appeared in paperback as separate volumes published by The New American Library. A hardcover edition of
The White Peacock was published by Hawthorn Books, Inc.,
and simultaneously in Canada by Prentice-Hall of Canada
Limited.

SIGNET, SIGNET CLASSICS, MENTOR, PLUME AND
MERIDIAN BOOKS
*are published by The New American Library, Inc.,
1301 Avenue of the Americas, New York, New York 10019*

First Printing (Double Gothic Edition), January, 1978

1 2 3 4 5 6 7 8 9

PRINTED IN THE UNITED STATES OF AMERICA

The White Peacock

Dedicated to Katharine Kidde

CHAPTER

I

"You realize, I hope, that my aunt won't be an easy person to deal with," Marian Russell said, maneuvering the red Austin skillfully through a village square lined with canvas-covered stalls and crowded with peasants. "She's been an expatriate for years. Portugal is her home now in every sense, but she still manages to remain a fine example of vintage British eccentricity. I'm only trying to say that you shouldn't take her too seriously."

I murmured something, uncomfortably aware that I was too tired to listen properly to what this woman was saying. My plane had landed in Lisbon that morning, and I had tried to see too much in the few hours before I was to leave for the northern part of the country. I had eaten green Portuguese oysters at the Floresta and walked about the harbor, watching gaily dressed women carrying baskets of silverfish on their heads as they climbed barefoot up the precipitous streets that led from the harbor. I had seen the magnificent bronze equestrian statue of King John I in the Black Horse Square and heard the screaming of the peacocks on the grounds of the Castilo, which looms over the capital city. And in the afternoon at five I had wandered into an arena on the outskirts of the city and seen a young matador nearly impaled on the horns of an angry bull. There had been too many new sights and sounds for a single day, and now I was reacting as any tourist might react. The only problem was that I was not a tourist.

"It slows us down, having to drive through these villages," the woman beside me said. "Unfortunately there's no other route to Alcombra. That's one of the things my aunt likes best about the estate. It's so isolated that not even her family can come to see her often."

The bitterness in her voice roused me. Half turning on the seat, I saw her profile: sharp-nosed, imperious, her deep-set eyes half visible from the side under thick dark glasses. She had, I suspected, once been beautiful, but now the skin of her face hung in tiny loose folds, like crumpled paper. She was about fifty, I guessed, although she looked older in the harsh blazing light of the afternoon. She had done everything that a woman can do to make herself younger. Her hair was skillfully tinted, clinging like a soft cap to her small head. Her beautifully cut silk dress clung to a figure as slim as a girl's. But one could not escape the grotesquery of that crushed face. I had never met her before she had picked me up at the Hotel Aviz as had been prearranged. That had been only half an hour before, and already I was aware that she was a deeply unhappy woman.

We were driving out of the market town now. The road was a steep alley that wove its way between narrow stone houses jammed into the hillside about which the town was built. From the upper windows brightly colored laundry hung like flags on lines that stretched across the cobbled street. Old women in black pressed back against the walls as we passed, eyeing us curiously. A peasant leading a mule up the narrow road before us gave up the right of way reluctantly, and through the open windows I could hear him shouting something after us. Still the road wound up until suddenly I saw a castle looming against the sky. There seemed to be castles everywhere in this country, pushing their walls out of the boulders as though they were an extension of the stone itself.

"Do you live with your aunt at Alcombra?" I asked her, aware that I should say something. If it were night, it would have been easier to close my eyes and doze surreptitiously. As it was, I had to keep myself alert any way that I could, even if it meant asking questions about relationships that, in a sense, did not concern me. The London solicitor who had made the arrangements for me to come to Alcombra had made it quite clear that it was the wish of the owner that the inventory be completed as quickly as possible, and that to facilitate this, I would be left quite alone to get about it.

The woman beside me laughed harshly. "The only people my aunt trusts are the people she hires. When you pay someone, you can tell them what to do—when to smile, what to say—and when you don't want them around anymore, you can tell them to go away, and they'll go. Servants aren't really people, according to my aunt. They're extensions of her ego, and she likes that. Oh, she really likes that."

She broke off and turned to stare at me through the two sheets of dark glass that covered her eyes. "Did you notice," she said, "how I managed to avoid answering your question directly? That's one of the many little things my aunt loathes about me. I'm inclined to hedge. The fact is that I don't live with her. She wouldn't have me, even if I'd agree to come. I'm only at Alcombra now because she's dying."

I stared at her incredulously. "But I was told——"

"You were told whatever she wanted you to be told,

and no more. You can count on that. Give me a cigarette, will you? You'll find a pack in my handbag."

The bag, like everything else about this woman, was expensive and in good taste. Distracted for the moment, I fumbled inside it for the cigarette, pushing aside a gold compact, a vial of perfume, a soft linen handkerchief with thickly embroidered edges, and a wallet fat with bills.

"Light it for me, will you?" the woman said sharply as I pulled out the pack. "I'm not that familiar with this wretched road."

We were high above the village now. The brown-tiled rooftops sprawled under the golden fingers of the sinking sun. Huge boulders jutted from the almost sheer drop at the side of the road. To our right rose the battlements of the castle. The woman beside me took the cigarette and leaned over the wheel, her eyes intent on the twisting, narrow road. And then, suddenly, we reached the peak, and in the distance in front of us there stretched a broad plain spotted with groves of olive trees and cork oaks. Beyond them a broad river cut a blue gash in the earth.

"That's the Mondego," Marian Russell said in a low voice. "Beyond it is another river, the Douro. You can see the Douro from Alcombra. This part of Portugal is one of the most beautiful places in the world. Sometimes I think that if I didn't hate her so much, I'd never want to leave it. But I'm a bit old for that sort of romantic nonsense, aren't I? A bit old for a good many things, according to her."

I would have made the monologue into a dialogue if I had known how. Obviously this woman hated her aunt. Obviously, too, she did not care who knew it—or, perhaps, for reasons of her own, she wanted to make it perfectly clear to me from the start what her position in the household was.

"Her solicitor told me that she was ill," I said, "but I didn't realize that she was dying."

"That's the reason that she feels she has to have the collection inventoried at once," Marian Russell said in a tight voice. A battered station wagon hove into sight as we rounded a corkscrew turn, and I heard her swear under her breath as she wrenched the car as close as she could to the boulders that lined our side of the narrow road. The station wagon lurched past us in a cloud of dust, and for a moment I thought that it would surely plunge into the gulf below. I caught my breath.

"She could have sent the chauffeur to pick you up," the woman beside me muttered, bending over the wheel and edging the car around another hairpin turn. "She knows how I hate driving on these roads. It's her idea of a subtle kind of punishment."

"Punishment for what?" There was something about the constant complaint in her voice that was beginning to annoy me.

"For coming to Alcombra. We all came, you see—as soon as we heard. All of what's left of the so-called family. Like vultures. That's what she calls us: vultures waiting to pick her bones."

Now the road plunged down toward the plain below in a long silver line, and I felt myself relax.

"You're a good deal younger than I thought you would be," Marian Russell said, changing the subject with a disconcerting rapidity as she pressed her foot harder on the accelerator. "Is it true that you have your own gallery in London?"

"Yes," I said, relieved that we had abandoned the topic of vultures. "It was my father's. He died two years ago."

"And you're a specialist on Iberian art?"

"It's what I deal in primarily, yes."

My companion flicked her cigarette out the window. "What made you agree to come here and do the inventory?" she demanded. "Did she offer you a sizable commission? You don't have to answer that if you don't want. It's probably unpardonably rude of me to ask, but you'll find that our family is always interested in the sub-ject of money—particularly money that we won't be inheriting."

It was becoming hotter and hotter as we plunged down toward the plain. Even the mimosa beside the road seemed to shrivel in the heat. Now that we had nearly reached the bottom of the mountain, the road veered to the west, and the red glow of the sinking sun seemed to burn my face. I pulled my long hair off my neck, coiled it into a bun, and dug in my handbag for a clasp—deliberately delaying. Certainly I did not want to tell this woman the real reason why I had come here. It remained to sort over in my mind other possible reasons that she might accept. As for the question concerning the commission, she was right. I had no intention of answering that. From what she had said it was clear that she and the other relatives would begrudge even a normal commission, which was all I was receiving.

"Lady Stewart's collection is well known," I said slowly. "Anyone who's interested in Iberian art would be inter-ested in examining it. As far as I know, no one has been allowed to see it for the past thirty years, at least. There are rumors, but that's all. That sort of situation was bound to intrigue anyone in my field."

We had reached the flatness of the plain now. In a grove of cork oaks men worked at stripping the bark from the thick branches. Around the base of the trees, oats bent red-gold heads to the sun. Oxen pulling carts full of drying cork lumbered along the side of the road. There was some-thing soothing about the peacefulness of the scene. It was a sharp contrast to Lisbon, and an even sharper contrast, I guessed, to what would await me at Alcombra.

"I hope," Marian Russell said in a voice sharp with amusement, "that you didn't delude yourself into think-ing that my aunt would let you have first pick of a few things. I mean, you aren't laboring under the misconception that she's going to do the sensible thing and sell the lot?"

"I understood that she intended to turn Alcombra into a museum," I said, stung by the implication of what this woman was suggesting. "I was told that nothing was to be sold."

"That's the way the situation stands now!" Marian Russell snapped. "Obviously it's an insane idea. The will can't be allowed to stand."

We turned to look at one another at the same moment. Above and below the dark glasses her face sagged in unattractive lines. I wondered how long it had been since she had laughed. Perhaps it was unfair to blame her. Perhaps she had had good reason to let bitterness consume her. For that matter, so had I.

"You'd rather I wasn't as frank, wouldn't you?" she asked, turning back to the road. "I suspect that you aren't particularly enthusiastic about self-revelation, Miss Haverlock—either your own or anyone else's—but you're going to have to take sides as soon as you reach Alcombra. You might as well know that in advance."

There was an arbitrary way about the way she treated me that infuriated me. I did not want to be analyzed, particularly not by someone who had known me a little over an hour. It had been difficult enough for me to have let Philip dissect me emotionally, to examine all my responses with microscopic care. In the end I had not been able to cope with that. Never again would I allow anyone to understand me as well as he had, because I knew now that there was no greater humiliation than in being understood.

"I don't know exactly what you mean by taking sides, Miss Russell," I said sharply. "It doesn't matter to me what you tell or don't tell me. I'm here to do an inventory, and that's all."

"In other words, you're my aunt's hireling," she taunted me.

"Yes," I said. "That's as good a word as any other. Why, what do you want me to be? Some sort of moral arbiter?"

She had not expected the attack, and I saw her hands tighten on the wheel. "Now you're angry," she said in a low voice. "I seem to have a certain flair for antagonizing people."

We had reached the banks of the river now. From the distance, perhaps because it reflected the sky, the river seemed blue, but now it lay before us like a strip of brown satin, skirted with yellow sandbanks. We crossed an arched stone bridge that spanned the sluggish, reed-spotted waters at a narrow point and found ourselves speeding past an orange grove, the ripe fruit hanging like small suns among the lush green leaves.

"I suppose I should apologize," the woman beside me said in a low voice. "I can't expect you to spend your life waiting for something, and then at the last minute to see all your hopes disappear in thin air. All that's left is the hatred, you see, and I can't bear what that's doing to me. What it's doing to all of us."

We were crossing the Seira da Gralheira range when the brakes of the Austin gave way. We had driven in silence since we had passed the Mondego, crossing fertile plains filled with prosperous looking vineyards, through an ancient town surrounded by chestnut trees, crossing the Douro over a curiously arched medieval bridge. The woman beside me seemed to see nothing but the road in front of her. Her mouth was grim. Obviously she was angry, although whether with me or with herself I was not certain. There had been times in my life when I, too, had rushed into intimacy too soon, as she had done. It was obvious that she was in no emotional condition to make valid decisions. Her nerves were brittle. I did not have to know the details to understand why. She had obviously waited for a long time, with the promise of her aunt's wealth glowing in the future. It was the sort of prospect which might have softened the blow of personal disappointments, such as her fading beauty. And now there were no more prospects at a time in her life when she needed them most. I knew enough about her aunt's affairs to be certain that there would be little set aside for the heirs to divide, despite the rumored value of her collection.

The solicitor who had contacted me in London was efficient but scarcely a master of conciseness. "Lady Stewart always makes her wishes very well known," he had told me, tapping his pencil against his goateed chin as he leaned across his desk, his spectacled blue eyes taking in every detail about me with obvious relish. "She has not lived in England for thirty years," he continued, his thin voice beating a staccato of sound against the silence of the dusty office. "However, our firm has continued to serve her through the years, and I do not think I am boasting when I say that we understand her particular—er—viewpoints, some of which are not absolutely conventional, let us say."

He had gone on then to tell me about her plans to establish a museum at Alcombra. "She knows, of course, that she has a limited time to take care of these details," he had said, and then he had colored and gone on to the subject of what would be demanded from me. I understood now the slip he had made. He had nearly told me that the old woman was about to die, but for some reason he must have been directed not to disclose that fact.

"Lady Stewart has spent her entire adult life collecting paintings and objets d'art, as I'm sure you know," the solicitor had told me. "At our insistence she has always kept a certain reserve of capital on hand, but every other shilling has gone into the upkeep of the estate in Portugal and the purchase of items of value. Actually, very little money has gone into Alcombra, in the sense that the estate takes care of itself. It possesses one of the largest vineyards in the Douro country, you see. Alcombra port is well known." He pressed his lips together as though savoring a remembered taste. "Lady Stewart is kind enough to send along several bottles every year at Christmas time. Not that she takes much interest in the vineyards and the bottling and all the rest of it. That was her husband's contribution. Now he's dead, of course, but there's an excellent manager, I understand, and the business carries on. Ah, yes, it carries on."

The light in his eyes had faded, and he sat isolated with his own thoughts until I tapped his hand to remind him of my presence. It had all been rather amusing, or perhaps I was simply trying hard to make everything in my life seem amusing. The idea of getting away from London for a few weeks had been especially tempting. Philip and I had the same friends. It was an effort to keep from meeting him accidentally. I had recently taken on an experienced assistant who was perfectly capable of keeping the gallery on Bond Street open. The commission that Lady Stewart offered was not particularly substantial, but there had been the temptation to examine the hoard that this legendary woman had spent a lifetime collecting. I had not lied when I had told Marian Russell that that had been my motive for coming. It was simply that there were other reasons as well—deeply personal reasons—and I would have to explain all of that to her if I were to make her understand why I did not want to become involved in the internecine struggles that were apparently going on at Alcombra.

So I had remained silent as we had driven through the fading sunlight, the road rising steadily through pine-shadowed hills. We had stopped once, just as the sun was setting, at an inn, a long, low stone building with pastel-shaded walls of pink and cream, the windows bordered with boxes of scarlet geraniums. Men in rusty black sat sipping wine at outdoor tables, and children with great bunches of poppies in their arms had surrounded us as we had ordered, offering the scarlet flowers for sale. It had been as peaceful as a scene painted by Patinir, but the tension between me and the chic, worn-faced woman who was my companion had been too great to break with casual words. I knew that she thought me cold, disinterested. I pitied her, but I did not want to become involved in anyone else's life—not now. I had come here for one purpose—the inventory—and I was determined that that was all there was to be to it.

I was dozing when I suddenly became aware that something was wrong. It was night, and the headlights of the little car thrust thin saffron fingers into the darkness, illuminating a narrow mountain road that seemed to plunge precipitously into a black void into which we were moving with frightening speed.

"It's the brakes," Marian said in a shrill voice. "They won't take!"

In the light of the dashboard I saw her wrench the wheel to the right as we approached a curve. I was thrown violently against the door. The moment seemed to suspend itself in time.

"Pump the brake pedal!" I cried.

She must have done what I told her to do, because the car began to slow. At the same moment the road seemed to level. There was a slight rise ahead. Beyond it lay nothing, and I knew that this was only a pause in the descent. We had to stop the car now, before the top of the rise.

"Pull on the emergency brake!" I said.

The woman beside me did not respond. I saw her bend over the wheel, staring into the beams of light. She saw, as I had, that in a moment we would be headed downward again, and yet she seemed to be incapable of responding. Reaching out, I pulled back the stick of the emergency brake with all my strength. The car came to a screeching halt, throwing both of us violently forward. I felt my head strike the dashboard, and then for a moment I was aware of nothing but the heavy warmth of the night air, and the silence.

Pulling myself back onto my seat, I turned and saw the woman beside me slumped over the wheel.

"Are you all right?" I asked.

She made no response. At first I had the absurd thought that she was stubbornly determined to maintain her angry silence, but it was not simply that she did not speak. She did not move either, and I was aware of a tiny thorn-prick of fear. Until that moment everything had happened too fast for me to be aware of fear—if fear was there—but now, when the real danger seemed to be past, I was afraid.

I took her gently by the shoulders and pulled her back from the wheel. There was not enough light, and it was only when her head was against the back of the seat that I could see that she was unconscious, her eyes closed, a trickle of blood running like a black line across her right cheek.

I have never been particularly good in emergencies. My mind seems to stop functioning. My only instinct is to find someone to help. And that was what I did then, even though reason would have told me that I was not likely to find anyone on the side of what appeared to be an uninhabited mountain at that time of night.

The futility of what I was doing struck me as soon as I stood beside the car, staring past the headlights at what I knew must be the edge of the sheer cliff that rimmed the road. And yet what else could I do? Even to move her would be risky. I had no way of knowing if she had suffered internal injuries, and yet I would have to pull her onto the other seat if I wanted to risk driving the car down what was left of the torturous road. Perhaps with the emergency brake half on, I could make it, even though it would burn out the brake linings. Still, I did not know this place. I was as likely to drive the car off the edge of the road as to reach the bottom of the mountain safely.

And once at the bottom, how could I be sure that there would be houses, a village? I did not even know how far we were from Alcombra.

The only other alternative besides remaining there, doing what I could for her and waiting for a car, which might not come for hours, was obviously to go on down the road on foot and try to find a house, a phone. Or perhaps it would be better to go back. Because I had been asleep until the moment when the brakes had begun to fail, I had no idea what we had passed as we had come up the mountain. For all I knew there might be a village somewhere behind me, its lights hidden by the boulders whose bulk merged with the night sky.

Certain that anything I might do would be wrong, I turned and saw a tiny pinpoint of light flare in the darkness above me. In the same moment there came the sound of rocks falling. One of them struck the car. I cried out, startled. Silence answered me. And then I became aware that something or someone was sliding down the rock surface toward the back of the car. I clasped my hands to my mouth and saw the shape of a man emerge on the road. Slowly he came toward me. It was not until he was beside me that I could see his face, fractured by the glow of the headlights. He was young, and there was nothing in his face of the square Celtic quality of the Portuguese. His blond hair was cut low on his forehead, the eyes deep set. He was wearing slacks and a light pullover sweater, and a knapsack was strapped to his broad shoulders.

"My God," he said in English, with a strong British accent, "I didn't know that anyone was here. Look, I can see that I've frightened you. I'm sorry. I was lighting a candle at a shrine up there—no special reason, but it amuses me. I often stop and do that when I'm traveling at night."

I drew my hands away from my mouth and nodded, aware of a great surge of relief. I knew the sort of shrine he meant. Tiny octagonal chapels sheltering stone figures

showing scenes from the Passion dotted the mountainsides.
When we had crossed the Douro, I had seen a woman in
black kneeling at one of them. It was, I thought, a strange
thing for a young hitchhiker to do at night—or in the
day, for that matter—but there was something about the
openness of this man's face which reassured me.

The stranger smiled. "I assume," he said, "you didn't
stop up here for the view. What's wrong? Car trouble?"

"The brakes gave way," I said and found that my voice
was hoarse, as though I had not used it in a long time. I
moistened my lips. "We nearly went off the road."

"We? Do you mean that your husband's gone for help?"

"No. The woman I'm with. . . . She's inside the car. I
pulled on the emergency brake to stop us, and she must
have struck her head against the wheel. She's unconscious.
I didn't know what. . . ."

He was no longer listening to me. Unloosening his knapsack, he threw it on the ground and slid into the front
seat of the car.

"She's still out," I heard him say. "Not much bleeding.
It feels as though there's a cut on her forehead. Listen.
Reach inside my sack. There's a flashlight in there. And a
flask of water."

I did what he told me, awkwardly, discovering that my
hands were trembling. There was a book in the knapsack
and a shirt. A package of sandwiches. I found the flashlight at the bottom and the flask. By the time I handed
them to him, my hands were steady.

"All right," he said. "Now, take this handkerchief and
pour some water on it."

He kept on talking as I uncapped the flask and tilted it
over the square of white linen. Through the open door I
could see him bending over Marian, shining the flashlight
on her. "She'll be all right, I think," I heard him say.
"She couldn't have struck her head very hard, or she would
have had more of a concussion. Here, give me that handkerchief. That's right. I'll just put it on her forehead,

folded so. That's right. I don't suppose you have any wine. Brandy. Odd sort of thing to be without when you need it in this part of the country, but I don't suppose two women traveling alone. . . . Is she your mother?"

The question startled me. Despite her lined face, I did not associate the intense woman slumped against the seat with motherhood.

"No," I muttered. "She's—she's a friend. An acquaintance really. But I can't bear to think of anything serious happening to her. I mean, it was my fault. I pulled the emergency."

"You didn't have much choice, did you?" the stranger said. "Not if the brakes are gone. It's better to have her concussed than both of you dead."

The narrowness of our escape had not struck me with full force until that moment. My legs suddenly threatened not to support me, and I leaned against the car.

"Look here," the young man said. "I don't like this. She should be coming to by now. How long had she been unconscious before I came along?"

"Not more than a few minutes," I murmured.

"Then this must have been the car that passed me up there," he mused. "Driving like a bat, she was. Don't think she saw me. I had to jump out of the way. It was your headlights that picked out the shrine for me. Does she always drive like that?"

"I don't know," I said. "We only met today. Perhaps the brakes had just begun to give way. I was asleep. But that doesn't matter now. What if she's seriously hurt? We've got to get her to a doctor."

"You don't know this part of the country, do you?" the young man said, turning to me. "The nearest town large enough to have a doctor must be twenty-five miles away, and the roads are like this most of the way."

"It's better than staying here," I said. And then, remembering: "But we can't drive the car anyway, not with the brakes gone."

"We'll be all right if we put it in first gear," he said. "Do you want me to drive? We'll get her in the back seat. You can sit in there with her and keep putting water on her forehead. That's all we can do."

He was right. It was all we could do. I watched him move the woman into the back seat as gently as though she were a child.

"That's right," he said. "You sit in that corner. Here, put her head on your lap."

Marian groaned.

"You see," he said. "She's going to be all right. You don't have to look like that."

Leaning across the seat, he put his hand on my arm. "It's going to be all right," he said. "You'll see. Look, before we start off, I'd better introduce myself. I'm David Ashor."

I tried to smile. "I'm Irene Haverlock."

"It's a great pleasure, senhora." He tugged at his forelock as I had seen peasants do. I felt a warm glow of gratitude. He was trying hard to make me relax, and, to a degree, he was succeeding.

"Now, one other thing," he said briskly. "The closest town is behind us, and that means negotiating the rest of this road and then turning around and coming back up it again. Where were you two going, anyway?"

"It's a country estate," I said. "Not too far from here, I think. It's called Alcombra."

For a moment he did not speak. In the light of the dashboard I saw his face suddenly grow set. The smile faded.

"Life is full of little surprises, isn't it?" he said, turning away from me, his voice grim. "Perhaps I should have guessed. As it happens, I'm on my way to Alcombra, too."

It was not until David Ashor had worked the car laboriously down the mountainside in first gear that he spoke again, and then the note of reassurance had returned to his voice.

"It's only about ten miles now to Alcombra," he said, "and on a straightaway we can make better time. Has she shown any signs of coming to?"

I pressed the damp cloth closer to the forehead of the woman whose head was cradled in my lap. "No," I said, "but she's breathing evenly, as though she were asleep."

The car picked up speed. In the glare of the headlights I could just see the even pattern of a narrow road, bordered with pine trees. The air coming through the open windows was cool, and I sensed that the descent from the mountain had not been as great as the original climb. We were, I thought, on some sort of plateau, apparently uninhabited. It was not so late that there would not be lights shining from houses if we were passing them. I felt a great sense of isolation, mixed with the ache of an anxiety that was not completely caused by what had happened to Marian Russell. There was exhaustion, too. I was tense enough so that it did not encompass me, but I felt it lurking inside. I did not want to think. I sensed that if I tried to examine the implications of what had happened, I might panic. And it was not the time for panic.

"Have you been to Alcombra before?" I asked the man in front of me. I did not want to be the one to ask questions, but I could not bear the silence.

"Many times," he said. "I should have explained. You see, I'm Lady Stewart's nephew—grandnephew, actually. She doesn't have what you'd call a strong family sense, but when I was a boy, I spent my vacations here. Partly because there was no other place to go. Partly because, I think, she wanted me."

I stared at the back of his head, bewildered. If both he and Marian Russell were who they claimed to be, how had it been that he had not appeared to recognize her? She had said that the family was descending on Alcombra like vultures. Was that his role, too? It did not seem to fit with what I had seen of his character, but then, people were seldom what they seemed to be. By this time I should have known that lesson by heart.

"What about you?" I heard him say. "Are you part of the family, too?"

"Wouldn't you know if I were?"

"Believe it or not, besides her stepson, William, I've met only one stray uncle who tried to force a visit on Aunt Lelia when I was staying there once. She sent him packing." He laughed. "The others either didn't try to come or were there when I wasn't. I don't know. Aunt Lelia always claimed it made her ill to think about her relatives, let alone discuss them."

It was an explanation of my unasked question—a rational answer, based on what I already knew of his great-aunt, Lady Stewart. And still I found myself wondering if the answer had not come a little too smoothly.

"If you're not a relative then, do you mind my asking who you are?"

"I suppose you could call me an art dealer," I said. "I have a small gallery in London."

He whistled through his teeth. "You mean my aunt is going to part with some of her collection? I don't believe it."

"No," I said. "I've come here to make an inventory. That's all."

"That surprises me, too," he said. "She's always talked about having that done, but she's always put it off, because, quite frankly, I don't think she likes to have strangers in the house. Particularly people who might realize the value of what she has there. I mean, she's talked a lot to me about making Alcombra a museum, but only after she's dead. As long as she's alive, she seems to want to keep it to herself. It's one of her little peculiarities."

When Marian Russell had spoken of her aunt's eccentricity, there had been an underlying viciousness in her voice, as though she would have rather referred to it as a manifestation of an unbalanced mind. With David it was obviously different. His tone was one of indulgence. It came to me, suddenly, that he might not know that Lady Stewart was ill.

"I think," I said carefully, "that your great-aunt is convinced now that the inventory ought to be done immediately."

"Why?" The road began to wind again, and I saw him grip the wheel tightly. His voice told me that he was only half concentrating on what we were saying.

"We aren't going up another mountain, are we?" I asked, catching my breath.

"In a way—but only halfway up. The house overlooks a valley. Don't worry. As long as we aren't going downhill, there's no danger. Can you tell me why the inventory has to be done now?"

"How long has it been since you've seen your great-aunt?" I hedged.

"Nearly a year now. I'm at Oxford, you see, doing graduate work. I have a fellowship. It's been quite a few months since I've been able to afford to take any time off. Then, instead of coming straight here, I took a walking tour of Spain. It's something I've always wanted to do."

"But she knows you're coming?"

"We don't correspond. Letters are almost as much of an intrusion as people as far as Aunt Lelia is concerned. Why? Has anything happened?"

"She's been ill apparently," I said.

"You mean she's dying?" He shot the words at me over his shoulder. It was almost as though he were challenging me.

"I—I don't know," I said. "I was told. . . ."

I broke off as the unconscious woman began to groan

again. I felt her eyelashes flicker under my fingers, and she began to roll her head back and forth in my lap.

"She's coming to," I murmured. "There, it's all right. Everything's all right."

"What happened?" I could scarcely hear her voice. I bent over her. Her face was a white oval in the darkness.

"You struck your head on the wheel when the car stopped," I said. "You've been unconscious."

Her hands pushed mine aside. "My head aches," she groaned. "I'm so sleepy."

She was not, I realized, alert enough to realize that the car was moving. She was dazed, able to think only about how she was feeling.

"Get her to sit up," I heard David say in a low voice. "If she's had a concussion, we shouldn't let her go to sleep."

If she heard his voice, she gave no sign. "Listen to me," I murmured, my lips close to her face. "Can you sit up?"

She did not answer me. I could not see whether her eyes were open or not. I brushed a finger over them and found them closed. Her breathing was heavy and slow.

"She's unconscious again," I said, "or sleeping."

"Push her into an upright position," David said crisply. "Try to get her to open her eyes. Put more water on her face. You have the flask, haven't you? Slap her if you have to, but keep her awake."

She was heavier than she looked, but I managed to make her sit up. The water did no good. I struck her once, gently, and then harder, stinging my fingers on her cheek. Her head lolled back against the cushions. There was no response.

"It's no good," I told him.

I heard him take a deep breath. "All right," he said. "I'm going to turn the car off the road and walk her. She's not complaining of pain anywhere but in her head. I don't think, considering what happened, that she could have any internal injuries. I may be wrong. You can argue with me if you want to, but I think she ought to be kept awake."

"I don't know," I said. "I just don't know. You said the house was only about ten miles farther on. Perhaps we ought to just keep going."

"Perhaps you're right. We aren't making very good time, but we ought to be there in another twenty minutes. Aunt Lelia's companion will know what to do. She's a gargoyle type, but she's a pretty competent nurse when she has to be. Her first reaction will probably be that we shouldn't have brought a stranger to Alcombra no matter what the reason, but I can talk her out of that."

"Miss Russell isn't a stranger," I said. "She's staying at the house."

"Russell!" He turned to face me, and for a moment he lost control of the car, which veered toward the side of the road. I cried out, and he jerked the wheel just in time to prevent us from striking a stone wall that formed a sort of terrace to our right.

"Russell?" he said again.

"Marian Russell," I said. "She must be one of those relatives you don't know. She told me she was Lady Stewart's niece. That makes her your aunt, doesn't it?"

"Does it?" His voice was tight with anger. We were going faster now, taking the curves wide. It was obvious that finding out who the unconscious woman was had upset him, but I had no idea why. I tried to tell myself it did not matter. I had been able to disassociate myself from Marian's problems. I had told myself I did not care about her bitterness and the reason for it, but somehow with David it was different. Perhaps it was because the woman had tried to confide in me. Obviously he had no intention of doing that, and yet I felt myself wishing that he would. I wanted to understand what had upset him.

"What's happening?" Marian Russell's voice was thick.

Now that she was sitting up, I could see her face more clearly. Her eyes were open.

"Talk to her." David's voice was grim. "Keep her awake."

"Who's that?" she said weakly. "Who's driving the car? Where are we going? Oh, my God, how my head aches."

"We'll be at Alcombra in a few minutes," I told her. "Everything is all right."

"Who's driving?" she repeated. Her voice was stronger now. I took her hand and began to rub it, but she pulled away from me.

"I came along just after the accident," David said before I could answer. "I'm taking you home."

"Who—who are you?"

I saw David shake his head slowly from side to side, and I knew that he was warning me not to answer her.

"I'm a hitchhiker," he said. "Just someone looking for a job harvesting grapes."

"But you're—you're British."

"The British hitchhike, too," he muttered. "Don't bother too much about me. All I'm concerned with is getting you home safely."

Suddenly she was reaching for my hand. Her fingers were like ice.

"Is he telling the truth?" she whispered. "Is he really taking us to Alcombra?"

"Yes," I said. "You don't have to worry."

There was a long pause. "But he doesn't know the way," she protested. Her voice was thick again, and her head swayed back against the seat. "It's not easy to find if you don't know the way."

"Tell her I'll find it," David snapped. "Tell her not to worry."

Without warning, he switched on the car radio. The strains of guitar music split the silence. They were playing a fado, and in a moment a woman picked up the

lament, her voice rising and falling through the quivering
static. The thick swish of her Portuguese filled the car:

> Don't speak to me of that street,
> The street
> That for me was the loveliest of all
> And still is.
>
> Yes, I'd rather you kept silent.
> Speak to me of the hours of today;
> Don't speak to me of the past. . . .

Marian Russell tightened her grip on my hand as the
man at the wheel twisted it sharply, and we turned off
the road onto what seemed to be no more than a narrow
path. We seemed to be driving through a forest. I could
smell the pines in the cool night air. The singer's voice
rose in sentimental agony.

"Turn it off!" I told him. "That can't be making her
head feel any better."

For a moment I thought that he meant to ignore my
demand, and I sensed why. Something about the course of
her questions had threatened him. Obviously he did not
want her to know who he was. But why?

Leaning over, he switched off the music, and at the same
time we came out from under the trees. I could see a few
pinpricks of light below us to the right. The headlights
picked up stone-terraced land on either side of us, and
I knew that we were driving through a vineyard.

"Are we there?" I asked him.

He did not answer me, and I realized that we were
crossing a small wooden bridge. Over the sound of the
motor I could hear the rush of water. Suddenly the horn
blared, and in response a hundred lights seemed to flash
on. There was a heavy iron gate in front of us. We approached it with undiminished speed, and it was thrown
open minutes before we reached it. There was the skid of
gravel under the wheels, and the smell of pines was re-

placed by the thick scent of mimosa. The lights lay directly before us, and through the shadows that they cast I could see a large stone house looming into the night.

"He knew the signal," the woman beside me cried. "Who is he? Why won't you tell me who he is?"

"I'm David," the young man said in a low voice as the car came to a stop in front of brilliantly illuminated stone steps that led to a thick oak door set deep into the stone. "You may as well know now."

"Oh, God!" Marian Russell mourned, swaying against me. "I've always been afraid that this would happen."

"You don't have to worry," David Ashor said in a hard voice, his back still against us. "I'll leave tomorrow. I've always known how difficult it was for you to accept the fact that you have a son."

CHAPTER

2

In the morning the shrieking of the peacocks woke me.
I got out of bed and went to the open window to look out
at them, only to find one of the great birds sitting on the
ledge outside my window. Startled, I drew back and pulled
the window down. The peacock began pecking at the panes
with its beak, and then, after staring at me arrogantly
with beady eyes, he turned and walked to the outer ledge,
spreading his tail as he went, until the window was check-
ered with scarlet and indigo.

When he flew off, I saw that the garden below my
window was filled with peacocks. Thirty or forty of them
paraded up and down the stone paths that led between
unkempt flower beds in which wild poppies struggled
with golden gorse under vast trunk-entangled camellia
trees, unclipped and overgrown with thick red flowers. The
birds swept along like royalty, their long tails sweeping the
ground, their blue breasts puffed. On the top of the stone

wall that enclosed the garden a peacock stood alone, his tail fully spread. His discordant cry shattered the morning silence.

It was a beautiful morning. The rich green of the giant pines that stood beyond the wall was touched with gold, and when the window had been open, I had smelled the perfume of sun-ripened air. I glanced at my watch and found that it was nearly ten. Usually I did not like to sleep that late but last night when I had finally gone to bed, I had known that it would be by far the best thing if I slept until I awoke naturally.

I turned away from the window and looked about the room. The night before I had been too exhausted to notice details. It was a comfortable room, but with something strangely reminiscent of pictures I had seen of 1920 drawing rooms. There was no particular style. The walls were white-paneled, the inset portions etched with gold, a touch of French Provincial which should have had a brightening effect but somehow made me feel that I was standing inside an overelaborately decorated box. There were two paintings on the walls, one a Watteau-like genre landscape by Pierra Quillard, the other a view of the city of Oporto by Quillard's eighteenth-century contemporary, José Carvalho. The furniture was in odd contrast to the room itself. A vast canopied bed—a monstrous affair with dusty green-velvet hangings pulled back with gold cords to disclose massive oak bedposts and an elaborately carved headboard—dominated one-half of the bedroom. Black-walnut chairs with straight backs were set formally at regular intervals along the walls, and a walnut vanity table lurked beneath a mirror that was so large there was scarcely a place in the room where one could escape its reflection. Last night I had felt as though the room was crowded with all the people who had slept in it in the past. Even with the bright morning light flooding through the windows, I felt as though I had somehow intruded.

There was something hostile, as far as that went, about the house itself. I had been aware of it as soon as I had followed David Ashor through the doorway the night before. A single servant had greeted us, an old man wearing a dull black suit. He had approached us across the black-and-white-tiled floor of the vast hall, his shoulders bent, his gait a shuffle. His faded black eyes, set in a plump face as wizened as a newborn infant's, had fastened on us as suspiciously as though we were all strangers. I would never have taken him for Portuguese, but it was with a shock that I heard the Scottish burr in his voice.

David had lifted Marian Russell out of the car despite her feeble protests, and he brushed past the old man with no explanation of what had happened.

"What room is she in, MacGregor?" he had demanded. Marian's eyes were closed, and it was impossible to tell whether she was unconscious again, or was simply blotting out the sight of the man who had called himself her son. David started up the broad, winding stairs that led up to a sort of balcony.

"What room?" he demanded when the old man did not answer immediately.

"The yellow room," the servant muttered sullenly. "We've not been expecting you," he added resentfully.

"We'll need Senhora," David said. As he reached a bend in the stairs, I saw his face set in angry lines. "Fetch her at once. And another thing: There's no need to bother my aunt about this tonight. Do you hear?"

Muttering something under his breath, the old man shuffled through a door at the far end of the hall, leaving me alone. Uncertain as to whether I should follow David or not, I stood where I was and wearily looked around me. The hall was lighted by a baroque glass chandelier that hung on a thick gold chain from a ceiling two stories overhead. The ceiling itself caused me to catch my breath. It had been painted in the style of Tiepolo. Angels and allegorical figures seemed to dart at me from among delicately etched white clouds, which appeared to drift against a background of vivid indigo. It was one of the most superb ceiling paintings I had ever seen, and to find it so unexpectedly looming over me was disconcerting.

I was still looking up at it when I heard the sound of steps on the tiled floor. A woman was coming toward me. Black eyes glittered in a broad, strong-boned Celtic face. Her coarse black hair was pulled into a tight bun, which seemed to strain at the skin of her forehead. She might have been any age. Her body, thick as a peasant woman's, was encased in a tweed skirt and a blue sweater. But if her dress was that of an English country woman, there was nothing British about the thickness of her accent, which was purely Portuguese.

"I am Senhora Sequeira," she said. Her mouth, set in a thin line, scarcely moved when she spoke. There was nothing of welcome in her attitude. "And you?"

"I'm Irene Haverlock," I said, aware of a rising anger. "I believe I was expected today."

She made no response to that. "What has happened to Miss Russell?" she demanded. "And why is Lady Stewart's nephew here? You must understand that the situation cannot be tolerated."

"I'm afraid that's no concern of mine," I said sharply. "As for Miss Russell, there was an accident. She appears to have suffered a concussion. Mr. Ashor has taken her upstairs to her room. She needs a doctor—or a nurse. Mr. Ashor said that Lady Stewart's companion is qualified to examine her."

"I am Lady Stewart's companion," the dark woman said, her deep voice tinged with sarcasm. "I assumed you would realize that."

Her deliberate rudeness infuriated me. "I see no reason why I should assume anything," I said sharply, "but if you are who you say you are, I think that you ought to go up to Miss Russell at once. And I would appreciate it if you would see that someone brings my luggage in from the car."

"You won't be able to see Lady Stewart tonight," her companion said with a certain grim satisfaction.

"I have no intention of seeing anyone," I told her. "I want, however, to be shown my room and to have some food sent up to me. I left London at two this morning, and I have been traveling on incredible roads for the past four hours. I want to eat and to sleep—in that order, and at once."

For the first time the woman smiled. It was not a pleasant smile. "I told Lady Stewart that she should not bring strangers here," she said smugly. "It's quite clear that you will never do."

"That is for your employer to decide," I snapped. "Did you hear anything that I just said?"

The smile faded. "MacGregor will see to you," she said. "As you so kindly advised me, I must attend to Lady Stewart's niece. And if David is here, there will be other complications as well."

MacGregor must have been listening to us, for as soon as Senhora Sequeira had ascended the stairs, he appeared with a young brown-faced boy, and between them my luggage and myself were deposited in a bedroom on the second story. The old man made no response except to nod his head when I reiterated my request for food. I did not adopt the same tone with him that I had with Lady Stewart's companion, but I was firm. Through a daze of weariness I was certain of only one thing—and that was that I establish at once the basis on which I demanded to be treated.

Adjoining the bedroom was an old-fashioned bathroom, with the toilet perched high on a raised platform and a tub so deep and long that I could not recline in it with any degree of safety. Still, the water was hot, and there was a thick bar of lemon-scented soap and bath salts. Lulled by the warmth of the water, I tried to put everything that had happened into some sort of perspective and found that I could not. I had not particularly cared for Marian Russell, but my overriding emotion was one of anxiety about her condition. In a sense I felt that I should be with her, but despite Senhora Sequeira's rudeness, I had sensed in her a basic competence. If a doctor was needed, she would call one. It was difficult to think she would welcome any intrusion on my part. I only hoped that before I fell asleep, someone would come to tell me how the injured woman was.

But they did not. While I was toweling myself, a sullen-faced girl in a black uniform appeared, without knocking, in the bedroom and set a tray on the table beside the bed. The meal was light but delicious: thin slices of cold roast lamb, a bun and butter, a small salad covered with a white dressing I had never tasted before, and a bit of pale-yellow, tart-tasting cheese. There were two small carafes of wine, one a sparkling rosé and the other a rich, mellow port. I drank only one glass of the port after I had finished my meal, savoring the rich, mellow taste and remembering what my father had often told me about Douro port being the finest in the world. Scarcely able to hold my eyes open, I had fallen into the huge canopied bed and slept.

Now I realized, however, that only exhaustion and the wine had made my first hours at Alcombra relatively simple to face. Quickly bathing and brushing my hair, I slipped into a pair of white-linen slacks and a blue-jersey tunic. If I was going to begin work at once, I might as well be comfortable. But first, I supposed, must come an interview with Lady Stewart. I did not find the thought reassuring and lingered for a while in front of the huge mirror, pretending to deliberate as to whether I should rub some color into cheeks that seemed unnaturally pale, whether I should leave my hair hanging straight about my shoulders or pull it back in a loose bun. I decided on the latter. I was twenty-six, but something about the sunlight or the mirror or the fact that I was completely rested made me look like a towheaded girl. I did not want Lady Stewart to lose confidence in me at first sight.

I was about to open the door when someone knocked. Senhora Sequeira stood outside in the shadows of the cavernous corridor. Before I could speak, she stepped inside the bedroom. The sullen-faced girl who had brought my supper the night before was behind her, carrying another tray, covered with a white napkin. Without as much as glancing at me, she placed it on the table by the window and left the room, closing the door behind her.

I found that the unpleasantness of the night before made it difficult for me to know what to say to the dark-faced woman who stood stolidly before me, wearing the same skirt and sweater she had worn when I had first seen her. There were gray circles under her dark eyes, and her hair was loosened about her face. There was something softer about her appearance this morning. Although she did not speak, she seemed more approachable. I hazarded a smile, which she did not return.

"I was about to come to find you," I began. "I thought that I ought to talk to Lady Stewart as soon as possible so that I can begin my inventory. I know that she is eager to have it completed as soon as possible."

"You must eat your breakfast first," Senhora said. "It has been especially prepared for you, which is something that is not usually done. You will find that we have a very regular routine, Miss Haverlock. Breakfast is served in the dining room promptly at nine. Guests are expected to eat there if they wish to eat at all."

There was something about this woman that reminded me of a headmistress I had particularly loathed. Under ordinary circumstances I would have apologized for oversleeping, but I had no intention of ever apologizing to Senhora Sequeira.

"Besides," she added when I made no response, "it will be a half hour at least before you can be interviewed by Lady Stewart."

She had, I knew, chosen the word "interviewed" especially to annoy me. Turning my back on her, I drew up a chair to the table near the window and flicked the napkin off the tray. She followed me and stood staring down at me, her arms folded across her thick breasts. In the full glare of the sunlight I could see that she looked incredibly tired. Suddenly I relented.

"Sit down and have some coffee," I said, making my voice as firm as hers had been. "You can have this cup. I only want juice and toast."

For a moment I thought that she would refuse, and then, her shoulders slumping, she drew up one of the black-walnut chairs and sat down across the table from me.

"Now," I said, pouring coffee from the ornate silver pot, "tell me about Miss Russell. Is she going to be all right?"

"It was not necessary to send for a doctor," the woman replied stiffly. "I examined her and found no signs of concussion or any other injury. I took the precaution, however, of staying with her through the night. When she awoke this morning, she seemed to be her usual self. There is no need to tell Lady Stewart of the incident. I wish to make that quite clear. Her doctor has impressed on me the need for her to be undisturbed by . . . minor problems."

There was an absurd note of authority in her voice, and for a moment I was angry again. But then I noticed that the hand that held the coffee cup was unsteady. For some reason this woman was not as assured as she wished to sound. I did not believe that she had come to me simply to warn me not to tell Lady Stewart about the accident, and if she did in fact have another reason, I intended to find out what it was, even if it meant controlling my temper.

I waited for her to go on, but when she did not, I asked her about David. "Has he gone yet?" I said. "He said last night that he was leaving this morning."

The woman's dark eyes narrowed. For a moment she did not answer, and then, clicking the coffee cup against the saucer, she said: "Lady Stewart has already seen him this morning. She will not hear of his leaving so abruptly. If anyone is to go, it must be his mother."

I drew in my breath. Somehow I had never quite believed what David had implied the night before when he had said that he had always known that she found it difficult to accept the fact that she had a son. It had seemed too incredible to be true when, up to that point, neither of them had given any sign of recognition.

"Then it's true?" I said. "Miss Russell *is* his mother?"

Senhora stared at me suspiciously. "I thought you were aware of that," she said. "I would never have spoken otherwise."

"David said something about it last night," I told her, "and yet when he first came across us on the mountain, just after the accident, he didn't appear to recognize her."

"There is no reason why he should," Senhora said in a tight voice, "since neither have set eyes on the other since he was a child in arms."

I stared at her incredulously. "She gave him up?" I said. "But why?"

"It is an old story," the woman said, "and like most old stories, better forgotten. Besides, you will understand me when I remind you that it is purely a family affair."

She had a masterful use of the barb. Obviously she saw herself as some sort of protector of Lady Stewart and, if necessary, of the entire family. She had told me enough to make me curious and then verbally slapped my hands for asking questions. If I had not sensed a certain viciousness about her, I would have been amused.

"But why is his name Ashor?" I insisted. "That wouldn't be a very intimate detail to divulge, would it?"

She did not take well to being mocked, even gently. Pushing her cup away from her, she rose. "David has taken his father's name," she said. "I answer these questions because I do not wish you to impose them on Lady Stewart. You will be in this house only a few weeks, Miss Haverlock. It is unfortunate, perhaps, that certain members of the family will be here at the same time, but I can see no reason why you should concern yourself either with them personally or with their affairs."

I rose, facing her. "And is that what you came to tell me?" I said in a low voice.

"I came to warn you, Miss Haverlock," Senhora said, her eyes flashing. "I guessed last night that you might be the sort to interfere, and I warn you: If you do, I will see to it that you leave Alcombra."

"Don't argue with me, Senhora," Lady Stewart said. "I won't stand for it. Do you understand? I won't stand for it."

Clutching the cane that leaned against the bed, she cracked it sharply across the legs of a small mahogany table, overturning a glass of water, which deluged a tray on which bottles of pills stood in neatly ordered lines. For a long moment the two women stared at one another with undisguised loathing, the one propped massively against lace-edged pillows in a high bed canopied with faded blue-velvet hangings on which the dust stood out like a frosting of snow, the other standing straight against the oak-paneled wall, her dark face scarcely visible in the shadows. Thick drapes were pulled across the windows, shutting out the day. The only light came from a small lamp beside the bed.

Lady Stewart turned her head against the pillows and stared down at me. My chair was lower than the bed, and the old woman's thick, hawk-nosed face seemed to jut, neckless, from rounded shoulders wrapped in a plaid shawl. Her black eyes darted from my face to that of her companion and back again.

"Since I've been ill," she said in a deep voice, "Senhora has seen fit to treat me as though I had lost my mind. On the whole, of course, that's more acceptable than the attitude my relatives have taken. I find it singularly disconcerting to have it assumed that since I am dying, I might as well be dead. Once you have met them, Miss Haverlock, you will understand what I mean. They wing about like vultures."

It was easy to see from whom Senhora had taken lessons in abruptness. Strangely enough, however, as soon as she had led me into the shadowy bedroom, she had seemed to shrink—to diminish in some way. Outside of this room she was obviously a power, but here she paled into insignificance beside the old woman, who seemed to rear out of the bed.

"Senhora Sequeira has been my companion for nearly thirty years," Lady Stewart said. "She has many excellent qualities, but she is inclined to be overly secretive. She has never learned to admire truth as I do." With an obvious effort, she pulled herself away from the pillows, gripping the edge of the bed with a hand that could have been a man's. "She doesn't want me to talk about my personal affairs now, do you, Senhora? You consider garrulity one of my many weaknesses, don't you?"

"What you talk about is your own affair, your ladyship."

"Quite right!" the old woman crowed triumphantly. "It *is* my own affair. And now will you tell me why you persist in hiding in the shadows? Come here."

It was a command, made deliberately as a show of strength. As long as an order was obeyed, there could be no doubt about where power lay. I guessed that the old woman was reminding the younger of that. Perhaps there was a message there for me as well. I watched the dark, tight-faced woman move out of the shadows and into the pool of light which encircled the old woman in the bed and myself.

Lady Stewart's eyes flickered over the companion as though she were presenting a particularly uninteresting exhibit. "I do not want you to misunderstand, Miss Haverlock," she said in a mocking voice. "Senhora is indispensable to me. She knows my ways. There will be times when my orders to you will be conveyed through her. But they will always be *my* orders, won't they, Senhora? Always *my* orders."

Her companion nodded, her dark eyes fixed on the blankets that bulked themselves over the old woman's body. I noticed that her hands were clenched.

"Senhora has always been afraid that someone new would usurp, as it were, her particular functions," Lady Stewart explained, a malicious smile twisting her lips. "I attempted to make it clear to her when I arranged for you to come here that your duties would be well defined. You are to catalog my possessions—nothing more."

"That was my understanding," I said. I had been in the room for no more than ten minutes, but I wanted nothing more than to leave it. The oil portraits that lined the oak-paneled walls oppressed me with their sightless eyes, and the air seemed to be heavy with the smell of dead and dying things.

"It wasn't necessary for you to bring in a stranger," the dark-skinned woman said suddenly in a loud, defiant voice. "I could have done everything that needs to be done. It's simply a matter of making lists."

Lady Stewart's laugh came from deep in her throat as she fell back against the pillows. There was something of a man about her, even discounting the thickness of her features and the way in which her white hair was cropped. Although I guessed that the bottom part of her body was lifeless, there was a restless vitality about her, a forcefulness that demanded attention.

"*You* see to everything?" she said scornfully. "You're a fool, Senhora, even to consider it. You don't know the difference between a Goya and a Velázquez, let alone a Patini and a Perugino. Miss Haverlock is an expert, or so I have been led to believe. She can do what needs to be done quickly, and time is of the essence. The doctor explained all that to you, didn't he, Senhora? As a nurse you shouldn't find it too difficult to understand what is happening to me."

"The doctor can't possibly be certain," her companion muttered.

"He knows all he needs to know about death," the old woman insisted, almost gleefully. "I have six weeks at the most. Let Miss Haverlock look after the collection. If you want to keep busy, you can plan the funeral." She laughed again.

"Don't!" her companion said harshly. "It's not good for you to upset yourself."

The old woman's face settled into heavy lines. "If I can't talk about my own death, who can?" she asked. "The point is, there has to be an inventory, or the bereaved will be off with all they can carry before I'm cold. Do you think you can get the job done in six weeks, Miss Haverlock?"

"I haven't seen the collection yet," I said. "I hadn't intended to spend longer than three weeks at the most."

"You see, Senhora," Lady Stewart said in a pleased voice. "This young woman knows what she has to do, and she wants to get on with it without any beating around the bush. She doesn't want to become involved with us and our quibbling. She's not even particularly impressed by the fact that I'm dying. It should be an object lesson to you, Senhora. You are inclined to take life much too personally yourself."

If she hoped to disconcert me, she was mistaken. I kept my face expressionless, but Senhora Sequeira flushed and seemed somehow, without moving, to falter. The old woman obviously knew by heart all the ways she could hurt her. Grinning, Lady Stewart pushed herself higher on her pillows, her face suddenly becoming a mask of pain. Senhora bent over her to help her, but the old woman pushed her away.

"Of course," she said to me, her voice weaker, "I may have less than six weeks—or more. These doctors don't know as much as they pretend. I may 'linger on,' as they say, longer than expected. That would be a nice state of affairs, wouldn't it, Senhora?"

"Don't talk like that," the dark woman said harshly, her dark eyes riveted on Lady Stewart's face.

"Does it really upset you to think of me dead?" the old woman said quizzically. "I can't think why it should, really. You'll be well provided for—not a rich woman, of course. You won't be able to live as you've been accustomed to living for the past thirty years. And you have developed a certain taste for luxury over the years, haven't you, Senhora?"

Shoulders stiff, her companion turned and hurried out of the room. I rose to follow her.

"No," Lady Stewart said impatiently, "I want to talk to you alone, Miss Haverlock. That was just my way of getting Senhora to leave the room. She never would have done so while you were here otherwise. I expect our little games don't make much sense to you, do they?"

"There's no reason why they should," I said sharply. I loathed these kind of female involutions, and I saw no need to pretend otherwise.

The old woman closed her eyes. It was as though someone had drawn a curtain. The forcefulness, the strength, the vitality—all disappeared. For the first time I realized that she was suffering. Her voice, when she spoke, seemed to come from a great distance.

"You're annoyed, aren't you?" she said.

"Perhaps," I said, "we ought to discuss where you want me to begin."

"Later!" Her eyes snapped open like a turtle's. "Tell me, what have you heard about me?"

I met her eyes. "That you're a well-known collector of art. That you have one of the largest private collections in the world."

"Yes, yes." Her thick, mannish face stiffened with impatience. "But what have you heard about me as a human being?"

I hesitated. "I've heard that you have a reputation for eccentricity," I said slowly.

"And what did you take that to mean?"

"That you go your own way, make your own rules."

"But not that I'm insane?"

It was not a casual question. Her voice burned with intensity. She lay motionless against the pillows, her gnarled hands clutching at the plaid shawl, but somehow she conveyed the sense of movement. She might have been pacing back and forth in front of me.

"No," I said, "I've never heard that."

Again she pushed a laugh from the back of her throat. "And what do you think now?" she asked. "Now that you've seen me?"

"I think that you're a very forceful person," I told her. "Very strong. You like to dominate other people."

"But I'm sane? You believe that I'm sane?"

I was suddenly aware of a feeling of exhaustion. "Of course," I said.

"Others aren't so certain," she muttered, "or perhaps they simply believe what they want to believe. I spoke of vultures a moment ago. You ought to know that by that I meant my family: my stepson, my niece, the lot of them. For a long time I've managed to stay clear of them. Now I can't even keep them out of this room, let alone out of the house. You'll meet them soon enough."

She paused and took a deep breath that was something between a gasp and a sigh. For the first time I realized that it was an effort for her to speak, but that she would not face the fact that she could no longer sustain her enormous vitality.

"I only mention them because you ought to know that all of them are opposed to your being here." She reached out and grasped her cane, pounding it against the floor as though she were afraid that she was losing my attention. "Do you understand what I'm talking about?"

I knew that it would be a kindness to her to pretend that I did, to leave her alone to rest. And yet, although I had lied a good deal at one time or other in my life, I found it impossible to meet those blazing black eyes and circumvent the truth simultaneously.

"I'm afraid I don't," I said, "but perhaps it would be better if you explained tomorrow."

"It would not be better!" the old woman said. "By tomorrow they will have gotten to you. You have to know that every one of them is opposed to my turning this place into a museum. That's what they're here for: to persuade me to change my mind before it's too late. The fools! I've spent my life collecting things of value for this purpose. The money was mine to spend. My husband left it to me because he knew that I was the only one of the lot that would put it to good use, and now they want to turn it into cold cash again—sell everything, divide the money. They're willing to go to any length. They'll try to prove that I'm not in my right mind if they have to. This inventory. . . ."

She broke off, gasping for breath. The cane fell from her hand to the floor. Rising, I went to the bed. The gnarled hand clutched my arm and pulled me down until my face was close to hers.

"Senhora!" She could scarcely choke out the words. "Call Senhora! She shouldn't have left me, no matter what

I said. But she's like the others. They hate me, all of them. They've been waiting for me to die for a long time."

When Lady Stewart was a girl, her portrait had been painted by Sargent. It hung now at the end of the long gallery that stretched the entire length of the wing where the major portion of the collection was evidently housed. I approached it slowly, scarcely noticing the other paintings on either side. The artist had painted her as she turned away from him. Her pale-golden hair was pulled back in an elegant chignon from her delicate, fine-boned face. She was smiling enigmatically, and her eyes sparkled as though something the artist had said had amused her. Her slender body was draped in a white evening gown, which swirled about her feet and left her translucent shoulders bare. It was incredible to think that this beautiful girl could have been transformed by time into the mottle-faced old woman I had just seen gasping for breath against her pillows.

It had not been necessary for me to ring for Senhora. She had come stalking into the room nearly as soon as Lady Stewart had called her name, and I assumed that she must have been listening outside the door. I had left her administering an injection into the old woman's arm. Since then I had been roaming this wing of the house with growing incredulity.

The sheer extent of the collection left me breathless. I had passed through five rooms before coming to this gallery, which formed the L of the wing, and each room had been crammed with objects of art, each wall thick with paintings. It was difficult to examine anything closely because of the poor quality of the lighting. The windows, which were set high in the oak-paneled walls, cut out more daylight than they admitted, ornamented as they were with iron fretwork, each with its own elaborate pattern of Moorish floral designs. Artificial lighting was restricted to wall lamps in the form of three-pronged candelabra supporting tiny flamelike bulbs that did little to illuminate even the largest canvases.

Each one of the five rooms was large and high-vaulted, with timbered ceilings on which painted panels were dimly visible. Hooded fireplaces jutted from the walls, and the floors were covered with beautiful glistening black tiles, genuine Moorish tile with a purplish cast. These tiles, called *azulejos*, were, I knew, common in Portugal. One found them in all colors—blue and yellow and green and pink—decorating the facades of houses and lining the inner walls of churches. The black tiles were rare, however, and I had never before seen them used as a floor covering. The moment I stepped into the first of these rooms I realized that what I was about to see was more amazing by far than anything rumor had prepared me to expect.

The rooms were furnished with antiques, which took the chill off what might otherwise have been a complete museum atmosphere, but it was difficult to imagine people sitting in the high wing chairs upholstered in faded tapestry. Long refectory tables—handsome, massive pieces, with lion-clawed legs—were set in the center of each room. Escritoires were dotted about in odd corners, but it was clear that it had been many years since anyone had penned a letter on their dusty tops. There were flat-topped glass tables everywhere, their surfaces covered with green felt. Various mementos, including letters, rested beneath the surfaces of the glass, but the light was too dim for me to see exactly what was there. It was clear that I would need some more adequate source of light before I could begin any sort of inventory.

One room had proved an exception to the general rule. Just before I had reached the long gallery, I had passed through a small chapel that appeared to have been transported piece by piece from an eleventh-century Romanesque church, with horseshoe arches and a delightful pregnant Madonna standing by the low altar. There were two arched windows set with brilliantly colored medieval glass, one portraying the Pentecost and the other an Annunciation scene. On the altar itself I found a doll-like figure of Jesus as a young boy, dressed incongruously in a black frock coat and knee breeches. On hooks beside him hung other costumes that I knew had been made, according to time-honored custom, by peasant women who had stitched each garment with piety to show their affection for their Lord. But perhaps the most surprising thing the chapel contained was a small stone tomb on which the alabaster figure of a young boy dressed in fifteenth-century costume lay sleeping. The effigy was so realistically carved that I had found myself brushing my hand over the sleeve that partially covered one delicately wrought hand as though to push back the cloth.

Nothing I had seen, however, had prepared me for the long gallery with the portrait by Sargent at the far end. Turning away from the beauty that had been Lady Stewart's when she was a girl, I stood on tiptoe to examine the other paintings, finding a treasure trove of sixteenth-century Portuguese art: brilliant group scenes by Gonçalves, showing the influence of the Flemish masters of the period; biblical scenes by Henriques, with their incredible clarity; and the static faces of Fernandes. For the first time since I had come here, I felt a sense of great excitement. Even if the inventory took me more than three weeks to finish—and it seemed clear that it would—it would be an experience that could not be duplicated. The tensions I had encountered here, the hatred, no longer seemed to matter. I would isolate myself as much as I could from the other people gathered in this house and concentrate on this extraordinary collection.

There was a narrow door set deep in the wall to my right, and I opened it, expecting to find myself in still another room, only to emerge into the glare of full sunlight. I was standing in a courtyard apparently formed by the wing I had been exploring on my right and the main house on the left. A cloistered walk, which must have once graced a monastery, ran along the two sides of the wing, and beyond the graceful columned arches was the court-yard itself, laid out in formal gardens through which ran gravel paths. Shade was provided by orange trees, their glossy dark leaves shielding the red-gold fruit. In the cen-ter of the garden stood the stone sculpture of a pig, ap-parently a smaller replica of the famous Pig of Murça. Crudely carved, its bestial quality struck an ominous note amid so much beauty.

"It's even more vicious looking than the Pig of Bragança, don't you agree?" a man's voice said.

Turning, I saw him coming across the grass, a tall, slender, dark-haired man, with a narrow, sharply boned face and dark eyes that were half veiled by oddly drooping lids. His skin was olive in color, and there was no more doubt than there had been about Senhora that he was Portuguese. But it was equally obvious that he was not a servant. His clothing was expensive and fashionable. His trousers were narrow and beautifully tapered, and his high-cut calfskin boots were glossed with a rich shine. Over a brown high-necked jersey he wore a tan thickly knit sweater, which was belted about the waist. Yet despite the foppishness of his dress, there was an enormous virility about the man. From a distance I had guessed that he was not much older than David, but now that he approached me and the statue, I saw that he must be in his forties.

"It's amazing how many of these artifacts you'll find scattered around this country," he went on. There was only the slightest trace of accent in his voice. "Any size at all. It's possible that the pig was worshiped in pre-historic times, of course—quite clearly possible. After all, primitive man frequently makes a deity out of any animal on which he depends for his livelihood. And the number of chestnut trees—particularly in Bragança, of course—

means that there was always plenty of forage for pigs. And we know that the pig's fat was used for soups and also for lamp oil, not to mention the meat itself."

Reaching past me, he stroked the granite side of the stone beast and looked directly at me for the first time, smiling.

"You must excuse me for not introducing myself at once," he said. "I am Jerez Caravels, Marian's fiancé. Probably she mentioned me to you during your long drive together yesterday. I was very much opposed to her making the trip to fetch you alone, you understand. Portugal's roads are a great deal better than they were a few years ago, but the mountain roads are still treacherous. And then, of course, there is Marian's driving to consider. She's quite competent, of course—I don't mean that—but she knows nothing about the machine itself, which is, I think, always a mistake. One would not qualify as an adequate horseman if one knew nothing about the beast itself. However, I might as well have kept my arguments to myself. She insisted on going alone." He made a wide expansive gesture, white teeth glittering as he laughed. "She said that she wanted to talk to you—alone."

I stared at him, bewildered. He had come upon me out of nowhere, obviously knowing who I was, and begun to talk as though we were intimate friends. What he had said about stone pigs and Marian jumbled together in my mind.

"And did she?" he asked.

"Did she what?"

"Talk to you."

Something about his confidence that I would respond openly to him irritated me. "Of course we talked," I said sharply. "One rarely travels that distance with someone else without exchanging some conversation."

"Ah, you are very much what I expected you to be, Miss Haverlock!" He ran his fingers lightly over the flank of the stone pig. The smile remained set on his face.

"Very practical, very businesslike, very English. A great deal younger than I had imagined, of course. And I had not even considered the possibility that you might be beautiful."

"How is Marian this morning?" I said stiffly.

He shrugged. "I am told that she is nearly recovered, but Senhora is seeing that she is guarded as closely as is the old woman. There is one way only to Senhora's heart, and that is illness, disaster, or catastrophe. Under ordinary circumstances she prefers to pretend that Marian does not exist. Last night she guarded her as jealously as a dragon guards a princess." He laughed and took my arm. "Forgive me for my awkward metaphors, Miss Haverlock," he said. "It is possible to envision Senhora as a dragon, but with all due respect to Marian, princess is not part of her image."

He was guiding me down one of the gravel paths away from the stone pig, toward the main house, as though we had a common destination. I wanted to pull my arm away to prove, if for no other reason, that I was not the sort of woman he could charm so easily. But I sensed that if I did so, I would only succeed in appearing gauche.

"No doubt you find me hopelessly garrulous," he was saying as he bent and picked a spray of mimosa and handed it to me, "but I am a man who likes the company of others, and without Marian around, this place is like a morgue. Worse. In a morgue people can talk freely. The dead will not be disturbed. But here. . . . Have you seen Lady Stewart?"

"I talked with her for a while this morning."

"How did she impress you?" Dropping my arm, he moved in front of me and stopped, blocking my path.

"She is an extraordinary person," I said slowly. Why was it that I should feel that everyone in this house wanted something from me? I knew before he told me that that was not the kind of impression he had wanted described.

"Ah, yes. She is certainly extraordinary. A woman with a vision is always extraordinary. Visions are the property of *men* under ordinary circumstances. There have been few Joan of Arcs, and that is, I think, a very good thing."

For the first time since we had met, he amused me. His mind was like a magpie's nest—or seemed to be. I had met women before who had flitted from the top of one topic to that of another but never a man. It occurred to me that this man might be being flip deliberately to put me off my guard—although that was absurd, of course. This was probably his normal manner toward attractive women. I had been only a few hours in this house, and already I was becoming paranoid. What could be more natural than that this man should want to know my impressions of Lady Stewart?

"I expect," he went on, taking my arm again and continuing our promenade down the gravel path, "that Marian told you yesterday her opinion of her aunt's idea to establish a museum here at Alcombra."

I avoided the question. "From what I've seen this morning," I said, "Lady Stewart has a collection that would do justice to a museum. Does she intend to leave the house and the contents to the care of the state?"

"No. No." Jerez Caravels was no longer smiling. "That is not her way, as you will discover, no doubt. A trust is to be established. The museum is to be privately operated and maintained. There will be no admission fee. An admirable idea, no doubt, although I find that no one else agrees with me. I expect you to help me convince them, Miss Haverlock, that Lady Stewart could do nothing better with her fortune than to leave the fruits of it to posterity. That phrase is not mine. The old woman is particularly fond of referring to posterity. One would think that the future was her own invention."

He broke off as there was a rushing noise in the flowers, and a great white peacock dashed away from us, emitting shrill screams of apparent outrage at having been disturbed. Involuntarily I found myself clutching the arm of the man beside me.

"Those peacocks are a nuisance," Jerez said blandly. "There must be over a hundred of them on the grounds. They'll overrun the place in time. As soon as the old woman's dead, at least half of them should be destroyed, but it won't happen. She's taken care of that in her will, I understand—the famous will. From what I hear, she's taken care that everything will go on here just as though she were still alive. It's her way of guaranteeing her own immortality. I've tried to explain all that to Marian, but she doesn't want to accept it. Perhaps you can make her see that there's nothing she can do to change things."

We had reached the shadows of the main house. It rose above us, the whitewashed walls glittering in the sunlight. I paused and looked back across the courtyard, past the hulking statue of the prehistoric pig. Beyond lay the cool cloisters that lined the wing where the collection was housed. I was aware of a sudden intense desire to hide myself away in those dusky rooms, to escape once and for all the insistence of these strangers that I involve myself in their personal affairs.

"I might as well tell you, Mr. Caravels," I said slowly, "that I have no intention of explaining anything to anyone. I'm here for only one reason: to make an inventory. As soon as that is finished, I intend to return to England."

For a moment he looked at me intently. There was something disconcerting about his heavy-lidded stare. "You find the personal affairs of strangers of no interest?" he said slowly.

"Precisely," I said. "You've put it very well. I'm aware that there are certain tensions——"

"Has anyone ever told you that you are a master of understatement?"

The faintly teasing tone he insisted on taking with me was infuriating.

"You'll have to excuse me," I said. "I want to start work as soon as possible."

"But surely you can't intend to begin now," Jerez Caravels said lightly. "It's nearly time for lunch, and I can assure you after a three-week stay in this house that if you intend to eat at all, you must put in an appearance for the three formal meals of the day."

I remembered what Senhora had said about it not being customary for breakfast to be served in one's room and nodded. "I think that today at least I'll skip lunch," I said. "I'm rather eager to begin."

"You have your instructions from Lady Stewart?"

It was none of his concern, and I wanted to tell him so. But at the same time I wanted to avoid outright rudeness. I had been frank with him a moment before, but rudeness was quite another thing.

"No," I admitted. "When I saw her this morning, she was not feeling particularly well, but I don't think that that presents any difficulty. I know how to proceed."

"Still," Jerez said, smiling, "I think that you will make a mistake in not appearing for lunch."

"Why?" I demanded wearily. "I can't think of any conceivable reason why it should matter one way or the other."

"There are a number of excellent reasons," he told me. "You will pardon me if I insist on telling you about them. I have a certain empathy with you, whether or not you care to admit it. We are in much the same boat, you and I. Neither of us are related to Lady Stewart, nor do we have any vested interest in her affairs."

"I thought that you said that you were Marian Russell's fiancé," I said caustically.

He laughed. "I suppose that does give me a certain interest—or would if the will were a different one. But no one here is going to inherit anything, other than the small bequests that go to Senhora and MacGregor. I am here only because Marian insisted, but that is not the point.

We were speaking of the small matter of luncheon. If you have met Senhora, you realize that she is a touchy, difficult woman. And her influence in this house is great. She supervises everything, even the housekeeper. As a consequence Alcombra is run with a certain monotonous regularity, and when that regularity is not observed, there is the devil to pay. The table will be set for six—that is, if Marian is well enough to come down—and if six do not appear, there will be ripples in the pool. And I assure you, Miss Haverlock, we do not at present need more ripples in this particular pool."

I believed him, even though it sounded absurd that it could matter one way or another whether I turned up for lunch. I remembered the reverberations that had resulted from my failure to appear for breakfast and felt my heart quite literally sink.

Jerez glanced at his watch. "Now," he said, "we have precisely twenty minutes before we will be expected in the dining room. Sit down here in the shade and let me continue to prattle. You are a difficult woman to carry on a dialogue with, Miss Haverlock, and I find that rather refreshing. Monologues have always been my forte, as you may have guessed."

I did as he said. The wrought-iron bench was draped with honeysuckle. The scent was overpowering. I smiled. This man had ceased to irritate me. He had tried to amuse me, and he had finally succeeded. Not that that changed my intention to remain aloof. But he had tried to be helpful, I knew, and I understood that if I wanted to work uninterruptedly that afternoon, I might as well follow whatever routine had been established and give neither Senhora nor anyone else an excuse to interrupt me. Perhaps, over lunch, I could make it clear to all of them that I had a good deal to do and that I had to be left alone to do it. Perhaps I had been wrong to think that without making myself clear, I could hope for any peace.

"All right," I said. "Now I *will* ask a question. Who

will the six be? Yourself, of course. And me, apparently. And perhaps Miss Russell——"

"Marian!" he exclaimed, sitting down beside me and smoothing the crease in his trousers with finger and thumb. "For heaven's sake, don't attempt to be formal. You may think it will make things easier, but I assure you that it will not."

"All right. Marian, then. Who else will be there? Senhora?"

"Good Lord, she wouldn't think of violating the conventions by dining with us. Senhora was born and raised in Lisbon, but somewhere along the line she was really inoculated with some firm Victorian values. No, she eats with the housekeeper—if she eats. I'm not at all certain that she doesn't sustain herself on her own venom."

Our eyes met, and we burst out laughing. He had the caustic humor of a woman, and despite myself, I responded to it. Obviously he was delighted. I guessed that he took great pleasure in making women respond, but there did not seem to be anything deliberate in the way he went about it, and for that I was willing to forgive him a great deal.

"There's another reason in favor of your lunching with us," he said. "And that——"

"But you haven't told me who will be there," I persisted.

"Well, there will be David, of course. I understand that you've already met David. He. . . ." Jerez broke off as though unwilling to break the mood.

"The others?" I encouraged him. I, too, did not want to talk about David. I was willing to spend a few minutes in light gossip, but not, for some reason, about him.

"William Stewart and his wife," Jerez said slowly. "Lady Stewart's stepson."

I no longer felt amused. Suddenly I remembered the old woman's voice when she had spoken of the vultures gathering. Jerez began to speak more rapidly, as though he was aware that he had begun to lose my interest.

"He was a grown man when she married his father," he said. "He's in his fifties now. Claire, his wife, is young, very young. Beautiful and greedy. A common combination in women, unfortunately. They are an interesting couple. Neither of them will have anything to do with me, of course. They consider my—er—position a compromising one. As a matter of fact you will find that few of us sitting around the table have anything at all in common—except, of course, Alcombra and what it contains."

He laughed, deprecatingly. "I am forgetting what I intended to say," he said. "Which was simply that there is a second reason that you should lunch with us. William Stewart considers that everything here is his—despite the will. After all, as he is so fond of saying, all of the collection was purchased with his father's money. He is here . . . well, who knows why he is here? Although one can guess. But one reason is certainly that he wishes to keep his eye very closely on what is going on, and he will want to talk to you. I suspect that he will want to talk to you very seriously—perhaps more seriously than you would like."

Leaning toward me, he took my hand. His hooded eyes were intent on my face. "I suspect," he said in a low voice, "that you find me a bit of a fool, Miss Haverlock. But like myself, I think that you came here imagining that you could remain the observer, and so I feel that I must warn you that it would be dangerous for you not to see quite clearly what is going on around you."

CHAPTER

3

The dining room opened off the tiled hall where I had been left waiting the night before. In the small anteroom between the hall and the dining room itself Jerez pointed out a miniature wine cask on a low table beside which was set a tray of glasses and a crystal decanter full of a ruby-colored liquid.

"Port," Jerez said, "from grapes grown here at Alcombra. You knew that this is one of the great vineyards of the Oporto region, didn't you? You wouldn't be aware of it unless you walked about the estate, but it's there, I assure you: rich, terraced lands. Lady Stewart may have devoted herself to her art collection, but her husband loved this land. The wine tells you just how much he loved it. Here."

Tipping the decanter, he poured the rich scarlet liquid into two of the tiny glasses.

"Try this." He raised his glass to his lips. Coming

straight from the brilliance of the day outside, I could not see his face in the dusk of the anteroom, but I sensed that he was on edge. Outside in the courtyard he had rattled on unselfconsciously. Now there was an edge to his voice that I had not heard before.

"Cheers."

Our glasses touched, and we drank. Port is a heavy wine to drink before any meal, let alone lunch, but my father had told me once that even the English wine merchants in the Oporto region imbibed their native product at any time of the day or night. Here in this house I guessed that the tasting had become a custom, probably begun while Lady Stewart's husband was alive. The decanter and the cask from which it was kept filled was placed where they were to ensure that every guest would be given the chance to appreciate the product of a famous vineyard. I held the wine in my mouth, savoring the rich bouquet.

"And now," Jerez said, taking my glass from me, "prepare for the direct encounter, my dear Miss Haverlock, or if you don't mind, I'll call you Irene. The others are waiting for us."

The dining room was cool and dim and elegant, its deep-set arched windows filled with elaborate grillwork, the plastered ceilings decorated in fluted patterns. The floor tiles were of a pale-blue that created the liquid impression of shallow water. A long black-oak sideboard stood against one wall, and the dining table itself stretched like a slender black finger down the center of the room. Pale-yellow place mats set off the sparkling silver. Crystal goblets caught and bent the few flickering rays of sunlight that penetrated the grilled windows. A huge cluster of yellow roses were at the center of the table.

David was standing just inside the door, still dressed as he had been the night before, in stained white chinos and a bulky sweater. His face was pale, and his long blond hair was pushed back untidily from his high forehead.

He started toward me, smiling, and then, apparently seeing Jerez behind me, stood by the end of the table and nodded stiffly.

Beyond him was a man whom I identified as William Stewart. Thick-set, with graying hair cut flat across his forehead, he stared at me with small pinched eyes that were nearly lost in his broad-nosed, fleshy face. Beside him the young woman who must be Claire, his wife, was talking vivaciously with another man whose back was toward me. She glanced for a moment in my direction, and I caught sight of the perfect oval of her face before she turned back to continue her conversation, throwing back her neck and shaking her long blond hair over her shoulders. Marian Russell was not in the room.

I heard Jerez introducing me, and I suppose I made the appropriate response. But I could no longer notice details. The man Claire Stewart had been talking to had turned so that I could see him full face, and I caught my breath as I saw his incredible resemblance to Philip.

Somehow we were all being seated. David was pulling out my chair. He slumped into a seat beside me and fingered the goblet closest to him with long, restless fingers.

"I tried to find you this morning," he said. "I wanted to tell you that I'm sorry about last night. I know you'll find it difficult to believe, but I didn't know who—who she was until you said her name. I haven't seen her since I was old enough to remember."

I felt a sudden rush of relief that he had chosen to be as direct with me as he had been the night before. With the others, I did not want to hear even the most superficial truths that influenced their lives, but with David it was different. And there was more to it than that. I welcomed the respite of talking to him. The man to whom Claire Stewart had been talking was seated at the far end of the table. I needed an excuse not to look at him again.

"You must think we're an odd lot," David went on as

a dark-haired maid bent between us to put a fruit salad in front of me. "I'm glad I'm not you, trapped here for weeks."

He spoke in a low voice, although there was no need. William Stewart was talking in a loud booming voice to Jerez, although I could feel his eyes on me. Beside him his wife was still intent in conversation with the man whose name I had not caught, the man who so closely resembled Philip. Her voice was high and light, sweeping over her husband's like a thin breeze.

"I had heard that you were going to stay," I said.

David's thin face hardened. "Who told you that?" he asked.

For a moment silence swept the table, and then the talk began again, louder than before, Jerez leading with a rapid staccato of words.

I shrugged. The salad was delicious, but I found I had no appetite. I put down my spoon. "I can't remember," I said. "Senhora, perhaps, or your great-aunt."

"Lelia probably," David said, scowling. "She enjoys nothing better than making an impossible situation worse. She pretends to hate having her family around her, and in a way, I think she's being honest enough when she says that. But once they are here, she has to control them. It's as though she relishes pitting them against one another, watching them tear one another apart." He laughed. "I expect," he said, "I'm being overly dramatic."

His eyes flickered, and then he looked down at his plate. He had not, I noticed, eaten any more than I had. "It wouldn't hurt me to stay," he said, "but my. . . ."

I realized suddenly that he found it impossible to say the definitive word.

"Your mother," I murmured.

"Yes." Now it was his turn to shrug. "I don't think she can bear to tear herself away now. I mean, I stayed in her room last night until Senhora came. She was talking a good deal—not to me, just talking. Shock, perhaps. But from the few things I heard, I don't think she'll let anything drive her away from here just now—even me. And if I stay——"

"Miss Haverlock."

If the man across from me realized that he was interrupting, he gave no sign. Leaning against the table, William Stewart somehow managed to give the impression that now that he had turned his attention to me, no one else was in the room.

"Mr. Caravels has been telling me that you have had an opportunity to visit the collection," he continued portentously. "I would be very interested in your opinion."

"It's even more impressive than I imagined it would be," I said.

"Yes, yes!" His thick voice was impatient. "We all know about that. What I want to know is, do you think it's possible for one person to complete the inventory in time?"

The folds of fat on his face seemed to envelope his small eyes, making it difficult to look at him directly. I felt a wave of repugnance.

"What 'time' did you have in mind?" I asked coldly.

I heard Jerez chuckle.

"He means, Can you get it done before Lelia dies?" David drawled.

"I see no reason for you to refer to your great-aunt by her given name," the older man said sharply.

David shrugged. The second course was being served: croquettes *ameijpas*, which my father had loved and sought out in the few Portuguese restaurants in London. MacGregor had appeared, making a shuffling, slump-shouldered circuit of the table, pouring wine with a hand that trembled. If it had not been for the way in which his sharp, dark eyes darted from one face to another, I would have thought him oblivious to what was

being said. Jerez held his wineglass in front of him as the
old man poured, watching the sparkling liquid subside
against the crystal.

"Bairrada," he said, letting the name of the wine slip
between his lips slowly. His hooded eyes darted from me
to David to William Stewart. It was obvious that he was
deliberately providing a distraction. "Like champagne in
appearance, don't you agree? But the bouquet is quite
different. It's a gayer wine. At least I've heard that said."

William Stewart eyed Jerez with undisguised disapproval. I guessed that Stewart was the sort of man who
took both food and drink for granted and was not apt
to become lyrical over either. There was, certainly, a
practical deliberation about the way he was consuming his
croquettes.

"What's all this about Marian?" he demanded, turning
on Jerez, a knife clenched in one hand and a fork in the
other. "How badly off is she, anyhow?"

Jerez put down his glass and gestured with wide-open
hands. It was as though, with this man, he was deliberately trying to accentuate the Latin qualities in his nature.
"I do not know," he said. "The dragon will not allow me
to see her. Not even last night was I allowed to be with
her."

It was impossible to tell whether he was genuinely worried or not. I glanced at David, thinking that he might
volunteer some information, but he was picking at his
food, his lips pressed tight together.

"Senhora told me this morning that Miss Russell—
that she was all right," I volunteered. "There's no concussion. It wasn't even necessary to call a doctor, although I understand Senhora sat up all night with her."

"Touching," Jerez muttered under his breath. "One
must toast such touching dedication."

He gestured to MacGregor, who stood waiting by the
sideboard. For a long moment the old man stared back

at him with what seemed to be rheumy defiance. Then, carrying a wine bottle, he shuffled toward the end of the table.

I became aware that William Stewart was delivering himself authoritatively on the subject of women drivers. "They can manage the straight-ahead sort of driving you find on dual carriageways quite adequately, of course," he boomed. "Even a child could do that. But when it comes to driving that requires snap decisions, the exercise of judgment——"

"It was my fault that Marian was injured," I said. "The brakes had given way. You must admit there was nothing either of us could have done about that. I made the decision to stop the car any way we could and put on the emergency brake."

The sharpness of my own voice startled me. There was a knot of tension inside me that my dislike of the thick-faced man across from me could not altogether justify. I was uncomfortably aware that Claire Stewart had stopped chattering, and that both she and the man who looked like Philip were listening to me.

"Don't pay any attention to William," Claire told me. For the first time I looked at her directly. She was incredibly beautiful, with porcelainlike skin and absolutely regular features. Her eyes struck the only discordant note. Oddly slanted, they were thickly fringed with dark-brown lashes that contrasted strongly with the near-white blondness of her long hair, but it was more than coloring. There was a shrewdness about those eyes which everything else about her belied. The way in which she wore her hair, the breathlessness of her voice, even the demure quality of the scoop-necked peasant blouse she was wearing, seemed deliberately to promote a childlike quality. But there was nothing childlike about those eyes. She giggled as she patted her husband's arm.

"William is absolutely dedicated to the belief that

women are basically incompetent," she went on. "Aren't you, darling?" She turned back to me. "It feeds his male ego," she said, "but you're not to take him seriously, Miss Haverlock. It's our only defense, you know: not to take men like my husband seriously."

"Don't talk nonsense, Claire," William Stewart said blandly, pushing his empty plate away from him and settling back in his chair, his hands clasped over his ample stomach.

"Darling," his wife said, "you know you like to hear me talk nonsense. You'd be appalled if I tried to be serious."

It was a light-enough exchange, but somehow it made me uncomfortable. A momentary silence fell over the table as the maids began to remove the plates. Even Jerez was silent, fingering the stem of his wineglass, apparently lost in thought.

"I was just telling Martin," Claire went on lightly, "that he must see the famous collection while he's here." Her fingers fluttered down her husband's arm. "If you've no objection, darling, I thought I might show it to him this afternoon."

So his name was Martin. Involuntarily I glanced at him, hating the fact that the simple combination of reddish hair and broad features should make my heart pound so. We were all types. There must be hundreds of men who would remind me of Philip. I was a fool to let it disconcert me.

"You won't be much use to Martin as a guide," William Stewart muttered. "You don't know the first thing about the stuff my stepmother has stashed away in that wing. Besides, it's an abominable way to spend an afternoon. I'm only quoting you. When I tried to show it to you, you lasted only through one room—not that I blame you."

"On the contrary," the man at the end of the table said. "I'd be interested."

I had not been able to tear my eyes away from his

face, and now he looked at me directly. "Perhaps," he said, "Miss Haverlock, as an expert——"

"Of course!" Jerez exclaimed, suddenly coming to life. "That's an excellent idea. From what I heard you say last night at dinner, Mr. Kubler, you already know something about Iberian art, and as you say, Irene here is an expert."

"She won't have time to give guided tours!" Claire snapped. "Isn't that right, Miss Haverlock?"

I knew that I should make some response, but instead I pretended to center my interest on the elaborate sweet that one of the maids was placing before me. Claire Stewart was right. I did not have time. More than that, I did not want to walk alone through those dimly lit rooms with a stranger who conjured up so many painful memories. But in order to respond I would have to assume a role. There was only one choice, of course: that of the crisp, no-nonsense professional woman. I knew that was what Claire expected of me, and yet for some odd reason I did not want to satisfy her. I had no intention of playing the foil to her girlishness. There was no particular difference in our ages. She and I and David were all in our mid-twenties, yet I was certain that if I gave her a chance, she would take delight in displaying me as an up-tight spinster.

I raised my eyes to Martin Kubler and smiled. "Perhaps," I said in a low voice, "if you can give me a little more time to become acquainted with the collection myself. . . ."

I quite deliberately did not finish the sentence. What I had said neither committed me nor freed me of involvement. Martin Kubler nodded, his eyes never leaving mine. Without looking at Claire Stewart, I sensed her anger. Beside me David remained silent. I heard Jerez laugh with a strange note of triumph.

"Fair enough," he said, "but perhaps Irene ought to know that she'll be doing a public service. As a psychiatrist, Mr. Kubler needs to know as much as he can about Lady Stewart before he pronounces her insane."

"Is it true that Jerez insulted Kubler?" Marian Russell asked me.

I shook my head wearily. I had spent the afternoon in the long gallery, and I was tired. It seemed the easiest part of the collection with which to start, since it contained only paintings, and most of those were large portraits. But the lighting was so poor that even with the help of the flashlight with which I had equipped myself, I had found identification difficult. At six, hot and grimy with dust, I had hurried back through the main part of the house, praying that I would not meet anyone. I had thought that I was home safe until I closed my bedroom door behind me and found Marian sitting in the chair by the window, looking as chic as when I had met her yesterday, except for the bandage that cut across the right side of her forehead.

"He implied that Kubler was deliberately going to find Lady Stewart insane," I said. "I suppose that if I had been intent on reading something into what he said, it would have been that Martin Kubler is unscrupulous."

"He is, of course," Marian said quickly. "William claims that he has an international reputation as a psychiatrist, but I've never heard of him. Bringing him here was William's idea, of course. He's determined to break that will. If anyone is unscrupulous, it's William. Still, Jerez shouldn't have said what he did, poor darling. He lets himself get carried away. Especially when he's here—he hates it so."

I stood just inside the door, looking at her. My bedroom faced the east, and the fading afternoon sun was kinder to her than the blazing sun of yesterday. Even so, her face seemed to be skinned with crumpled parchment. The deftly applied makeup accomplished nothing. One could be distracted only by her dress, a tailored white-silk sheath with a high shirtlike collar that plunged to a deep V, disclosing the lightly tanned flesh between her breasts. There, at least, the skin was smooth. I wondered what had drawn Jerez to her. When he had spoken of her in the courtyard, there had been a certain impersonal quality to his voice. But when she talked of him, it was tenderly, with an overlay of ruefulness that a woman might express in speaking of a careless child.

"Jerez told me all about it this afternoon," she went on, bracelets jangling as she reached up to touch the bandage, "directly after lunch. I believed his version of the affair, of course, but I wanted to hear it from someone else as well. For a sensitive man, Jerez is sometimes quite oblivious to the effects of what he says. And, of course, people like William irritate him so—that terrible British condescension. Jerez has his own career. Perhaps he told you. He's an interior decorator—quite well known in Lisbon. That was where we met, you see. I have an apartment there where I live part of the year, and when I wanted to redecorate last year, one of my friends recommended Jerez."

She told the story proudly, with the triumph of a woman who has quite unexpectedly attracted a personable man. For Jerez was personable. So much so that I wondered for the second time what had drawn him to this woman. I did not know her well enough to make judgments, but there was a brittle quality about her, a lack of depth. Even last night, when she had discovered that David was driving the car, she had collapsed into simple hysteria. Whatever else Jerez was, he was a complex individualist with a subtle sense of humor which I doubted whether Marian was capable of appreciating. Somehow, listening to her talk about Jerez disconcerted me, as though I sensed that at any moment she might say more than she meant to say and end by embarrassing both of us.

"I'm glad you're better," I said, deliberately changing

the subject. Going to sit on the edge of the high bed, I caught a glimpse of myself in the broad gilt-edged mirror and saw that my hair was pulled back in a tangle, that my face was dirt-stained, and that I had clearly been a fool to have worn white slacks, which in the few hours I had spent in the long gallery had turned gray. I wished that this woman would leave me alone. After a bath I knew that I might feel more human.

"It was nothing," Marian Russell said quickly. Clearly she was no more certain of how to cope with my lack of interest now than she had been yesterday. I remembered how she had washed her hands of me the day before and hoped that she would do the same thing again. This time there would be no need to sit in awkward silence in the confines of a car. All that she had to do was to get up and leave the room—my room. I waited, silent, for her to do so.

"You mustn't blame yourself for what happened," she said, crossing and uncrossing her slim legs. "Jerez told me that you defended my driving to William." A faint smile flickered across her worn face. "You kept us from going over the side of that road, you know. What we should have done—what *I* should have done—was to shift into first gear. Jerez told me that this afternoon. But I would never have thought of it—never. It was clever of you to pull the emergency brake, even if it meant I had to bang my head."

She looked at me in that same expectant manner I had been aware of yesterday. There was something curiously girl-like in these moments, as though she expected some sort of spontaneous response from me—and this in the face of my having snubbed her the day before. I gave up the idea of a bath and offered her a drink, taking the bottle of Scotch I had brought with me from the top drawer of the dresser.

"You should ring for ice, really," Marian chattered happily, "but I know why you might hesitate. I mean, one feels as though one is here on sufferance, don't you agree? At least I do. And Jerez feels the same way. The only person who's made to feel at home here is—is David."

The moment she said his name I knew that all the rest—all the concern over what Jerez had said to William Stewart, all the hesitant offerings of friendship—had been for this purpose. Yesterday she had wanted me to take sides in some kind of vaguely defined internecine struggle, and now she wanted something from me again. Only this time it involved her son. My first response was of resentment mixed with a feeling of helplessness, and she sensed this.

"Jerez told me that I shouldn't talk to you about David," she said, draining her glass and getting up to pour more. "He likes you, you know—very much. He says that you're very sensible. That's something that I'm not, I'm afraid. I act from instinct." She went into the bathroom, and the rest of what she said was lost in the sound of running water as she mixed her drink.

"And so," she said, coming back into the bedroom, "I decided that no matter what he said, I'd ask you to help me."

I sank back on the bed and lit a cigarette. "I don't know what I could possibly do to help you," I said.

I was not trying to repulse her as I had the day before. What I said was the simple truth, but she shook her head and came to stand by the bed. She looked down at me, and her face sagged into even deeper lines. Despite the eyeliner and the mascara, her eyes had that strangely exposed look of one who usually wears glasses. Yesterday there had been a veneer of hardness about her that had made it easier for me to explain that I did not want to involve myself in her affairs. Today she seemed to be doing everything that she could do to put herself in as vulnerable a position as possible.

"Jerez overheard part of what David said to you during

lunch," she said slowly, "about whether or not he should stay at Alcombra as long as I'm here. Jerez told me that David said that he didn't want to hurt me."

"That's true," I said.

She turned away from me restlessly and paced to the window. A peacock was seated on the ledge, pressed against the glass. As she approached, the bird turned and stared curiously at her with beady eyes. Marian did not appear to notice him.

"You don't know what it meant to me to hear that," she said, bowing her head. There was, I thought, something schizophrenic about her appearance. Standing with her back to me, so slim, her hair so beautifully coiffured, she might have been a young woman. Then she turned, and the illusion was broken.

"You must have been curious last night," she said, almost defiantly. "The fact that he didn't recognize me——"

"It doesn't matter," I said.

"But it does to me! This is the only time I've been in the same house with him since three weeks after he was born. I mean, it's a chance, the only chance I may have, to make him understand why I—why I gave him up, let my aunt take the responsibility for him. I know from what she's told me that she taught him to hate me. Now I have to explain it all to him. You don't know what it's been like all these years, knowing that I made a mistake."

"Go to him now, then," I said in a low voice. "Talk to him."

She raised her glass to her lips, and I saw that her hands were shaking. "That's what Jerez said," she whispered. "With him everything is so simple. He doesn't understand that I can't. I can't! But David will talk to you. You're the same age. He likes you. He wouldn't have said the things he said to you during luncheon if he didn't trust you."

"He and I are strangers," I protested. "He was only explaining to me why he couldn't stay here."

"He wouldn't have tried to explain if there wasn't some —some rapport," she insisted. "If you won't help me, he may leave, or I will have to go myself—one or the other. If her ladyship has anything to do with it, it will be me."

"Perhaps," I said, "it would be better if you left Alcombra."

For a moment her eyes narrowed. It was the first time I had seen guile in her face. "You don't know what my position is," she said slowly. "If my aunt insists on this— this insane idea of turning Alcombra into a museum, it's going to mean that every cent of the estate, except for what she leaves Senhora and MacGregor, will be involved. I've got to try to salvage something for myself. It's only fair that I should. My mother was her sister, after all. When Mother was still alive, she always promised her that there would be something. . . . But then she became obsessed with this collection. It's gone on for fifty years. When I was a child, we were poor. I mean, really poor. Probably you don't understand what it means to go without everything that makes life civilized. I could have had a proper education if her ladyship could have spared one moment's thought from all this." She wildly waved the hand in which she was holding the glass, and what was left of the drink was spilled onto the carpet. She did not appear to notice.

"My mother swallowed her pride and came here begging. My father was dead. We needed help, and she promised. And in the end there were a few hundred pounds. We could have managed better if we hadn't always had to remember that she was sitting on a fortune. If she had been what she should have been to us, there never would have been a David."

She broke off. Sinking down on a chair, she buried her face in her hands. "His father was no one I could have married," she said in a muffled voice. "The kind of man I never would have met if we hadn't had to live the life we did: cheap pensions, always on the move trying to find some place less expensive, the odd jobs. I didn't even have the training to be a secretary. It killed my mother in the end. It wasn't my having David. *She* always said that it was, but that's simply not true."

The way in which she spat out the word "she" told me that the reference was to Lady Stewart. Marian was making herself quite clear—too clear. I did not want her to go on, and yet I did not know how to stanch the flow of words.

"I couldn't keep him—not with things the way they were. My mother wrote to her, and she offered to take him. I thought at the time that it was—it was the first really kind thing that she had done, until I realized that as far as she was concerned, I was never to see him again. Not even when I married Arthur Russell. That was the only reason I married him. I thought that then she would let me have the child back. He was a doctor—a fairly good practice in England. When he died five years ago, he left me enough to live on. But there's always been this to think about. Alcombra. And her. She always took everything she wanted, including my child."

It was a magnificent performance, and it was false as hell. I did not even attempt to say anything when she had finished. For the moment I no longer pitied her. She had had no right to make me play audience to this kind of act, and yet I knew that I might be making a wrong judgment. Obviously she had been possessed for years by her own obsessions. The point was that I had never wanted to make any sort of judgment about her at all.

Her hands collapsed from her face, but she did not turn to look at me. The room was warm with the captured sunlight of the day. Outside the window the peacock still stared in at us. I felt the same uneasiness I had felt the night before, as though we were not alone in this room.

"Will you talk to David?"

I realized that I would be willing to do anything to make her leave me alone.

"Yes," I said wearily. "What do you want me to tell him?"

"I don't know." She spoke almost impatiently. "Tell him what kind of person I am."

"I don't know what kind of person you are."

"You know enough about me. Just let him know the kind of pressures I'm under. He's only known her side of the story. I don't know what he thinks of me. Don't you see? I tried to explain this to Jerez. I can't talk to David until I know what he thinks about me, how he'll react. I couldn't stand it if he simply shut me off. I have to be certain that he'll listen."

"All right," I said. "I'll talk to him tonight if you like."

She rose and started toward the door, with her face still averted from me.

"He can't leave," she said, "not now. Make him promise he won't leave until I've talked to him."

"I'll try," I said.

She did not thank me, and for the moment I did not care. As soon as the door closed behind her, I leaned back against the pillows and fell into a dreamless sleep.

When I awoke, the room was dark. Outside the window a thin streak of moonlight touched the pines. The air was stuffy with the smell of cigarette smoke, and my head was thick with unremembered dreams. When the tapping came, I remembered that that was the sound that had awakened me. Stumbling off the high canopied bed, I switched on a light and went to the door, but there was no one in the long, dimly lit corridor. Somewhere in the distance a woman laughed, and then there was silence.

The door closed behind me, and I heard the sound again and realized that something was striking one of the windows. My first thought was that a peacock might be pecking at the glass. Still groggy with sleep, I went first to one window and then to another, throwing them open to the coolness of the night. As I opened the last, some-

thing struck me lightly on the arm, and I saw a pebble
fall to the carpet at my feet.

"Irene."

It was a man's voice. Leaning out into the darkness, I
saw someone standing below, a shadow faintly touched by
moonlight.

"It's me. David. Are you all right?"

Instantly I was wide awake.

"You woke me," I whispered.

"Sorry. I was worried when you didn't turn up for
dinner."

Dinner. It was later than I thought, then. I was suddenly uncomfortably aware of hunger.

"Come outside," David hissed. "It's a beautiful night.
I've managed to round up some food. We'll have a picnic
on the hill."

I laughed. The idea was suddenly irresistible. As though
to urge me on, the moon broke through a thin veil of
clouds, splashing the courtyard with white light.

"Wait for me where you are," I said, not bothering to
mute my voice. "I won't be long."

It was strange to feel like a schoolgirl again—strange
and exhilarating. Throwing off my crumpled slacks and
shirt, I showered quickly, forgetting in my rush to cover
my hair. Standing naked in front of the long bathroom
mirror, I combed the long, damp strands straight down
about my face in dark sheets. There was nothing of the
competent professional woman in the image that stared
back at me. My eyes were still heavy with sleep, and my
cheeks were flushed. I knew that I looked more like
eighteen than twenty-five, and I was glad.

Quickly I slipped on a pair of brief lavender-jersey
shorts and a matching long-sleeve top. A long wrap-
around flowered skirt, which opened in the front to my
waist, and sandals completed the outfit. During the past
few years I had bought most of my clothes to please

Philip, traditional classic dresses and suits, but this outfit had been chosen as a deliberate act of defiance the day after we had broken off our engagement. I had told myself as I stood in the shop on Oxford Street, watching the girl wrap the package, that the moment marked my emancipation from him. But that had not been true, of course. No one can purchase for twelve pounds one's freedom from another human being, but as I hurried out into the passageway, the full skirt billowing about my bare legs, I thought that perhaps there was just a chance my release would come sooner than I had dared to hope.

I turned to the left. When I had come back that afternoon from the wing where the collection was housed, I had come across the courtyard and discovered a side door that led to a deserted hallway from which narrow stairs ran up to the second floor. The route suited me much better than the front approach, which meant crossing the vast hallway under the penetrating glare of the cherubs who flitted across the painted ceiling. Using the front door increased the chance that I might meet someone, even if only the dour MacGregor, and tonight I particularly did not want to meet anyone. When he had thrown those pebbles against my window, David had set a mood—a mood I did not want broken.

It was only when I reached the bend in the hallway that I realized that one of those closed doors I had hurried past this afternoon was the door to Lady Stewart's bedroom. I had been so new to the house when Senhora had first taken me with her that directions had eluded me, but now I heard the booming resonance of a voice that could be no one but her ladyship's, raised in anger. At the same moment a door ahead of me opened to disgorge her stepson, with Senhora close on his heels. Without rationalizing what I was doing, I drew back behind one of the innumerable pieces of statuary which lined the hall and held myself motionless, expecting them to pass

me. Instead, they drew together only a few feet away from
the door and began to talk in low voices. At first I did
not even try to listen. My own impatience to get outside
seemed to stop my ears. Then I heard Senhora spit out
the name of Martin Kubler.

"You should have known better than to have brought
him here," she said. I could not see her, but I could
imagine all too well the glittering eyes, the taut, dark
face.

William Stewart answered her, but the words blurred together until they lost themselves in undertones.

"She'll never agree to seeing him now that she knows
what he is," the woman hissed.

"That's not my fault," the man replied, no longer making an attempt to whisper. "I brought Martin here as my
guest—nothing more. How Caravels found out that he's
a psychiatrist I don't know. Marian always did associate
with fools. He put a screw in things, blurting it out that
way at the table—the idiot. It's to his advantage as much
as it is to ours to have her declared incompetent. I suppose it was MacGregor who told her."

"Keep your voice down," Senhora told him. "Of course
it was MacGregor. He reports everything. He always has.
Why do you expect she keeps him on? Not that it matters
now who told her. You might as well send Kubler back
to wherever he came from."

"You said you'd help. . . ."

The voices were nearer now, and I knew that the two
must be moving toward where I stood. I pressed myself
closer against the wall, realizing that I had been a fool
to have hidden myself like this in the first place. I should
have walked past them and kept on going. It would be
humiliating to have them find me like this—and David
was waiting.

"I promised nothing," the woman was saying. "As far
as I'm concerned, she's no different than she has been for

the past thirty years. I told you before that if you brought this to court, I'd swear that she's as sane as I am."

They were beside the statue now. I could see Senhora's sweatered arm. In another moment. . . .

I must have been involuntarily pressing to the left, because suddenly the statue gave way, rocking on its base. Reaching out to steady it, I found myself looking straight into Senhora's scowling face.

"So," she said triumphantly, "you were eavesdropping, Miss Haverlock."

I opened my mouth to protest and realized suddenly that there was no explanation I could reasonably make. They would not understand if I told them that I had wanted to leave the house without seeing anyone. Why should they? Yet I could not bear the thought that they should be left to believe that I was interested enough in their affairs to want to overhear anything they might say. Trapped, I answered one question with another.

"Why should I want to eavesdrop on you?" I said carefully. "Actually I was on my way out of the house."

"By way of the side door?" Senhora's eyes were narrow slits of suspicion.

"Front way, back way, what does it matter?" William Stewart said gruffly, and I realized that he was as disconcerted as I, as anxious as I to end this encounter. He plunged his hands nervously in and out of the pockets of his blue blazer, which was buttoned tightly over his stomach.

"If you intended to try to see Lady Stewart tonight, you must understand that it's out of the question," Senhora said sharply. "She's not at all well. There are far too many people in this house making demands on her. From now on, any instructions that she has for you will be conveyed through me."

"That's perfectly agreeable to me," I said, trying to pass her.

"It's not at all certain," the woman said, moving to the left so that she blocked my path, "that Lady Stewart will wish the inventory to be completed after all."

"I'm afraid," I said stiffly, "that if it comes to that, she will have to instruct me personally to leave. There are certain instructions that I would be willing to have 'conveyed,' as you put it, through you, and others that I would not. In fact, I think that her solicitors in London would be very much concerned if I were dismissed without a personal interview with her."

"Are you threatening me?" Senhora's voice slashed its way through the silence that followed my remark.

I had not intended to be drawn into any sort of altercation with this woman, but I found myself possessed, quite suddenly, with an absorbing fury.

"I'm explaining to you what will and will not be acceptable to me," I said. "If there is any question about the inventory being completed, I will have to know now. My time is valuable. I don't intend to put in weeks of work here for nothing."

William Stewart cleared his throat nervously. "I think," he said, "that we ought to talk this out in private."

"There's nothing to 'talk out,'" I told him. "Under the circumstances I'm going to have to insist on seeing Lady Stewart in the morning."

"She's much too ill," Senhora began.

"I'll take her doctor's word for that," I said. "She *is* being attended by a doctor, I take it. If she's had a serious relapse since I saw her this morning, he should have seen her today. *Did* he see her?"

The hall was very dimly lighted, but I could see that Senhora's face was flushed with anger.

"I think that we must trust Senhora in this affair," William Stewart said hurriedly.

"You may prefer to trust her, but I see no reason why I should," I snapped. "I intend to get in touch with her doctor tomorrow, and unless there is any reason why I should not see her, I intend to get this matter of the inventory settled once and for all then."

Senhora reached out and gripped my arm, her nails digging through the jersey into my flesh. "Marian Russell put you up to this, didn't she?" she asked, and then, turning to the man beside her: "I told you. . . ."

I did not want to hear any more. It took all my self-control not to push her away from me. My hand settled on hers, disengaging her fingers, and then I was running down the passageway and down the narrow stairs and out through the narrow door into the caressing warmth of the moonlit night.

I did not see David until he caught me by the shoulders and turned me to face him. His face was a white streak in the darkness.

"Where the devil have you been? It's been at least fifteen minutes since you switched off the light in your bedroom."

I shook my head. The night air settled like a gentle touch about me, and although David's voice was impatient, his hands were gentle, too.

"I don't want to talk about it now," I said. "I met someone when I was coming out of the house. That's all."

Instantly he was alert. He moved away from me, and I could hear a thin edge of hostility in his voice. "My mother?" he said.

"No. Only Senhora—and William Stewart."

David whispered an exclamation. "What were those two doing together?" he demanded. "They hate one another's guts."

"It was something about Kubler," I said. "They were coming out of your great-aunt's bedroom."

He whistled softly. "Why in God's name——"

"I don't want to talk about it now," I repeated, keeping my voice light, trying to recapture the mood in which I had left my room minutes before. "Besides, I'm hungry. Remember, I didn't have any dinner."

"I remember." He laughed and took my hand, bending at the same time to pick up what appeared to be a wicker basket. "All right. Let's go."

Weaving our way along the gravel paths, we passed the stone pig and emerged from the courtyard at the back of the wing where the collection was kept. Soon we were climbing up a narrow track between the pine trees. It was too dark for me to see where we were going, but David seemed to know the way. I was out of breath by the time we reached the top of the rise and emerged into the full glow of the moonlight. Below us the house stretched itself like a massive shadowy hand, dotted with a few lights.

"Here," David said. "Just over the top a bit. There's a hollow. I used to come here when I was a boy. I don't expect we can see the river."

But we could see it. Far below us in the distance it sparkled like a thin trail of white silk. On either side of it the land seemed to rise in terraced steps.

"The vineyards," David said. "My God, it's beautiful. I'd almost forgotten."

We sat down on the rough grass, and he groped in the basket for a white cloth, which he spread carefully in front of us. "There's cold chicken," he said, "and cheese, rolls and butter, and wine. I took the decanter from the alcove outside the dining room. It was all I could lay my hands on. MacGregor guards the wine cellar like a gorgon."

I ate as though I were famished, and he watched me in silence. We drank the thick, rich port from wineglasses he had brought wrapped in napkins. A slight breeze rose, brushing my still damp hair. Perhaps it was the wine or the food or the moon-glossed view, but I felt incredibly happy.

"Well," David said, throwing himself supine beside me, "what do you think of the menagerie now that you've seen it? God knows, if I'd known they were all here, I would have turned around and let you and my mother make your own way down the side of that mountain."

"Even if you'd known that your great-aunt was dying?"

He laughed. "You don't mince words, do you? No, if you want the truth, I still wouldn't have come—to appropriate one of her terms, not if it meant joining the vultures."

He raised his hands, cupping them to his lips, and a shrill whistling sound pierced the night. I realized that he was blowing on a piece of grass, and suddenly I remembered long summer afternoons at the house my father had rented once in Kent and lying flat on my back for hours, watching the clouds change their shapes. I had amused myself then, as David was now, by blowing on strips of grass—and watching ants crawl over my fingers. For a moment I ached with the awareness that for so long there had been nothing in my life to remind me of those long sunlit hours.

"No," David said abruptly, rolling on his side toward me. "No, I take back what I just said. I would have come anyway if I thought that she needed me, and I think, you know, that she does. Oh, she can keep up the old facade when she's not in too much pain. She always did like to play the tyrant. But she's losing her grip on Alcombra, and she knows it. And that's why I'm going to stay. If she wants this place turned into a museum, that's the way it's going to be."

"Do you think the others could stop it from happening? I know what her stepson is trying to do, but——"

"You mean his bringing Kubler here? That may have already backfired on dear old William, you know."

"Because Lady Stewart knows that Kubler is a psychiatrist?"

David shifted onto his back again, spreading his arms wide over his head. "No, although that will present problems if she finds out."

"She already knows," I told him. "MacGregor apparently told her what Jerez said at luncheon."

David chuckled. "What about Jerez?" he said. "I haven't seen much of him, but he seems like a genuine character —too much of a character to have latched onto my mother."

"You can't really say that," I murmured. "You don't know her, do you?"

"No! No, I don't know her!" He threw himself into a sitting position, pressing his face against his knees. "But I'm talking about Kubler. I had a chance to talk to him this afternoon—not about why he's here, not directly. But I got the impression that William didn't give him the whole story. I take it that he thought he was here at Lelia's request. Now that he knows that isn't so, I think he'll leave. He's not a bad sort—no charlatan, at any rate. It's like William not to let his right hand know what his left hand is doing. That's why he's in financial trouble."

"What do you mean?"

"Oh, he hasn't talked about it to me. We aren't what you'd call friends. He was in his early thirties when I first remember him. He lived here at Alcombra until I was ten and his father died. Presumably he helped manage the vineyards, but I don't think that he actually did anything much. He certainly wasn't a happy man. Young as I was, I realized that. He and Lelia never did get along. She likes people who perform—who do something."

David took up the decanter and poured us both another glass of port. The moonlight flickered on the glasses.

"Anyway, when his father died, he was furious because he'd been left only enough to set himself up in business. In the end Lelia told him to get out. He went to England and bought into an export-import firm that deals in Portuguese wines. Now and then he'd turn up here begging for a handout in a refined kind of way. When I was sent away to school, I lost track of him. We never happened to visit Alcombra at the same time. This is the first I've seen of him for nearly ten years, and I can't say that I think age has particularly improved him."

"How do you know that he needs money?"

David laughed. "That's thanks to Claire," he said. "I don't know where William found her, but I'm willing to bet that he handed her a story about being heir to Lelia's fortune. She doesn't strike me as the sort of girl who'd have attached herself to someone like him without pretty substantial motivation." He rolled over to face me again.

"More wine?" he said.

I shook my head.

"Listen, Irene," he said in a low voice. "Do you really want me to talk about this? From what Jerez said tonight, I take it that you'd rather not be too involved in the family's little crises."

"Jerez!" I smiled and let myself slide down until I was lying, looking up at both David and the moon. "He's incredible. What did he say about me?"

"He gave us all a little lecture over the soup, as a matter of fact," David told me. "I think he got it into his head that you hadn't come down to dinner because you felt that we were, somehow, bearing in on you. He said that he had made a mistake himself in suggesting that you show Kubler around the collection. In fact, he went on at considerable length about how you should be let alone to do what you came here to do."

I turned my cheek against the grass and smelled the warm thick scent of summer. The moonlight was so bright that I could see the small white flowers nestled close to the ground. I was not certain whether I wanted David to go on talking about the family or not, but so far it was the only link between us. And besides, I had promised Marian. . . . I swept the thought of her to the back of my mind. I owed her nothing, and I did not want to risk anything that would destroy this moment.

"Tell me about Claire," I said. "I'm a woman, and you know about women and curiosity."

"Yes, you're a woman," David said slowly. I closed my eyes against the moonlight as he bent closer over me, and I felt his lips brush my face. For a moment neither of us spoke, and then with a sudden sharpness, he repeated Claire's name.

"She had a lot to say to me over dinner," he said. "I think she's more interested in enticing Kubler, actually. But he wasn't interested. I don't think he had a word for anyone—probably wondering how he was going to extricate himself from all this."

I opened my eyes and saw that he was sitting up again, staring off across the valley.

"Claire?" I said gently.

"When you get to know me better," David said, "you'll find that I have a very annoying habit. I rarely speak directly to the point. It takes a long time for me to tell a story properly, and tonight for some reason I think that it's going to take longer than usual."

He turned and looked down at me, grinning. "Claire," he said, "apparently decided that I was the only halfway-acceptable substitute for Kubler and monopolized me during the meal—not that she had to compete with anyone else to do that, you understand. William never did care for me, and I think Jerez hasn't quite made me out. And then, of course, there was my mother. Under the circumstances there wasn't much chance that the two of us would launch into a stimulating conversation about old times. In fact, she scarcely looked at me."

"Claire," I said.

"Yes, Claire. Well, as I said, she talked nonstop—not about herself, you understand. She's far too clever for that. But about London and the latest shows. I take it she wishes she were back there, and it's only a guess, but I think she was trying to make it appear that when she is there, she and William circulate in a far more glamorous circle than I think is probable."

He shrugged his shoulders. "Another thing I ought to warn you about," he said, "is that I'm inclined to be a little intolerant of people I don't like, and I don't like Claire. I think she guessed as much, but she kept up the game. Asked me about my work at university. Actually pretended an overwhelming interest in Georgian poetry. God!"

Pushing himself to his feet, he revolved in a circle, arms outstretched, and flung himself back on the ground, face down in a pool of moonlight, laughing. "What are we doing talking about someone like Claire Stewart? Let's discuss the relationship between a full moon and madness."

"Don't be a fool," I teased him, sitting up and wrapping my skirt around my bare legs. The clouds had appeared again, and as I spoke, one swept across the moon. The river below disappeared, and so did he. The breeze was stronger now, and I felt suddenly chilled. "Come on, now," I said. "What did Claire say that makes you think that her husband is desperate for money?"

"I didn't say he was desperate." David's voice seemed far away. "I said he needed it. Claire told me that the bottom had fallen out of the business he invested in. She just slipped that detail into the conversation in the process of telling me she had been trying to convince William that she should go back to modeling—high-fashion modeling. She made a great point of that. Irene. . . ."

In the darkness I could not even see the outline of him, but suddenly his hand was cupping my face. If the moon had not been behind a cloud, it would have been all right. If I could have seen him, I would not have conjured up Philip's face. I leaned to the side and drew my face away.

"Sorry," I heard David say. "Sorry! Sorry! Sorry!"

The moon sped into view, windblown now, in flight. Before it disappeared, I saw that David had risen to his feet and that he was holding the decanter to his lips, draining the last of the wine. I suppose I was confused. Otherwise I would never have mentioned Marian at that precise moment. But I had to say something—anything.

"Your mother came to talk to me today," I said.

"Did she?" His voice was cold.

"She wanted me to speak to you. I——"

"Is that why you came out here with me tonight? Carrying messages?"

"No," I protested. "No. I came because I wanted to. It doesn't matter about her now. I'm sorry."

"But it does matter," he said. For a moment his face was illuminated in a glare of white light, and then the darkness engulfed him again. "What did she want you to say to me?"

"She wants to talk to you herself, but——"

"Then why doesn't she?"

Suddenly I wanted to weep. What was it Philip had said to me once? That in the end I spoiled every moment. That had hurt, but I had been so certain that it was just because he was he and I. . . .

"She wants to explain," I said in a low voice.

"I imagine that she does. It's a good time for it now, isn't it? Now that I'm no longer a responsibility. Now that there's just a chance that I may inherit some of that money she's had her eye on for so long."

"But you aren't going to inherit anything. Senhora and MacGregor will have something, but all the rest will go to maintaining the museum." The words burst out of me involuntarily.

"And how do you know that?" He might have been a stranger. Whatever our relationship had been, it had floundered when I had drawn away from him.

"I can't remember," I said. "Someone said. It doesn't matter."

"That's one of your favorite phrases, isn't it? 'It doesn't matter.' But everything does matter, you know—to someone."

The bitterness had gone from his voice now, leaving it flat and expressionless.

"She simply wanted me to tell you that she—she doesn't dare approach you. She thinks that Lady Stewart has turned you against her. She doesn't want to be rebuffed."

For a moment he did not speak. "I suppose," he said, "none of us want to be rebuffed, but sometimes you have to take the chance. Come. We'll go back now."

He did not speak again as we made our way back down the hill. He took my hand but only to help me find the way. And the moon stayed behind the clouds.

CHAPTER

4

It must have been past midnight when I reached my bedroom to find MacGregor waiting for me outside the door. The house had seemed totally silent. Sleeping. The front door locked. David had opened it with a large key that fitted noiselessly in the old-fashioned keyhole, and we had parted at the top of the stairs, leaving the silence in the vast hall below us unbroken.

I was so lost in my own sense of depression that I did not notice the old man until my hand was on the knob of my bedroom door. Only a single table lamp glowed at the far end of the long corridor, and when he moved out of the shadows that had hidden him, I cried out, startled. His creased face was set in its usual grim lines of disapproval.

"Her ladyship wants to see you," he said in a low voice thick with a Scottish burr. "Come with me."

I wanted to protest. I wanted to tell him that I would

see her in the morning. But then I remembered what Senhora had said to me about the fact that from now on she would act as a messenger for her mistress, and that there was some doubt about whether or not Lady Stewart would want the inventory to be completed. I had taken a bold line with her in my anger, insisting on my right to see the woman who had employed me. I had made threats that involved contacting an unknown doctor. It seemed as though all that had happened years ago, and now—now I was not at all certain that I wanted to stay at Alcombra. Perhaps it would be best to put the matter straight now, no matter what the time.

And so I followed the old man to her room. The thick carpet muffled our footsteps. Only when I saw the light shining around the rim of her door did I realize that I was tense with nervousness. If Senhora was with her, there would be difficulties. And I did not want any more difficulties.

But there was no one in the long high-ceilinged room except the old woman, propped up in the canopied bed as I had seen her that morning. She nodded past me at MacGregor as I came toward her, and he went outside, closing the door noiselessly behind him.

"He will see that we are not interrupted," Lady Stewart said when I reached the bed. The single light that burned on the table beside her made a white mask of her face. "Sit down. Yes, there. Move the chair up a bit. Senhora has ears like a hawk."

"She told me earlier this evening that you weren't well," I said. The chair was so close to the bed that I was caught in the pool of light. Beyond us the room receded into darkness. The air was heavy with the smell of medicine, harsh acrid odors.

"It escapes me why a dying woman should be expected to be well, as you put it," Lady Stewart said dryly. "Hand me that handkerchief, will you, my dear? There, on the table."

There was something different about her tonight, I realized. This morning she had been tense, defiant, determined to demonstrate that she was a powerful woman. Perhaps it had been the presence of Senhora in the room which had made her so harsh. Even physically she seemed to have changed. I remembered the way her gnarled hand had gripped the shawl about her heavy shoulders, the way she had kept pushing herself up from the pillows, the sudden viciousness with which she had struck out with her cane. Now she seemed to exude only an overpowering weariness, which softened the thick, hawk-nosed face. There was nothing in those dark eyes except a certain curiosity as she looked at me. I guessed that this morning she had been too intent on creating an impression to consider me as a person. I waited, but she did not speak. Uncomfortably I glanced down at my crossed legs and saw that the slit skirt had fallen away from them and that my skin was flecked with bits of dry grass.

"I've been outside," I said with sudden awkwardness.

"I thought you might have been." Her lips curled in a sly smile. "Do you think it's wise to walk about alone at this time of night?"

"I wasn't alone," I said.

She waited.

"I was with David."

"Ah, yes." The smile faded. "And what do you think of my grandnephew?"

"He's. . . ." I realized suddenly that I did not know what to say. Somehow I did not want to make the usual pat comments.

"I think a good deal of him," Lady Stewart said. "Tell me, Miss Haverlock, do you think it's wise of him to stay here?"

"If he wants to stay. . . ."

For the first time since I had come into the room she moved restlessly against the pillows.

"I told him that he needn't feel obliged to see me

dead," she said with sudden harshness, "but I didn't ask you to come here to listen to me ramble on about matters that can't possibly concern you. Tell me. Have you looked at the collection?"

"Yes," I said, relieved. "I spent the afternoon in the long gallery."

"Ah!" Patches of color came into the white cheeks. "You saw the portrait of me, then."

"It's a magnificent thing," I said truthfully.

"I'd like to see it again before I die," the old woman said slowly. "I expect you'll think I'm a fool, but every day of my life that I've been in this house, I've gone to look at it. I haven't looked in mirrors for years if I could help it, but that portrait. . . . I was just twenty-five when it was painted, and as I got older—one doesn't change that much inside, you know. When I looked at that portrait, I could forget what the years were doing to me. Time is cruel, my dear. You don't know that yet, but you will."

She paused, and for a moment her broad face was convulsed with an expression of pain.

"No," she said as I started to rise. "It's all right." And then, pressing the handkerchief to her mouth: "I hate this, you know. It should have happened suddenly. I always hoped that it would happen suddenly. Now everything's failing me. It's hard to remember. . . . What were we talking about?" Her voice rose desperately. "You see, I can't remember what we were talking about."

"The long gallery," I said in a low voice, "the Sargent portrait. You'd asked me——"

"If you'd started with the inventory. Yes, that was what I wanted to know." Her eyes softened with relief. "Can it be done in the time I set? Can you do it in three weeks?"

"I think so, yes," I said, "if you still want it done."

She seemed to stiffen against the pillows. "Why would you ask that?" she demanded. "Of course I want it done."

I decided to be frank. "I talked with Senhora tonight,"

I said. "She implied that you might change your mind."

"Don't listen to her!" The old woman tried to push herself away from the pillows. "Do you understand that, Miss Haverlock? Don't listen to her."

She let herself grow limp again, breathing heavily. I knew that I was taking a risk to go on. I was not even certain of the nature of this woman's illness. I did not want to bring on any sort of attack, and yet. . . .

"She told me that I would not be seeing you again," I said slowly, "that any directions you might want to give me would come through her."

"I thought I knew what I could expect from her," the old woman muttered, her voice so low that I had to lean forward to hear her, "but she's like the others."

"She may simply feel that it would tire you to talk to me," I said soothingly.

She shook her head back and forth against the pillow. "Would you have believed her," she said, "if I hadn't sent MacGregor for you? I suspected that something was wrong, you see. The doctor should have come today. I don't know what's going on any more. I. . . ." Her voice trailed off into silence.

"No," I said. "I wasn't willing to accept what she said. I told her that I was going to insist on seeing you in the morning, that it would be necessary for your doctor to tell me himself that you were too ill to see me."

The old woman's eyes caught and held mine, and suddenly I could see the remnants of the beauty Sargent had captured. "I like you, Miss Haverlock," she said. "No, it's more than that. I trust you, and besides David, there's no one else in this house I can trust. I suppose I can't be certain even about the doctor." She paused. "Do you know about the man William brought here?"

I nodded.

"He's not going to see me," she said, her voice cracking on the words. "I'm not mad."

"No," I said slowly, "you're not mad."

Her clawlike hand crawled across the coverlet toward mine. Her fingers were cold despite the oppressive warmth of the room.

"They may say," she whispered, "that I imagined—oh, a good many things. And it's odd, you know. I haven't admitted this to anyone before, but I do have the feeling that—as though the walls were closing in."

"You could tell them all to go," I said. "You could dismiss Senhora."

She laughed then, although the sound she made was very unlike a laugh; it was deep in her throat. Then the sound turned into a racking cough, which she tried to stifle with her handkerchief.

"No, it's all right," she gasped as I half rose from my chair. And then: "What was that?" Her voice sank to a whisper. "Do you hear someone outside the door?"

I listened, aware of a sudden chill of fear. There was no sound.

"Senhora's room is next to this one," the old woman murmured. "Thank God there's no communicating door. MacGregor will give us some warning, at least, if she comes."

"But that shouldn't be necessary," I insisted. "All of this shouldn't be necessary. If you don't trust her, let her go. It shouldn't be difficult to find a nurse. You could. . . ."

The old woman closed her eyes. "No, my dear," she said. "You don't understand, and I should warn you. For your own sake, you shouldn't let anyone know that you've said what you have to me. I know these people better than you could ever know them. I know what they're capable of."

In that moment it occurred to me that I might have been wrong. Perhaps, I thought, she is mad. Her situation was difficult. I could see that. She had been a woman accustomed all her life to controlling others, but she implied a threatening situation that could not exist. In all probability Senhora simply wanted to keep her from becoming excited. Lady Stewart had deliberately over-tired herself with me during that morning interview, as she was overtiring herself now. As for Marian and William, they were probably both clinging to the hope that something would happen that would change this woman's plans for Alcombra. But that was natural, too.

"You're tired," I said, rising, "and everything is settled between us. I'll complete the inventory. You can depend on me to be as quick as I can be. And then——"

"Wait." Her eyes flickered open, and her grip on my hand tightened. "There was something else. I've made a list—a list of all the things in the collection that I can remember. It's not at all complete. I wouldn't have needed you if I could have remembered everything, but I've been afraid. . . . It was the real reason I wanted the inventory made. There are so many things of value. It would be so easy for someone to take what they wanted. I have to know. . . ."

She began to cough again. Leaning over her, I smoothed the white hair back from her forehead.

"Don't talk any more," I said in a low voice. "I think you're probably wrong. They wouldn't have stolen from you, but I'll make a careful check. You only have to give me the list, and I'll do what you want me to do."

The eighth item on the list was missing. I stood staring at the spidery handwriting on the sheet of white-linen stationery for many minutes before being struck by the full significance of the simple fact that an eighteenth-century silver snuffbox was not in the glass case where it should have been.

The list that Lady Stewart had given me the previous night described about a hundred of her possessions. There was a smattering of everything: antique candelabra, bits of furniture, small bronzes, and jewelry. Paintings, how-ever, predominated the list. Beside each item she had indicated where it should be found. Evidently there had been some doubt in her mind whether she would be able to talk to me as she had, for a letter accompanied the list, a letter explaining why she wanted me to make this particular check. "No one has been given permission to move a single object," she had written. "If any one of these things is not in its proper place, I must know at once. If for some reason it is impossible for you to see me personally, send a message through MacGregor."

I remembered how the old man had been standing patiently outside Lady Stewart's door last night when I came into the dim light of the corridor. He had not answered when I murmured goodnight to him, and as I went down the corridor, I had heard a door click open. When I looked back, he had disappeared, presumably into Lady Stewart's room. The relationship of the two old people was an intriguing one. There was something in Mac-Gregor of the caricature of the loyal family servant, and yet, as I had undressed, I remembered suddenly that when she had said that she trusted me and that she trusted David as well, she had not mentioned Mac-Gregor's name.

I took out my notebook and began to jot down a message, and then I paused. I had no way of knowing how she would react when she knew that something was missing, and it was all too possible that the snuffbox was actually there somewhere in the five rooms. Her memory could have failed her. With the mind's eye, it was simplicity itself to see an object in a place in which it had never been. I decided to check the rest of the list as quickly as I could. If there were a number of things missing, I would have no choice but to let her know, but with the reminder that the completed inventory might find them rediscovered.

It was so early in the morning that I did not feel as though I was taking any time from what I should be doing in the long gallery. I had hoped to complete the inventory of the gallery today, and with that in mind, I had set my alarm for six. The events of the night and day before had accomplished some sort of change in attitude in me, or perhaps it was simply that I felt a new assurance. I had taken a sleeping pill to get to sleep so that I would not think of David and the picnic in the moonlight. I had often taken sleeping pills when I had been engaged to Philip—and afterward, as well. It was like a welcome return to sink into a dreamless sleep. I had awakened determined to do what I had come here for as quickly as possible, and with no interference. As for the sort of restriction that Senhora and the housekeeper set on the serving of meals, I was no longer willing to put up with that nonsense. I intended to start work at seven, and I was not about to do so without having breakfast.

Dressed in brown slacks and a blouse which would not show the dirt, I had descended promptly at six-thirty to the kitchens at the back of the house. The servants were having their breakfast, seated around a long rough-wooden table in the center of a dark-beamed room equipped with a massive old-fashioned stove and an iron sink. A plump, gray-haired woman was seated at the head of the table, MacGregor at the foot. Four neatly uniformed maids lined the sides, and at a separate small table nearby sat a man whose weather-wrinkled face seemed to indicate that he was the gardener; beside him was the boy who had carried my luggage the day before. Everyone except MacGregor had stared at me in astonishment when I introduced myself and explained why I was down so early. The housekeeper had been obviously flustered and protested in Portuguese that I should be served in the dining room. The name Senhora punctuated her flurries of protest. But I insisted on staying where I was, and in the end a chair was drawn up for me beside the maids, and I consumed my eggs and tea and toast with relish. MacGregor had not spoken, but once I had caught his rheumy eyes fixed on me with an expression of what I thought, for him, might be amusement.

Now I stood in the first of the five rooms in which the collection was kept, staring at the ninth item on the list, which was a landscape painting by Fernandes. Lady Stewart had designated the rooms in which each treasure was to be found by a letter, and in order that there would be no mistake, she had drawn a sketch of the five rooms, the chapel, and the long gallery on the back of the first sheet. Her descriptions were quite clear. By eleven I had checked off every item except five; those five things, as far as I could determine, were not in the places where they should have been.

There was no possibility of my doing more than make a rough estimate of the value of what was gone. Besides the snuffbox, I could not find a small painted panel by Lopes which Lady Stewart had described as being a representation of the death of the Virgin. Also missing were two fourteenth-century bronzes of saints and a ruby ring that was supposed to have belonged to Dona Constanza, a Castilian who had been married to Don Pedro, the heir of Alfonso IV. Every one of the missing things was small, small enough to be taken from these rooms while tucked under a sweater or placed in a pocket. I guessed that the total worth of what was gone might be about ten thousand pounds—not, of course, if it had to be sold secretly. At an open auction such as those at Christie's, however, ten thousand pounds was a modest estimate.

There was no question in my mind but that I must let Lady Stewart know, and it struck me as somehow wrong to send a note until I was certain that Senhora was determined to prevent me from seeing her. Tucking the checked list into the pocket of my blouse, I left the dimly lit rooms of the wing by way of the long gallery and crossed the sunlit courtyard to the side door of the main house, refusing to think of the beauty of the place by moonlight and the eagerness with which I had left my room to meet David in the shadow of the white walls.

I could hear a man's voice speaking beyond the door of Lady Stewart's bedroom, and my first thought was that the doctor was with her. But when Senhora opened the door to me, I saw Martin Kubler standing by the canopied bed. His broad face was set in sober lines as he bent over Lady Stewart, who, no longer propped high on her pillows, lay flat on the bed, her body muffled by layers of thick blankets. He raised his eyes to meet mine, and for the first time I saw him as a man in himself, an individual. The resemblance to Philip no longer struck me, perhaps because under no circumstances could Philip have managed to convey, as Martin did, the impression of quiet command.

"So it's you!" Senhora hissed as I closed the door behind me. She was wearing the same crumpled skirt she had worn the day before, and the same shabby sweater was bunched about her leanness. Her dark skin was even darker under her eyes, and her face was molded in hard lines.

"Have you come to see the damage you've done?" she demanded. "She's unconscious. See for yourself."

I moved slowly across the long room to the bed. The drapes of the long windows were drawn; it could have been midnight outside. The same small lamp cast an oval of light over the gray face of the old woman. Her eyes were closed, and she was breathing heavily.

"You were here last night, weren't you?" Senhora asked accusingly from behind my shoulder. "Don't deny it. I heard you leave the room. I watched you leave with my own eyes. It's no good MacGregor trying to lie about it—or you, either."

Ignoring her, I spoke across the bed to Martin Kubler. "What's happened?" I asked in a low voice.

He had been holding the old woman's wrist, but now he placed her arm gently on the blanket. The light from the bedside lamp fired the red of his hair as he raised his head. His eyes met mine. "I want to speak to you for a moment, Miss Haverlock," he said.

"Irene," I murmured. Somehow I did not want to maintain the fiction that I was a stranger to him. No one who could arouse such strong responses of confidence in me could ever be a stranger. I went with him to a shadowy corner of the room, not aware, until she spoke, that Senhora had followed us.

"Don't let this woman lie to you," she said shrilly, pointing a finger at me. "I told her that it would not be possible for her to speak directly with Lady Stewart. She is responsible for this."

"Be quiet!" Martin spoke in a low voice, but there was no mistaking the absolute nature of the command, the command of a doctor accustomed to dealing with people who followed orders, at least in the sickroom. "I intend to talk to Miss Haverlock in private. As for you, it would be best if you sit by Lady Stewart. I should be informed if there is any change in her condition. Is that clear?"

"It is not for you to give orders!" Senhora spat out the words. "I will not be treated——"

"If you find it impossible to control yourself," Martin Kubler said, "perhaps it would be better if one of the maids watches her. We can send to Oporto for a professional nurse. Yes, on the whole, I think that would be best."

For a moment the dark woman glared at him, and then she turned and stalked across the room to the bed.

"Perhaps," Martin Kubler murmured, "it would be better, under the circumstances, if we talked outside." In a loud voice he said to Senhora: "I'll be in the corridor if you need me."

She made no response, nor did he speak to me until we were outside the door. A maid was dusting the statue behind which I had hidden the night before, but on seeing us, she scuttled down the corridor. It was better here in the full light that poured in at the long window at the end of the passage. I was not sorry to have left the bedroom and Senhora behind me.

"First of all," Martin said in a low voice, "I should explain why I'm attending Lady Stewart this morning. I realize that after what was said at the luncheon table the other day, you may find my presence in her bedroom somewhat irregular."

He was the sort of person whose eyes address you as directly as their voice. "No," I said. "After all, you're a doctor, and Lady Stewart is ill."

"She has a regular doctor," he reminded me, "and technically, I'm a psychiatrist. The fact remains that you must wonder why her regular doctor hasn't been called in."

I found that I could not play a hedging game with this man, even under the guise of politeness.

"Yes," I said, "I did wonder."

He smiled as though my frankness delighted him. "There's a simple-enough explanation," he said. "Lady Stewart's regular doctor lives in Oporto, which is a fair distance, and at the moment, he's ill. I'm a medical doctor as well as a psychiatrist," he said. "I'm quite qualified to attend her." He hesitated. "I know there's probably no need for me to try to justify my presence here, but I want you to understand that when I arrived—when I realized the situation for what it was—I wanted no part of it. I intended to leave Portugal today, to return to London. Under the circumstances I have no choice but to stay until another doctor is found who will be willing to come the distance from Oporto, or until Lady Stewart's own doctor recovers. He is, I understand, an elderly man who has been treating her for years."

It was all straightforward enough, and I found that I wanted to believe him. I had been a fool to let the atmosphere of mistrust in this house affect me. I instinctively trusted this man.

"How serious is her condition?" I said. "Senhora is

right, you know. I came to see Lady Stewart last night—very late—but it was at her request. If it's anything that I did——"

"No," Martin said gently. "I'm certain that you weren't responsible, but the thing is this: Apparently you were the last person to see her conscious. Senhora claims she found Lady Stewart in the state she is still in early this morning. Whatever you can tell me about her condition when you talked to her will be important."

I stared at the window reflectively. What was it that Senhora had said to me? That she had seen me leaving Lady Stewart's room the night before? If that was so, how did it happen that she had not gone directly to her mistress? I could not imagine her not doing so, and if she had, then I was not the last person to have seen her during the night.

"What's wrong, Irene?" Martin murmured. In the clear light that flooded us from the window I saw that his face was drawn. Obviously he was under a great deal of tension—and no wonder. The entire responsibility for this situation had been suddenly cast on his shoulders.

"Senhora found Lady Stewart unconscious, you say?" I asked him.

"Yes, this morning."

"She did not see her last night, after I had left the bedroom?"

"No. Or if she did, she saw fit not to tell me."

His eyes were brown like Philip's, but Philip had never looked at me in precisely the way this man was looking —as though he really saw me. Yes, that was exactly it. With Martin it was as though there were so much mutual understanding between us that we could talk on two levels at once. Perhaps it was because he was accustomed professionally to searching for the real person behind the mask, the real meanings in words strung one after the other. Whatever the reason, I knew that he would not misinterpret anything that I said. I decided not to pursue the subject of Senhora. Both of us realized that she might well prove a liar.

"When I left Lady Stewart," I said, "she seemed to be well enough. A bit tired, I think. I imagine that she found it a strain to talk, but there were certain things she felt that she should say to me. She coughed some while I was with her, and once I thought that she was in pain."

Martin nodded. "She's a dying woman, you know," he said.

"That was what I was told."

"She had a massive stroke a few months ago," he said. "That much is obvious. She's paralyzed from the waist down. Since then there have been other slight strokes. Fortunately—or unfortunately perhaps for her—the strokes have not affected her mind. There's heart damage as well. That's undoubtedly why she coughs a good deal."

"But—but how do you know about her mind?" I asked him. "You haven't talked with her since you arrived at Alcombra, have you? And she was already unconscious when you were called to her this morning."

"I confess that what I know about her mental condition is based on hearsay," Martin admitted. "You're quite right. I haven't talked with her. When William suggested that she see me, she refused. I'm basing my estimation of her lucidity on what her grandnephew told me."

"David?"

"Yes. Forget that I mentioned the state of her mind. I was brought here, as you probably know, because her stepson felt that her mind had been affected by the strokes. He claimed to have no faith in the doctor from Oporto. I had no idea when he talked to me in London that there was a question of vested interest on his part. I mean I was not aware that he was interested in breaking her will on the basis of my testimony. You've talked with her. Did you find her rational?"

"Yes," I said, "completely rational. She had the feeling that she was losing her control over the household. I think she may have felt that Senhora deliberately intended to keep her from any contact with anyone besides herself, but I think she had good reason for feeling that way."

"Yes," he said. "I sense something. . . ."

For a moment he was silent, staring past at the window, his broad face intent with concentration. He was, I thought for no reason, taller than Philip. My head was level with his shoulder. But it was not a matter of small differences. There was something solid about this man, something unutterably reassuring.

"It would be best," he said, almost as though he were talking to himself, "if she were in a hospital. I think that she's suffered another slight stroke, but I can't be certain. Senhora tells me that she's always refused to consider leaving Alcombra. However, I don't think that I can take the responsibility. I'll be honest with you, Irene, I want to leave this place as soon as possible."

I felt a sudden unreasoning shock of anxiety and realized that for some reason I did not completely understand myself, I did not want him to go.

"And you," he said, his eyes meeting mine, "are you quite certain that you should stay?"

It was as though a tape recorder had been set off in my mind. I seemed to hear Lady Stewart's voice telling me that she trusted me.

"No," I said. "I can't explain why, but I feel that I must stay."

To my surprise, lunch was brought to me on a tray while I worked in the small chapel. The maid muttered something about Senhora having said that I should have my midday meal here in the future and disappeared. I was glad enough of the chance to continue my work uninterrupted by a foray into the main house, but at the same time I found it rather strange that Senhora had changed her mind—unless she wanted to keep me away from the others as much as possible. The night before, when I had come upon her and William Stewart, she had dropped the fact that she knew Marian and I had talked together. She had gone further than that, actually, implying that I was helping Marian—whatever that was supposed to mean. Senhora had obviously determined to keep me as much as possible away from the others as well.

Whatever her motives in having given the order, I had no complaint. I did not want to see David again so soon. There was little room in my mind now for anything except the necessity of finishing the inventory as soon as possible. I wanted to be certain beyond any doubt that those parts of the collection which I had not been able to find were, indeed, missing. If there actually was a thief in the house, the knowledge that I was listing the contents of the rooms could act only as a preventive to further theft —assuming always that Lady Stewart's memory had not played her false, that she had had in her possession the ring and the painted panel and the other things I had not been able to find. It occurred to me that since she was not able to take steps to prevent anyone but me from entering these rooms, perhaps I should do so. The wing did not appear to be locked, either at night or at any other time. There had been no necessity to give me keys to these rooms. Even the first time I had come here, everything had been open, vulnerable to anyone who might wish to come here. Yet all the rooms had locks. I determined to talk to MacGregor that night and see that this part of the house was protected. Surely that would have been the order that Lady Stewart would have given.

I sat on the small altar beside an elaborately carved fourteenth-century lectern and ate the lunch of cold meat and salad. A carafe of rosé had been provided, and I sipped it slowly, lost in thought, while beyond the stained-glass windows the afternoon light faded. A shower was evidently approaching, for I heard the crack of distant thunder.

The question of the missing pieces of the collection

was, I found, beginning to obsess me. It was reasonable to suspect theft—only too reasonable, considering the situation. William Stewart needed money if what David had told me was true. There was every chance that he would not be able to invalidate his stepmother's will after her death. David had implied that he was an unscrupulous man. It would not have taken any particular creativity on his part to have come up with the idea of safeguarding his future by taking what he could from this wing. If that was true, he must have been upset when he had discovered that I had been hired to do the inventory. Certainly Marian had made no secret, during that first day's drive here with me, that she was opposed to the idea. She had subsequently admitted to me that she had for a long time grudged the fact that none of Lady Stewart's wealth had been shared with her side of the family. William had an even more direct claim in that it had been his father's money that had allowed the collection to be accumulated in the first place. Either one of them could have easily formulated a rationale that would have excused their taking what they wanted.

But, I reminded myself, pouring out the last of the wine, it was scarcely fair to restrict the list of suspects to Marian and William Stewart. The house was full of people, not only guests but servants. Senhora had told William that she would not be party to an attempt to prove Lady Stewart mentally incompetent, but would she have necessarily rejected the opportunity to help herself to a few small objects of art while she still had the opportunity? Perhaps, when Lady Stewart saw my final list, she would realize that many more of her possessions than five were missing. Perhaps someone had been helping himself for years. I knew nothing about MacGregor, for example, except that Lady Stewart had trusted him to keep us uninterrupted the night before. Still, it might be that the old man could be depended upon to do anything that would foil Senhora. There was likely to be a certain amount of rivalry between two long-term retainers such as they were.

It was all hypothesis, however. I put the tray aside and rose, reminding myself that it was too early for accusations. I could try to see to it that the wing was locked in the future, but other than that my only responsibility was to complete the inventory. Luckily the chapel was not going to take much time. Most of the objects were large, like the sarcophagus and the altar screen.

The thunder was closer now, and the light was so dim that I had to turn on all the small electric tapers and use the flashlight as well. Usually the air in the rooms where I was working was cooler than outside because of the thickness of the stone walls, but as the storm approached, the atmosphere became more and more oppressive. The silence, which until now I had welcomed, seemed somehow ominous.

I was intent on reading the Latin inscription at the base of a small twelfth-century statue of the Virgin when I heard the sound. For a moment I thought it was simply the cracking of the thunder, and then I heard it again and realized that someone was walking about in one of the adjoining rooms. I got to my feet and went to the door, and as I did so, the sound unmistakably became that of heels clicking on the tiled floor.

My first thought was that the maid had returned to take the tray back to the kitchen, but then I realized that all of the servants, with the exception of MacGregor, Senhora, and the housekeeper, wore cork-soled native sandals. I stood in the arched stone doorway that Lady Stewart had brought from God knows what decaying country chapel and stared into the next room. The lights were not on there, and I could see only shadows, all of them immobile in the dusk.

In order to switch on the lights in the room I would have to cross to the other side, and the idea held no appeal for me. Thunder rumbled overhead, and the room was plunged into deeper darkness. Rain began to splatter against the stone grilled windows set high in the walls.

I waited, uncomfortably aware that I was afraid. It was the kind of fear I had known as a child when my parents had put me to bed in the room on the third floor of the town house in Chelsea where we had lived, a room that was part of an old nursery, with iron bars on the small windows and deep dark corners and closets. I remembered how my heart had pounded as I had huddled under the covers, casting reason aside, certain that someone was in the room with me, plugging my ears so that I could not hear them if they moved, pressing myself into the mattress, as though by some miraculous effort I could become part of the bed. Now the same feeling was rising in me, the same panic, the same certainty that I was not alone.

"Who's there?" My voice sounded harsh and unfamiliar to me. "Is anyone there?" There was no answer, no sound, until a thin white line of lightning ripped its way across that small portion of the sky visible from the window above me to the right.

I tried to will myself to move, to turn back to the chapel and continue my work. Or if I did not have the courage to stay here alone, I could go out through the long gallery and cross the courtyard to the house. Run away. I taunted myself with the words.

No, I would stay. It was only three in the afternoon, and I had another good three hours' work ahead of me. With any luck, I could finish the chapel today, and that would leave me with only the five rooms—the hardest rooms to deal with, granted. But the psychological value of having done the long gallery and the chapel in the first two days would be valuable.

The detailed remembrance of what I had already done and what I meant to do gave me confidence. Tomorrow I would lock this wing off from the rest of the house not only during the day but also when I was working here. The maid could leave the luncheon tray outside the door at a certain time. I need never go through this particular experience again if I could be given the keys, and even if Lady Stewart did not regain consciousness soon, I was certain that MacGregor would give them to me.

In the meanwhile I could reassure myself by beaming the flashlight around this room—reassure myself and go back to translating the inscription, which would give me a more positive identification of the Virgin. It was as simple as that. The flashlight was in my hand. How strange that it should be necessary for me to literally force myself to move my finger over the switch. Suddenly it was done, and a pool of light shone on the tiled floor. I raised the torch abruptly and sent it scanning about the crowded room, flickering over the hooded fireplace, the cabinets, the statues. Everything the light touched seemed to be given a life of its own as it was propelled out of the darkness, and then there was a face peering out at me, a black-mustached man with cruel eyes and a ruff. . . .

I heard myself laugh shrilly as I realized that it was only one of the portraits that lined the walls. The laugh rebounded off the stone walls and seemed to flood against my ears, and over the echo I heard another laugh—that of a man—and something inside me seemed to freeze. I lowered the flashlight, my arm gone weak, and Jerez Caravels stepped into the glare. His teeth glittered in his swarthy face.

"I must apologize," he said. "I think, perhaps, that I have frightened you."

I turned my back on him and went into the chapel, where the electric tapers made spots of light in the dusk. Overhead the thunder growled to a crescendo of discordant sound. I leaned against the stone wall, aware that my legs were shaking so that I could scarcely stand. Out of the corner of my eyes I saw Jerez standing in the arched doorway. I turned to face him.

"Why didn't you answer me when I called?"

"You must accept my apologies, Miss Haverlock," he said, coming to take my arm. "Irene. Here, there must be somewhere you can sit down."

I let him lead me to the altar and sat down, clasping my hands about my knees to keep them from trembling. Relief was succeeded by anger. He had no right to frighten me as he had done. There was no reason. . . .

"It was the storm that brought me here," he said, sinking down beside me, pinching the crease in his trousers in that same gesture I had noticed in the courtyard when we had first met. He was wearing a gray lounge suit and a white shirt and tie. There was something foppish about the way he dressed—foppish and at the same time oddly old-fashioned. His elegance had amused me before, but now I found it annoying. He had lost my indulgence by standing silent in the shadows as I flashed the light around that room.

"The storm?" I said coldly.

"Ah, you are annoyed. I guessed that you *would* be annoyed at being disturbed. That was why I did not answer you when you first called. I thought that I could simply creep away. . . . Forgive me. It would have been much better for me to have identified myself at once and left you to your work, as I intend to do now. I realize, you see, better than the others that you must be left alone. It was I who encouraged Senhora to send you your luncheon here. I——" He was on his feet, moving toward the door.

"Why did you come here in the first place?" I demanded. "What has the storm to do with it?"

He smiled down at me. "It is only right," he said, "that under the circumstances I satisfy your curiosity. No, don't look at me like that. You terrify me."

He laughed again, but uneasily this time. The thunder and lightning seemed to have ceased, but the rain dashed heavily against the stained-glass windows.

"It's very simple, really," Jerez said. "When it started to rain, I was outside in the courtyard, and I happened to look over at this wing of the house and thought—thought, mind you, that I saw one of the windows open. Naturally I imagined the kind of damage that any sort of seepage might do, and so I came in here. I could hear you moving about in the chapel here, but as I said, I didn't want to disturb you. I'm making that my campaign, you see, to guarantee that you not be disturbed in your work."

He smiled down at me confidently, and I, in turn, looked down at the stone floor. It was a lie, of course. Did he expect that I did not know that it was improbable that any of those heavily grilled windows could be opened? He was here for some other purpose, and yet I found I could not challenge him. It was not that I was afraid. I simply sensed that it would be unwise to press the point. Something else lay under that smooth, smiling mask that this man presented to the world, but I did not want to know what it was.

"But, of course, I should have realized that you would be frightened when you heard me moving about," he went on. "It's a bit—eerie in here, don't you think? And then, of course, there was the thunder. The peacocks don't like it, you know—storms. I expect you heard them screaming a few minutes ago."

I felt as though his eyes were burning my face. I rose and went to the sarcophagus, running my hand over the alabaster fingers of the boy's effigy. "No," I said slowly. "I didn't hear the peacocks."

"I thought you might have." He took my arm, and it was all that I could do to keep myself from pulling away. "Am I forgiven, then?"

I forced myself to look at him. "Of course," I said.

"Then I will leave you to get on with your work," he said. "I must find Marian, at all events. I haven't seen her all this afternoon, and she's terrified of storms, you know —positively terrified. No, don't see me out. I can find my way. One is always afraid, of course, in these rooms that one will knock over some absolutely priceless piece of bric-a-brac, but there's more light now." He paused at the arched door. "Yes, the storm must be passing. Go on with your work. Believe me, my dear, I'll find some way to make amends for this unpardonable interruption."

I waited until I was certain that he was back in the main house, and then, flashlight in hand, I went through each of the five rooms, switching on the lights as I went. It was only by chance that in the last room, as I turned to go back to the chapel, I happened to see Marian Russell's body wedged behind a fifteenth-century coat of arms.

CHAPTER

5

At first I thought that for some reason Marian was hiding there. I actually spoke her name before I realized that her eyes were not focused on me but set in death. Lines of blood criss-crossed the wrinkled face, and her mouth hung open as though she were about to utter one last terrified protest.

I suppose I must have screamed. I remember only the sound of running feet, and suddenly the room seemed to be full of people. The body was being pulled out from its hiding place, the arms and legs limp as a puppet's. Someone laid her on the tiled floor, and I saw the blood-matted hair about the crushed skull. Then Martin Kubler was bending over the body, and someone's arms were about me, someone's hand shielding my eyes.

"What's happened?" David murmured.

"I switched on the lights, and she was there," I gasped. "Oh, my God! What happened to her?"

"Marian!" It was Jerez's voice. I saw him come through the door and push aside one of the staring maids.

"She's dead," Martin said as Jerez knelt, white-faced, beside the body. "Someone's beaten her skull in."

"No!" Jerez protested. "No! That can't be true!"

"Someone had better call the police," Martin said quietly. I glanced at him with gratitude. Something about his tone took an element of the horror away from the situation. A woman was dead. The police must be called. Terror would retreat, step by step. "Where's Mac-Gregor?" Martin continued.

The old man detached himself from the group and started toward the door, shuffling as always, his face set in what appeared to be an expression of grim satisfaction.

"Call the police and tell them there's been a murder and that they should get up here right away," Martin called after him. "The rest of you get out of this room. Nothing should be disturbed. I'm sorry, Mr. Caravels, but you must go, too. You can't do her any good now."

I fastened my eyes on Martin, drawing strength from him.

"He puts everything into perspective, doesn't he?" David said bitterly, but he kept his arm about me. We turned toward the door just as Claire stepped inside. She was looking more beautiful than usual in a pale-blue linen dress, her blond hair hanging loose about her shoulders.

"What's going on?" she asked, her voice shrill. "I thought I heard someone say. . . ."

Then she saw Marian's body. I suppose I expected her to react as violently as I had done, but she simply stared down at what was lying on the floor, her face expressionless. Behind her William hove into sight. It was he who cried out, and I saw her whirl to silence him by pressing the tips of her fingers to his mouth.

"If everyone will leave . . ." Martin Kubler said again, helping Jerez to his feet. The broad-boned Celtic face of the man who had been Marian's fiancé was twisted in a mask of grief. In the doorway he turned to me.

"Why did you do it to her?" he demanded.

"Are you insane, man?" David snapped, tightening his arm about me.

"She was found in this room, wasn't she?" Jerez cried hysterically. "I was here only a few minutes ago looking for her and——"

"I thought you were looking for an open window," I said in a low voice.

Jerez ignored me. I had the sense that he quite literally did not know what he was saying.

"Irene Haverlock was the only person in here," he said. "I went through all the rooms. If Marian was killed here, she must have done it."

"Miss Haverlock may have been the only person here when you came into the wing," Martin Kubler said, "but if that was only a few minutes ago, as you say, it proves nothing. It's my professional opinion that Miss Russell has been dead for a matter of hours. Now, everyone out into the hall, please. I'm going to see about locking this room at both ends until the police arrive. That's right, outside."

Propelled by the authority in his voice, we all crowded out into the corridor that led to the main part of the house. MacGregor sood waiting for us. I heard him mutter something I did not catch, and three maids scurried past him and disappeared.

"Did you call the police?" Martin demanded.

The old man nodded.

"Good. The next thing are the keys. I want to lock this room."

Slowly the old man reached into a pocket of his rusty-black suit and brought out an immense bunch of big old-fashioned keys. Detaching two with great deliberateness, he handed them to Martin.

"I want to stay with her," Jerez said in a shrill voice. "We can't just leave her in there alone."

"You can't do her any good now," Claire Stewart said in a hard voice.

"She's quite right, you know." The bluster in her husband's voice was only a thin echo of his usual heartiness. "Come along. What we all need is a drink."

For the first time since I had come to Alcombra, there was no talk of wine. In the long drawing room, with its broad windows draped in green-velvet hangings, William poured out Scotch for all of us. Martin Kubler joined us immediately, and we sat in silence in a semicircle of chairs and wide old-fashioned sofas around an empty fireplace lined with green tiles. I had not been in this room before, and to steady myself, I studied the paintings that lined the oak-paneled walls. Snatches of watery gray light illuminated two Vandykes, a Gainsborough, and several watercolors by Constable. I guessed that this room reflected the taste of Lady Stewart's husband, for everything in it down to the smallest cabinet reflected British craftsmanship and artistry. It was absurd, perhaps, to attempt to pretend to myself that I was back in London, with this horror behind me, but I did—until Jerez began to talk again.

"I told her that she ought to leave," he said. His voice was low now, even. He drained his glass, and William Stewart rose to pour him another drink. "She laughed at me when I said there was something wrong in this house. I sensed it from the first." His dark eyes fastened on me. "I'm sorry that I said what I did about you, Irene," he said. Then he laughed with a sudden wildness. "I seem to have spent a good deal of my time today apologizing to you."

"The thing we've got to think about," Claire said in a clear voice, "is making it quite clear to the police that none of us could have been responsible for this—this thing."

She was sitting on one of the two sofas that faced one another in front of the open mouth of the fireplace. As she spoke, she tucked her legs under her and looked around at us with clear, untroubled eyes.

"I doubt whether it will be as easy to do that as you may think, my dear," her husband said, handing Jerez his drink and coming to sit heavily beside his wife.

"Nonsense!" Claire snapped. "It should be quite obvious that none of us could have done such a—such an uncivilized thing."

"Who would you suggest, then?" David asked her. He was sitting on a footstool at my feet. I could not see his face, but his voice was hard and unwavering. Still, I knew that he more than any of us, except possibly Jerez, was torn to shreds inside. Despite his alienation from his mother, he had cared for her—cared, perhaps, more than he had realized until this moment. Martin's pragmatism might have reassured me, but there was no reassurance for David—only the agony of loss. I knew that he could not trust his own reactions. Thus the hardness in his voice. Perhaps it was asking too much to think that Claire could realize what he was going through.

"Of course, you can't be expected to be completely rational about this right now," Claire said brightly. "After all, I suppose, she *was* your mother."

"She was as much a stranger to me as you are," David said.

"That simply isn't true," Claire said vivaciously. Having taken the stage, it was clear that she intended to captivate us all. "You might not have seen her since you were a child, but she was your mother. Martin will tell you that certain strong emotional ties——"

"I think, my dear . . ." Her husband began, patting her knee.

"What I'm trying to say," Claire went on, flashing him an angry look, "is that one of the itinerant workmen who are helping with the harvest must have done it. Remember when you took me around the vineyards the other day, William? I told you that they looked like a very shifty lot."

"That's absurd, my dear," her husband said heavily. "Those men are never anywhere near the house. They're lodged well over a mile away, and they would have no reason to come here under any circumstances. The vineyard and the house itself have been kept entirely separate since my father died."

"It's common knowledge that your stepmother has a valuable collection," Claire snapped. "Now, you can't deny that, William. Anyone could have gone into the wing hoping to steal something—not necessarily the workmen but, well, anyone. Any stranger. Probably Marian surprised whoever it was as he was taking something, and he killed her. It's quite a logical explanation, and——"

"Shut up, Claire!" At first I could not believe it was William Stewart speaking. His face was deeply flushed, and he was breathing heavily. "For God's sake, shut up! You don't know anything about any of this."

"She knows as much as any of us, I suppose," Martin Kubler said easily. The man had been slow in formulating any sort of distinct personality as far as I was concerned, but I had sensed an inner strength in him when we had talked earlier today outside Lady Stewart's bedroom, and now I realized that we might very well all come to depend on him for our stability in what was to come. The feeling of numbness which had crept over me after the first shock of seeing Marian's body was wearing away now. When Jerez had leveled his accusation at me, I had scarcely taken it in. The only thing that had meant anything to me in those first few minutes of recognition that a murder had, in fact, been committed had been the protection of David's arm. All the antagonisms of the night before on the hillside had fallen away—for him, I thought, as much as for me. He was no longer touching me, and yet I knew that he realized that I needed him close to me.

And so, for me, Claire's outburst meant little. I could rely on Martin Kubler and David to provide some sort of perspective on what had happened. I reached out and touched David's shoulder, and he turned and smiled at me.

"The first thing that I think we ought to agree on is that this should be kept from Lady Stewart as long as possible," Martin said. His voice was calm. I had never been more aware of the fact that he was a doctor, accustomed to dealing with crises of this sort. "I don't know whether you all realize that she had a stroke during the night—a slight stroke, I think, because she was conscious and rational when I left her an hour ago. But I doubt whether this would be the right time to subject her to any sort of shock."

Claire laughed bitterly. "From what I hear," she said, "I think she might find it a relief to know that there was one less of us to bother about."

Jerez muttered something unintelligible, and I saw William Stewart's hand close firmly over his wife's knee.

"I don't know why we shouldn't be frank," Claire protested. "Surely even Mr. Caravels realizes that all of us are unwanted guests."

"Be that as it may," Martin Kubler interrupted, "I think we can agree that Lady Stewart should not be told. The next thing to consider—and consider seriously—is that the police will undoubtably ask us a considerable number of questions. I would suggest that all of us stick to the facts as we know them and avoid any sort of verbal surmising as to what may or may not have happened."

"I can't see any reason why we shouldn't give them our opinions," Claire said stiffly, sweeping her hair back from her face. "I shall certainly tell them that I think they would do well to question the workmen—and to see if anything is missing from the collection."

"All else aside, my dear," William Stewart said wearily, "if the murderer was a thief, there would be no way of telling whether anything is missing or not, except in the unlikely event that my stepmother should be well enough to be brought down to the room herself. And even then —" he made a sweeping gesture with one arm—"even then I doubt very much if she could remember the exact location of every item. Even when she was well, I think that there were times when she was not certain what she had purchased and what she simply had meant to purchase."

"There's always Irene's inventory," David said in a low voice.

"Ah," William said ponderously, "but Irene hadn't inventoried that room yet, had she?"

"I don't know," David said evenly, "but I'd be interested in knowing how you reached that conclusion—unless she told you."

The fat man shifted restlessly on the sofa, his thick fingers fumbling with the buttons of his blue blazer. His small eyes darted toward me and away. "Actually—" he began—"actually——"

"I don't have any record of what was in that room," I said flatly. "I completed a list of the paintings in the long gallery yesterday, and I was working in the chapel this afternoon."

Claire laughed and curled herself more tightly into the corner of the sofa. "Poor William," she said, "you're always putting your foot in it, aren't you, darling?"

"Tell me, Miss Haverlock," Martin Kubler said abruptly. "Were you working in the wing during the entire day?"

"Yes," I said. "My lunch was sent to me there. I started work at seven this morning, and except for the few minutes that I spoke with you. . . ."

I broke off. I could have been mistaken, but I thought that his eyes flashed me a warning.

"And you say that during that time you were in the

chapel?" He stressed the last word as though he had mis-understood me.

"We're forgetting that Martin here hasn't had a chance to make the grand tour," William Stewart said heartily. "Yes, she said 'chapel'—a little something my stepmother had brought stone by stone from some place south of Lisbon. My father put up with most of her nonsense, but he nearly drew the line at that."

I stared at Martin Kubler curiously over the top of David's blond head. Had Martin, I wondered, made a deliberate point of the fact that he had not yet seen the collection? This was in all probability true, however, because yesterday, during luncheon, Claire had suggested taking him to see it. For a moment I remembered vividly the way Jerez had interrupted to make the point that I should be the one to act as guide.

"All that doesn't matter," Jerez said impatiently to William Stewart, who was still rambling on about the role of his stepmother as scavenger. "The thing is, if Irene was there all day——"

"Except for the 'few minutes' she was with Martin," Claire said sarcastically.

"That was in the morning," the doctor said flatly. "If you'll remember, Miss Russell was at lunch. We are concerned with what happened in the five hours between then and now."

"I wanted Marian to go for a walk with me," Jerez said, rising and going to the liquor cabinet. I noticed that his voice was slurred. "But she said that she was tired. She wanted to take a nap. I could have insisted that she come with me." His voice broke. "Something was bothering her. I could tell. . . ."

He broke off, the bottle of Scotch in his hand, as the double doors to the drawing room were flung open and Senhora appeared, her hair, loosened from its knot, straggling on her swarthy cheeks. She was breathless, as though she had been running, and her dark eyes seemed to be starting out of her face.

"What are the police doing here?" she asked. "Who called them? What do we want with the police? She was an old woman. Everyone knew that she was going to die."

There was no time after Senhora's announcement to gauge the immediate effect of the news on those of us gathered in the drawing room. MacGregor showed the police inspector into the room on Senhora's heels, and even she kept silent as the inspector doggedly explained to us in heavily accented English that it would be necessary for him to be shown the body at once, and that he would hear what we had to say afterward.

"Bodies," Claire said brightly, "in the plural." The inspector—a slight, weary-looking man with sunken cheeks and bloodshot eyes behind thick gold-rimmed spectacles —asked her to explain with a flatness that quelled Claire instantly, whereupon the little man, whose name it later developed was Soria, listened to what she had to say with the attitude of having expected something of this sort. One had the feeling that life was constantly playing this kind of trick on him: two dead women instead of one, a talkative young Englishwoman who preened herself as she rattled on interminably. Even Senhora, standing trembling with God knows what pent-up passions, did not escape his notice. When he heard enough of what Claire had to say, he left, and through the open door I saw three policeman standing awkwardly in the wide hall, one of them, the youngest, staring up at the painted ceiling with a gaping mouth. Then MacGregor shuffled into view in the hall, and the inspector moved forward to speak to him. Orders were obviously being transmitted. We watched in silence as one man was sent upstairs in the company of a white-faced maid, and the inspector and the other two policemen disappeared in the direction of the wing in MacGregor's wake.

If the situation had been awkward before, it was impossible from that point on. Martin left the room at once, pausing by the door to snap some questions at Senhora, who was still trembling, her sweatered arms crossed about her chest, apparently incapable of making him coherent answers. Martin slammed the doors behind him, and I realized that under the circumstances he had no choice but to go up to Lady Stewart's room to verify her death.

But I did not doubt that what Senhora had said was true, nor, I think, did the others. David was silent, his hands clenched between his knees. Jerez put down the bottle of Scotch without pouring himself another drink and stood rubbing his face with his hands and staring out one of the long windows at the wet lawns that rolled away from the house, gray under a glowering sky. A wind had begun to rise, and the pine trees that bordered the lawn were waving their boughs as though in an attempt to ward off the gathering storm. Claire uncurled herself from the sofa and started toward Senhora with the obvious intention of questioning her, but William heaved himself after her and led her, protesting, from the room.

As the doors closed behind them, Jerez appeared to make some sort of decision. Going to Senhora, he took her arm and led her to a chair.

"Marian is dead," he said simply. "Murdered."

I was not sure that the woman was able to take in what he said, but she refused the offer of a drink by shaking her head so violently that what was left of the bun tumbled loose in disheveled greasy strands about her face.

"The other was murder, too," she hissed, staring at David and me with eyes that did not quite come into focus. "Someone was in that room with her before she died."

"I thought that you were watching her," I said. As always the only emotion she aroused in me, even now when she was obviously distraught, was anger. I tried to keep my voice even. "Dr. Kubler told you to stay with her."

"I was only in my room for a few minutes," she said shrilly. "Someone must have been watching, someone who wanted her to die."

"You'd better make it clear exactly what you're saying," David said, rising from the footstool and jamming his fists into the pockets of his wrinkled slacks. "You mentioned murder. Are you saying that someone killed her—beat her head in, perhaps—as they did my mother?"

Jerez made a sound deep in his throat and covered his face with his hands.

"They may as well have done!" Senhora cried. "She's just as dead as if they had."

"Listen," David said with an ominous mildness, "are you trying to tell us that Lelia was attacked?"

"I don't know!" Senhora spat at him. "I only know that she is dead."

There was a momentary silence, broken only by the beating of the wind against the long windows. The room was wreathed in shadows, shadows as dark and threatening as the clouds that shadowed the sky.

Bending over Senhora, David put his hands on her shoulders. His face was pale. "Were there any signs that she had died of anything but a natural death?" he asked, spacing his words as though he were speaking to a child. It was obvious to me that he was desperately trying to maintain his self-control. There were deep currents in this man. I had sensed that the night when we had sat together on the hillside. His emotions were strong and complex. He had loved and hated his mother. Even his relationship with his grandaunt had been ambiguous. But there was no doubt in my mind that he despised and mistrusted Senhora. I knew that in this moment he wanted to hurt her, and I also knew that if that thin thread of self-control snapped, he might do so. Unlike Martin, he was a passionate man, capable of great hatreds—and great loves.

Senhora pulled herelf away from him, her eyes glittering. For the first time I could really understand how much she loathed all of us.

"Are you even certain that she's dead?" David asked. "She was not breathing," Senhora said defiantly. "I held a mirror to her lips, and there was no pulse. I am a nurse. Do you not think that I am capable of telling when death comes?"

"Don't you think that it's probable that your grandaunt had another stroke?" I said quietly. I did not want David to go on with this interrogation. In some obscure way I wanted to protect him against himself.

"I think that it is very probable," he said grimly, turning to me. "I simply want to make this woman admit that she's making wild accusations, and this is not the time."

"Perhaps," I said in a low voice, "this is not the time for anything, even questions."

For a long moment our eyes met, and then I saw his face relax. He held out his hand to me then, and I went with him. As we reached the door, I heard Jerez say something to Senhora in a low voice. But I had no interest in what passed between them. In the storm-darkened hall, at the foot of the broad stairs, we met Martin, who told us, grim-faced, that it was true Lady Stewart was dead and that although under the circumstances he imagined the police would order an autopsy, he was satisfied it had, in fact, been a second stroke that had killed her.

I listened to him explain the case as he saw it and heard a clinical detachment in his voice which somehow horrified me. Yet why should it? An old woman was dead of a stroke. Implicit in what Martin was saying was that there was nothing unusual about it, nothing to wonder at. David asked questions. "Yes," Martin said, it was possible that a sudden shock could have killed her, but

it was obvious that he intended to take no part in speculation. Why, I wondered, should I have expected anything
else of him? There was no reason why he should deal
with the matter in a more imaginative manner because he
was a psychiatrist and not simply a medical doctor. Still,
whatever the reason, his encounter with us left me angry
and frustrated.

David's response was to insist that I go with him to his
grandaunt's bedroom. David and I stood silent, looking
down at Lady Stewart's body as fingers of rain tapped
impatiently against the thickly draped windows. I had
mistaken Marian's staring death for life, but there was no
mistaking what I saw here. The corpse lay slumped side-
ways, the white head flung to the side of the sloping mound
of pillows as though she had made one last frantic
struggle against oblivion. The broad, coarse-featured face
seemed to have shrunk, and for the first time I could see
the fine body structure of the girl Sargent had painted
so long ago. An hour had passed since Senhora had burst
into the drawing room to tell us that the old woman was
dead, but on the orders of the police the body had not
been moved. On their orders, too, a policeman had been
stationed in the hallway outside the door. When David
and I had come into the room, the man had followed us,
protesting in rapid Portuguese. But David had ignored
him, and I had understood. It was necessary that David
see for himself that she was dead.

Fretful with the realization that the guard was not
willing to leave us alone with the body, I broke the suffocating silence. "I'm sorry, David," I said, "truly sorry."

He gave a half laugh, his eyes fixed on the waxen face
on the pillow. "Why should any of us be sorry?" he said
in a low voice. "She was dying—in pain, helpless. It's
better this way, although I suppose she would have enjoyed
hearing that my mother is dead. She always hated my
mother."

"Don't," I begged. "Don't torture yourself."

"We all torture one another," David said, "pretending love where none exists. The only reason Lelia kept me here was because it was a way of hurting someone else. Yet my mother never really wanted me. She never made any real effort to get me back, no matter what she may have told you. All that she was interested in was the money. All that either of them were interested in was money and what it would buy." He turned to me, and it was as though he were forcibly tearing his eyes away from the dead woman on the canopied bed. "I suppose that sounds a little too dramatic for you, doesn't it?" he asked. "It's the sort of thing people don't say—particularly not men. It's not the sort of thing that the admirable Doctor Kubler would tell you."

"Who?"

He had taken me by surprise with his sudden transition. Even the bitterness in his voice was disconcerting.

"Our friend the doctor," he said, "or should I say, 'Your friend the doctor'?"

I looked at him in the dim light. "You're upset," I said. "Whether you want to believe it or not just now, your mother and your grandaunt meant a good deal to you."

"I'm not talking about me," David said in a low voice, taking my arm. "I'm talking about you, Irene. You're really not too interested in having people tell you the straight truth, are you? When I said that neither my mother nor my grandaunt was interested in anything but money and what it would buy, I meant it. But a man like Kubler wouldn't have offended you by speaking the truth. That's my only point. I——"

"Don't be absurd," I interrupted him. "If you believe something to be true, you should say it."

"Ah, but there's the rub," David said as though he were talking to himself. "It's sometimes difficult to know what *is* truth and what we simply want to believe. I suppose if Lelia had been happy in her marriage, she might not have developed her passion for collecting things. She wasn't that good a judge of quality, you know. You'll find there are a good many things in that hoard of hers that are worthless. She simply wanted things because if she had them, no one else could. It was the same with me. She wanted me because my mother pretended to want me."

"You've got to consider that you may not be being fair," I said quickly, "to them or to me." He was doing what he had done the night before on the hillside: going to extremes. First the blanket condemnation of two women whom, whether he knew it or not, he had loved and needed; then the unwarranted attack on Martin, which had involved the statement that I could not bear to hear people speak the truth. "From what your mother told me," I went on evenly, "she gave you up of her own accord when you were an infant."

"Not of her own accord," David said harshly. "She gave me up because she couldn't face society with me. It wasn't that easy, twenty-five years ago, being an unmarried woman with a bastard."

"Tell me," I said softly. "Did you talk to your mother before she died?"

He might have answered me, but at that moment the guard chose to accost us again, reminding us in rapid-fire Portuguese that we were not supposed to be in the room. He was the young man I had seen earlier staring at the ceiling in the hall below, and he waved his arms frantically in an attempt to make his point.

"All right," David muttered. "Let's get out of here. My God, when are they going to see to settling this? They can't just leave her like this indefinitely."

"Probably they have to wait for a coroner," I told him as we walked out of the dimness of the room into the corridor, where last long drops of rain were streaking the windows. Below us in the courtyard a peacock screamed, and I suddenly remembered Jerez asking me if I had heard them scream just before the storm began.

It occurred to me that what he might have heard was Marian screaming, but that was absurd. If she had cried out, I would have heard her—if she had been killed in the room in which her body had been found, that is. And that did not have to be the case. She could have been somewhere else, carried there, and hidden. Perhaps the murderer had hoped that since the wing was so unfrequented, she would not be found for some time. Still, he had been taking a chance. Everyone in the house, including the servants, had known that I was working there. I had heard Jerez moving about in the room next to the chapel. I might have heard the murderer as well—unless it was one and the same person, unless Jerez had killed her, and having hidden the body, deliberately alerted me, albeit in another room, with a feeble excuse about closing a window. But no. That did not make sense. I wanted desperately to think clearly, but my mind felt as though it were wrapped in cotton wool.

I realized that somehow we had reached the top of the broad staircase, and that David had stopped, putting out his hand as though in warning. Looking down past his shoulder, I saw the inspector and one of his men coming up the stairs, heads bent, not seeing us. Martin Kubler followed them, and behind him came another man, wearing a wrinkled white suit, a bald man with a few tufts of white hair standing up behind his ears.

"Quick," David whispered, "in here."

It was apparently his bedroom. A knapsack lay on the floor beside an old-fashioned brass-railed bed. It was a high-ceilinged, spacious room, but unlike mine, it was full of shabby, comfortable furniture, had a desk littered with papers, and was lined with bookcases. The windows were open, and two peacocks sat on one of the sills, craning their necks in our direction. David made a dash at them, waving his arms, and they disappeared with a flash of vividly colored tail feathers.

"Look," David said, turning back to me. "I wanted us

to have a chance to talk before we encounter the inspector again. It's my bet that the old fellow is the police doctor. They'll probably be holed up in Lelia's bedroom for a while, so we have time. Sit down."

I did as he said, passing a mirror and looking hastily away from my own reflection. My face was smeared with dirt, and my slacks were wrinkled. Suddenly I was uncomfortably aware of the fact that I had not even combed my hair since seven o'clock that morning. Suddenly I felt not only dirty but also exhausted, and yet I was glad that David and I had made our escape. I did not want to risk going to my own room just now if it meant risking an encounter with the police.

"It's just this," David said, dragging his easy chair close to mine. "Once they get started, the police are going to ask a lot of questions. They're going to want to know when you last saw my mother, for one thing."

"Not since yesterday evening," I said wearily, leaning my head back against the cushions and closing my eyes. It was strange how long ago yesterday could seem.

"And Lelia?"

"Last night—after I left you. MacGregor was waiting outside my door when I got back. She wanted to see me."

There was a long pause. I did not open my eyes. I wanted to believe that David was asking me these questions out of genuine concern for my protection from suspicion. If I looked at him, I knew that there was just a chance I would see something else in his eyes.

"What about?" he said in a low voice. "Tell me, Irene. What did she want to see you about?" I felt his hand on my arm. "Whoever else you lie to, don't lie to me—because I think we're in danger, you and me. Someone obviously believed that my mother had to die, and I don't believe that it's going to end there."

The thing that I could never explain to myself later was why I did not tell him about his grandaunt's fear that

her collection might have been pillaged, nor did I tell
him about the five items I had already found missing. It
was not because I did not trust him; I think it was because
there had been no time for me to think about the possibility of such thefts having been committed in the context of Marian's murder. Granted that Claire had suggested a relationship when she had spoken of the possibility
of Marian's having surprised someone in the room where
she had died. But Claire had been attempting to place the
blame for murder on one of the workers in the vineyard,
a stranger, and I did not think that was true.

So because I needed time to think about how I would
deal with a knowledge that at present was only mine, I
had told David that Lady Stewart had wanted to see me
about the procedure the inventory would take, and that
she had sent for me at the unlikely hour of midnight because she knew Senhora was opposed to having me in the
house in the first place and wanted our talk to be undisturbed. I don't think he had believed me, but there had
been no time for him to probe, because we had been interrupted by William Stewart, who had made it clear, in
his heavy-handed way, that he wanted to talk to David
alone about "family business."

I had gone to my room then, thinking that I would take
a long bath and lie down for a while—and try to think.
But on my way from David's room to my own, I had encountered two white-jacketed men carrying a stretcher, and
I had been overcome by the feeling that this house and
what was going on inside it were stifling me. The rain had
cleared now, and when I opened a window, I smelled the
fresh dampness of the earth. Pausing only long enough to
shower and slip on a loose white-linen shift, I had run a
brush through my hair and hurried out of the house
past the ambulance waiting in the gravel drive.

Wondering where to go, I hurried to the west side of the
house and stood in the shelter of a huge mimosa bush out
of sight of anyone who might be looking out the drawing-

room windows. There was the hill behind the house which I had climbed with David the night before, but I did not want to go there alone. Besides, there was always the possibility that if he decided to come looking for me when William was finished talking to him, he would look on the hill if he could not find me in my room.

The front of the house was lined with green turf, which stretched away into a park, the park through which we had driven the night I had come to Alcombra. I started in that direction but then changed my mind. There was too much chance that I would be seen leaving if I took that unprotected route, and besides, I suddenly remembered the way the car had brushed its way under the low limbs of the pine trees that crowded the narrow road that led up to the house. The rain would have made the trees wet and dripping.

I looked to the west again, to where the enveloping distant hills were turning purple in the first fading light of the sunset. The air was fresh and cool, and now that I was out of the house I already felt better. All that I needed to do was to walk for a while alone, and what better place to walk than westward, where the terraced vineyard faded into the hills?

Hurrying down the sloping lawn in the shelter of the shrubbery, I paused twice, once to turn aside to avoid one of the peacocks who fixed himself defiantly in front of me, his exotic feathers spread in a fan, and once more to look back at the house. The setting sun turned the long windows into panels of flame, which seemed to leap out from the gray stone. There was a brooding quality about the house, a quality that incorporated the ominous mood of what had happened there. A peacock screamed in the distance, and suddenly I seemed to see Marian's face, the mouth open in a cry of terror. Stumbling, I pushed my way through the hedges and found myself on a dirt path that led down into a bowl-like valley lined with terraced vines.

It was quiet here. To my left the granite wall that supported one of the terraces gave out the captured warmth of the day. To my right the ground fell away to the next terrace. Once when I had been a girl my father had taken me to visit a friend who lived in Bordeaux. His vineyards had been less extensive than this, but I remembered the absorption with which he had explained the complexities of wine-farming. In the autumn, as soon as the grapes were harvested, it was necessary to dig hollows around the vine trunks to catch the rain. "There is never enough rain," he had told my father, "except in those years when there is too much, and then the landslides. . . ." He had waved his arms in Gallic desperation, and I remembered how my father and I had smiled at one another.

Leaning against an outcropping of the granite wall, I let the fading warmth of the sun strike my face. It was odd how, quite suddenly, I could remember so much of that long summer day when I had walked with the two men among the vines, intrigued by the description of how blue lupine had to be sown between the rows of vines, of the process of careful pruning, the replanting, the grafting—and then at last, the vintage. Reaching up, I plucked a bunch of purple grapes off the vine and ate them, staring into the past. It was all so familiar, this moment— and so deceptive. Try as I might, I could not retreat into a time when all my decisions had been made for me, when security was as close as my father's hand.

I shook my head impatiently and continued to walk along the dirt path. I could not remember a time when I had not tried to escape reality when it became too unpleasant. It was a fault, and I knew it. Yet habit was strong. I had known that I did not want to marry Philip for months before the final break came, and in the end he had been the one who had had to make it, because rather than take a stand, I would retreat into the protection of the past or into dreams. He had called me a coward, and he had been right.

I stopped walking again and struck my hands together

impatiently. I was doing it again: first the memory of my
father and then of Philip. One consoling, the other painful.
But both were conjured up deliberately to keep me from
thinking of Alcombra and violence and death.

Pulling myself up on the wall beside me, I sat and
stared out over the valley. For the first time I noticed in
the distance the red-tiled roofs of a string of low, barrack-
like houses and heard from far away the faint sound
of an accordion being played. That must be where the
workers were housed, I realized—a long distance from
the house. I remembered what Claire had suggested about
one of the workers having attacked Marian. Even though
they were in the fields during the day, closer to the
house, I found that the idea of one of them coming inside, particularly into the wing, to steal anything seemed
absurd to me—certainly not in broad daylight. The risk
would be too great. Besides, if the items I had checked
off on Lady Stewart's list had been stolen, they had been
stolen by someone who knew enough about the value of
such things to have chosen items from the collection
which, although small, were of great value. And David
had been right when he had said that his great-aunt had
accumulated a mass of bric-a-brac. I had seen enough of
what was in those rooms to know that was true. Whoever
had taken the ring and the panel and the rest had been
someone of some degree of artistic discrimination.

Yet if that was true, who did that leave to suspect, even
if one narrowed one's suspicions to the members of the
household? Neither Marian nor David had ever mentioned
anything that might indicate that he was interested in
art. The same held true for Marian herself, and for Claire.
William had obviously never taken any interest in what his
stepmother collected. His only attitude toward her possessions seemed to have been one of resentment, if what
David had told me about him when he was still living at
Alcombra was true. And David himself? His field was
Georgian poetry. Certainly it did not follow that he

knew anything about Iberian art. In my talk with him he had never mentioned a single one of Lady Stewart's acquisitions. As for Martin Kubler, what did I know of him except that he was a psychiatrist or claimed to be a psychiatrist? He had expressed an interest in seeing the collection, but surely that was only natural. Even Claire had apparently seen it. I expected that every visitor to Alcombra had at some time or other taken the grand tour. Besides, Martin had been in the house for only a few days. Or had he? It occurred to me that I did not know exactly when he had arrived, even whether or not he had accompanied William and Claire from London. I had accepted him at face value because—because of the quiet confidence of the man and because, from the very beginning, there had been a certain rapport between us. And yet . . . and yet there were so many things I did not know. In the end I ought to admit that I knew so little that there was no use in my speculating over what had happened.

But I was certain of one thing. Although I had not chosen to tell David about the fact that certain parts of the collection were missing, I would have to tell the police if for no other reason than to ensure that the wing be locked during the times I was not there, and that the key be placed in safekeeping—even though it might occur to them that I had ample opportunity to take what was missing myself. Certainly I would rank high among their suspects as a person who would know what was most valuable, and therefore most worth stealing. It was, I realized suddenly, entirely possible that once the police knew of the thefts, they would not allow me to conclude the inventory. I would simply have to convince them that it was an essential step if Alcombra was to become a museum.

But why did I have to do any such thing? Presumably Lady Stewart's will provided for a particular procedure that was to be followed after her death. Perhaps a curator had already been appointed—someone who would immediately take over after the will was probated—but legal processes were slow. Even if William did not dispute the terms of the will, there was no question of the museum's being established within a few months—not even, perhaps, for years.

I pushed my hair back from my face. There was a cool breeze. The part of the vineyard that lay below me in the bowl of the hills was gray-green in the growing shadows. Only a sliver of the red sun showed above the distant hills. Back at the main house the police might be looking for me. The inspector had said that he would want to talk to all of us. It had been unwise, perhaps, for me to leave without telling anyone where I was going. I had to face the fact that Lady Stewart's death and the will, even the thefts, were secondary to the question of who had murdered Marian Russell.

They could not suspect me of that, at any rate. I had no reason to have wanted her dead. She was a stranger to me, as were all the people in that house. They would see that, surely. But what would they see as well? That David had a life-long reason to hate his mother? That perhaps Jerez had agreed to marry her under the impression that she was an heiress, and that this visit to Alcombra might have disillusioned him? But surely disillusionment alone would not have been an adequate reason for him to have murdered her. Still, they had been close to one another. There could have been other reasons for him to want her out of the way. What use was there in my thinking about it? I knew so little, and even that little was more than I wanted to know. Had it been only two days ago that I had so ruthlessly attempted to keep Marian from drawing me into this little world? This terrifying world.

I slid down from the wall and started slowly back toward the house. Far below me an accordion pulsed out a wailing song. The breeze rippled the leaves of the vines, and an unutterable sadness engulfed me. Lost in thought, I wandered up the dirt path, my eyes on the ground. It was only by chance that I heard something falling above me, only by chance that I stepped aside as the jagged granite missile plunged past me and lodged itself among the vines below.

CHAPTER

6

The inspector was, surprisingly enough, not willing to admit that anything unusual had happened to me. "There is a Douro saying," he told me. " '*Ano sem sapada, não da nada.*' Which means, 'A year without a landslide is a year that gives nothing.' Vineyard walls are always collapsing, particularly after such a rain as we had this afternoon. You were fortunate to avoid being hurt, Miss Haverlock, but I find it difficult to believe that that stone was dislodged deliberately. It is quite natural, you realize, after a murder has been committed for everyone to see danger in the corners, so to speak."

MacGregor had been waiting in the hallway at Alcombra when I had reached the house, breathless from having run all the way—breathless, perhaps, from panic as well. Because I had been certain when that piece of granite had shattered its way past me that someone wanted me to die, and that that someone was hidden above me, behind one

of the layers of walls. I had scarcely listened to Mac-
Gregor as he muttered something about someone—perhaps
the police—having looked for me. I had wanted only one
thing: to see the inspector and tell him what I knew—
everything I knew. I had left this house in order to think
about what I should do, how much I should tell. The piece
of falling granite had decided me. I would trust the police
and no one else.

I think I would have insisted on seeing the inspector
whether he had been waiting for me or not. He had set
up what seemed to be a sort of temporary office in a little
room toward the back of the house, a room that had
apparently been someone's study, perhaps Lady Stewart's
husband's. Whoever's refuge it had been, I had the feeling that it had not been used for a long time. There was
no dust, but there was something about the bareness of the
massive oak desk, something about the symmetry of the
books that lined the walls, which hinted at desertion.

I had not waited for the inspector to begin to question
me before I told him about what had just happened in
the vineyard. He had listened, puffing on a cigarette, his
thin, exhausted face illuminated by the white light of a
metal desk lamp. Then he had discounted the incident,
putting out the cigarette and lighting another, his dark
eyes never leaving my face.

He asked questions then—about my relationship to the
family, about the gallery in London, about what I was
doing here—chain-smoking all the while, leaning on the
desk in a manner that seemed to convey nothing but weariness and an incredible boredom. It was as though he had
been investigating Marian's murder for months instead of
a few hours, as though nothing that I could tell him would
come as a surprise. Even when I told him about the list
Lady Stewart had given me, and that some of the possessions seemed to be missing, there was no real reaction
on his part.

"Yes," he said. "That's very interesting, Miss Haverlock. I shall want to see that list, of course. We shall have to ascertain whether or not those things are really missing. As you say, they might simply have been misplaced. It is quite possible that Lady Stewart did not remember their location accurately."

"The collection should have been kept locked," I said. Now that I had blurted out everything I knew that could possibly be of any importance, I felt a great sense of relief. It was as though I had conveyed a burden to someone else—as, of course, I had. Yet there was no sense of relaxation. I sat on the edge of my chair across the desk from him, tensely twisting my fingers together.

"Under ordinary circumstances one does not suspect one's servants or the members of one's household capable of theft," he said wearily, "but now, of course, you are quite right. The rooms have been locked and will be guarded until this matter of Miss Russell's death is resolved. Tell me. Will you be willing to complete the inventory?"

"Surely," I said, "that will be a matter for the executor to decide, and I have my own affairs to see to in London. I will not be able to wait here indefinitely."

"Under the circumstances—" the inspector said, "and you must forgive me if I continue to remind you that there are 'circumstances'—I think that I will take it on myself to direct that such an inventory be completed. You are, I take it, well qualified to do the work. From what I have heard of Lady Stewart, she did not tolerate incompetence. And there is, I'm afraid, no possibility of your being allowed to return to London immediately. You understand that, of course."

"All of us will have to stay here?"

He nodded his head slowly. His dark hair was thinning at the temples, and there were gray pouches under his eyes. I thought that I had never seen such an emaciated, tired face. "Even Dr. Kubler, who seems to be particularly anxious to leave," he said.

"We stay because we are suspects?"

"Yes." He broke into a fit of coughing which wracked his thin body. "All suspects. And now, if you please, Miss Haverlock, we will speak of motives and of opportunity."

"And means?" I added in a low voice.

"The means are known to us," he said. "Perhaps you may have noticed in the course of your work the gold cross which sat on a pedestal in a corner of the room where Miss Russell was killed?"

"Yes," I said. "It's a beautiful piece—sixteenth century. I think she must have found it in the Tagus area."

"I'm sure that you are right," the inspector said wearily. "To me it is simply a good cross—small enough to hold in one's hand, heavy enough to kill."

An hour before, when I had been outside and a peacock had screamed, I had visualized Marian's mouth open in a cry of terror. Now I saw more. A faceless form. The cross descending. The battered head. My hands grew icy cold, and the cigarette smoke seemed to choke me.

"You do not like to think of what happened," the inspector said. "Well, that is natural enough. Even the murderer did not care to see her face when she died. She was struck from behind—one blow only. It was enough. Tell me, Miss Haverlock. I am informed that you were working in the wing today."

"In the chapel," I said, finding as I spoke that my lips were numb. "Four rooms away."

"Away from what?"

"From—from the room where she was murdered."

For the first time there was some animation in that thin face.

"What makes you think that the murder was done there, in the room where she was found?"

"I simply assumed——"

"One can assume nothing. The cross was found there, true—matted with her blood and hair at its tip—and the body was found there as well. But that tells us nothing about where she was killed." He lit another cigarette. "You found the body?"

"Yes."

"It's position?" The weariness was gone from his voice now. The boredom he had conveyed was replaced by an intent eagerness.

"Wedged behind a suit of armor."

"Yes. I have seen it. There are traces of blood there, too. It must have been a shock."

His voice was sly now, insinuating.

"I thought she was alive," I whispered. "Her eyes were open."

"Alive? A curious impression, Miss Haverlock. Was she the sort of woman you would have expected to find in such an unusual place?"

"I thought that she was hiding," I protested. "I know it's absurd, but it never occurred to me that she might be dead."

"Hiding? And why should she be hiding?"

"I don't know," I told him. "That was my first impression. It lasted only a second. I shouldn't have mentioned it."

"You should mention everything," he told me. "Come. Think, Miss Haverlock. You may not consciously have thought of a reason that she might be hiding, but subconsciously——"

"Her fiancé had been looking for her," I said quickly.

"Ah! And is there any reason why she should have been hiding from Mr. Caravels?"

"Of course not," I said impatiently. "You're making something out of nothing. The last words that he said to me were about his having been looking for her, and naturally when I saw her——"

"Naturally?"

"Considering the fact that Mr. Caravels had apparently just walked past her without her calling attention to herself."

"It is somewhat difficult for a dead woman to 'call attention to herself,' as you put it, Miss Haverlock."

A thin smile etched itself on his lips.

"You can't possibly be making a joke out of this!" I said.

"No. There is no joke. I went too far, perhaps, but I was attempting to demonstrate that one may know—or intuit—more than they think. Perhaps this will be more meaningful to you later. For the moment you have been forced to remember more than perhaps you might have done about the events of this afternoon. You were many rooms away from the room where the body was found, you say."

"In the chapel." I did not know how to react to this man. His air of ennui had returned, but a moment ago I had been so tense that I could scarcely talk to him. Then he had confused me, made me angry. And now, surprisingly, I found that I could relax. I leaned back in the chair.

"You had been there all day?"

"No. Dr. Kubler will tell you that I talked with him for a few minutes in the morning upstairs."

"Where upstairs?"

"Outside Lady Stewart's room."

"And why had you interrupted your work to go there?"

"I wanted to see Lady Stewart to tell her that I had not been able to locate five items on the list she had given me."

"She had given you a list of her possessions?"

"No, only of about a hundred of them."

"She had asked you to check those particular items?"

"Yes."

"And may I ask why?"

"I think that she was afraid that some of her things might be missing."

"And it appears that she was correct. That is very interesting, Miss Haverlock. You went to tell her this?"

"Yes, but she was unconscious."

"And so you talked to the doctor instead. He is, I think, a psychiatrist?"

Despite the inspector's laconic air, the questions were coming fast, and each question was carefully chosen. I felt a sense of rising admiration.

"He is also a medical doctor," I said.

"You have proof of this?"

"It is what he told me."

"I see. And when you discovered that Lady Stewart was unconscious, did you tell him why you had come to see her?"

"No, certainly not."

"Why not? Did you think that Dr. Kubler might have been party to the thefts?"

"No. That had nothing to do with it. The conditions under which Lady Stewart had given me the list—well, I knew that this was a private matter."

I realized, too late, that he had made me say more than I had meant to say. No, that was not it exactly, but he had twisted things ever so slightly.

"What were these 'conditions' under which she gave you the list?"

I took a deep breath. There was no telling with this odd little man where my answers would lead me. "She called me to her room last night," I said, "at midnight."

"Awakened you at midnight?"

"I didn't say that. As it happens, I was outside the house until that time. When I came back, MacGregor was waiting for me with her message."

"And what were you doing outside alone? I would not think that a young woman such as you, a stranger to this place——"

"I was with David Ashor," I said. "We had taken a walk."

The inspector stared at me through a veil of smoke. "You are a good friend of Mr. Ashor's?"

"No." Now it was my turn to let exhaustion creep into my voice. "I met him for the first time when I came here."

"But it is perfectly natural that you should become friends quickly," the inspector said. "He is a handsome young man, and you . . . but I expect that is beside the point."

"I think that it is," I said stiffly.

For the second time he smiled that thin smile. "You will pardon me, Miss Haverlock," he said, "but you can see that one thing leads to another. But you have made your point. Lady Stewart wanted to speak to you in private—although, I take it, she was not usually surrounded with people."

"Senhora was always with her," I said, and I realized once again that I had said more than I meant to say.

"So Lady Stewart did not want even her companion to know that she suspected that certain of her possessions had disappeared?"

"It doesn't necessarily follow that she thought that Senhora might have been stealing from her," I said tartly.

"Many things do not necessarily follow," the inspector said, pulling a handkerchief out of his pocket and rubbing it across his bony forehead. "Only a few more questions, Miss Haverlock. To return to Mr. Caravels. After you returned from talking to Dr. Kubler . . . what time would that be, do you think?"

"I don't know. Perhaps eleven-thirty. It was before lunch at any rate."

"Yes. And Miss Russell was alive at luncheon. Did you have occasion to speak to her during that meal?"

"I ate in the chapel," I said. "A maid brought me my lunch."

"At your request?"

"No. Senhora had ordered it. She knew—they all knew —that I did not want to be interrupted."

"And she was eager that you finish the inventory as soon as possible?"

"I don't know," I told him. "The first time that I talked with Lady Stewart about the matter, Senhora was in the room, and she gave some indication that she was opposed to the inventory being made."

The inspector started to light another cigarette and then, sighing, returned it to the package. "And so you were in the chapel from eleven-thirty until the body was found—until you found the body, I should say."

"Yes."

"And the doors were open between the adjoining rooms?"

"They were."

"Did anyone interrupt you there?"

"Only the maid when she came to bring my lunch at about one."

"And Mr. Caravels. We must not forget Mr. Caravels. What time would you say he came?"

"I don't know. It was during the storm. We couldn't have talked for more than ten minutes, and directly after he left, I went to turn on the lights in the other rooms and found—found the body."

"I see." The inspector tapped his fingers against the top of the desk, staring at them as though they were moving without his consent. Then, with an impatient movement, he took another cigarette out of the crumpled package and lit it. "And Mr. Caravels came to see if you had seen his fiancée?"

"No," I said in a low voice. "He only mentioned that when he was leaving. He said that he had been outside in the courtyard when the rain had started, and that he thought that he saw that one of the windows in the wing was open."

The inspector stared at me over the flame of his match, letting it burn until it scorched his fingers. "But," he said, "those windows are set in grilled stonework. They do not open."

"I know," I whispered.

"Very well, then." The inspector pushed back his chair. "You have been most helpful, Miss Haverlock. I will not forget that you have been most helpful. There is only one further thing."

I rose, my hands clenched in front of me, tension pouring back into my body.

"I would not be as open with the others as you have been with me. You may feel that you know little that is of importance, but to the murderer small things may seem of the utmost importance. And it has always been my opinion that one murder is more than enough."

Instead of a formal dinner, a buffet was served in the dining room at nine. When I left the inspector, it was being set out, apparently under Senhora's supervision, together with the housekeeper, for I saw them both standing by the massive oak sideboard that lined one side of the dining room as I passed its open door. For the first time since I had met her, Senhora was not wearing the wrinkled tweed skirt and stretched-out cardigan but was dressed instead in black. I saw her face, drawn and haggard, as I paused in the hall, and for a moment her dark eyes met mine, and I saw the familiar flare of hostility in them before I hurried up the broad stairway to my room.

I lay for a long time in a hot bath, trying not to think, aware that my emotional exhaustion would allow no high degree of rationality to my thoughts. I would, I determined, live the time that was left for me at Alcombra on a day-to-day basis, completing the inventory as quickly as possible and keeping my own counsel, as the inspector had advised. Whatever else I did, I would not play guessing games with myself or anyone else about the identity of Marian's murderer. It would be enough for the inspector to point the finger of guilt, and from what I had seen of him, I thought that it would not be too long before he did so. I loathed the thought that anyone in this house could have committed an act of violence, but I believed that one of us had. And I wished that it would soon be over.

When I came down to the dining room, dressed in the most subdued article of clothing I had brought with me, a pale-gray cocktail dress cut in simple lines, I found only Claire there before me. She intended to make no pretense of being in mourning, if the red-velvet pants suit she was wearing was any sign. Her blond hair was high on her head in a mass of curls, and what appeared to be diamond earrings dangled about her face. She smiled over her shoulder at me as I came into the room and continued to heap her plate with food.

"I don't see why we have to wait," she said in the husky voice she usually assumed only with men. "I suppose it's dreadful of me to say it, but I'm famished. Make sure you have some of these prawns—they're absolutely delicious—and this dressed crab. *Santola recheada*, I think they call it. Ummm." She dipped a spoon in a casserole dish and closed her eyes as she tasted. "I don't know what this is," she said, "but it's simply marvelous. Whatever else you have to say about this place, the food is first rate."

I suppose that until that moment I had thought of her as simply a beautiful, rather silly woman who was accustomed to having her own way. But now, as she helped herself greedily to some sort of aspic, I found myself appalled by the extent of her self-absorption. It was not that I would have thought any more of her if she had made a pretense of caring that either Marian or her mother-in-law was dead. If she had worn black and come to dinner tearful and pretending to a lack of appetite, I would have been equally repelled. But she could have struck some middle course.

There were several decanters of wine on the sideboard, and while she took her plate to the table, I poured myself a glass of rosé. "There is a great deal about this house that wants changing, you know," Claire said, taking a seat at the head of the long table. "I shall have to get the decorators in as soon as it's possible. I don't expect Jerez would like to take on the job, but then one never knows."

I tried to keep my face expressionless, but she must have seen that she had surprised me. She laughed, delightedly. "Pour me a glass of Chablis, will you?" she said. "Why shouldn't I have the house redecorated if William and I are going to spend part of every year here?"

"No reason at all," I said, pouring her wine and taking it to her. It occurred to me that she was probably the sort of woman who finds it impossible to establish any sort of relationship with anyone unless she could somehow put them in the position of waiting on her in some way. It would, I determined, take more than this for her to arrive at any state of intimacy with me. Necessity dictated that for a while we would have to live in the same house, but I would make it quite clear, if I had to, that I intended to be neither her servant nor her confidant.

"I expect you're surprised that I should be making plans about the house," she said, patting her full mouth with her napkin and plunging her fork into the aspic on her plate.

"Why should I be?" I said crisply. I had thought a few minutes ago that I was hungry. After all, the last meal that I had eaten had been eight hours ago. But now, looking at her heaped plate, I found that my appetite had disappeared.

"Don't be so up-tight," Claire advised me. "You're really quite attractive, you know—or would be if you'd let yourself go. A woman should have a certain amount of—well, vitality. William always says——"

"Does he?"

With her mouth full, she looked up at me with slowly

narrowing eyes, and I knew that I had made myself quite clear, and that there was no longer any question of our being "girls together," if that was what she had had in mind.

"Everyone thinks that Alcombra is going to be turned into a museum," she said in a hard voice, "but that simply isn't true. The old woman had no right to make that sort of plan. The fact that she did is proof enough that she had totally lost her grip on reality."

That last phrase did not sound like her. I wondered whom she was quoting.

"She didn't have a thing when she married William's father," Claire said triumphantly. "Not a shilling, except some paintings her father had left her. William's father never cared anything about this absurd collection of hers except that it kept her out of his way. William told me that."

I expected that William had told her a good many things in whatever ratio of truth and falsehood was necessary to convince her to marry him. I wondered if he was sorry now that he had been so successful.

"And so," she continued blandly, "William deserves to have Alcombra. It's what his father would have wanted. As soon as these silly legal technicalities are out of the way——"

"Claire!" I looked to the door and saw William Stewart standing there. Ordinarily I saw him as only a stock figure—a fat, pompous man with a too-young wife—an ineffectual, bombastic middle-aged man who, I suspected, knew his own weaknesses only too well. But there was something in his face as he came into the room, his eyes pinned on his wife, that made me think there might be more to him than I had imagined. And Claire's reaction seemed to substantiate that. She seemed to shrink a bit, and the smile that she assumed was conciliatory.

"I was just telling Miss Haverlock that the crab is delicious," she said, rising. "Let me get you some, darling.

Here, sit down beside me and tell me what you'll have. There's some marvelous salad and. . . ."

He let her run on as she began to scoop bits of this and that into a plate, her back to him. But his eyes never left her, and there was a brooding expression in them, a pensiveness that I did not associate with the man. Then, suddenly, as she set the plate in front of him, he seemed to switch off whatever his thoughts had been.

"Soria's gone," he said heavily, addressing himself to me. "I expect he talked to you."

I nodded.

"He's a good man," William Stewart said, unfolding his napkin and placing it carefully over his stomach. "I expect he'll get this thing settled without too much delay. He's not leaving anything to chance, I can tell you. Two of his men are staying here the night."

"Why on earth would he do that?" Claire said lightly. "He doesn't think there'll be another murder, does he?"

Her husband ignored her. Taking one look at his plate, he pushed it aside. "David was looking for you a while back," he said to me. "He's down talking to Teles now— about the vintage. It's due to come off any day now, and we can't have it held up because of what's happened here."

"Who on earth is Teles?" Claire said with demanding playfulness, biting into a roll.

"He's the estate agent," her husband said. "I've told you that before, Claire. Don't you ever listen to anything I say?"

I took it from the triumph in her voice that her husband had a stance with which she was familiar, and that she knew she could deal with him now. But she had not been so sure of herself a few minutes before, and I knew that for some reason I would remember that.

"Teles is a good man," William Stewart said heavily, stabbing a bit of crab meat with his fork. "My stepmother never liked him. My father hired him to manage the vineyards before he died, you see. She had nothing to say about it. I don't know how many times since, I've heard her threaten to let the man go, but she never dared. Teles knows how to make those vineyards work, you see, and she needed the money to complete that collection of hers. Besides, she never liked to think about the farming aspects of this place. You see the way she cut it off from the rest of the estate with that stand of pines and the shrubbery. Not that when the vintage comes there's any way of forgetting what's going on down there. You can even smell the fermentation in every room of the house." He lifted the fork tentatively to his mouth and then put it down, the food untouched. "Not that she didn't try: windows closed tight, no matter what the weather. You've got to say this for her, she was a damn strong-minded woman."

I think that when he said that, I really realized for the first time that Lady Stewart was dead. I had known it before, of course. I had seen her body. But I had not, until that moment, had the sense that she was really gone. I think that was why he was reminiscing—to help to convince himself that only her memory lingered on in the house.

Jerez joined us then, taking a place beside me at the farther end of the table from William and his wife. He did not help himself to any of the buffet but sat, silent, his face ashen, steadily drinking glass after glass of port, which he poured from the decanter he had brought to the table. The silence was oppressive. William ate balefully, his eyes fixed on the wall. Even Claire had nothing to say until Martin Kubler came into the room, and then there was a little flurry while she advised endlessly on his choice of food and insisted that he sit beside her.

"The thing is," Jerez said to me suddenly in a low voice, "I can't understand why anyone would have wanted to kill Marian." He spoke as though we had been in the middle of a conversation. At the other end of the table Claire chatted vivaciously to Martin about her impressions

of the inspector, caricaturing him in a shrill voice, while
the doctor obviously did his best to change the subject. I
realized suddenly that as far as the others were concerned,
Marian might never have existed. Even David, when he
had talked to me in his room, had spoken only about the
way in which her death might affect us, not of the woman
herself.

"She didn't have any enemies," Jerez continued. His
dark eyes seemed to be imploring me to believe him. "Not
here, not anywhere. No one is going to benefit from her
death. I've been trying to reason it out. All afternoon I've
been trying to reason it out, but it doesn't make sense."

His voice broke, and he drained his glass. I found
myself wishing that David were here to help me with this
man, because he obviously needed help. David would
have known what to say to him, but I had always been
worse than useless in the face of the strong emotions of
others.

"I want to tell you that I'm more sorry than I can say
that I had that—that first reaction," Jerez said. "Accusing
you of being responsible. I didn't mean it, of course. It was
simply the shock."

"I know," I said. "It's all right." I could scarcely remember what he had said. That afternoon seemed so
very far away.

"I was extraordinarily fond of her, you know," Jerez
went on under the cover of Claire's laughter. "My God,
hasn't that woman any feelings?"

He glared at Claire, but her attentions were focused on
Martin Kubler, who had evidently managed to divert her
from the subject of the police. I heard her say something
about the wine going to her head. Her husband seemed
to have forgotten to eat and was still staring straight in
front of him.

"Perhaps she's nervous," I suggested with a generosity
I did not feel. "People act in strange ways when there's
been a—a tragedy."

"You feel it, too, then." Jerez put one hand over mine. "I know you hadn't known Marian long, but you did sense, didn't you, that she was a very unusual woman?"

I had felt no such thing, but it was impossible to say so.

"The only thing that I can think of," Jerez said rapidly, "was that whoever killed her thought that she was someone else. I mean, it was dark in that room. The murderer could have made a mistake."

"They would have known she was a woman," I said, startled. "And besides Claire and myself——"

"Someone could want her out of the way, couldn't they?" Jerez asked in a loud voice, glancing at the other end of the table. "She's a silly, malicious, self-centered woman."

He spoke at a moment when Claire had stopped talking. His words seemed to echo off the walls. Even William was startled into awareness. There was a long moment of awkward silence.

"I don't suppose you'd like to have a hand of cards, Kubler," William said. "Gin—or cribbage. There's a board about here somewhere."

"I think that I'll go to bed," Martin Kubler said, rising. "It's been a difficult day for all of us."

I left the dining room with him, eager to escape and yet hating myself for not having been able to say something to have mitigated the agony Jerez was going through —if it was agony and not simply a clever act. He had said that no one had had any reason to kill Marian, and I was willing to admit that as far as I knew, she had not constituted a threat to anyone in the household—except, perhaps, in some way I did not understand, to him. She had had no ties with William or with Claire. Martin Kubler was a stranger to her. Even her own son did not know her. She had been close to only Jerez. If anyone had had a reason. . . .

Martin Kubler was silent as we climbed the stairs together, but when we reached the top, he touched my arm. "I wanted to say one thing to you," he said. "It's about Senhora. From something that she let slip when we were seeing to—to Lady Stewart's things, I think that you should avoid her as much as you can. Probably this sounds overly dramatic, Miss Haverlock, but she's a vindictive woman, and in my experience vindictive women can be dangerous."

I think I knew the moment I stepped into my bedroom that someone had been there while I was at dinner. There was no overt sign of this. Nothing had apparently been moved. My cosmetics were still arranged as I had left them on the bureau, and when I opened the drawers slowly, one after another, my underwear and handkerchiefs were still in neat piles. Nothing seemed to have been disarranged in the closet. Even my notebook was still on the bedside table where I had left it. It was only when I looked inside it that I realized that the sheet of notepaper on which Lady Stewart had listed part of her possessions was gone.

I looked everywhere for it—in my purse, in the pockets of the slacks I had been wearing that afternoon, even on the shelves of the drug cabinet in the bathroom—though I remembered quite clearly having placed it, folded as she had given it to me, in the notebook just before I had come upstairs this morning to tell her about the missing items. When I had talked to Martin Kubler outside her room, the notebook had remained in my hand. And later, when I had been working in the chapel, I had tucked her list in the pocket at the back of the notebook so that the list would not slip out.

I sat on the side of the bed and tried to remember if I had kept the notebook in my hand when I had gone to turn on the lights in the five rooms. I thought that I had. I had certainly had it when I had gone with David to his room. I remembered placing it on the table beside my

THE WHITE PEACOCK 153

chair. And when William Stewart had interrupted us, had I brought it away with me? Obviously I must have done so, because it was here on the table beside my bed. There was the possibility that I could have left it in David's room, of course, and that after I had left, he had found it and brought it here. If that was so, he could have found the list and taken it. Was it simply because I did not want to believe such a thing that I imagined that I could recall placing it here myself?

There was no lock on my door. Anyone could have come in and taken anything while I had either been walking in the vineyard or been at dinner, or it was conceivable that despite the fact that I had tucked the list in the pocket, it could have fallen out. Whatever the answer, it was gone. And the realization made me tense with frustration. I needed that list. Obviously it was important, and although I could easily remember the five items I had not been able to locate, the list was my only proof that anything had been removed from the collection. From the interest the inspector had shown in what I had told him, it was more than possible that the fact that certain things were missing from the wing might be vital to his case— might, in fact, provide a motive for Marian's murder. Without the list, how could it ever be proved that anything was missing? Even with it, someone could always argue that Lady Stewart's memory had played her false. Perhaps, among her things, one could find bills of sale for what she had purchased over the past years. But even then there could be no certainty that some things had not been resold. No, her written word that certain items had been in her possession, or should have been, was the best proof of theft which could be provided. And whoever had taken it must have considered it incriminating evidence against him.

I felt a pricking of resentment. The inspector should have realized the importance of the list. He should have asked for it—taken it from me—but he had not even expressed a desire to see it. He had taken my word, and that seemed strange. He had not impressed me as a man who was overly impressed by people's words. Now I would have to tell him that it was missing, and I did not relish the thought. Apparently he had trusted me to keep it safe, just as Lady Stewart had trusted me. I had failed both of them—and myself.

And then there was another consideration. As far as I knew, no one but myself and Lady Stewart and now the inspector knew about the existence of the list. On those grounds alone, he might jump to the conclusion that I had destroyed it myself, for reasons of my own—incriminating reasons. There was no way I could convince him that anyone else could have known. I could not even convince myself. It was possible, of course, that MacGregor, watching outside Lady Stewart's door that night, had taken the occasion to listen to what she had been saying to me. He might have subsequently told Senhora. I only guessed that there was some antagonism between them. Or perhaps Senhora had not told the truth about not having gone into Lady Stewart's bedroom after I had left. I had found that odd to begin with. Perhaps Senhora had gone to her and demanded why I had been sent for at that time of night, and perhaps, weak and ill, the old woman had told her. Perhaps that had brought on the stroke, and Senhora, frightened at what she had done, had gone back to her room and pretended subsequently not to have discovered Lady Stewart's condition until the next morning.

And then there was David. When I had gone with him to his room, he had appeared curious about why his great-aunt had wanted to see me. Perhaps he had had some reason for suspecting the existence of the list. She had been fond of him. They had talked together the day before. She had told me herself that she trusted him— and me. If she had told me about her suspicions, there was no reason why she might not have told him. Perhaps the list had not been drawn up then, but she had told him that she was going to make it out and give it to me. He could have come into this room as easily as anyone. He was supposed to be talking with the estate agent, but how could I be sure. . . .

I undressed slowly, my mind moving in diminishing circles. Only when I was in bed, with the lights off, did I come to the full realization that someone had actually been in this room, that some faceless person had gone through my belongings with prying fingers and eyes—or perhaps through only the notebook. But that was enough. Suddenly I was afraid. I discovered that I was lying stiff, every muscle tensed, gripping the sheets.

I forced myself to relax: took deep breaths, turned on my side, played all the tricks that I had played during those first long weeks of restless nights after Philip had left me. My thoughts had tormented me then, and they tormented me now as well, although in a different way. And now, added to the rest, there was that thin knife-edge of panic. I tried to think of something that would soothe me, and searching, I found only the dark corners of my mind. And then someone screamed. I sat bolt upright in bed, but it was minutes before I realized that it had been one of the peacocks.

Something or someone had disturbed them. I forced myself to get out of the high bed and went to a window. The moon was shining as brightly as it had shone the night before, when David and I had sat on the hillside. I could see the gray stone of the granite figure of the boar in the center of the courtyard. Even the white blossoms of the mimosa bushes were visible, speckling the darkness. And to the left of the courtyard, close to the cloistered walk that lined the wing, I saw the figure of a man.

For some reason, my first thought was that it was David. I had an unreasoning urge to throw open the window and call to him, but I waited, clutching the window-sill, and then he moved and began to cross the courtyard.

The moonlight fell full on him as he reached the figure of the pig, and I saw that it was one of the policemen Inspector Soria had brought with him. I could not see his face, but the cut of his uniform was unmistakable, and I remembered what William Stewart had said about two of the officers having been left behind.

I lit a cigarette then and paced the room in the darkness, trying to relax. But in that moment when I had thought that the man outside might be David, I had conceived a desire to see him, to talk to him. The night before on the hillside his presence had brought me a sort of peace. Perhaps if I could talk to him for only a few minutes, my nerves would uncoil.

Slipping on my black-silk wrap, I hurried out of the room, not giving myself time to think. He would surely be in his room by now. For some reason I knew that part of my tenseness was due to his having left the house. It would be something to know, simply, that he had returned. I turned the corner and saw the black-and-white-tiled floor of the hall stretch below me. I had forgotten the openness of the approach to his room. I knocked at his door and when no one answered, turned the knob, only to find the door locked. My first reaction was one of resentment. Why should he be able to lock his door when I could not lock mine? I turned and hurried back the way I had come, and as I did, I heard the sound of Claire's voice from below. Standing in the shadows of the bend in the corridor, I waited, listening, and heard William respond to her. There was no mistaking his voice, although I could not catch the words. And then I heard David speak—harshly, abruptly. My reaction was one of relief. He was back, then. That was really all I had to know: back safely. As I started toward my room, I heard Claire's voice again, and then Martin Kubler's.

They were all down there, then. Probably in the drawing room. Perhaps I should join them. Martin had said that he intended to go to bed, but obviously he had changed his mind. Or had he simply wanted to give me the impression that that was what he meant to do? Had they deliberately caucused without me? I laughed at my own paranoia—or tried to laugh. But the idea sparked a decision. I would not go down. I needed sleep, and I intended to get it. Closing my bedroom door firmly behind me, I went into the adjoining bathroom, took a sleeping pill, and climbed into the refuge of the high bed.

My mind was just beginning to unfocus when I heard a sound, and instantly I was wide awake. I opened my eyes and incredulous, saw the door swing open. A woman's figure was silhouetted against the dim light from the hall. Then, before I could speak, she was inside the room, and the door had clicked behind her. I lay motionless, hearing her heels click on the parquet floor. Where had I heard that sound before? Where. . . .

Then the light beside my bed flared on, and Senhora was standing not an arm's length away from where I lay. She saw me in the same instant that I saw her, and it was she who cried out. For a moment neither of us spoke. She was the first one to collect herself, smoothing her dark face into expressionless lines.

"I thought you were downstairs with the others," she said, her accent thickening her voice. "I came to turn down your bed. I'll leave at once."

She reached out for the light switch, but I caught her arm and at the same time pulled myself up against the pillows.

"Wait," I said. My heart was still pounding so hard that it was difficult to speak. "What did you really come here for?"

"I've told you," she said sullenly, pulling away from me and starting toward the door, a thin, straight-shouldered figure in black.

I was determined not to let her go without an explanation. I had always disliked and mistrusted her. How many times had she leveled accusations against me? Now it was my turn. Throwing back the covers, I slipped out of bed and ran across the floor, my tissue-thin nightgown tangled about my legs. I reached the door before her and pressed my back against it.

"I've been here two nights," I said, "and on neither of those nights has my bed been turned down. If it had been done, I would expect one of the maids to do it. Tell me why you came here. What did you expect to find?"

I expected some sort of sullen refusal, but instead she stopped where she was in the center of the room, her stiff figure duplicated by her reflection in the gilt-edged mirror.

"Proof," she hissed, her eyes glittering. "I expected to find proof!"

The venom in her voice struck me like a cold wind. I had realized when I had first met her that she hated me for what I represented—an interference in the pattern of life that had been established in the house—but I had never realized until now that she hated me for what I was. I remembered Martin Kubler's warning me that I should stay away from her, that she was a vindictive woman. But it was not my fault that she was here. She had come under her own volition, and now I wanted an explanation. I intended to have one.

"Proof of what?" I snapped.

"Proof that you're responsible for—for what's happened here." For the first time her eyes wavered from my face.

"A great deal has happened here," I told her. "What, precisely, do you mean? Do you think I murdered Marian Russell? Is that what you're saying?"

She shrugged her shoulders. "As if that mattered," she said scornfully.

"Then if you're not concerned with Miss Russell's death, you must be talking about Lady Stewart."

Her dark eyes seemed to slash at my face. "You killed her," she said. "She didn't have to die when she did. You killed her!"

"How?" I demanded furiously.

"You drove her to that stroke," Senhora cried. "When you went to her last night, you deliberately upset her. She was dead before you left her room. Why don't you admit it?"

I stared at her incredulously. "Because it's not true," I said. "She was perfectly well when I left her. You know that. You must have seen that she was all right when you went into the room yourself after I left."

The cords in Senhora's throat stood out as she tensed herself. "I did not go to her room until the next morning," she said shrilly. "If MacGregor told you that I did, he lies."

"Then there was a chance that he might have seen you."

"*Meu Deus*!" she hissed. "If you have told your lies to the inspector, you will live to regret it!"

"Just as Marian Russell lived to regret coming here?"

I was striking out wildly now, but she reacted. Throwing herself toward me, she tried to push me away from the door. Her nails tore at my arm. She was twenty years older than I, at least, but she had the strength of a peasant. Only by catching hold of the back of one of the walnut chairs did I manage to keep my balance.

"You said that you came here because you wanted proof," I said breathlessly. "Is that why you searched my room earlier? Is that why you stole the list?"

She seemed to freeze where she stood, her hand clutching the knob of the door. She turned her head toward me slowly, her eyes narrowing.

"What list?" she said in a low voice. "I know nothing about any list. Good night, Miss Haverlock. I advise you to say nothing of this to anyone."

It must have been a half hour after she had left me when, still pacing back and forth across the bedroom trying to regain my self-control, I found the list that Lady Stewart had given me tucked under a bottle of perfume on top of the massive oak bureau.

CHAPTER

7

The next morning the wind was high. It woke me with its shrieking, and from my windows I could see the pines bending under its force. My dreams had been full of the same sort of mindless fury, and I dressed quickly and hurried down to the kitchen, determined to spend the day engrossed in work. There would be no brooding over what had been done and said the day before. The events of yesterday had shaken me more than I cared to admit, and there was no escape from those memories except in total concentration on the inventory.

The talk in the kitchen was all of the wind and the storm that was approaching. The harvesting of the grapes had obviously taken precedence over murder and sudden death. For the first time since I had come to Alcombra I was aware that the farming of grapes was the major function of the estate, more important to the people who worked there than the personal tragedies of the inhabitants of the house. The word *roga* was repeated frequently, and the housekeeper explained to me, stiffly, that they were the men and women who served as additional pickers, called from the villages that dotted the mountains above the Douro. More of them would be needed if the grapes were to be harvested in time, and I took it, from what I overheard as I ate my eggs and freshly baked rolls, that David had gone to collect as many extra pickers as he could.

I had been afraid that I would meet Senhora in the kitchen, but she did not put in an appearance. As I crossed the broad expanse of the black-and-white-tiled hall, there was no sound in the house, or if there was, it was blotted out by the wailing of the wind. By the door that led to the wing I found one of the young policemen sitting listlessly in a straight-backed chair, his eyes shadowed with fatigue. It was necessary for me to explain who I was before he would unlock the door. Evidently the inspector had given him instructions to stay with me, for we made our way to the chapel together. As we passed through each of the five rooms, he carefully unlocked and then locked each door again. I realized with a sting of self-consciousness that the inspector did not trust even me to be alone here. It might be, of course, that he had ordered the officer to stay with me for my own protection. It was, I thought, more probable that the inspector entertained the suspicion I might be as capable of theft as anyone else in the household.

In the chapel, with the wind hammering at the stained-glass windows, I worked with absolute concentration for over an hour. The police officer did not speak, and when I entered the last item on my list, a sixteenth-century ivory relic portraying a figure that I thought I could identify as Saint Francis, I saw that the young man had fallen asleep, huddled in an old choir stall, with the carved face of a gargoyle leering at me through the shadows over his shoulder. I woke him reluctantly, realizing that he had been up guarding the house all night but always aware that if any charge of theft were ever brought against me, I did not want him to testify that he had not been watching. I had just touched his shoulder when I heard a key turn in the heavy arched door, and the inspector came into the chapel.

A cigarette was hanging out of the side of his mouth, but he bent and butted it out on the floor at once with a curiously guilty expression as though he was not certain whether or not the proprieties should be preserved, even though the room that he was in was no longer a place of worship but only an exhibit of sorts. The young officer pushed himself to his feet and stood at attention, staring at his superior with eyes still thick with sleep. The inspector muttered a few words of dismissal in Portuguese, and in a moment he and I were alone. I waited for him to say something, and when he did not, I expressed my appreciation that he had appointed someone to stay here with me while I worked, carefully keeping my voice free of irony.

He responded by shrugging his thin shoulders. His eyes were even more heavily shadowed than they had been the day before, and his thin face was like a gaunt mask. "I don't suppose," he said, "you've come across any of the missing items this morning."

I shook my head. "The few things that Lady Stewart designated as being in the chapel are here," I said, and then, remembering what had happened the night before: "Don't you think, Inspector, that you ought to have her original list? If it becomes necessary to prove that certain thefts have occurred——"

"Yes. Yes." His voice was impatient. "You're quite right, of course. Perhaps if you will make a duplicate list sometime today and give me the original——"

"I'd like you to have the original now," I said flatly,

taking it out of the pocket of my notebook and handing it to him. "You can provide me with a duplicate, or if you like, I will copy it in your presence. But I don't want the responsibility of keeping it any longer."

"Perhaps," he said, his fingers creasing the edges of the cigarette package that he had drawn involuntarily from his pocket, "you will tell me why you feel the sudden urge not to keep the list any longer, Miss Haverlock."

"It's a vital piece of evidence, isn't it?" I said sharply, certain that he was being purposefully obtuse. "At least it might very well be."

"It is your opinion, then, that Miss Russell's murder had something to do with the missing pieces?"

"I have no opinions," I said. Should I, I wondered, tell him that last night the list had been—for some short time, at least—taken from my room? Would that be fair? Because if I told him the entire story, it would carry with it the implication that Senhora had returned the list, and that, in turn, would imply that she had taken it. The question had nagged me last night until, with the help of another sleeping pill, I had fallen into a drugged sleep. Could I be absolutely certain that the list had not been there, tucked under the perfume bottle on the top of the bureau, all the time?

"All right." The inspector leaned against the wall, and it was as though his body caved in to meet it. "If you have no opinions, you may have convictions. A great many of your friends have these—er—convictions. Tell me, who do you believe killed Miss Russell?"

I stared at him, appalled, as the wind thundered against the glass above my head. I did not presume to understand this man, but I had never expected him to ask that question. "I have no idea," I said stiffly.

"Let me put it this way." He took a cigarette out of the crumpled package and smoothed it lovingly between his fingers. "Do you know of any reason that anyone here might have had to kill her?"

"No," I said positively.

"But you will agree that someone must have had a reason?"

"It may have been a mistake," I said, "an accident. There might have been a quarrel."

"And yet you heard no quarrel."

"People don't necessarily have to shout at one another."

"True. What you say is very interesting. Can you think of any other circumstance in which no motive would have been necessary—no long-term motive, that is? Assuming that it was manslaughter and not murder."

He was doing just what he had done with me before: making me draw hypotheses. I wanted to protest, but in a sense what he was presenting me with was an intellectual challenge, the sort of thing I had always found irresistible. It was a horrifying thought, somehow, to think that he could have so quickly taken my measure.

"She could have come upon someone in that room," I said quickly, "seen something she should not have seen."

"Another theft, perhaps?"

"Perhaps, or perhaps," I went on, unable to stop myself, half remembering another conversation, "the murderer mistook her for someone else."

He smiled thinly and giving up the struggle, lit the cigarette, immediately breaking into a spasm of coughing. "I see," he said when he could talk again, "that you have been giving this a good deal of thought, Miss Haverlock. And yet, as you say, you have no convictions in the matter."

"Have you?" I said boldly.

"A few, Miss Haverlock, a few. For example, I am convinced that she was killed near the spot where she was found. Her handkerchief, embroidered with her name, was found near the body, you see. Since you heard nothing, no sound of any quarrel, it might have been conceivable that she was killed elsewhere, and her body brought to that room to be hidden—to give the killer time."

"Time for what?"

He inhaled deeply. "Ah, about that, unfortunately, I am like you. I have no opinions, no convictions. That is why I had hoped that you might help me. You are the sort of person I find invaluable in such investigations, Miss Haverlock. You have an imagination, but a well-disciplined one—unlike others I might mention. Unlike Lady Stewart's companion, for example."

"Senhora?"

"That is what she is called, I believe. Her imagination is quite uncontrolled, and as a result, she has many answers—but not, I think, the right sort of answers."

He eyed me curiously, as though he had just made an important move in a game of chess and was waiting for me to make a predictable response. I thought that I knew the question that he wanted me to ask, and instinctive caution made me remain silent.

"Very well," he said, "if you will not ask me what I mean, I will tell you. The woman you call Senhora was waiting for me outside when I arrived a few minutes ago—in a rather agitated condition. She seemed to think that you would be telling me some tale or other about something that happened last night, and she wished to talk to me first, although as any woman should know, last words are often better than first."

"What did she tell you?" I said in a low voice.

He shrugged, grinding out the butt of the cigarette with his heel on the stone floor. "What do you think she told me, Miss Haverlock?"

"I don't like guessing games," I said briskly. There was a limit to the extent to which I could let this man manipulate me. "If you don't want to tell me, I'll start my work in the next room."

"She said," the little man purred, "that she had gone

to your room to turn down the bed and that you accused her of having come to steal something. At least that was the general tenor of what she told me. Is it true?"

"In a sense, yes," I said wearily, "but she was mistaken about my intention of going to you with the story."

"But why?" He mimicked disappointment. There was, I thought, something unpleasantly playful about his mood, despite his exhausted appearance. "Why should you not come to me with any story? You must know that I have a certain interest in what goes on in this house."

"Very well," I said. "Shortly before Senhora let herself into my room—she was under the impression, you understand, that I was downstairs with the others at the time—I had discovered that the list that Lady Stewart had given me was missing."

He stared at me in what seemed to be mock confusion. "How can that be, Miss Haverlock?" he said. "You have just given me that list."

"After Senhora left, I found it on the bureau," I said. "I decided not to mention the—the incident to you because I cannot be absolutely certain that it was not there all the time."

"But you do not think so." He was serious now, his eyes growing smaller in his thin face.

"What I think," I said crisply, "would not be admissible evidence in a court of law, and I find it difficult to understand how you could accept—"

I broke off as the little man raised one finger to his lips. Over the sound of the wind I heard someone's footsteps outside. They paused before the door, and then it slowly opened, and David appeared, his hair tousled, a streak of dirt smudging the right side of his face. It was obvious that he had not expected to find the inspector here.

"Ah, Mr. Ashor," Inspector Soria said happily. "To what do we owe the honor——"

"The storm is going to break in a few hours," David interrupted him. "I don't have time to talk. We've got to get as many people as we can into the vineyards to pick. I came to ask you if you'd help, Irene."

I stared at him, startled. He was tense, drawn to a fine edge of excitement. There was none of Martin's quiet confidence about him, but there was something that I found even more appealing, a sensitive response to the situation— an impulsiveness, the same impulsiveness that had made him shoot pebbles at my window that night. I remembered with sudden vividness the white of the moonlight on the hill, and I remembered the way he had opened himself to me. How curious that I had not realized until this moment that I loved him.

The inspector was saying something, but I did not hear the words. My eyes seemed to be caught to David's by invisible webs.

"Will you come and help, Irene?" he repeated in a low voice. "Will you come down to the vineyard with me?"

Again the inspector spoke, and I caught only the word "interview." Perhaps he was reminding us both that what he was doing was important, too. But questions and answers about death could wait. My life was what mattered now, and for the first time since I could remember I knew that I could do what I wanted to do rather than what I should do. Conscience was in retreat. What I wanted most to do was to be with David.

"Yes," I said eagerly.

The inspector rose. 'Before you run away with Miss Haverlock, Mr. Ashor, perhaps you might tell me how you were able to get in here. My officer had orders to lock each one of the rooms of the wing as he left us here and to stand guard outside."

"You kept the man up all night and failed to relieve him this morning," David said, taking my hand and leading me to the door. "It shouldn't come as any surprise to you that he's asleep on a chair in the hall. As far as the locked doors are concerned, I used my own keys. I have a key to every room in this house."

There was a silence. I knew the implication that the inspector would put on the admission. David would be suspect now, if he had not been before. But I did not suspect him. That was the important thing. Together we left the room, and neither of us looked back.

Five hours later the storm broke. There was no time to get back to the main house as the sky broke its hold on the rain, which descended in torrents, battering the vines and beating against the bent backs of the workmen carrying the last tall dark baskets full of grapes down the twisting yellow paths to the wine-press shed. I followed them, stumbling on the wet stone of the ladderways that jutted from the terrace walls, the rain dashing against my back. There were other women running, dark-faced peasant women, their black skirts swaddled about their thick bodies. Watching the men dump the loads of purple grapes, the women huddled under the eaves of the shed, their weather-beaten faces twisted in smiles as each man, ridding himself of his load, shouted "Io!"

Inside the shed a concertina played a melody that challenged the beating of the rain against the tin roof. The mood was one of gaiety because the grapes had been harvested in time. These people had been picking and carrying grapes from dawn till dusk for days. Clearly their lives had known little but back-breaking labor and poverty. The thin, unshaven faces of the men told their own story as they stood talking together in rapid Portuguese, their frayed trousers and patched shirts clinging, rain-drenched, to their bodies. But they were exhilarated because the harvest was in.

"You can't stand out here," a man's voice said in English. "Come on. Let's get inside."

It was Jerez, his usually immaculate clothing mud-spattered, the tightly cut trousers torn at the pocket, his dark hair clinging flat to his high forehead. He and Martin Kubler had, I knew, responded to David's request for help, but I had not seen either of them since we had come out to the vineyard that windblown morning. I followed him through the crowd of workmen and through a low door into the shed.

We found ourselves in a long, low-ceilinged room with a plank floor and the unhidden tin of the roof above us. At the far end of the shed were the vats where I knew the grapes gathered earlier were fermenting. There was the thick, acrid smell of fermentation in the air, an overpowering smell that made me catch my breath. In another corner a man was sitting on the floor, playing the concertina I had heard outside. Around him a few barefooted men were dancing a native dance, probably as old as the hills outside. It was incredible, I thought, that after their arduous toil they could have any strength left for dancing. Vitality seemed to exude from them as they laughed and clapped their hands in time to the music.

It was not until my eyes became accustomed to the shadows that I saw David talking with a broad-shouldered man, better dressed than the others although in work clothes. I guessed that he was Teles, the estate manager, or as David had spoken of him as we had left the house, the *caseiro*. Teles had apparently been shocked when David had suggested soliciting help from the main house. "And, of course," David had said grimly, "he was right as far as Claire and William are concerned. They'd rather let the entire crop be destroyed than dirty their hands."

Now he turned his head and saw Jerez and me standing just inside the door, but there was no sign of greeting in his eyes. Turning away, he continued his animated conversation with the *caseiro*.

"It's a good thing we didn't do this for thanks," Jerez muttered. "Here, here's a bench. Sit down. You must be exhausted. I don't know about you, but I find it difficult to make out that young man—and just as difficult to think of him as Marian's son."

I made no response, but I knew precisely what he meant. I leaned back against the board wall, beginning now to be uncomfortably aware of my aching body. Jerez was right. I had not done this for thanks, but David's attitude bewildered me. When we had first met on that lonely mountain road, he had been gay and confident. Then that night on the hillside, with the moonlight holding us in its embrace . . . but it was better not to think of that. Better to remember that he was a stranger to me, a man who was capable of hatred for a woman who had abandoned him, a man who soon after her brutal murder could warn me that we would have to think of ourselves first. A man who had ignored me since he had tried to question me in his room. A man who, whatever else I might feel about him, I found I no longer understood.

"He's acting as though he were owner of this estate," Jerez said laconically, looking down at his hands, which, like mine, were scarred and red from the vines. "I suppose he may be the executor. Have you heard anything about the terms of the will?"

I shook my heard wearily.

"I suppose," Jerez mused, "someone had to take over although from what I hear, Lady Stewart left this business up to Teles completely. I wonder how he feels about David making his presence felt."

I glanced at the two men. Teles was talking, bending forward so that his broad face was close to David's. He was not smiling, and he gave the impression of someone making firm pronouncements, but the concertina was playing so loudly that I could not hear. More of the workmen had crowded through the door, and the air was thick and damp with the press of drenched bodies. Suddenly I felt as though I were suffocating. I started to rise from the bench, but Jerez caught my arm.

"You aren't planning to go back to the house just now,

are you?" he said. I could scarcely hear him over the sound of the music and the clapping of men's hands. At any other time I might have found this scene colorful, but I was exhausted, and my head was beginning to ache. If David had given any sign of gratitude, I knew that I might have felt differently. There was exhilaration in the air. I could have shared it.

I realized that Jerez was still speaking, enunciating carefully to make himself heard over the sound of the concertina. ". . . drenched. We might as well wait until the rain lets up a bit. Those dirt paths we'll have to climb will be pure mud. As far as that goes, we shouldn't have to walk back at all. I mean, it would be unreasonable of David to expect us to, wouldn't it? After all, even if it weren't for the rain, it means climbing back up those terraces again. There must be a road that goes back to the main house, and some sort of truck. I'll ask him about it."

"No!" I felt suddenly that I would not under any circumstances be a party to begging David to find us transportation. I started to push my way through a cluster of peasant women toward the door. I had just reached it when someone caught my arm. Thinking it was Jerez trying to dissuade me, I tried to pull away. Then, turning, I found that it was David. His blue eyes seemed to be sunk in his narrow face, and he was not smiling.

"Where are you going?"

"Back to the main house," I said. "It's too crowded here, and I'm tired."

"Look," he said impatiently, "there's no need for you to walk. I don't even know if you could get back up the paths with it raining like this. If it's too crowded for you in here, there's Teles's office."

"I don't want any special favors," I snapped.

As soon as the words left my mouth, I was bewildered as to why I should have spoken them. David frowned.

"What's wrong with you, Irene?" he said. "I'd take you

back now in Teles's truck, but I can't leave until we get some details straightened out."

"I thought he took care of this part of things single-handed," I said, "and has for years."

"'With Lelia dead, he wants some assurance that he won't have to take the blame if something goes wrong with the vintage," David said angrily. "Believe me, this isn't easy for me. I don't know a damn thing about wine-making, but somebody's got to give him the authorization he wants. And since William wouldn't consider coming down here among the riffraff, it has to be me. Now, are you going to wait for me in his office, or aren't you?"

I wanted to tell him that I was not, but I knew that the only thing I would prove by going was that I was capable of playing the fool. I let him lead me across the crowded room to a small office containing only a battered desk, a file cabinet from which the drawers lurched drunkenly, and two chairs. A cracked piece of linoleum covered the floor. Only when David had left me there did I realize that Jerez had followed us.

"Well, this is more comfortable, isn't it?" he said with an attempt at cheerfulness. "I hope you don't mind if I keep you company. I heard David say that there was a ride back to the house in a truck in the offing."

He sat down on one of the chairs, and I saw the fingers of his right hand automatically begin to crease his trousers, mud-spattered and wet as they were. He caught my eye on him and laughed. For a moment he was like the Jerez I had first met that sunlit morning in the courtyard.

"Old habits die hard," he said. "I'm sure you'll believe me when I tell you that I haven't done any manual labor for—oh—twenty years at least. And even then, helping my father hoe a few rows of potatoes was about the extent of it. He's a poor man, my father. A small farm south of Lisbon. Even as a boy I didn't fit in, as you can guess. When I got my first job in an interior decorator's shop in the city, my family treated me as though I'd had some sort of mental aberration. Now that I have my own business—well, I might as well be living in another world as far as they're concerned. In a sense, of course, I am. Oh, I send them money, but we rarely meet. I learned a long time ago to loathe the stench of poverty. You can smell it out there, can't you?"

He waved his hand in the direction of the room we had just left. With the door of the office closed, the sound of the concertina was muted, but some of the men had begun to sing, and I could hear the words clearly enough. It was a fado, the words strangely formal, the tune melancholy:

> My eyes are two tapers
> That give sad light to my face,
> Marked by martyrdoms
> Of *saudade* and sorrow.

"It's just a familiar song to them," Jerez said scornfully. "They don't even understand what their lives are. They'll take the pittance they're given when the vintage is over and go off happy enough. They don't have any concept of the profit that a farm like this makes."

"How could they have?" I snapped. He was rambling on just as he had done when I had first met him, and, as then, he irritated me. "Do you expect them to understand higher finance when most of them haven't been given the beginnings of an education? My father loved Portugal, but he used to say. . . ."

"Yes?"

"It doesn't matter." It would, I realized, be easier for me to speak of Philip to a stranger than of my father. A few words of his, repeated, would do very little to show the sort of man that he had been, and I prefered to present him whole or not at all.

"You're annoyed with me," Jerez said. "I can't say that

I blame you. It isn't any good trying to explain to someone who's never been poor what it's like. Did Marian ever talk to you about that, about what it felt like for her to have nothing, with her aunt sitting on a fortune?"

I sat down in the chair behind the desk and propped my chin on my interlaced fingers. If there was anything I did not want at the moment, it was to be forced to remember—to remember anything. There had been one excellent result to having put in five hours of hard physical exertion. During all the time I had struggled with the vines, my mind had remained as nearly blank as possible. It had been enough to have been forced to concentrate on the elusive grapes. There was something about this man's directness, however, that made it difficult to rebuff him, as I had discovered before. And who could blame him for wanting to talk about the woman who had so suddenly and violently vanished from his life? There were, I guessed, few other people at Alcombra who were willing to talk about her in the way one talks in order to deliberately conjure up a sense of sustained reality. I remembered with a twinge of guilt how I had left him in the company of Claire and William in the drawing room not an hour after Marian's body had been found, without having uttered one word of consolation.

"Yes," I said slowly. "She mentioned how difficult it had been for her."

"In what context?" Jerez said eagerly. "Forgive me. I don't mean to pry, but somehow it's important that I know what she said and what she did and what other people said to her during those days just before she died. She hadn't talked much to me, you see. There was a—a misunderstanding, I wanted her to go back to Lisbon with me, you see. I didn't think she should stay here—unwanted, without even the chance to talk to her aunt. Senhora made it quite clear, you know, that the old woman considered us intruders. I'm a proud man. I've never wanted to stay where I wasn't wanted. Somehow Marian—

she got it into her head that I meant to leave without her."

The words seemed to pour out of him, hammering at my ears as the rain hammered against the tin roof. Obviously he badly needed to talk about something. I suspected that this was no idle conversation, and yet I could not see precisely where he meant it to lead. Whatever else, although I was willing to let him talk to me about Marian, even to ask me questions, I did not want to hear about their personal difficulties. Hurriedly I thought back to what his question had been.

"She had come to my room," I told him, "the day after we arrived here. She was upset about David being at Alcombra, too, of course. She wanted to talk to him, but I don't think she dared. She told me that Lady Stewart had prejudiced him against her. I think she talked about her past life because she wanted me to understand why she had given him up."

Jerez frowned, but he was obviously more comfortable now that I had shown my willingness to talk about Marian with him. He was, I guessed, a man who was happiest talking. It was one of those touches of the female about him.

"I don't understand," he said. "She didn't mention having this conversation with you. I don't know why. She used to tell me everything, but she'd changed since she'd come to this damn place. It was as though she was—was struggling with something inside herself, and she couldn't share it with me. When I wanted her to go, she said she couldn't run away. That was when we began to quarrel."

I could see that it was going to take a good deal of effort on my part to turn the conversation away from whatever had happened between him and Marian. Surreptitiously I glanced at my watch. It was after five. Surely David would be leaving soon.

"She wanted me to talk to David first," I told him, "to see just how hostile he really was to her. I think she wanted me to lay the groundwork. I mean, I think she wanted me to explain to him that as far as she was concerned, she had had no choice except to give him up when he was a baby."

Jerez shook his head. "Poor Marian. She had a very difficult life, you know—not just as far as David was concerned. When she finally married—well—she wasn't at all happy. I think, although she never admitted it, that she wanted desperately to give herself some sort of financial security, to prove to her aunt that she didn't have to be as much an inferior as the old woman had always made her feel."

He paused, buffing his fingernails against the palm of his left hand. "Did you?" he asked.

"Did I what?"

"Did you talk to David?"

Suddenly, over the drumming of the rain on the tin roof, I heard the silence of the night when David and I had sat together on the hillside. How difficult it was now to remember precisely what had been said and left unsaid. Only the memory of the mood remained, and it was bitter to think that that could never be recaptured.

"Yes," I said in a low voice. "I—I mentioned that she wanted him to understand why she wanted to give him up."

"And I suppose he made it clear that he didn't want to talk to her," Jerez said in a hard voice. "It was unforgivable what he did to her, you know. That next morning I saw her just after she'd talked to him. She'd lost her head, I think. Marian always was too emotional. I think she'd said things that never ought to be said. Anyway, she was completely distraught. She told me that she wanted to die, and then, just a few hours later, she was dead, wasn't she? You may think I'm a fool, but I can't help but wonder if her own son didn't have something to do with it."

The drive back to Alcombra was a nightmare of mud-slicked roads and blinding rain. I sat between Jerez and David in the cab of the truck and clenched my teeth to keep from crying out as we slid from one side of the narrow road to another. Only when we reached the gravel road that led directly to the house was there any traction for the wheels, and only then did I breathe easily.

The two men did not speak to one another during the drive. David bent grimly over the wheel, trying to see through the rain that battered the windshield, and Jerez pressed stiffly against the door. Occasionally I felt his eyes on my face, and I knew that he was trying to decide what my response had been to what he had said about David. In the tiny office I had turned the conversation aside with a determination that had kept him from pursuing the subject of David's possible guilt. I had tried to dismiss the subject from my thoughts as well, but I knew already that it was going to gnaw at my mind during the long lonely hours of the night. I did not think David capable of murder. Despite the fact that he might have quarreled with his mother, I could not think of any possible reason why he might have wanted to harm her, even assuming that he would have done so. And yet. . . .

When we climbed out of the truck, the wind caught us at the back and propelled us toward the rain-shadowed house. Inside, with the thick oak door shut against the storm, we found the hall in semidarkness. Muttering something under his breath, David clicked the light switch, but the chandelier overhead remained sightless. I heard a shuffling sound behind me and turned to find MacGregor coming toward us.

"What's wrong with the lights?" David asked.

The old man's bent shoulders moved in a hint of a shrug. "It's the storm," he muttered.

David ran his hands through his drenched hair. Behind

him Jerez stood stiffly, his dark face expressionless. Somehow he gave the impression that he was waiting.

"Where's the inspector?" David said. "He's still around, isn't he?"

MacGregor shook his grizzled head. "He went back," he mumbled.

"Back where?"

"To the town."

"I'll call him, then," David said as though talking to himself. "He ought to know——"

"Telephone's out," MacGregor muttered, and turning, he shambled away from us.

"I'm glad you're back." It was William. He came down the long stairs, his thick face set in worried lines. "I was afraid you'd been marooned down there. Did MacGregor tell you we're cut off completely? I don't like it, you know. I tried to keep the inspector here, but he said he couldn't risk being cut off from his office. In case of trouble, I suppose—trouble from some other source. The thing is, he'd sent those two men of his back earlier, and two other officers were supposed to have come to replace them—but no sign. I suppose the road to town is a stream of mud by now. I'll never understand why my father allowed himself to be talked into buying this godforsaken place, and now Claire——"

"The harvest's in," David snapped. "In case you wondered."

"Fine, fine." Clearly William was trying to present himself to us in his usual hearty manner, but something rang false. He was worried about something, on edge. But why shouldn't he be? I asked myself. Why shouldn't all of us be on edge? The storm and the sense of isolation it had brought with it would not, I knew, improve the situation. I was suddenly aware of my total physical exhaustion. I would take a long hot bath and lie down. And think. Or try not to think. I started toward the stairs.

"It was you I was really waiting for, Miss Haverlock," William Stewart said. "I know you must be tired, but I'm worried about Claire. Perhaps if a woman could talk to her. I mean, she admires you. You could make her see reason."

Throwing his cousin a look of disgust, David passed him and ran up the stairs. Jerez held his ground, watching and listening with what appeared to be intense curiosity but, for once, not intervening. I imagined that I disliked William Stewart almost as much as David did, but I found that I could not be as rude to the man as he had been. In fact, in some strange way, although my back was aching and I felt as though dirt were ingrained in every pore in my body, I sensed that I should make up in some way for David's abruptness.

"What's wrong with her?" I said wearily.

"That's the thing," William said, his plump fingers roaming up and down the line of buttons that pulled his tweed jacket tight about his bulbous stomach. "I don't know. She was in her room when the storm started, and when I went up to see what she was doing, I heard her talking to someone. I thought perhaps it was Martin." For a moment his pale-blue eyes were shielded by his lids as though he did not want me to look too directly at him. "She often talks to him to pass the time, you know. He's been our friend in London for some time, ever since Claire went to him. . . . But that's neither here nor there, is it? She's been upset, of course, because of what's happened here. I know that to you she seems quite—quite cool, but actually she's very sensitive. I thought that she probably wanted to talk to Martin alone, and so I went away. But then I came upon him reading in the drawing room, and I realized that she must be with someone else." He cleared his throat nervously. "And that was odd, you see, because you and Jerez and David were down in the fields, and I couldn't think of anyone else. . . ."

He paused and made a wide helpless gesture with his plump hands. "I'm not putting this very well, am I? But you see, I'm worried about her. Because she's locked the door, and I can't hear anything. I mean, she might be napping, but I'd like to be certain that she's all right. I mean, under the circumstances——"

"Surely," I said, "someone must have a key to the room."

"MacGregor has them," William Stewart said with sudden violence. "I know he has, because my mother always did trust them to the old fool, but he claims he gave them to the inspector."

"Did you ask the inspector for them?"

He stared at the tiled floor. "I didn't want to involve him," he said. "She might simply be angry with me. She's done this sort of thing, locking doors. You know what women are." He looked past me at Jerez as though seeking confirmation. "And later, when I became really concerned, the inspector was gone."

"But what do you think I can do?" I asked him.

"Well, you're a woman," William said with the air of having answered my question. "Claire's never had many women friends. Even when she was modeling, she didn't ever seem to be close to any of the other girls. There was too much competition, you know. It's a difficult business, that. I made her give it up as soon as we were married. She's had a hard life in many ways. And now—well, sometimes she doesn't seem to be able to talk to me. Even those sessions with Martin . . . and he's a fine psychiatrist. It was Claire's idea that I bring him here." He rubbed one hand across his forehead. "I'm rambling," he said. "I always do that when I'm upset. Claire says. . . . You could at least knock on her door and see if you can get some sort of response." There was a sudden belligerence in his voice. "You could do that, couldn't you?"

Nothing that he had said had given me any reason to think that I would be more successful than he had been, but he was right. I could do what he asked. I could understand why he was worried. I only wished that I was not so incredibly weary. That the inspector were here. That the wind and rain would stop beating at the windows.

He followed me up the stairs, and so did Jerez, both of them hesitant, as though they were expecting me at any minute to tell them to leave me alone. But I didn't want them to go. Without lights the house assumed the same ominous quality that I had sensed in the wing. It was nearly dark in the upstairs corridor. Someone would have to bring candles soon, or lamps. William indicated a closed door with his outstretched arm and then stood a little distance away with Jerez beside him as I knocked.

There was no answer. At the end of the hall the long window rattled under the onslaught of the wind. Then there was a pause. A silence. I do not think that I had ever heard a silence so complete. I called her name, softly at first and then, in response to my rising concern, more loudly. When she answered, her voice was muffled as though something was pressed to her mouth.

"What do you want?" she said. I could scarcely make out the words. "Leave me alone."

At least she was alive. I had not realized until that moment that in the back of my mind had been the memory of Marian Russell's lifeless eyes as her body had slid from its hiding place behind the coat of armor. I glanced at William and saw his heavy body sag with relief. I pointed at the door, asking him without words if he wanted to take my place. He shook his head, and I saw him mouth the words "Ask her to let you in."

And so I asked, expecting refusal, but without warning, the door was flung open. She was wearing a crumpled pink nightgown that hung off one shoulder, disclosing most of one breast. Her hair was disheveled, her eyes red-rimmed —and riveted on me. If she was aware that anyone else was in the corridor with me, she gave no sign.

"Very well," she said in a hard voice that bore little

relationship to the childlike wispiness she usually assumed. "Come in if you want to. You're supposed to be clever, aren't you? Perhaps you can tell me what to do."

There was no way of refusal. After all, I had sought her out, not the reverse. What excuse did I have for having bothered her if I now refused to talk to her? It did not occur to me until the door closed behind me that I could have simply left her with her husband. But if what William had said was true, in all probability she would have slammed the door in his face.

"You're wet," Claire said accusingly, throwing herself down on the bed. "That's right. You went along to the vineyard, didn't you? I told David that I wouldn't think of playing peasant, even if it meant losing every grape."

She said it triumphantly, as though she had accomplished some coup. I did not answer. I had not come into this room for the purpose of admiring her strength of mind.

"You'll find a housecoat in the closet," Claire said. "You'd better change, or you'll catch cold."

I ignored the suggestion. If I were going to change my clothes, I would do so in my own room.

"Your husband is worried about you," I said. "He asked me to find out what's wrong."

She laughed scornfully. "That's like William," she said, "to send someone else to do the dirty work."

I had never disliked her more intensely. "He knocked on your door several times," I said, "and when you didn't answer, he was afraid that something had happened to you."

The bedroom was a near duplicate of mine, with the addition of a single easy chair. There were four long windows against which the rain pounded with monotonous steadiness. What light there was, was slate-gray. Every chair and table seemed to be covered with discarded clothing and cosmetics. In the shadows of the far corner I detected an open suitcase. I wondered if, for some reason, Claire was preparing to leave Alcombra in spite of the inspector's order that all of us should remain.

"What's wrong with the lights?" she said now, querulously.

"The storm has evidently knocked down a line," I said wearily. "Since you seem to be all right. . . ." I started toward the door.

"Don't go!" She propped herself erect. "I want to talk to you."

"About the lighting arrangements?" I said dryly.

"No. I'm sorry. I'm not behaving very well, but I've had a shock."

I waited, my back to her.

"You don't really care, do you?"

"No," I said, "not really. But if I can help you, I will."

"It's that woman," she murmured. "No. Look at me. I'm trying to tell you something important. I can't tell William—not now. He may have had something to do with it. Don't you understand how terrible it is not even to be able to trust your own husband?"

I turned and looked at her. She had pulled the pink nightgown up over her shoulders and was busy wrapping a quilt around herself. "It's so cold," she said. "Ever since she came, I've been so cold."

"I don't know who you're talking about," I said, trying to keep my voice even. I was cold, too. My clothes felt like a wet shroud.

"Senhora. Who do you expect? She had the nerve to come in here and accuse me of. . . ."

"Of what?"

Throwing off the quilt, Claire slipped off the bed and made her way across the shadowy room to a low table littered with clothing. As she passed me, I realized that she had been drinking. Her pink nightgown billowing about her slim body, she left behind her the odor of whiskey and expensive scent.

"Have you ever seen this before?" she asked.

She had taken something from the mess on the table and was holding it out to me. Whatever it was, it was too small for me to see through the dusk. I went to her and saw, cradled in the palm of her hand, a ring. Taking it from her, I saw the glitter of a dark stone—a ruby. The gold band was very thin, molded as it touched the stone into what appeared to be two dragon claws. I recognized it immediately from the description on the list Lady Stewart had given me. It was the ring that was missing from the collection.

"Well, have you ever seen it?" Claire asked shrilly.

I chose my words carefully. "Where did you find this?" I said.

"I asked you a question first," Claire said petulantly.

"No," I told her. "I've never seen it before." That, at least, was true. I wanted to hear what else she had to say before I volunteered any more information.

"That woman said that I'd stolen it," Claire muttered. "That's a lie. I told her it was a lie."

"Where was it found?" I repeated.

"She *said* she found it here," Claire said defiantly, "in the top drawer of that bureau."

I took a deep breath. "What was she doing looking in drawers?" I asked her, trying to keep my patience.

"That's what I wanted to know," Claire said angrily. "She may think she's mistress of this house now, but she had no right to go through my things. Of course, she had an excuse. She said that she was helping the maids, putting away some of my clothes. A likely excuse. She was prying. I told her straight out that I wasn't going to put up with it. I told her that William would see that she was sent on her way. That was when she accused me of having stolen this from the collection."

I folded my hand around the ring. She seemed to take no interest in having it returned, and it was just as well,

I thought, that I keep it. "How did it get in the drawer?" I said slowly.

"How should I know? I never set eyes on it before. Who'd want an old thing like that? That's not the sort of thing I care for, someone else's castoffs. If you ask me, I think she put it there herself—to try to make William and me look bad. She said she was going to take it to the inspector, you know. That was before I took it away from her. I thought I was going to have to knock her down. She knew I meant business. There are some things I won't put up with, and being called a thief is one of them." She was talking with random spitefulness, but all the time her blue eyes were clinging to me. "Why doesn't someone do something about the lights?" she asked plaintively.

I had one more question: "Why didn't you tell your husband about this instead of frightening him the way you've done?"

"I won't be told what I should or shouldn't do," she said, flaring up, and it took me a moment before I realized that it was me and not him that she was talking about. "Oh, all right," she went on, sullenly. "I didn't want to tell him because he'd make a fuss. He never thinks I handle things properly. I mean, that woman may have gone to him and told him God knows what lies about the way I treated her."

"Because you took the ring away from her?"

"I may have hurt her a bit," Claire muttered. "I don't know. She said she was bleeding."

I clenched my fingers so tightly together that the ring hurt my hand. "Bleeding?" I said. "But you said——"

"I tried to frighten her," Claire said, suddenly furious. "Do you blame me? She was trying to blackmail me, wasn't she? I was simply protecting myself. I had a letter knife, and I——"

"You stabbed her with a letter knife?" I said incredulously.

"No, I didn't stab her. I may have cut her arm a bit. I

don't know. She deserved it. I had to make her give me that ring. She was staying terrible things: that there was a lot else missing from the collection, and that she wouldn't be surprised if all the things were hidden in this room. That's what I've been doing: hunting for anything that shouldn't be here, turning out the drawers."

"But why not tell your husband?"

"Don't talk like a fool," Claire hissed. "Don't you understand? If she really did find that ring in the drawer, it wasn't me that hid it here. And if it wasn't me, it must have been William. He could have done it, you know—stolen things. He told me when we came here that he didn't intend to go back to London empty-handed."

CHAPTER

8

___

It was when I turned away from Claire to stare out the long window that I saw, through the gray threads of rain, a flickering light. Her room, like mine, looked over the courtyard, now lost in the thick shadows of approaching night. It took me a moment to realize that the light came from one of the windows of the long gallery in the wing where the collection was housed. I caught my breath as the red glow turned to orange, spreading like an opening hand. It was not a candle flame that I was looking at or the glow of a lamp, but fire—fire raging out of control.

I ran to the door, threw it open, and smelled the faint musky scent of smoke. Behind me I could hear Claire babbling something about my not leaving her. I ran down the corridor toward the balcony that overlooked the main hall, hearing my own voice, shrill and unfamiliar in my ears.

"Fire!"

As I reached the head of the stairs, David came out of his room. The smell of smoke was more powerful. There was no need for him to ask me any questions. Together we ran down the slippery marble stairs into the dusk below. At the bottom he paused.

"The collection!" I gasped breathlessly.

I did not remember until much later that the door to the wing should have been locked. David threw it open, and over his shoulder I saw nothing but darkness. The smoke was thick, stinging my eyes. By the time we reached the second door and found it open, I could see, far ahead of me, the flickering tongues of flame.

David shouted something at me, but I did not take in the words. The house was stone on the outside, and I did not think that even the tile of the roof would burn easily, but the interior of the wing was paneled in old oak that would burn like tinder. It might be pouring rain outside, but in here it made no different. And someone had opened the connecting doors. As I ran behind David through the crowded rooms, I realized that someone had deliberately wanted the fire to spread, that it must have been set.

But there was the chapel! As we reached it, my mind seemed to work with a sudden clarity. The floor was stone here. Even the walls were of stucco in an attempt to create the original effect. Beyond, in the long gallery, I could hear the flames crackling. The smoke made me gasp for breath. If we could shut the gallery off, there might be a chance. . . .

In the doorway David came to a stop, shielding his face with his hands. Looking past him, I saw that the long velvet drapes that lined the window farthest from us were in flames. At the end of the room the painted face of Lady Stewart as a girl stared blankly at us through the welling smoke.

"Get back, Irene!" David shouted at me. "I told you to go back! Get help!"

"Too long," I gasped, the smoke choking me. "It will take too long, even if the telephone were working." I grabbed his arm. "The walls haven't caught yet! We've got to try to put out the fire in the drapes."

For a moment he stared at me through the swirling smoke, and then, reaching past me, he slammed the heavy oak door behind us and ran toward the flames. I followed, coughing and gagging, knowing that I should cover my face with something but knowing, too, that if we were to do what must be done, we would need both hands free.

We started to tear at the drapes, I on one side of the long window, David on the other. Where it touched the floor, the thick velvet was not yet aflame. I sank to my knees, tugging, twisting, struggling with the heavy cloth, scarcely aware of the tongues of fire licking the air above me until I heard David shout my name. Looking up, I saw the great mass of blazing cloth descending. It was too late for me to get out of the way. Before I could throw myself to the side, a blanket of flames engulfed me, suffocating me in blazing heat, wrapping me in a fiery cocoon.

Then I was being torn out of the layers of flame, and David's body was heavy against mine as we rolled together across the floor. My eyes still closed, I felt him press his hands over my head, felt his long fingers in my hair, and knew that the fire must still be blazing there, although I could feel nothing but his hands and body.

"I'm all right," I gasped. I opened my eyes and saw nothing but his. We rolled apart. I forced myself to my knees and reached for his outstretched hands. Together we rose. Across the room the drapes were smoldering into ash on the parquet floor. I watched, unable to move, as David went to the window and wrenched it open. I saw him gather the blackened cloth in his arms and shove it out into the courtyard.

After that there was silence. David was standing by the window, looking out. The wind pressed his blond hair close to his narrow skull. I went to stand beside him, letting the rain drench my burning skin as the storm swept through the gaping glass-toothed window. It was dark now. No lights showed from the windows opposite. I wondered if Claire was standing where I had stood a short while ago. Had she watched the flames being extinguished with relief, or had she wanted the wing to be gutted? Was that why she had not followed me, had not brought help?

I remembered the ring then. It had been in the palm of my hand when I had stood talking to her in the bedroom. I could not remember putting it down before I ran out of the room. Could I, in my panic, simply have dropped it? My heart seemed to stop. I had been frightened a few minutes before. No, terrified. Until the last tongue of flames had been extinguished, I had been terrified. But this feeling of dread was as bad—worse. I groped in the pocket of my slacks. It would have been natural if I had automatically put it there. Thank God. I had.

David, a stranger with a smoke-blackened face, moved away from the window to face me.

"Are you all right?" he asked.

I wanted to give him the simple answer he expected. I knew that simply because we had come through this together there was no reason for me to expect that we would suddenly be as close as we had been that night on the hillside. We *had* been close then—and gay. It seemed a very long while ago.

"I'm fine," I said, choking on the words. Or was it the smoke?

"You've burned yourself," David said in a low voice, "on your forehead. Let me see."

His hands cradled my face, and suddenly he was no longer looking above my eyes but into them. Then his mouth was warm on mine. Only for a moment, but after that I clung to him. Until I could breathe again. Until the door at the end of the long gallery creaked open, and I saw William Stewart coming toward us, a candle in one hand, the other pressing a handkerchief over his nose and mouth.

"My God!" he sputtered. "This is terrible, isn't it? Really terrible. Claire just told me. I've directed the others to stay outside until I could find out how bad it was. You don't mean that the two of you———"

David released me. "It wasn't as bad as it looked," he said coolly. "The drapes were on fire, and the Sargent of Lelia is completely destroyed. But there isn't much other damage—unfortunately."

The candle made a hollow of light in William's face, stripping it of its plumpness. His eyes seemed to waver in the flickering glow. The wind bursting through the broken glass was dispersing the smoke rapidly. Hesitantly he lowered the handkerchief. Except for the pool of candlelight, we were in total darkness.

"I don't know why you say 'unfortunately,'" William protested. "This was a very brave thing for you and Miss Haverlock to do. When you think of what could have been destroyed. . . ."

"If it had been," David said, "there wouldn't have been any bother about trying to break Lelia's will, would there?"

"I don't know what you're trying to say," William said stiffly. "If you're implying that I have any reason to want these—these beautiful things destroyed, then you're quite mistaken. I may have thought that my stepmother put entirely too much time and money into collecting them, but I assure you that I know their value."

"I'm sure you do," David said. I stared at him curiously. Too much had happened in too short a time. I was not certain what was happening now or what he was trying to make happen.

"Well, then, I don't know what you meant by using the word 'unfortunate,'" William said stubbornly.

"Someone is going to think that it was most unfortunate that the fire was put out," David said with slow deliberation, "and that person is whoever set it in the first place."

"But surely you can't believe——"

"How else would it have started?" David asked. "Spontaneous combustion? I think you'll have a difficult time convincing our friend the inspector of that."

"Look here!" William exploded. "It's not my function to convince him of anything. The fact remains that I don't believe that this fire was set."

"Don't you?" Bending, David scooped up some of the charred remains of a drape and held it to his nose. Then, passing it to his cousin: "Don't tell me you can't smell what I can smell. This cloth has been drenched in oil."

He was right. Even at a distance I could smell it, a pungent, sour odor.

"You can't hold me responsible!" William said, waving the candle back in front of us excitedly. The wavering light caught, for a moment, the painted sneer of a seventeenth-century Portuguese nobleman. "I wasn't anywhere near this gallery. I can't imagine who would do such a thing."

"Perhaps the inspector can," David said grimly, taking the candle from the fat man and starting up the long hall toward the door. "I'm going to send a messenger into the town to inform him of what's happened. It wouldn't surprise me if he came trotting back here, pronto—storm or no storm. You can tell him where you were or were not when the fire started."

"And so can you!" William Stewart bellowed, and then, to me: "Come along, Miss Haverlock. It's obvious that he's quite capable of leaving us here without a light."

We followed David like obedient children, back through the chapel and the five crowded rooms, their contents lost in darkness. My legs were weak with exhaustion. I was too tired even to remember with clarity the moment David had held me in his arms. Whatever he had felt in that moment, he was obviously capable of ignoring me now. I loathed this grim determination into which he seemed so easily to slip. It was a pity that Alcombra had not burned to the ground. At least then all of this would be over, and we could go our separate ways—all of us. And forget.

What appeared to be the entire household was waiting for us in the grand hallway. They huddled together in the center of the black and white expanse, Jerez standing a little apart from the others, his eyes watchful. Someone had set out candles on the tables that dotted the sides of the huge room, and the flickering light threw shadows on the floor, a clustered set of shadows like stalagmites.

"Is the whole house going to burn down?" Claire asked shrilly. She was standing a little apart from the housekeeper and the gaggle of maids. "Because if it is, I want to have my things removed from my room immediately."

"The fire's out," David snapped, "but the inspector should be sent for immediately."

"I've sent the gardener's boy, sir," a creaking voice announced as MacGregor stepped out from behind the women, his old head jutting forward like a turtle's from his hunched back. "He'll see that the village fire department is alerted as well, although with the roads in the condition they are, I shouldn't think their trucks could get through."

It was the longest speech I had ever heard the old man make. Even in the dim light I could see that something about him had changed. He still tottered back and forth on his feet, as though it was an effort for him to remain alert. There was still the air of feebleness. But beyond that there was a certain excitement, as though, had he been able, he could not have prevented himself from breaking into a jig. He shuffled on toward David until he could look directly up into the younger man's face.

"You shouldn't have put the fire out, sir," he said, his voice heavy with the Scottish burr that I had noticed before. "There's something evil about those things. Satan's playthings, that's what I called them. Told her to her face they'd bring her nothing but God's wrath. 'Thou shalt not covet,' I told her, but she didn't listen. Not her."

"That's enough, MacGregor," William Stewart said stiffly. He was, I could see, priming himself to take command of the situation. His chest puffed like a pigeon's as he confronted the servants. "As my cousin has told you," he said, "the fire has been put out. There is nothing to be concerned about. All of you are quite accustomed to doing without electricity. That should present no problem. It is now eight o'clock." He peered at his watch as though it were important that he verify the fact. "We will expect dinner by nine. There will be six of us, won't there? Tell me, where is Dr. Kubler?"

"I'm here." The voice came from the darkness of the upper reaches of the stairs. Like a Greek chorus, we turned to look into the shadows. There was a long pause, a silence. Martin Kubler neither descended nor spoke again.

William Stewart cleared his throat. "I think, my dear," he said to his wife, "that you had better see about changing. The housekeeper or MacGregor here will provide you with a candle. Hurry along now."

His voice took on a sharp edge, and I realized that Claire had not bothered to throw on as much as a negligee over the pink nightgown she had been wearing when she and I had talked in her bedroom. The strap had slipped off her right shoulder, revealing the top of her breast, as it had done when I had first gone into her room, and now, with her husband's eyes on her, she pulled it up angrily and started toward the stairs, a wraithlike figure in the dusk.

"Wait," David said in a loud voice. "No, I mean all of you. Dinner can be a bit late if necessary. Until the inspector arrives, I want all of you gathered in the drawing room. Yes, everyone. You, too, MacGregor. And Martin."

He spoke up into the darkness, and slowly the tall figure of the doctor emerged into the reach of the candle-light. He moved toward us slowly, reluctantly, his face expressionless.

"I'll be only a moment," Claire said. "Look here. I need a light if I'm going to go upstairs."

"You're not going upstairs," David said.

"Well, then, one of the maids can go," William said, puffing. "I can't have my wife——"

"No one is going anywhere," David told him. The candlelight threw his eyes and forehead into pale relief. "All of us are going to remain together until the police arrive. There'll be no more fires, no more murders, no more violence—at least until the inspector takes over again."

"See here, David," William Stewart said heavily. "You have no responsibility for what goes on here. If anyone should take control of this situation, it should be me."

For a long moment David simply looked at him. I heard Claire laugh softly near the stairs. When I glanced at her, I saw that Martin Kubler had bent to say something to her. The smile vanished from her face.

"We'll wait in the drawing room," David said in a low, evenly paced voice. "When the inspector arrives, he can decide what ought to be done next. Until then everyone is to stay together."

As the housekeeper and the maids turned to cross the hall, MacGregor muttered something under his breath. He was still standing in front of David, dwarfed by the younger man's height. I could not catch everything that he said, but I heard the name Senhora, and suddenly I realized that she was not here with the others.

"Missing?" David said. "What do you mean, she's missing?"

The old man raised his head. His hooded eyes were lost in the shadows, but his sunken mouth was twisted in something like a smile. "Gone," he chortled. "Look for yourself if you don't believe me. She's nowhere in this house."

While the others trooped into the candle-lit drawing room, William wearing a belligerent expression and draping his jacket over his wife's bare shoulders, David talked to me alone.

"You don't have to do this, Irene," he said in a low voice, "but you're the only one I trust—even Kubler. I can't be sure about him because of his relationship to William. I don't want any of them roaming about this house, but I can ask you. . . ." He took a deep breath. He had picked up one of the candles in its silver holder, and the light flared upward over his drawn face. "I want you to go to Senhora's bedroom. You know where it is, don't you? Next to Lelia's."

I nodded.

"I only hope I'm not making a mistake," he said, "asking you to do this, but I believe MacGregor. He may know more than he's saying about where she is, but I believe him when he says she's not in this house. We've got to find out what's happened to her, where she's gone. We can't wait for Inspector Soria to turn up, and there may be some indication in her room, some indication of where she's gone. If she's taken her clothing, well, that will give us some hint. Will you do it?"

I did not relish going anywhere alone in this shadow-stricken house, but I understood him. I knew that we had to make some attempt to find her. I had sensed for some time that she was a desperate woman, although I did not know why. The fact that she had searched Clarie's room and subsequently confronted her with the ring meant something. There were so many puzzle pieces that did not seem to fit, but perhaps they had fitted for Senhora. Perhaps she had made some sense out of what had happened here. And if she had, she was in danger. The least I could do was to go to her room.

"No," David said before I could answer, "I haven't any right to ask you to walk around this house alone. Listen. You go into the drawing room with the others. Make them stay there."

"I can't do that," I murmured. "William's chafing at the bit. It's hard enough for him to take orders from you. He certainly won't take them from me. Give me the candle. I'll see what I can find in her room. I'll be all right. If Senhora isn't in this house, well, then there's no one here but them." I pointed at the door to the drawing room and tried to laugh. "I can't be hurt by ghosts."

For a long moment his eyes met mine. "All right," he said, "go on, but don't take more than ten minutes at the most. If you can't find anything in that time, well, at least we did what we could."

He stood in the hall watching me as I mounted the long stairway. At the top I turned and looked down at him, and then I hurried along the corridor, past Claire's bedroom, the door ajar. Past my own. The candle cast jagged fingers of light on the carpeted floor as I turned the corner, moving soundlessly. Past the marble statue behind which I had hidden the night William and Senhora had stood there talking. She had said that she would not help him prove that Lady Stewart was mad. Had she, I wondered, already suffered the penalty of that refusal? I tried to keep a tight rein on my imagination. Simply because one woman had died was no reason to think that Senhora had been harmed. For all I knew, she might have fled Alcombra because of her own guilt. In the end we were probably all capable of any enormity.

I twisted the knob of her door, not giving myself too much time to think, aware that my own panic was lurking just beside my consciousness, as nebulous and yet as real as my shadow tottering on the wall behind me. The door swung open, and I stepped inside. There was a strange odor in the room—an acrid smell. A mirror hung opposite me on the wall, a gilt-edged mirror high on the wall. I could see my face. And then another. Another face! I could not breathe, could not move. It was a man. Dark, glittering eyes met mine in the glass. It was the man David had been talking to in the wine-press shed. The estate manager. Teles! In the glass he seemed to loom over me, and I saw the reflection of the long, thin knife in his hand.

I threw myself to the side, at the same time pressing my hand over the flame of the candle. We were in darkness. And then the silence! Yet I knew that he was there beside me. In a moment he would move. Or speak. Every sense straining, I waited. Not breathing. Aware that in a moment I must scream or die.

He moved at last. I heard his feet on the parquet floor. Shuffling. I heard him shuffling toward me. I knew that at any moment the knife might be at my throat. Involuntarily I screamed. Heard the scream. Unrecognizable. An animal's cry. I threw myself out into the corridor, bruising my arm against the edge of the door. I heard the pounding of feet. But in the distance. Not behind me. I heard David calling my name. And I ran, stumbling, toward the sound of his voice.

We met at the bend of the corridor. He held the candle away from my hair as he caught me against his side.

"It's Teles!" I gasped. "He's in her room!"

But he was not. Within minutes David had circled the room, opened the closets, and come back to where I stood, watching his candle throw light against the empty mirror.

"Are you certain?" he asked grimly.

"I saw his face!" But I was already doubting myself. I had been afraid, and in my fear I had imagined Teles. Was that what had happened? David lowered the candle toward the floor, and I heard him mutter something. Looking down, I saw a stain of yellow mud on the carpet. I followed David as he moved slowly down the corridor in the opposite direction from which he had come. I followed him closely enough to see the marks left by the mud.

"He's gone down the side stairs," David said. "Probably he's halfway back to the shed by now. I'm going after him, Irene. You go back downstairs and tell the others it's all right. When the inspector——"

"No." I said. My throat was so dry that I could scarcely speak. "I won't let you go."

For a moment his face seemed to soften, and for that moment he was the man I had known by moonlight. "I have to go," he said in a low voice. "I've got to find out what he was doing here. You know that, don't you?"

"Then let me go with you."

"That's impossible. I'm going to have to walk down there. It's no use expecting to get the truck back there. You can't——"

"I can."

"No." He paused. "Irene, you do know what you mean to me, don't you? If there were some way I could get you out of this house now and keep you out, I would. Now go back to the others. Tell them. . . . Don't tell them anything. Say that you screamed because you saw your reflection in the mirror. Tell them I'm searching Senhora's room, and after that I'm going to search the house for her. MacGregor's an old man. They'll understand that I might think I couldn't take his word for her not being here. That's all. Don't tell them anymore than that. Whatever you do, don't mention having seen Teles."

"But you do believe I saw him."

"At first I thought you were imagining things, but the mud convinced me."

"Do you think he knows where she is?"

David shrugged. "Listen, Irene. I've got to go down

there, and you must join the others. Keep them together
if you can. I'm not sure about Kubler, but I think he'll
help you. And, Irene. . . ."

"Yes?"

For a long moment we stood in silence, caught in the
oval glow of the candlelight. And I knew that whatever
he wanted to say, he could not say it.

"You'll need a flashlight," I said brusquely, stepping
back into the shadows.

"I know my way," he said and put his hand on my arm.
He did not look at me, nor did I look at him. Slowly his
fingers slipped down to my wrist, and then, for a long
moment, our hands met, palm to palm.

"Be careful," he said in a low voice. "For God's sake,
be careful, Irene."

I repeated the words under my breath as he disappeared
down the narrow flight of stairs. I remembered all too
vividly the night I had run down those same stairs to
meet him in the courtyard. The moonlight had made the
night a silvered day. Now the candlelight was warm and
golden. And what I felt for him had changed from silver
to gold as well.

Holding the candle at arm's length, I went to the
window overlooking the courtyard. But I could see nothing. I might have been staring into a void. Even the
stone pig was not visible. The panes of glass rattled under
the prodding of the wind, and the rain beat a wild tattoo.
Pressing my hand against my mouth, I slowly turned and
looked about me: at the drapes, spots of crimson in the
flare of the candle flame; at the thin line of the hallway,
narrowing itself into a black pencil-line of nothingness.
I was no longer afraid. Even if Teles had not really left
the house, even if he was hiding in one of the rooms,
behind one of the closed doors, it did not matter. What
mattered was the ache inside me, the burning of tears
against my closing eyelids. Oh, God, why was it such a

terrible thing to me that David should have gone without me?

Slowly I made my way back down the long corridor. Time seemed to have stopped inside my mind. It seemed that I had lived forever among these shadows. Fear and exhaustion had ceased to have any meaning to me. I knew that my hands and arms and clothing were caked with mud, that my face was blackened with soot. I had seen that in the mirror in Senhora's room in the moment before I had glimpsed Teles's face. Why he had been there did not interest me. I was numb. My body and my mind were numb—except for the ache inside my chest which had begun when David had disappeared down the stairs.

When I reached the top of the wide staircase, I began to hear their voices. Apparently they had stayed in the drawing room. There was something odd in that, surely. I had screamed. David had left them and not returned. Yet they had stayed where they were. Because he had told them to, or did they remain together out of fear? What did it matter? What did any of it matter?

I had no real reason to blow out my candle. Probably there was every reason not to. There were no lights burning in the hall. The candles that had been there had been taken into the drawing room. Yet I preferred the darkness. Perhaps in the darkness I could think. Slowly I groped my way down the marble stairs, one hand on the railing. By the time I reached the bottom step, I could hear their voices clearly, Claire's shrill and penetrating, William's gruff in response. Then Martin Kubler was saying; "No, we'll wait here—for another few minutes at least."

I caught a glimpse of them as I passed the door, moving soundlessly across the tiled floor in my soft-soled sandals. The candlelight cast a yellow glow on the frightened faces of the maids, who huddled together near the fireplace. Martin was standing in the center of the long room, his back to me. William and Claire were seated on the sofa, and I saw that he had his arm about her. The house-keeper was perched stiffly on the edge of a chair facing them. She was speaking, but I could not make out the words. I paused. David had told me to go to them, but he had been wrong. He had been wrong not to let me go with him.

The groping fingers of light illuminated the anteroom that led into the dining room. I saw the glitter of the crystal decanter and went to it. Slowly. Silently. The richness of the port was sweet in my mouth. I drained the glass and set the decanter back on its tray, my decision made. In a moment I was at the thick oak door that led outside. They were arguing now; William's voice was raised petulantly. I slid the latch down, and the door swung open. Rain battered me as I stepped outside. I could not see the truck until my hand touched the fender. If only the key had been left in the ignition. That was all that mattered now.

The cab smelled of grapes and gasoline. I felt for the key and found it there. The motor turned over with a rattling sound. I groped among the knobs protruding from the panel and found the light switch. The windshield wipers were inadequate to deal with the torrent of rain, but as the truck began to move, I did not think of that or the muddy roads ahead. I knew where David was going, and I had to get there. That was all that mattered.

I don't know whether the drive took minutes or hours. At the time it seemed like an indefinite nightmare. The first part went easily, although I could scarcely make out the twisting gravel road that led between the pines. But I reached the gate intact. There were only two choices then as far as roads were concerned. Straight ahead of me stretched the tarred road down which I had made my first approach to Alcombra. The other, the one I took, swerved to the left. The headlights caught the rich yellow of the mud. Once I was on it, I found it was like oil.

The truck skidded from one side of the narrow track to the other. I had no way of knowing what lay on either side, but I understood now why David had estimated that there was more chance of his reaching the shed through the vineyard on foot than in this way. Struggling to keep the wheel under control, I stepped as heavily as I could on the accelerator, determined not to bog down in the sea of mud even though the alternative might be to skid off the road completely.

Not until I saw the shed ahead of me did I realize that my teeth had been set so hard that my jaw ached, but only the warm flood of relief mattered. I switched off the motor without bothering to turn off the road. Lights glowed from the shed window. Whoever was there, I did not want to warn them. For a moment I simply leaned on the wheel, pressing my forehead against my arms, taking deep breaths to calm myself. It had been one thing to follow David here. It would be another to ruin whatever plan he had through my own carelessness. He did not even need to know I was here. If he was inside with Teles, I would not break in on them. I only had to know that he was all right. I simply had to be near him until this nightmare was over.

The wind buffeted me as I stepped down from the cab of the truck. I had switched off the lights, but the sound of the rain drumming on the tin roof of the shed told me I was even closer to it than I had guessed. The lights behind the dirty windows were too steady to come from candles. Ankle deep in mud, I made my way toward the lights. When one sandal was pulled from my foot, I kicked off the other and went on in my bare feet.

I stopped only when I had reached the corner of the long low building. Gasping to regain the breath the wind had whipped away, I wrenched back my long hair, wringing the water out of it to keep it from draining down over my face. I began to shiver uncontrollably as I moved to the first window, although whether from the bite of the wind on my wet skin or from a rising dread, I did not know.

The window was high. Only by taking hold of the sill and pulling myself up on the tips of my toes could I see inside. What I witnessed was a scene of horror. Directly across the room from me stood the mechanical press, illuminated by gas lamps that lined the walls. The press was round, the barrel composed of wooden staves with thin gaps between them. I knew that inside, the barrel was packed with trodden grape skins. When the press was not in use, there was a heavy wooden lid on the top. I had seen it there this afternoon. But now the lid was not visible, and I knew that it had been screwed down into the press by the turning of the long metal rods that projected from the rim of the barrel. As the rods were turned, the lip would be screwed tighter and tighter against the grape skins, squeezing the liquid out of them. Perhaps even before Teles stepped into view, I knew what was really happening.

He was naked to the waist, his dark skin glistening with sweat. As I watched with horrified fascination, he leaned against one of the metal rods and slowly began to turn it. Behind him his shadow moved grotesquely against the wall. Teles's face was toward me, and I could see the grim concentration in his dark eyes as he threw his entire strength against the rod. Over the sound of the wind and the pulsing beat of the rain on the tin roof, I heard the sharp click as the ratchet was engaged and the heavy lid was forced down farther against whatever lay beneath it.

I could only think that he must be stopped, and yet I am sure that I did not deliberately strike my hand against the window. At the time I thought that it was an accident, that I had lost my balance and that in my trying to regain it, my hand had hit the glass. But whatever the truth, I can still remember the shock of terror that I felt as Teles, hearing the noise, looked up. Perhaps he could not see me through the darkness beyond the room, but his black eyes seemed to burn into mine. Slowly, with his left hand, he reached across the top of the barrel and without drawing his gaze from the window, twisted a sort of latch. Only when he took his other hand off the rod and started to move with a rough shambling gait toward the door did I push myself away from the window and start to run.

The mud was thick under foot, and I slid to the side and nearly fell. By the time I had reached the corner of the shed, I heard the door slam. Fear blinded me, or perhaps it was the night. I could not see the truck. Hesitating, I knew that I was lost. I felt the man's hands on me, twisting my shoulders. I struggled, and it was like a nightmare repeating itself. This was the man who had been lurking in Senhora's room. The sour, acrid odor of crushed grapes was the same. I felt the rough texture of his shirt as he pulled me against him.

"Stop!" I cried. "Let me go!"

"Teles! What in hell do you think you're doing?"

It was David's voice. David's arm was about me. I sank back against him, breathless. In the dim light sifting through the dirty windows of the shed I saw Teles hunch his shoulders and turn away from us. In a moment the door of the shed slammed behind him.

"You little fool!" David muttered. "I told you not to come."

"You've got to stop that man," I gasped, pulling myself away from him. "He's working the press, and Senhora. . . . I think he's killed her. I think her body is inside the barrel. . . ."

I did not have to finish. Together we ran through the mud to the shed. Teles had not bothered to bolt the door. David tried to push me back, but I followed him inside. The odor of fermenting grapes was overwhelming. Teles, bent over the rod again, did not turn even when David slammed the door behind us. The ratchet creaked into place, and the gas jets hissed.

"Teles!" David shouted.

The broad-backed man bent farther over the rod.

"Teles," David said again, this time in a low voice, "I want to talk to you."

"I can talk and work," the man muttered. "Why have you come back here at this time of the night? And the woman. It is no place for a woman to lurk about. How did I know that it was she? How did I know that it was not someone bent on doing damage to this property? It is my duty to protect——"

"Let me ask the questions, Teles," David said grimly. "Why are you working this press now?"

"The grapes must be processed," Teles replied, pulling the rod upward slowly with an effort that made his muscles strain. "It is not unusual for me to work at night during the vintage."

"I know that," David said sharply, "but not alone. Where are the men who should be helping you?"

Teles paused, the rod raised to the height of his shoulder. "They have refused," he said. "This press is dangerous, and I have told them so, since it is only fair that they should know. You saw the condition of the slats this afternoon. If one should burst. . . ." He shrugged. "It happened once five years ago. Perhaps you remember. Three men were killed, one of them decapitated. Not a pleasant sight, I can assure you."

"There are presses in the other sheds," David retorted. "I thought we had agreed that this one was not to be used."

"I do not mind the risk," Teles muttered, pushing the metal rod downward.

"Teles!" Leaving me, David went toward the press. "An hour ago you were at Alcombra. You were seen in Senhora's room. I want you to tell me why you were there."

"Stand back," Teles warned. With an effort he pushed the iron rod into its lowest position, and the ratchet clicked again as the lid descended lower into the cask. "I have told you that this press is not safe."

"If it explodes, it won't make much difference where I am standing," David said grimly. "I think if you were really concerned with our safety, you would stop working that thing."

"Perhaps," the man said, "it would be simpler if you and the lady would leave."

"Wouldn't you rather explain why you were in Senhora's room to us than to the police?" David said in a low voice.

The estate manager stared at him blankly. "You are threatening me, Mr. Ashor?"

"Senhora is missing," David said. "Do you know where she is?"

"Why should I know where she is, Mr. Ashor?" There was something taunting about the man's voice. He began to lift the metal rod upward.

"Because," David said in a loud voice, "she is your wife and has been for the last ten years."

Teles must have loosened his hold on the rod, for suddenly it began to spin. He threw himself on it, holding it in position with all his strength. Sweat poured down his swarthy face, and on his right hand I saw a red gash where the rod had struck it. Teles began to laugh wildly. The sound made me grow cold inside.

"You are dreaming, Mr. Ashor," he said, taking great gulps of air between each word.

"No," David responded quietly. "It is true. Lady Stewart told me about it two years ago. I know that it was intended to be secret, but she found you once in Senhora's room, and the truth came out. She was angry. You knew her feelings on the subject of Senhora. Senhora's only allegiance was supposed to be to my great-aunt. She told you that she would dismiss both of you if you attempted to live together as man and wife."

For a moment there was silence except for the hissing of the lights and the pounding of the rain against the tin roof. Teles remained motionless, holding the rod in a down position. "She was an evil woman," he muttered finally. "She wanted to control the lives of everyone about her. And in return for what? A few *escudos*."

"Is that why you stole from the collection?" David asked. "To get from her what you thought you deserved?"

I stared at him, puzzled. How could he have known that anything was missing? I had not told him. For some absurd reason that I could not remember, I had not told him.

"My great-aunt told me she suspected that was what was happening," David said as though in answer to my unspoken question. "She told me that the day before she died. She intended to make a list——"

"She made one," I said.

David turned toward me, grim-faced. "You should have told me," he said. "A good many things would have made sense before this if you had told me." His voice hardened. "Was that why she talked to you that night?"

"Yes."

"And did you check the list?"

"The next morning. Five pieces were missing. I—I have one of them here." I dug in my pocket for the ring and held it out to him. He backed toward me, not taking his eyes off Teles, and took it from me.

"Where did you find it?" he asked.

"Senhora claimed to have found it in Claire Stewart's bedroom," I said.

"Have you seen this ring before, Teles?" David asked, stretching out his hand.

"I do not have to answer your questions."

"If you do not give me answers, you will give them to the police. I think I understand now, Teles. You began to steal from the collection when you knew my great-aunt was going to die. You must have felt very safe—until she decided to have an inventory made."

"Senhora didn't want me to come," I said, following David closer to the cask. "I heard her tell Lady Stewart that she could make the inventory herself. She wanted me to be sent away."

The flash of hatred in Teles's eyes as they met mine stunned me. I looked past him at the cask, its wooden staves straining against the rusting iron bands that held them in place.

"Senhora failed you, didn't she?" David asked. "You counted on her to have more influence on a dying woman than she did have. Miss Haverlock stayed."

Suddenly I remembered the piece of granite tumbling down past me as I stood in the vineyard the afternoon of Marian's death. Had that been Teles's attempt to put an end to the threat of discovery which my presence at Alcombra presented? And Marian's death. Was that. . . ?

David voiced the words as though our minds were working in unison. "You killed my mother," he said. "You thought that only Miss Haverlock was in the wing that afternoon. It was dark because of the storm. You saw a woman, and you killed her."

Teles made a strangling noise deep in his throat, and I saw his hands grip the metal rod as though he wanted to rip it out of the cask.

"Someone took the list out of my room the night your mother was killed," I said in a low voice to David, touching his arm. "Senhora returned it."

"She wouldn't go along with you, would she?" David said to Teles. "I've known Senhora for a good many years. She's capable of a good deal, but not of murder. She fought against what you were doing to cover the thefts, didn't she? And in the end she was more of a liability than an asset. She couldn't even manage to put the blame on Claire. That was why you tried to burn the wing down tonight, wasn't it? You must have left here as soon as I had gone. And when that failed, Senhora had to die, didn't she? She was the only person who could give evidence against you. What have you done with your wife's body, Teles? Is it in the press?"

Pushing all his weight against the metal rod, Teles suddenly groped out with one hand and grabbed a hammer from the floor. I saw him strike at one of the bulging staves. And strike again. In the same moment the door behind me was thrown open to the roar of the storm and someone fell against me, knocking me to the floor. Over the sound of the storm came the thunder of an explosion, and the scream of a man.

It was Jerez lying on top of me. I saw his face as I crawled free into a sea of cold slippery grape skins and a thick liquid that was like blood. Coated with wine, I pushed myself upright. The blast of the exploding cask had thrown David against the wall, but the flying staves had not struck him, as they had Teles. We stared in horror at the body of the man on the floor, his neck nearly severed from his body. Beside him, half-buried in the remains of the pressed grapes, was the mutilated body of Senhora.

It was dawn when we walked back to Alcombra. Above the hedges and the pines the house loomed over us, drenched in the faint white light of early morning. We came up through the vineyards, pausing sometimes, but never to look behind us. It was as though we both understood that if we did not look back, the deepening light would drive away the shadows in our minds. When we had started up the terraced slopes, I had been numb inside and so physically exhausted that it had been an effort to move. Jerez had gone back to the house with the inspector in his car, knowing perhaps that David and I needed to heal one another, and that to do that we had to be alone.

As we reached the dew-drenched lawns of the house,

I felt life spring up inside me, as warm as the tentative touch of the sun's rays on my back. David's arm was about my waist, and my head was on his shoulder. We moved so slowly, as though we were one person, that the peacocks did not seem to notice us. Only one, his white breast flaring, spread his tail feathers as we passed, flaunting the mosaic of his colors.

There was so much that we could have said. Yet there was no need for either of us to speak a word. It was, I knew, a fresh beginning. The past could never be forgotten, but it had already begun to fade. Philip? The woman who had loved him had been another woman, unsure of herself, uncertain of what she wanted from life. I felt as though I had been reborn. The future held the fulfillment I had only dreamed of before. David. I raised my head, and our eyes met. The scent of flowers hung heavy in the morning air as we turned into one another's arms. Somewhere the call of a peacock broke the silence, and for the first time the sound came to me not as a scream but as a cry of joy.

Shadow Over Grove House

For Mary Jane
and
Andrew Dillon

Chapter One

HE WAS standing on the District Line platform of the Charing Cross underground when I saw him. It was Van. I knew it at once. Ever since they had told me a year before that he was dead, I had felt numbed inside. Now, suddenly, impressions rushed in on me. I smelled the fetid air. The distant roar of a train vibrated in my ears. The vividly colored posters on the curved wall at the other side of the tracks leaped into my consciousness. I was alive, just as he was alive, and the pain inside me twisted and cut until I felt I must cry out.

Instead I reached. Reached out to touch his arm. And as I did so, he turned and walked away from me, down the platform, and the thunder of the approaching train stole the dimension of sound. I called out to him against the explosion of noise. The great circular cavity shook as the train thrust its way out of the tunnel, gathering the flat, stale air into a warm, dust-filled wind, until we were all caught in a shifting whirlwind of sound and gray air and movement.

Then with a shrieking of brakes it was all over. The train was motionless in front of us. Motionless and silent. Inside the brightly lighted cars men and women talked and read and stared sightlessly at the platform. Van was four cars away from me now, striding toward the end of the train. I could just make out the light tan of his raincoat, that thick shock of black hair. People

5

were pushing past me, funneling themselves through the doors of the cars behind me, while I struggled with the realization that I had found him only to lose him again.

I began to run, thrusting people away from me with my hands. My eyes burned with the effort of concentrating on his back. I could not lose him. If I were to look away for only one second he could disappear into a car and I would lose him. In a moment the doors would slide shut. Unless I could manage to get into the same car with him, I would be left here on this platform, not knowing where he was going, helpless as the city swallowed him.

He turned into a car and disappeared. Gasping, I pushed past an old woman carrying a straw market basket, and tried to work my way through the crowd near the door.

"There's no more room, luv," a man's voice told me. "Try the next car."

I was back on the platform, my eyes searching the inside of the car from which I had been rejected. Where was Van? He had to see me. He would come to me. He would never go off like this without me. He had to see me!

And then I realized that the doors were closing. There was no time to think. I only knew that I did not dare let his train go without me. I threw myself toward the car on my right and pushed through the narrowing gap. The metal doors closed on my dress, and I pulled it away, ripping the primrose silk, not caring.

The train was moving now, and I was thrown forward against a neatly dressed Pakistani who smiled and murmured something in a gentle voice. Automatically, I reached up and groped for the strap, bracing myself against the side of one of the seats. The car was full of people and light and the thick smell of cigarette smoke and perfume and damp raincoats and umbrellas. I was conscious of all of it, and yet I could not look at it, take it into my consciousness. I did not dare. I wanted to close my eyes, to keep that image of Van's retreating back free from the overlay of other things seen. I did not dare to let words intrude, or the tenuous thread between myself and the man who had once been my husband might be broken.

I pressed the palm of my right hand to my forehead and waited for my mind to clear. The train was moving rapidly, twisting and curving under the city like a serpent in a vast labyrinth. What was the next stop? My mind wouldn't seem to work. I had taken this underground route countless times. When Van was alive. After they had told me he was dead. I asked the man beside me. My voice was hoarse.

"St. James Park," he said, his dark face tilted down toward me. "Is something wrong? You look . . ."

"No," I said over the rattle and the creaking of the swaying train. "Nothing's wrong."

St. James Park. I must get off at the platform. Watch for Van. The train was already slowing. I swayed toward the door. The blackness of the tunnel gave way to the dim lemon light of the station. A sudden jamming of the brakes. The blue and white sign marking the station. A small clump of waiting people further down the platform. The doors slid open and I stepped down onto the cement. And turned. But which way should I turn? Had he gone into the next car to my left or to my right? I couldn't remember. Why couldn't I remember?

There were so many people. Getting off. Pushing past me. I ran to my left. The next car was still nearly full. I stared desperately through the windows. And he was not there. But of course not. It had been the other car, the one further toward the end of the train. But the doors were already beginning to close. Confused, I pushed through the one closest to me. The Pakistani was still standing there. Watching me. Obviously wondering what was wrong.

"Did you want the next station, then?" he asked me. "Sloane Square?"

I don't know whether I replied to him or not. I was sealed inside the car again and the train was starting up. Like a recurring nightmare that begins again and again and never ends. Had Van got off at this station? Had I missed him? There were so many people. So many people. He had to be on the train still. He had to be.

I closed my eyes and kept them tight shut until I felt the train beginning to lose speed once more. Again the jerking stop came. I had not moved from my position just inside the door. I scanned the platform desperately. No Van. Again the train lurched forward. South Kensington. Earl's Court. We were above ground now, heading out of the city. The stations were country stations now. Few people were left in my car. My body ached with tension. One platform after another. And no Van. I must have missed him. He had disappeared among the crowds at Sloane Square station or Earl's Court. The countryside was a blur of random lights. And then we were at Kew. My stop. A single man pushed past me. And then I saw Van on the platform, his back to me.

Relief overpowered me. For a moment I felt dizzy with it. I started to run and found myself propelled into the front of a broad-busted matron who shrilled something after me as I jettisoned myself away from her and down the steps off the platform. Ahead of me stretched the darkness of the tree-lined street. A passing car illuminated the figure of a man. Was it Van? It had to be Van! There had not been time for him to have disappeared again. Unless he had seen me. Unless he was trying to escape me. Was it possible that he did not want me to find him again?

There was so much that I did not understand. He was supposed to be dead, and yet he was alive. He loved me. Had loved me. Why would he have come here to Kew if he did not want to see me? And yet, although I was nearly running now, my heels clicking on the sidewalk, beating a staccato in the silent night, he seemed to be moving away from me faster and faster. This sort of thing had happened to me before in nightmares. But this was real. I was awake. My side began to pain me. I was gasping for breath.

I called his name, and the sound of my voice was lost in the darkness as the man turned to the right and was gone. It could have taken me no more than a minute to reach the spot. There ahead of me was the familiar narrow road which led into the open country. But it was so dark here that I could see nothing. Nothing.

My heart pounding, I turned onto the narrow footpath which led up the terraced hill on which Grove House was located. Grove House, where I had been living with Van's father since my marriage. I walked without looking up, aware of nothing except the grief welling up in me. I had thought that I had suffered twelve months ago when the telegram announcing Van's death had arrived. But, strangely, the shock had been nothing to what I felt now. Then I had been numbed by his loss, and in a sense I had never since regained a total awareness of myself. But now sensation crowded in on me, and the tears that ran down my cheeks did nothing to soothe the terrible ache inside.

By the time I reached the gate of the park that surrounded the house, my mind had begun to function again, bringing the realization that it could not have been Van that I had seen. Rationally, practically, I knew that I must have been mistaken. Granted that after the fire in the villa in Milan his body had never been found. But then there had been nothing left but charred ruins. Four witnesses had testified that they had seen his face at the window of one of the upstairs bedrooms just before the walls collapsed. It was impossible that he could have escaped. Anthony had assured us of that.

No, what had happened tonight must have been a hallucination. I had yearned for him for so long that my subconscious mind must have created a myth which had forced itself into my consciousness. I had wanted desperately to be with him when I had left the concert hall. For two hours I had been listening to Chopin, and the music had brought back so many memories that I had even then been aware of his presence. When I had walked out into an evening warm with spring, I had had to supress the urge to put out my hand to him. I had needed him desperately, and as a result my mind had conjured him up. If I were to tell Anthony, he would explain it in clinical terms. I must never tell him.

Suddenly the night clouds seemed to split in two, and the moonlight dashed itself against the house looming above me. It rose like a thin shaft above me, pricked by the slits of lighted windows. It was a Victorian horror, tipped by a peaked cupola, like the turret of a ghostly castle. I had always hated it for its ugliness. Now, more than ever before, it seemed like a prison.

I had nearly reached the steps when I saw the man silhouetted against the door. The lamp overhead caught the curve of his face. I caught my breath. I could not have spoken if I could have thought of any words to say. Only when I was standing beside him did I manage to whisper his name. He turned to face me just

10

as the door was opened, and I saw him clearly in the blaze of light from the hall. And saw that it was not Van, but a stranger.

It was a devastating moment. And an awkward one. I could not take my eyes from his face. The hair was like Van's, thick and trimmed long in the back. And there were the same square sideburns, like smudges of charcoal, along the sides of his cheeks. Even the shape of his face was the same, square with blunt chin and broad forehead. But every other feature was different. This man's lips were thin and sensitive. His nose was blunt. His eyes penetrating. There was a certain heaviness about him that I had never sensed in Van. And there was more. When Van had looked at people, even at me, we knew that the most important things in his life were going on inside him. This man, this stranger, seemed to turn his full attention on me. It was as though he were absorbing me.

The maid who had opened the door shifted restlessly, and I tore my eyes away from him to the girl standing eyeing us curiously, one hand still on the doorknob and the other adjusting her small white apron. I nodded. That was all I could do. I could not speak. Could not move. But she knew what I meant, and turning, she left us standing there on the doorstep in front of the open door.

"I'm Michael Kyd," he said. His voice was very low-pitched, very gentle for a man.

Michael Kyd. The name was somehow familiar to me. Was it a name I should know? Was it because of my confusion that I could not place him? I had never met him before. I was certain of that. Perhaps he was a friend of Van's father's. But surely if he had known anyone in the family, they would have mentioned his extraordinary similarity to Van. Or was that all in my mind? Was I simply seeing what I wanted to see?

"I'm—I'm Amanda Harcourt," I said. It was difficult to keep my voice level. I felt torn apart inside, my emotions shredded. But that added sensory perception that had come with the first sight of this man, thinking, as I had, that he was my husband, was still with me. I was intensely aware of the quality of the light blazing out on us from inside the house, the faint smell of the river which the spring breeze was bringing in its wake, the cold dampness of the iron railing under my fingers.

"Van's wife." He did not sound surprised. "I should have recognized you from your pictures. He must have told you about me."

Instantly I remembered. When Van had first arrived in Italy over a year and a half ago, he had written me that he had enlisted the help of an expert of the Etruscan period, a professor at the University of Milan. But he had not described Michael Kyd, and I had simply assumed that he was an older man, an absorbed academic. As this man might be.

"Van—Van wrote about you often," I said. "I'm sorry that at first I didn't recognize the name, but . . ."

I had been on the verge of telling him how upset I was. If I had not stopped myself, I realized that I would have told him everything that had happened that evening, beginning with the moment I had turned my head and seen him standing on the underground platform, his head turned away from me. He would think that I was mad, if I told him. Still, there was something about him that invited confidence. And he wanted to know what was going on inside me. I could see that in those eyes that had never once left my face, eyes that seemed to trace patterns over my lips, my nose, my mouth, as though they were memorizing me.

"Come inside," I told him.

"Are you certain that I won't be disturbing you?"

He knew that something was wrong. But he was sensitive enough to realize that whatever it had been that had happened to me, his presence was somehow reassuring.

I shook my head and led the way down the scarlet-carpeted hall to the little sitting room at the back of the first floor, which I preferred over the larger, more ornate rooms that Van's father had so carefully furnished. The curtains had been pulled against the May night, and a single light glowed in the further corner by the armchair where I had sat sewing before the concert.

"Let me take your raincoat." Michael's hands were on my shoulders. I turned my head and looked at them as I slipped out of my coat. They were like his face. Square. Blunt. Comforting hands.

He was the sort of person who makes himself at home at once. I rang for drinks, but he was the one who mixed them. When I began to turn on the other lamps, he said that he found the shadows restful. Instead of sitting on the armchair opposite mine, he sat on the footrest. I was glad. When he looked up at me his face was even less like Van's. Among other things, he was older. In the light that came over my shoulder I could see the wrinkles at the corners of his eyes, the lines of white in the dark hair.

"Actually," he said, "I came to see your husband's father. I know that I should have called or written first. I just flew into London this afternoon, and I intended to contact him tomorrow, but this evening I had an odd impulse—"

He broke off, staring at the glass in his hand as though he had suddenly been caught up in his own thoughts. I did not speak. I was glad of the respite. Gradually I was feeling calmer, but there was still the difficulty of acclimating myself to the situation. This man who only a short while ago I had so vividly identified as a dead husband was now a personality in his own right. There was no more confusion in my mind, and the ache inside me was subsiding. But he was still a man who, according to Van's letters, had been an intimate, someone who had shared parts of my husband's life that I knew little of.

"I'm sorry," he said, detaching himself from his own thoughts and smiling. "What was I saying?"

"You said that you wanted to see Mr. Harcourt," I prompted him. "He's not here just now. He and Anthony, Van's brother, went down to Devon for the weekend."

"Ah, yes. Anthony." Again he seemed lost in thought.

"You knew him, of course."

"Yes. Yes I did." Michael frowned. "I'm not so certain whether he'll want to see me or not. Tell me, are you feeling better now?"

"What made you suppose—"

"When I first saw you, outside on the steps, you looked as though you had had some sort of—of shock, I suppose. When I turned to face you there was an odd look in your eyes. As though you had expected to see someone else."

I set my drink down on the table beside me, because quite suddenly my hands had begun to tremble and I did not want him to see. And yet, in a strange way, I did not mind his questioning me.

"And just before I turned," he said in a low voice, "I thought I heard you call me Van."

I took a deep breath. "I did," I murmured. "There's something about the look of you. . . ."

"You're not the first person to say that," Michael said. "When we were working at the dig, bent over, examining something, people quite frequently confused us." He paused, and I could feel his eyes on me. "I'm sorry. It must have been a shock."

Suddenly I felt a great sense of relief. He had accepted the hallucination for what it had been with no questions. There was no need to tell him that I had followed him on the underground, run after him, called his name. But if I were to tell him that, he would understand.

"I know he's dead," I said in a low voice. "I know that there was no chance that he escaped from that house. Anthony said—"

"Anthony was the one who told you about it?"

I tried to answer him and then did not, realizing that my throat was knotted by a sudden anguish, and that if I spoke I would break into sobs.

"I'm sorry," Michael said again. "Look here. I've taken enough of your time right now. Perhaps later, after I've seen Mr. Harcourt, we can talk again."

He rose. And I with him. "Don't go just now," I said. "Talk to me awhile. Not about Van. Not right this minute. Tell me what you're doing in London."

The words spilled out of me in broken pieces. I only knew that I did not want him to leave me so soon. He would probably think me an hysteric, but I could not bear, just now, to be alone with my thoughts. I was feeling too much awareness still. If memories forced themselves into the forefront of my mind now, they might be too vivid for me to endure.

"All right." We smiled. We sat. And for a few minutes we did not speak. It had begun to rain again, a light spring rain. I could hear the faint tapping fingers on the window. Somewhere in the silent house a clock struck the hour.

"You're a good deal younger than I thought you would be," Michael said. "I never saw your picture, but Van talked a good deal about you. Never an outright description, of course. Except your eyes. He said that they were violet." He laughed softly. "I thought that he was being a bit lyrical. Lonely men are sometimes. But now I see that it's quite true."

He shook his head. "Probably I shouldn't have said that either. You said that you didn't want to talk about your husband yet, but everything I say . . ."

"No. It's all right." I picked up the embroidery I had been working on earlier, and then put it down again. I felt a calmness that had nothing to do with the calm I had tried so hard to induce all these many months with such things as senselessly drawing a needle through a bit of cloth. "I was wrong when I said that. Wrong about myself. I do want to talk about him."

I paused, wondering whether I should try to explain to him that everyone had seemed to conspire against me for so long whenever I tried to talk about Van that I had long since ceased to do so. Even Anthony had told me that I should not brood. And, for him, brooding seemed to consist of verbalizing memories. Or asking questions about that last day, about the way in which his brother had died.

"Are you certain?"

I nodded. It was strange, but I felt as though the two of us were isolated in that single pool of light, cut off from the house itself, the rain outside. I searched to identify my own feelings and found that for the first time in as long as I could remember, I felt safe. And yet, emotionally, I was in as much jeopardy as I had been since Van had died. Against my will at first, and then voluntarily, I had been sequestered against the truth. I knew the bare facts of his dying, but nothing else. The doctor who had been called in when I had collapsed after hearing the news of his death had told me that, in all probability, Van had not suffered. He had explained as carefully as one would to a child that

16

my husband had been overcome by the smoke. That he had been unconscious when the fire had engulfed him. He had repeated over and over again that I was not to imagine that he had suffered. They had all said the same thing. Anthony. Van's father. Until I had brought myself to believe that I believed them.

There had been the nightmares, of course. Nightmares in which I seemed to inhabit Van's body. Dreams in which I had been he, struggling to the window, staring in an agony of desperation at the crowds surrounding the burning villa. But he had not even tried to break the glass, if what Anthony had said was true. Was it, as the doctor said, because the smoke had, at that moment, pushed him into unconsciousness? Or had there been a paralysis born of fear when he realized that no matter what he did, he was about to die? Had the flames seared his flesh before unconsciousness barricaded him against agony?

"You're shivering," Michael said. "I think that I was right at first. We should put this off until another time."

"It's been put off too long," I told him. "It would have been better in the first place if someone had told me about it."

He looked at me for a long time before he spoke. And then only after he had crossed the room, into the shadows, and refilled both his glass and mine.

"You loved him very much," he said.

My laughter quavered. "More than I knew, apparently. We were married when I was only eighteen. Anthony claims—"

"Let me guess." His voice was hard. "I know your brother-in-law, too, remember? As a psychologist he would probably have told you that your very immaturity made it improbable that you could have had any really deep feeling for Van. That your reaction to his death was only superficially emotional. Dangerous, of course. Dangerous enough to keep you from having the answer to too many questions. But, in the end, superficial."

I closed my eyes. He had paraphrased exactly what Anthony had said to me only two nights ago. Here. In this room. It was what he had said before he had asked me to marry him. And the revulsion I had felt for him then returned to me now as vividly as though his hand were still on my arm.

"All right," Michael said. "I may be wrong in saying this to you. But if you want to know what I suspect to be the truth . . ."

"Yes," I said. "I want to know the truth."

"Then it's this." His eyes met mine. "I came to London because it's my belief that it was no accident that your husband died. I believe that he was murdered."

I caught my breath. Involuntarily my hands flew to my mouth, and I felt the ice of my fingertips against my lips.

"I'm sorry," Michael said, touching my arm, "but I thought that if it had to be said, it should be said straight out. And you have to remember this. I said that I believe that Van was murdered. It's only a suspicion. I can't prove anything yet. And I may be wrong."

I continued to stare at him, disbelievingly. When I had first had the news of Van's death, I had not been willing to accept it. I had kept asking, "Why?" and there never seemed to be enough good answers. But I had never thought of murder. And now, strangely enough, once the word had been spoken aloud, I did not rebel against it as I had against the knowledge of an accidental death.

"I've known that something was wrong ever since

the day that your husband died," Michael said. "But I couldn't decide whether to come here. I knew that I would disturb people's lives. Yours. Anthony's. His father's. And, of course, the longer the time that passed, the less easy it was for me to rationalize that there would be any value in my coming."

He rose and moved out of the ring of light, his back toward me. "But I've decided," he said in a low voice, "that I can't go on not knowing any longer. Your husband was a good friend to me. I know that revenge is an outdated word, and revenge isn't exactly what I want, but if someone did deliberately kill him, I want him to pay for it."

"But why should you have thought that he was murdered in the first place?" I demanded. The original shock had passed, and I felt clear-headed. "His body wasn't found, they tell me."

"It was the fibula," Michael said. "When I couldn't find any sign of it, I knew that something was wrong. I knew that Van had it with him that night. And then when it turned up in Paduolo's estate, I was sure. . . ."

He turned and came back toward me, smiling. "I'm sorry," he said. "I've started at the wrong end. I'm not making sense, probably. It all began when your husband wrote to me. It must have been two years ago, because it was spring then, too. I was in Milan then. As a visiting lecturer. My major interest is the Etruscan culture, and when I saw the name Harcourt—well, I was excited."

I stared up at him steadily. He had not had to tell that when he had seen Van's name, he had thought at first it was his father's. V.J. Harcourt was a well-known name among archaeologists, not only because of his association with the British Museum, but because of the books he had written. Van had told me a good many times that perhaps he had been wrong to follow

19

the same line as his father. At first there had been only pride in his face when someone had made the usual remarks about his father, but later, after his first book had been published, after the results of that first dig were made public, then there had been the comparisons. The measuring. The weighing. Always him and his father. He had come to hate it. I had actually seen him stiffen whenever a stranger mentioned his father's name in sudden recognition of the relationship.

"When I saw that it wasn't V.J. Harcourt, but Van, I was still interested," Michael was saying. "The idea for the dig sounded like the kind of thing I wanted to be involved with. And I liked his ideas. They were fresh. He seemed to have the capacity to avoid the system. But then, you know all this. I don't have to tell you about your own husband. The point is, he wanted me to act as a consultant. There was only the problem of money."

I nodded. I remember that problem about money vividly. When Van had first begun setting up archaeology digs on his own, his father had been helpful in an indulgent sort of way, although it was obvious that he would rather have Van stay under his control. But he had helped. With his own money. Getting grants from various societies. Arranging for the backing of museums. And that had gone on until Van began to establish his own reputation. And when his book had come out and his father had seen that Van was actually daring to attack some of the sacrosanct ideas that he had spent a lifetime trying to protect, the assistance stopped. Money was suddenly difficult to come by. Not that Van needed his father as a go-between any longer. But when he went to the museums, the directors were unresponsive. It was obvious that they had been urged by his own father not to continue their support. And V.J. Harcourt was still the ultimate authority in Etruscan affairs.

I had not lived in this house then. But I had come here with Van. And hated it, as I did now, for its vast, dusky rooms and pretentious ceilings. And most of all for the museumlike quality that Mr. Harcourt had deliberately imposed on it. The amounts of money spent on the artifacts he collected appalled me. And particularly after he had not only seen to it that Van could not raise money, but had refused his own personal financial support—then I had scarcely been able to enter the drawing room with its Etruscan vases and its lighted cases full of Roman coins and jewelry. There was so much obvious wealth in this house, wealth that went to feed an old man's passion to possess the stuff of antiquity. An old man who would not accept any challenge, even that of a son.

"All right," Michael said. "Then you know that for a while we had to postpone everything. Your husband and I met in Paris once. He tried to get backing from someone there. Private backing. Anyway, we met and talked, and we found out that we both had been thinking along similar lines in regard to how much the Etruscans were influenced by Greek art forms. It's been an accepted theory for a long time that, even at the height of their cultural development in the sixth century, the Etruscans were never more than imitators." He broke off, laughing. "Sorry. I'm probably boring you with too many details. It's an academic hang-up, details."

I could have told him that it was anything but boring, that it was a relief to be treated like an intelligent human being again. Van had always treated me that way. I had heard the details of all his enterprises, all his schemes, although I had no background in either history or archaeology. But he had always

21

talked to me as though I were a colleague. Until the last dig. That was one of the reasons why I had hated his involvement with it right from the start. When he wrote me about it he was always indirect, as though he were hiding something. Only then did he begin to treat me as his father and Anthony treated me now, as a person who could not or should not understand their affairs.

"And then," Michael went on, "when it appeared that we would have to give up the idea of the dig entirely, Greene turned up."

"Greene?"

"Your husband never mentioned him to you?"

I shook my head. "I assumed that a museum somewhere had decided to sponsor what he was doing. But he didn't offer any information, and so I didn't press him. I mean, I knew it was a sore point with him—the backing. Because of his father."

"All right." Michael started to sit down on the sofa out of the pool of light and then changed his mind and continued to pace, his hands jammed in his pockets. "Well, Winton Greene apparently turned up out of the blue. He's American. Wealthy. Or, at least, that's the impression he gives. He came to Van while he was still in Paris. I don't know how he heard of what we were going to do. In fact, I'd gone back to Italy by that time, and never met him until the dig was under way. But, according to your husband, he was willing to accept our terms. Whatever we turned up of value was to be presented to museums for their consideration. We were to proceed in a certain way. Excavate where and how Van decided. It was a completely open-ended contract. Except that Greene wasn't willing to put anything on paper. And that bothered both of us."

Michael shrugged his shoulders. "But, in the end, it was either accept the money or forget the project. And

Van thought that he could handle Greene once we had started. That was his—our first mistake."

He turned and came back across the shadowy room toward me. His eyes were intense. "Look here," he said, "will you mind if I ask you some questions? There are certain things I have to know before I talk to your father-in-law. I know the kind of man he is. I know he won't accept a stranger suddenly appearing with the news that his son may have been murdered. And I've got to make him consider it as a serious possibility."

I understood what he meant. Even if he had never met Van's father, he must have heard a good deal about his reputation. Mr. Harcourt was a near fanatic about his interests, a man who would never take a stand without having answered every question that presented itself and proving every answer beyond any doubt. Considering his scientific background, that was natural. But he was also a man of violent belief. Once having accepted a hypothesis, he would not readily relinquish it. His reaction to Van's challenge of his theories concerning the Etruscans was proof enough of that. He had been willing to risk the professional destruction of his own son rather than let his own theories be challenged in public.

But there was another point to consider, too. Michael had said that Van's father was not likely to consider the possibility that Van had been murdered, having accepted as he had long since that the death was accidental. And perhaps he was right. Why had I so willingly agreed to talk to this man who was, as he had reminded me, a virtual stranger? Why was I willing to consider that he was sincere in his claim that because Van had been close to him he was now unwilling to let any question of how Van had died remain? Why was I so able to consider that murder was, in fact, a possibility? If it were true, it would not bring my husband back. Michael spoke of revenge. Yet what did I care for revenge?

I didn't know how to answer those questions. I only knew that I instinctively trusted this man. And perhaps because I am a woman, I was willing to trust those instincts. And to help him.

"What do you want to know?" I said in a low voice.

He did not bother to hide his relief. He came back to sit at my feet, back into the light. How strange that I could ever have mistaken him for Van.

"Your husband's brother turned up in Italy shortly after the dig started," he said. "I don't think he had met Greene before that time, but he appeared to become very good friends with him in a short time. Still, that's beside the point just now. What I want to know is, do you have any idea why your brother-in-law should have turned up there, and why he should have stayed so long? As far as I could make out, he knew very little about what we were doing and cared less. Although he was always around."

I shook my head. I had wondered about that at the time. Anthony was a man who took very little interest in anything except his own enjoyment. Although he was accredited, he did not practice psychology. He was ten years younger than Van, but even so he had earned his university degree six years ago. And in those six years he had never worked. He lived here in this house, and supposedly assisted his father. But precisely what he did had never been clear to me. He was an attractive man. And he knew how to be charming. But I had never trusted him, less than ever now that he had made it clear that his interest in me was not strictly what it was by virtue of my being his brother's widow. Still, I knew that I was perhaps being unfair to him. He and Van had never agreed about anything, and that would have been enough to have set me against him subconsciously.

"I'm not certain," I said. "Neither he nor Mr. Harcourt ever explained why he should have gone there. I thought perhaps that Van might have sent for him. To help with the dig in some way. Or with the paper work. But no, I don't know."

"As far as you know," Michael went on, "your brother-in-law never knew a man named Greene before the dig began."

I shook my head again. "I don't know many of Anthony's friends," I told him. "I expect that he knows a good number of people of whom I've never heard."

"All right. Now, tell me this. Do you think it's possible that your father-in-law sent him to join us in Italy for the express purpose of finding out what we were doing—what we were turning up?"

It was a clever idea. Even though Van's father had always made it a point not to talk about his private concerns in my presence, I knew that he had been concerned that Van would draw what he called "maverick" conclusions from his finds.

"Perhaps," I said. "If he wanted to know, and couldn't get the information from Van, that would be the sort of thing he would do."

"I can tell you the rest of it in a very few words," Michael said. His face was expressionless now. If he was disappointed at the extent of the information I was able to give him, he did not show it. "We found a good many artifacts that could have possibly been supportive of our premise, which was that in some of the Etruscan city states an individualistic art form was developed, one that owed little to Greece. It was a rich dig. But nothing really definitive until the sixth month. And then we found the fibula."

I nodded. I had been around this house long enough

to know a good deal about Etruscan art, and I knew what a fibula was. There were a good many of the clasps in the cases that crowded this house, and I had seen them in the museums Van and I had visited. Fibulae were found in a great variety of designs, but their function was always the same—to serve as a pin, and, at the same time, as an ornament, a brooch.

"You know what they are, then?"

"Yes. I thought that they were quite a common find."

"They are. That's not the point. This one was gold, which isn't in itself unusual. It was obviously Etruscan work. But far more sophisticated than anything that's been uncovered before and the design was more abstract. What I'm trying to say is, put simply, it was evidence that the Etruscans, in this one city state, at least, had succeeded in breaking through the Greek tradition to produce something original."

He was silent for a moment, and I held my breath. This was important. Terribly important. And yet neither Van's father nor Anthony had let me know about it. Van's overriding ambition at the time he had died was to prove conclusively that the Etruscans had been capable of producing an art form which was uniquely their own, and that those art forms had developed to a far more sophisticated stage than any of the artifacts that we possessed would indicate. I had been led to think that he had died a disappointed man. The dig had not been continued, and someone had seen to the disposal of whatever artifacts of value had been turned up at that time. I had asked no questions. Some of Van's notes had been sent to me by him from time to time, and Van's father had asked me for them. They were too technical for me to understand, and so I had given them to him. And later I had heard him tell someone who was interviewing him that it was unfortunate that Van's last premise was one that it was so impossible to validate scientifically.

"But it's not possible," I said, leaning forward in my chair. "I've heard nothing of any such find. Anthony's never said anything——"

I broke off. A few minutes ago Michael had implied that Van's father might have sent Anthony to Italy to watch what was going on and to report on it. And I had agreed that that was possible. If Michael were telling the truth, Anthony must have known about the fibula. Why then had he said nothing to me about it? It occurred to me that this stranger was making charges by implication which were far more complex than simply that of murder. Something inside me tightened.

"Have you the fibula in your possession?" I asked him.

"No." Michael's eyes met mine. "You're perfectly justified in refusing to believe me without the evidence of that find. That was one of the reasons that I didn't come to England before now. I knew that I would be asked for proof, and I had none. It was probable that Van had made notations in his records. It's hard to believe that he would not. And I was led to believe that those records were destroyed in the fire. He kept them in his room."

I stared at him, puzzled. "But some records must have been kept in his office," I told him.

"There was no office," Michael said. "He kept everything in that villa. And it was burned to the ground. I was there. I watched it burn. There was nothing left but ashes."

He conjured up the scene too vividly, and I shuddered. This might be simply some sort of puzzle to this man, but it had meant my happiness. He had said that he was reluctant to stir up old passions. Well, he had done that, and for a moment I resented him.

"Some ledgers were sent to me," I repeated helplessly. "They were technical. I couldn't read them. His father asked for them, and I gave them to him."

For a long moment neither of us spoke.

"And Mr. Harcourt never mentioned the fibula?"

"No."

"Nor did Anthony? Because Van's brother knew about it. He saw it that first day, and although he may be no archaeologist himself, it was clear that he understood its significance. But I wondered about him, even then. On another account. You see, the next day, an agent contacted your husband. He wouldn't say who he represented, but I saw him, too. A stout little man wearing a shiny black suit. He told Van he was prepared to offer him a quarter of a million pounds for the fibula."

I caught my breath. "But no museum—" I began.

"He didn't represent a museum," Michael said quickly. "I told you that it was a private client. Someone who wanted to remain anonymous. And two things disturbed Van. How anyone had known about the find, in the first place. The student who had uncovered it had been asked not to say anything. And he's a completely trustworthy chap. Other than that only Van and I and Greene knew. And Anthony."

"But it wasn't you or Van who let the word out," I said quickly. "So what you're implying is that it was either Greene, who'd already promised that he'd let Van decide how the finds were to be disposed of, and—"

"If you'd met Greene you'd know he's not the sort of man whose promises can be taken too seriously," Michael said grimly. "Van and I realized that from the start. We suspected from the beginning that he was primarily interested in getting whatever we turned up into the hands of private collectors. Even significant

28

finds. Even finds which would change the records, the history, of a culture. There are a good many kinds of collectors, you know. And the most dangerous as far as men like myself are concerned are the men who collect for the sake of collecting, and who value most keeping from the researcher, from the expert, evidence that would change basic theses. It's a form of corruption, but there are some very wealthy men who practice it. Men who will buy the work of a great painter which has been lost and which the texts describe, but which cannot be documented. It would be easy enough for these men to let the world know that the supposedly lost painting had been found. Easy enough to loan it to galleries for displays, to make it possible for men whose life work depends on their knowledge of art to look at it. But these collectors don't do that. They hide what they have away. It's like a perversion."

He broke off and stared down at his clenched hands. I knew that it must be very late, but I also knew that I was not likely to sleep that night.

"All right," Michael said, taking a deep breath. "So someone knew about the fibula and was willing to offer a fortune for it. Van insisted that we refuse, of course. But that's when the second problem manifested itself. Greene wanted to accept the offer. And your brother-in-law supported him."

"But it was Van's decision to make."

"There was nothing written down to that effect. Remember? And Greene had the money. Van was willing to quit the dig on the spot. After all, he had what he wanted. He didn't need any more evidence to prove his thesis. But Greene turned nasty. Said that he'd sue."

"Who had the fibula?"

"Your husband." Michael lit a cigarette, and I noticed that his hands were not quite steady. "It was

29

found on a Tuesday morning. We knew what it was by that afternoon. That night he kept it in his bedroom at the villa he'd rented. The next day the agent came. And that night there was the fire."

I rose from my chair. My body ached from sitting so long in the same position, but my mind was clearer than it had been for months. It was as though I were doing a mental puzzle, and the pieces were falling into place before I could even properly conceptualize them.

"What was the fibula made of again?" I demanded.

"Gold."

"And the fire totally destroyed the house?"

"I know what point you're trying to make." Michael came and stood beside me. "In that sort of heat the gold would probably melt. Still, I searched for a sign of it the next day. And I would have assumed that that was what had happened to it—until last month."

We were standing close together now in the shadows, far away from the pool of yellow light that fell on my empty chair. I had spent too many nights in that chair, reading, remembering, trying to make the time pass, while in the drawing room Van's father puttered among the artifacts that meant more to him than people. Now I felt as though I never wanted to sit in that chair again, never again pick up that piece of embroidery. Michael was about to tell me something that would change my life. I felt certain of it. And I might be more unhappy because of it. The even pattern of my life might be disturbed. But I wanted it to happen.

"Last month a lawyer in Rome contacted me," Michael said. His voice was very low now. Both of us, for a long time, had been speaking in near whispers. "He was settling the estate of a very wealthy man whose name I recognized as a collector of art objects. A man named Paduolo. And he wanted me to look at one particular item in order to give an estimate of its value. As an expert."

Michael took a deep breath. "Ordinarily I don't do that sort of thing, but when he mentioned the word 'Etruscan', something clicked in my mind."

"The fibula," I breathed.

"The last time I had seen it, it was in Van's hands." Michael was looking past me at the light. It was clear that the moment he was remembering was far more vivid to him than the present. "It was evening, and he was going into the villa he had rented near the dig. We said good night, and four hours later there was the— the fire. And he was gone. And the fibula with him. Except that it wasn't really gone. I saw it just two weeks ago in a house in Rome. And according to the private records of the man who had bought it, he had paid exactly a quarter of a million pounds."

Chapter Two

IN THE morning it all seemed like a dream. The pattern of my life seemed so unchanged. I lay in that vast bed, watching the gray light that crept around the side of the curtains flicker on the high, ornate ceiling. A window was open, and I could hear the sound of birds cracking the shells of snails against the brisk walk of the garden. The leaves of the poplar trees that encircled the house beat thickly against one another. There was the musty smell of damp earth.

The clock in the hall downstairs struck nine as Grace came into the room, carrying a tray. Always she followed the same routine. Good mornings murmured in a tone of subdued cheerfulness. Curtains pulled briskly. A comment about the weather, which I answered automatically, my eyes fixed on the light gray of the sky and the shimmering quality that the rain gave to the leaves of the poplar trees outside my window. Then she was gone, as quietly as she had come, and I was sitting propped up against two satin pillows, the tray braced across my knees, the tray that, like so much else in my life, was always the same, with its single rose in a silver bud vase, the silver-covered platter of scrambled eggs, the rack of toast, and the small crystal dish of marmalade. Finally, a pot of tea and the *Times* folded at the side of the tray. Just as I liked it. Or had I ever put so much importance in details?

It seemed absurd to me now that I could have ever followed this routine day after day since Van had died. Had there really been some comfort in it? A lingering breakfast in bed. The paper skimmed. Then letters read with a fresh pot of tea. By then it would be nearly ten thirty. Time for a hot, lingering bath. From eleven thirty to twelve thirty a walk. And then lunch taken alone in my sitting room, with the windows open to the garden, or a fire roaring, depending on the season. After that I usually read, and then perhaps took the underground in to London to a gallery, or to an afternoon concert. Then back to that little sitting room, that refuge from the world, for tea. And so the day passed through a stiff formal dinner with Mr. Harcourt and Anthony, and my ultimate escape into my own affairs. Last night had broken the thread of my life. And I was glad. I felt alive. Not happy, but simply alive.

I pushed the tray away from me and climbed out of the bed. The breeze from the open window was damp and cool against my skin. I went to the mirror, seeing myself for the first time in a long time as a woman, pulling my long black hair tight back from my face, letting my nightgown slip off my shoulders, drop to the floor. I was thin. Too thin. But other than that I had not changed too much. Van had called me beautiful. But that was because he loved me.

And Michael. How had he seen me? As a timid, easily excitable woman who chose to hide from the world? He would be right, in a way, if he had thought that. But he must have sensed some of the old vitality, the old tenacity in me, or he would not have been as frank. Not as open. He must have trusted me, or he would not have made the implications he had made.

But perhaps I was not being fair. He had told me

what had happened. And it was puzzling. It did have
to be explained. And it would be too easy to draw
conclusions now. I must not do that. I had always
disliked and feared Van's father. And felt distaste for
Anthony. It would be too easy to find them somehow
implicated in the events that had led to the fibula being
found in a private collection. Someone had received a
good deal of money as a result of that transaction. But
Van's father would not have cared about money. What
he would have cared about was keeping the artifact out
of the public eye until he could refute the argument
that its very existence presented to his theories. And
Van. Who was responsible for his death? That was the
danger of drawing this sort of conclusion. One thing led
to another too easily. Michael was coming back that
afternoon. Van's father and Anthony should have returned from Devon by then. I wanted to keep my mind
open until I saw him again. Saw him with them. I
could tell a good deal more when I saw him with them.

I drank some of the tea, and dressed quickly but
with more care than I usually took. The violet-colored
sweater hung loose on my shoulders. It had been one of
Van's last presents to me. And the gray tweed skirt.
Was I wearing it because I really liked it, or because it
had been one of his favorite things? There was more to
reevaluate about myself than simply the idleness of my
days. It was time that I stopped dressing like the kind
of English matron Van would have liked me to become. I had my own tastes. Strong tastes in clothes,
which I had subdued while he was alive. Tomorrow I
would shop. And perhaps have my hair cropped short.
I was tired of that thin black frame to the oval of my
face, tired of twisting that mass of hair into a smooth
knot at my neck.

Once I had closed the door of the bedroom behind
me, the usual suffocating feeling came over me. My life

had changed, perhaps, but this house affected me as it always did. The corridor with its red plush runner seemed endless, lined with door after door shutting me out like so many closed eyes. The landing was dusky, with only a little gray light creeping in from between the scarcely drawn curtains of the long window that faced the terraced hill. Mr. Harcourt did not like light. Not natural light. It faded the carpets and hurt his eyes. Or was I only assuming that? Had he ever said as much? Probably not. Van's father was a man who did not believe that anyone of character should ever bother to apologize or explain.

Whatever the reason, he had created an atmosphere inside the house that matched his own forbidding character. The stairway was wide and curving with graceful shallow steps, but the brown walls hung with black-framed photographs of various digs did nothing to lighten the effect. In the hallway itself, potted ferns brushed against my dress. Mr. Harcourt's touch had been felt in the drawing room as well. The door was open, and I stood on the threshold looking down the long, display case-lined wall to the elegantly tiled fireplace. Black and orange Etruscan vases glowered at me from the corners. I knew that if I went close to them I would see the charm of elongated beasts and silhouetted dancers. I knew all too well the wealth of miscellany that crowded the cases. I could switch on the light over any of them and see the irregular shape of a copper mirror, the rough handle of a goat-figured stamnos, a gold armlet once worn by a dusky, sharp-nosed woman under a blazing sun. Once those things had fascinated me. Van had explained them all, and brought the past to me with a vividness I had never imagined possible. But now that he was dead these remnants of a nearly forgotten past weighed on me. Crowded against my life. What did I care about a culture so long since dead, about the objects made by men and women long since turned to dust inside their tombs? Why should I let them, even for a moment, drag me into their past, when I could not even release myself from my own?

I stood in the gray of the corridor then, realizing suddenly that the determination to change my life, of which I had been aware in the bedroom, had somehow eluded me here. It would be so easy to get my coat and walk my usual walk up through the gardens. So easy to fall back into the routine. Michael was coming this afternoon, but until then, what did I do? Shop, perhaps. It was so difficult to begin. But I had to free myself from the atmosphere of this house, with its shadows and its silence.

I turned back toward the closet to get my coat, and suddenly I heard the sound of a drawer closing. It had come from inside Mr. Harcourt's office to the left of the stairs. But that was impossible. He was not at home, nor was Anthony, and the maids had long since been directed never to go in there. Even I, in the few instances when I had crossed the threshold, had felt uneasy. Unwelcome. Yet someone was there. Odd that my mind should so quickly go to Michael. And yet it was possible that he might be anxious enough to prove what he suspected to break into Van's father's office. After all, I knew nothing about him. I had often in the past played the fool by taking people on trust.

I opened the door quickly, noiselessly, my heart pounding. The office was a largish room, but crowded with desks and file cabinets. Etruscan masks stared sightlessly at me from the walls, and a bulky statue of a naked warrior loomed ominously in a further corner, one raised fist clenched.

"Who's there?" I cried, and turning to the left, saw

Bernice hastily replacing a drawer in the desk that Van's father most often used.

For a moment we stared at one another without speaking. The lights were not on in the room, and her long, thin face was a patch of white set against gray, the gray of a scarf that blended with the general gloom.

"God, you startled me," she said in a shrill voice. "What did you think I was, a burglar?"

Bernice Woodring had been Mr. Harcourt's secretary for ten years. Because she was the only woman besides the maids whom I saw daily, I thought of her as a friend. But only because of that. There was something brittle about her which I had never liked. And she had never liked me, particularly during these past weeks when Anthony had made all too clear his interest in me.

"I didn't think you were supposed to come in today," I said breathlessly.

Her dark eyes narrowed behind her glasses. "There's no particular time that I can't work," she said. "There were a few odds and ends. . . ."

"Were you looking for something?" That was the kind of question that I never asked. Ordinarily I ignored the work that was going on in this house. And she knew that. Her expression was one of surprise and annoyance.

"Only a letter that Mr. Harcourt wanted answered," she said sharply. "He forgot to leave it out for me. No matter."

After that there seemed to be nothing left to say. Nothing was wrong, and yet there was an extraordinary tension between us. She cleared her throat.

"One of the maids told me that Mr. Harcourt had a visitor last night," she said abruptly.

I turned away from her and went out into the hall. Opened the closet and took out my raincoat. To give myself time. How could the maid have told her any such thing? I had met Michael on the doorstep before the door was opened. As far as the maid was concerned he was someone who had come to see me. Or was I remembering correctly? I had whispered Van's name and then the door had opened, and I had seen Michael's face. The maid had stood there for a while, until I had nodded to her. What had he and I talked about at first? Had he said that he had come to see Van's father? I slid my arms into my raincoat. It was useless to try to remember. I had been too disturbed at that moment of meeting Michael to remember anything in sequence.

"I don't know," I said, going toward the door. "If someone did, I wasn't told."

It was my first lie and I felt, somehow, as though it had plunged me into some sort of an abyss from which it would be difficult to extricate myself. If the maid had told Bernice that—and how would she have known about Michael otherwise?—then she would know now that I was lying. And she had a prying mind. I knew her well enough to realize that she would not rest until she found out the truth, or something close enough to the truth to satisfy her.

I opened the door and found that she was behind me, her umbrella in her hand. Only then did I realize that she had apparently been in too much of a hurry to do whatever she had intended to do in Mr. Harcourt's office to remove her raincoat. And only then did I realize that I did not believe the story she had told me about searching for a letter. She had been searching for something, all right. But for something far more important to her.

We walked across the rain-soaked gravel drive to the spongy, close-cropped turf which rolled in gentle terraces to the foot of the hill where the high iron gate marked a boundary to the estate. The air was thick and gray but there was no fog, and I could see the Thames in the distance, and the red roofs of the town of Kew. Bernice moved closer to me, sheltering me with her umbrella, but I stepped quickly to the side, tossing my hair against the rain. The damp earth smelled of liberation.

"You know," Bernice said, "you ought to get out more, see more people. You've isolated yourself for the past year, and it hasn't been good for you. I've seen the change."

And had she seen today's change with her sharp little eyes? Was that what she was probing to find out? I did not want to walk with her. I wanted to be alone. But outside of directly asking her to leave me, there was no way to get rid of her. I seriously considered making the request.

"There's something I've been meaning to ask you," she went on. I did not look at her, but her voice was sharper, and I knew that she realized that she was being snubbed. "Do you spend, perhaps, too much time with your mementos? I mean, you kept all of Van's letters, didn't you? All the letters he sent you from Italy. That was the first time you had been apart, wasn't it? I mean, it would be understandable if you might find yourself brooding over them now?"

What on earth was she trying to get at? She had always been a woman who pried, but never without reason. Did she want to know what was in those letters? Or was she urging me to destroy them? And, if so, why?

"I expect you're thinking that I'm being unreasonably curious," she went on, breathless now with trying to keep up with me. "But I'm only interested in your well-being, Mandy. All of us are interested in your well-being."

"I'm perfectly all right." I threw the words back at her over my shoulder. We had reached the gate now, and I turned abruptly, and saw her lose her balance, put out her hand to support herself against the wet rails, her umbrella waving perilously.

But she was not to be put off that easily. Nearly running, she moved in front of me, her black eyes snapping behind rain-spattered glasses. She was angry. That was clear. But her voice was sickeningly sweet.

"Incidentally," she said, "I met a perfectly delightful man a few days ago. At a party. Someone who knew Van in Italy."

Something seemed to drop inside me. Not Michael. Please let it not be Michael.

"He said that he wanted to meet you," she went on. Something about my face had made her triumphant. She was smiling a thin smile. "And I promised I'd introduce you. You'll find him perfectly charming, I know. His name is Winton Greene."

When I finally returned to the house it was after two, and Burrell, the chauffeur, was unloading suitcases from the trunk of the black limousine. I stood for a long time staring at the house. It was not raining any longer, and a fresh breeze was blowing. But the sky was overcast, and I was aware of a curious depression settling over me.

I had spent nearly an hour over lunch at a little Italian restaurant near the library, trying to come to some conclusions. Either I had become totally paranoid, or something that I did not understand was going on around me. Perhaps it had just started, or perhaps it had been going on for a long time, and I had been too much involved with my own feelings to notice. After all, today was not the first time that Bernice had asked me questions about my mementos of Van. And yet, before this morning, it had never occurred to me that there might be something among those letters which I kept locked in the wall safe that Van had had put in our bedroom early in the first days of our marriage, something that Bernice or someone else wanted to know. Once she had asked me where I kept his "things," as she referred to them, and when I told her, without thinking, that they were in the safe, she had gone on at a great rate about how odd Van's father had thought it that he had had it done. "He could have used his father's big desk in the office," she said over and over again. "Van was a marvelous person, but inclined to be a bit secretive, don't you think?"

Yes, this had not been the first evidence of Bernice's prying. But I had been insensitive to it. And why? I had ordered a half carafe of red wine and asked myself that question over and over again. It was surely too simple to say that Bernice's questions could suddenly seem ominous because of my meeting with Michael. Under ordinary circumstances I would have taken her presence in my father-in-law's study this morning for granted. Or not noticed. That was more likely. Surely it was not simply because of Michael that I had suspected her of trying to look at something that she had no right to look at? Still, he had used the word *murder*. But he had never directly implied that Van's father or Anthony or anyone who was close to them was involved. I would be insane to think in those terms.

I had sat lingering over coffee and tried to decide what my role was to be now. Michael was convinced that Van had been killed. Now he was obviously determined to prove it. I could either decide to join him on the basis of the information about the fibula, or I could go to Van's father now and tell him everything that Michael had told me. And, in so doing, let him prepare himself before Michael came to see him. But the point was, that way I could relinquish responsibility. Van's father could make the decisions. He could listen to Michael or he could ask him to leave. And I? I could wait. I had always been the waiting sort.

But now, standing under a poplar tree the branches of which dripped rain onto my hair, I knew that I was no longer content to be dormant. To wait and let things happen. I wanted to cause things to happen. I wanted to help Michael. And that did not mean that I necessarily accepted the premise that Van had been murdered. I would make that clear to him when I saw him next. It only meant that I thought that the matter should be investigated, particularly the matter of the fibula.

But for the present, I did not want to see anyone. Not Bernice with her prying eyes, nor Anthony with his smooth dark face and insinuating smile. And particularly not Van's father. There was no need to tell him that Michael was coming. Michael had told me the night before that he would call this afternoon and make his own appointment. And until he saw Mr. Harcourt, I did not want to. He was an old man. But too shrewd. Too shrewd by far for anyone with secrets to be around.

There was no difficulty in getting into the house unnoticed. I had done it a good many times before. I crossed the gravel drive quickly while Burrell was still bent over the trunk, and slipped around the corner of the house where an alley separated it from the loose boxes where horses had once been stabled, a building that was now a warehouse for Etruscan statues, many of which were being examined before being sent on to museums in this country and abroad. It was dank and gray there, but it would take me to the servants' entrance at the back of the house with the least likelihood of being seen. I walked along for ten feet on the flat cement, and then up three steps to an odd little landing just beside the window that opened into Mr. Harcourt's office. The landing was small and led immediately to three steps leading down, whereupon the alley continued for another twenty feet to the yard at the back of the house. But for a moment, when one was standing in that raised position, one could look through the iron-barred window to his office. From habit I did so, and caught my breath.

Anthony and Bernice were there together. The door was closed, and they were standing in the corner to the left of it, slightly behind a cinerary urn of terra-cotta. Anthony's thin face was twisted in rage, and as I looked, he took Bernice by the shoulders and shook her. I could not hear them, but I had the impression that they were not speaking loudly. Suddenly he released her and I saw her remove her glasses and wipe her eyes with the back of her hands while Anthony watched her dispassionately. And then he turned his head. Impossible to tell whether or not he saw me, for in that same moment I stepped out of view on the tiny landing and ran down the stairs to press myself against the wall of the house.

The suffocating quality of fear rushed over me. And why? Why? Standing there motionless, my eyes closed, I asked myself that question. I had broken no laws. I had a perfect right to enter the house by the back entrance if I wished. I had, in fact, been doing that a good deal during the past year. It was only normal for anyone passing that way to glance in the window. But no one beside myself did pass that way. And Anthony and Bernice had not planned on being observed. It was useless for me to tell myself that it was a lovers' quarrel. If Bernice had ever meant anything to Anthony, that time was passed. And she must know it, too. For weeks she had gone around with red eyes and a persecuted expression. She had been jealous of me then, even though she must have realized that I tried to avoid him. But recently she had seemed to behave very casually with him, and I had thought that all the emotional traumas were past.

I forced my muscles to relax, forced myself to walk slowly down the alley to the back of the house. Slipping through the door that opened into the hall next to the kitchen, I ran up the back stairs to the second floor. Perhaps the servants noticed me. It scarcely mattered. They were accustomed to seeing me enter the house this way. For them, at least, nothing had changed.

When I was standing in the dusk of the second-floor corridor, my feet sunk in the thick red carpet, I breathed a sigh of relief. For the moment, at least, I had avoided whatever issues were in store for me. But when I turned the corner toward my bedroom, I saw Van's father standing there, waiting for me.

I was certain that he had been waiting, even though he was pretending to be examining the bronze statuette of Apollo that stood on a stand beside the wall. He was stroking it as he often stroked his treasures, as though they were living things. The green patina of the tiny object glistened in his hands as he turned to face me. He was a tall man and slender, dressed as always in the height of fashion, in a gray business suit cut along Edwardian lines. His face was like Van's about the eyes, which were blue and penetrating, but his nose was a thin beak, and his mouth only a line that scarred his face like a wound.

My reaction to him was what it had always been, a combination of fear and dislike. Fear because he was a powerful man, powerful in intellect and determination. The slight bend of his shoulders and the sparse white of his hair did nothing to mitigate this. Anyone who had ever had dealings with him must realize the sheer force of his personality. As for the dislike, this was born of many things. He had hated me since the day Van had brought me to meet him. God knows why except that, perhaps, he detected in me Van's first signal of independence. And I disliked him, too, because of the barriers he had put in Van's way concerning the Italy dig, barriers that had made it quite clear that his professional reputation was far more important to him than his son's success.

"My dear," he said, putting the statuette carefully back on its stand. "I wondered where you'd gotten yourself to. I do wish you had gone to Devon with Tony and me. The weather was superb."

Perhaps he had forgotten that he had not asked me to go. But then, this man forgot nothing. I smiled and murmured something about being glad. Moved level to him. Past him. Hoping for nothing but to reach my bedroom without any real encounter.

"You're looking particularly well," he said, stretching out his long arm and cupping my face in his hand. I hated the touch of his fingers. Cold and dry. Dead things. "In fact, I don't think I've seen you looking so—so vibrant since poor Van . . ."

"I've been walking," I said desperately, drawing away from him, pressing myself against the wall.

"Perhaps it was the company that stimulated you," he said quietly, moving with me, refusing to relinquish my face.

"What company?" Why should so many waves of fear wash over me? So many times today I had felt afraid. I, who for so long had felt nothing but a certain numbness.

"Bernice tells me that you had a guest last night," he said. His fingers trickled away from my face, but now his thin body blocked my way. "One of the maids verified that you had a visitor."

I felt panic. I wanted to lie. To say that I had seen no one. But I had lied once today, and I refused to lie again. Lies were traps. And I did not want to be trapped by anyone.

"Yes," I said. "Someone called."

"At eleven at night?" His eyes were quizzical and cruel. There would be no snubbing him as I had snubbed Bernice.

"Actually he came to see you," I said. "On impulse. He's someone who knew Van. In Italy."

"Someone who knew Van in Italy?" His voice was amused. Patronizing. He had always patronized me. But that particular game was over now.

"His name is Michael Kyd," I said.

"And who, might I inquire, is Michael Kyd?"

"He's an expert in Etruscan art," I said defiantly, "I think you must know that. He agreed to work with Van in evaluating the artifacts on that—that last dig."

"And he came here?"

I could not look the old man in the eyes, and yet wherever I looked, the blank Etruscan eyes of statuette after statuette seemed to stare back at me. And which was worse?

"Yes."

"Why?"

"I'm—I'm not certain."

"Not certain? And yet I understand you talked to him until one in the morning."

For the first time it occurred to me that a house with servants is a house with jailers. And I had had so little feeling of having been observed when I had said good-bye to Michael.

"We talked about Van," I said in a low voice. "They were friends."

"Ah, yes, friends." The old man's voice was quite steady. Unlike my own. "Van had a great facility for gathering friends about him, didn't he?"

I did not answer. As so often happened when I talked to Van's father, there was nothing to say.

"And what did this—this friend talk about?"

I was moving down the corridor now toward my bedroom, but the old man was following me. I had the desperate feeling that he would never stop following me until I told him what he wanted to know.

"About Van," I said in a low voice. "About those last days."

"And what about those last days?"

Was it my imagination, or did his voice hold a note of menace?

"He'd better tell you himself," I said. And in that moment I had a desperate feeling that Michael was not real. That he was a product of my imagination. That he would never appear again.

"I think, my dear," the old man said, "that I should warn you——" I heard someone behind me and I turned to see Bernice staring at us, her eyes magnified by her glasses until she became a caricature.

"Mr. Harcourt." She was breathless. More breathless than the trip up those long, winding stairs would have made her. "There's someone on the phone," she said. Not looking at me. Deliberately not looking at me. "Someone who wants to know if he can see you this evening. Someone named Michael Kyd."

I knew that I had to get out of the house. It was no use shutting myself in my room now. That had worked before, but it would never work again. Mr. Harcourt and Bernice were watching me. Wondering, perhaps, if I would react to Michael's name. They were always watching me. I had felt that for a long time without ever admitting it to myself. I did not move until Van's father started toward the stairs. Even then, Bernice remained behind. I turned my back on her. Started toward my bedroom.

"Anthony's looking for you," she said. Her voice was shrill. Whenever she spoke of Anthony to me she sounded that way. And I knew why. She hated the attention that he paid to me. She was suffocated with jealousy. And yet she consented to act as go-between. She brought messages from him. Urged me to see him. Because there was no limit to her curiosity. And, perhaps, to her masochism. I was not built that way, and I found it difficult to understand, let alone sympathize with. I had seen her and Anthony together in the office only moments ago, seen his fingers dig into her arms. But I did not want to know why. I did not want to know what had gone on between them. Turning now to look at her, I saw that her eyes behind the thick glasses were red-rimmed. She had been crying. But that was her affair. Not mine.

"I'm going out," I said.

"Where?"

"I'm not certain," I said. And then fled, locking my bedroom door behind me, taking off my sweater and skirt and slipping into a jersey dress, fingers slipping on the zipper as though someone were about to force himself in on me. I knew that was absurd. I was not a prisoner. But I could not let them talk to me now. I knew my own limits. In the end, if they persisted, I would tell them about Michael.

I paused in front of the mirror, comb in hand. My eyes were like dark blots in my face. I looked like what I was, a frightened woman. And I despised myself for that. I could tell them about Michael's visit, tell them what he believed to be true about Van's death. In a sense I owed it to Van's father. He had a right to know before he encountered Michael face to face. Michael was nothing to me. A stranger. Someone who had known my husband. And many people had known Van. The old man had given me a home. He had been kind to me in his own way. He had never complained about the way I had gradually withdrawn from my friends. And from his. I owed him something.

But I hated him. I hated all of them. I had never admitted that to myself before either. I had hidden for a year behind the belief that it was only indifference that I felt as an aftermath to my grief for what I had lost. Now I could no longer hide from myself. If I did not tell Van's father now what I knew about Michael's mission, I must at least face why I refused to do so.

Once I was outside the house it was better. The sky was a faded blue now, and the sun was drying the leaves and the daffodils. I wandered down the hill without thinking of where I was going until I realized that I was beyond the gates of the park. Turning, I looked up through the iron fretwork at Grove House. Gray stone. Gaping windows. A mausoleum. My mausoleum.

I had to get as far away as I could. Just for a few hours. During the long subway ride into London, I told myself that I would be all right in a few hours. I simply needed to be distracted. To see people. People I did not know. And to forget that there was any such thing as Etruscan artifacts.

I went to the Tate Gallery. There were crowds in the foyer, tourists speaking a babel of languages massed about the huge circular desk buying postcards. Skirting them, I hurried down the corridor to the left to the room at the end where the Pre-Raphaelites were displayed. There were never many people in this room. And the lights were muted. I sat down on the bench in the center of the room and let the vivid colors of the paintings press in on me. There was comfort in reverting to what I habitually did here, tasting the room as a whole without letting my eyes focus on any particular painting. And then, at last, I let myself concentrate on that painting I liked best. "The Wedding of St. George and Princess Sabra." It was a choice that only a romantic would make. I knew that. Van had laughed at me a good many times for my taste in art. But what did it matter, as long as these brilliant canvases still had the power to draw me into them?

Suddenly I was aware that someone was sitting down on the bench beside me. Too close. It was not crowded. There was no reason for anyone to let an arm touch mine. I moved away in annoyance, my eyes still drawn toward the painting. And then Anthony spoke. And I went cold inside. Cold with rage. He had followed me. He must have followed me. What right had he to do that?

I turned to stare angrily at him. He was not a tall man and, sitting, his eyes were level with mine. Some people might call him handsome. He had that particularly upper-class British face. Full-featured. Sallow-skinned. Eyes that were blue and expressionless. An arrogant mouth. He was smiling. My dislike for him had never seemed to penetrate his consciousness.

"This is probably the best collection of second-rate stuff in this gallery," he said, obviously amused. "You're too beautiful a woman to have such rotten taste, Mandy."

I started to rise. I could leave. He could not force me to talk to him. But why should I go? This was where I wanted to be. There was a limit to the number of places I would be willing to run from to escape these people. I sank back on the bench, but further away from him.

"If you don't like it, why don't you go to another room?" I said.

He whistled softly between his teeth. "I've never seen you this fiery," he said. Still amused. "Bernice said that you'd changed. I don't suppose it has anything to do with your nighttime visitor, has it?"

I had ignored the question when Bernice had asked it. And only an hour ago I had refrained from giving Van's father any information about Michael. But they knew he had been to see me. They all knew. In a sense, in refusing to talk about him, I was humiliating myself. And I had been too willing to humiliate myself in the past.

"Are you talking about Michael Kyd?" I said defiantly.

"So it was Kyd." For a moment every pretense of amusement fled from Anthony's face. I felt a sense of power over him that I had never felt before. Van had told me once that, when attacked, I should take the offensive. He had tried so many times to cure me of meekness. Well, he had been right. My anger was replaced by exhilaration.

"You knew him, didn't you?" I demanded.

Anthony raised his eyebrows. Obviously it was not my role to ask questions. "I could scarcely have avoided knowing him," he said. "After all, he was Van's right-hand man in the Italian project, as he must have told you."

"He told me a good many interesting things," I said. My voice had risen slightly, and a man and woman who were examining a small portrait in the corner turned to stare at us. For a moment I reacted as I customarily would have, pressing my lips together and staring straight in front of me. I have always hated drawing attention to myself in public. As for Anthony, he apparently cared as little as he ever had about anyone else. He reached out and took my arm, and for a moment I felt his fingers bite into my flesh as they must have done to Bernice.

"Don't touch me!" I hissed. The man and woman gave us another curious glance and wandered out of the room. We were alone again.

"What was that remark supposed to mean?" Anthony demanded. He had lost all that humorous condescension now. There was no mistaking that he was angry. The dark skin was flushed, the eyes hard.

"Why don't you ask him yourself?" I retorted. "He said that he was coming to the house again. To see your father."

"Tonight? He's coming tonight? Listen, Mandy. Obviously he's managed to upset you. He—"

"I'm not upset," I said.

"You're putting on a pretty good act of being disturbed, then," Anthony told me. He was in control of himself again now. Deliberately being gentle with me. I hated him in this role as much as in any other.

"Don't worry about me," I said, rising.

"Don't go." He was imploring me now. Pretending to implore. Trying to find some chink in my armor as he always did. "You know I hate having you upset," he said. "You know how much you mean to me, don't you? And I know this man, Kyd. Know him much better than I imagine you do after one meeting. He has a lot of appeal, doesn't he? Even Van was completely taken in by him. But he's trouble, Mandy. Believe me."

"Perhaps he is," I said. "As far as you're concerned."

Once again I saw that flash of anger in his eyes, anger quickly overlaid with an expression of concern. But the anger was real. The other was not. Anthony might dupe a good many people, including his father.

53

But I was not going to let him dupe me. The only person he had ever cared about was himself.

"Listen." I was walking toward the door and Anthony was following me. An old man, bent over a stick, came shuffling past us and went to sit where we had sat on the bench in the center of the room. "You ought to know that Kyd hates me. You can't believe anything that he says about me."

"Why does he hate you?" I threw over my shoulder. Why hadn't I learned this trick before, to answer question with question?

"Because he was busy playing Svengali with Van," Anthony muttered. We were blocking the door to a family group, and a passing guard glanced at us.

"Just stop for a moment," Anthony said. I had never seen him less in command of himself. His face was flaming red now, and his eyes had narrowed into slits. Before I could avoid him, he had manipulated me into a corner of the long corridor, blocking my escape with his thick body. "Michael Kyd may have been able to convince you that he was sincere as hell," he said. "I've seen him play that trick before. He had your husband eating out of his hand before he was done."

"You're not making sense," I said. "What influence could he have had over Van?"

"He managed to convince him that that insane theory about independent Etruscan cultural development was true."

"No one had to convince Van of that," I said. "It was his idea in the first place, and the fibula proved it."

I had said more than I intended. Staring at the man in front of me, I automatically pressed my hand over my mouth.

"So that's it." Anthony's voice was triumphant. "He told you that cock-and-bull story about the fibula."

"What story?" How much did he know? Obviously

he could not realize that the fibula had turned up in private hands. Michael had just discovered it himself a few weeks ago. And that piece of information was, I guessed, Michael's ace in the hole. He had not asked me to keep it secret. But I could at least do that. I had gone too far already. Said more than I had meant to say.

"The story about its uniqueness. Kyd told you that the finding of it proved Van's theory, didn't he? But whose word do any of us have for that? Only his. He was the so-called expert who authenticated what Van wanted to believe. And where is that fibula now? He couldn't tell you that, could he? It was a stroke of luck for him that it was destroyed in the fire."

He didn't know that it had been found, then. I took a deep breath of relief. Now the only thing left was to make him think that I knew no more about the matter than he did. That and to escape.

"I don't see why it would have concerned him one way or the other," I protested, edging past him. The guard was watching us, frowning. After all, Anthony couldn't keep me here by force.

"Don't you? Don't you really? Sometimes I wonder if you're really as unsophisticated as you pretend to be, darling." Something had happened to restore Anthony's self-confidence. The arrogance was back in his face. In his voice. "Kyd led Van on because he liked that fat salary he was getting as expert in residence, or whatever the hell his title was. But even Van was getting suspicious. Do you know what your husband was going to do the next day? If he hadn't died in the fire, he would have gone to Rome to verify what Kyd had told him. And when he found out how he'd been deliberately misled, he would have exposed your new friend. Ruined his reputation. Destroyed him professionally. If you ask me, that was why he died. If you ask me, that fire was no accident. And if you don't stay away from Kyd, Mandy, you may find out more than you want to know about murder."

Chapter Three

WHEN MICHAEL came that night I was in the drawing room with the others waiting for him. I had thought that it would be a private interview, but apparently Mr. Harcourt had decided to make it, at least in part, a social occasion. He had not gone as far as to invite Michael for dinner, granted, but there was a tray of bottles on the low stand by the fireplace, and not only Anthony and I but Bernice as well had been asked to be in attendance.

I had not seen Anthony since I had run from him at the Tate that afternoon. It had been for the purpose of avoiding him, as well as to give myself a chance to think about what he had said concerning Michael, that I had taken dinner in my sitting room alone. Now I avoided his eyes. But I had seen the sullen look on his face when I had entered the room, and I knew that he would not forget for a long while the way I had treated him.

Perhaps to compensate for the snub, he was paying a good deal of attention to Bernice, the sort of attention he had not given her for months. And she was blooming as a consequence. She had removed her glasses, and the silk dress she was wearing was attractive. Only when she looked at me did her face draw itself into ugly lines. When she looked at Anthony, she was almost beautiful. Whatever had gone on between them that morning in the office had, apparently, been settled.

As for Van's father, he was more restless than I had ever seen him. Moving about the perimeter of the room, bowing his white head over first one case of artifacts and then another, he kept clearing his throat, always a certain sign that he was nervous. But his long face was as enigmatic as ever. Those cold blue eyes gave nothing away. I sat watching him, my hands folded in my lap, my throat tight with anticipation. I could see myself reflected in the glass front of a display case in the far corner. I had drawn my long dark hair back from my face and twisted it in a soft knot at the base of my neck. My face was very pale, but my eyes were bright. It was a cool evening, and a fire had been lit in the fireplace. In the glass I could see the reflection of the flames juxtaposed against my face. And I looked away. Flames made me think of Van and those last moments. What was it that Anthony had suggested? That Michael had set that fire?

Suddenly one of the maids opened the door and Michael appeared. I was amazed at the extent of my own relief as he stood outlined by the bright light of the corridor behind him. Smiling, he walked into the room. Handsome. Self-possessed. More than that, he was real. I could see him, touch him, listen to him. Had I ever doubted that? And if not, why this sudden swelling of thankfulness? The light was dim in the long drawing room, and we were at the further end of it. It took him a minute to see me, but when he did, he moved his lips in greeting.

There was no question of his coming to me first. Van's father had gone to meet Michael, his hand outstretched. As soon as he spoke I knew that he was going to be difficult to deal with. Not that he was not pleasant. He would be very tactful, very suave. He would be the perfect host. But impervious to the ideas of anyone except himself.

"I believe that you've met my son, Anthony," he said, taking Michael's arm and leading him toward us. "But I don't believe you know my secretary, Miss Woodring. It was she you spoke with on the phone today. Of course, I realize that you've met my daughter-in-law, Amanda. She's been telling us all about your visit."

Michael had been bending over Bernice, who was seated on the couch. He turned to me as Van's father finished his last sentence. And the warmth in his eyes faded. Slightly. Or was it my imagination? I extended my hand, as had Bernice, and he took it. But that was all. Damn the old man for making it appear that he was my confidant, for implying that I had told them everything. That they, instead of Michael were my allies.

It was clear from the moment of introduction that Mr. Harcourt did not intend to lose control of this meeting. He directed Michael to a seat, one which, I noticed, kept his face directly in the light, while the old man sat close to him in the shadows. Anthony was told to pour drinks. And then Mr. Harcourt proceeded to question Michael as though this were a legal cross-examination.

"You were, I believe, the 'expert' whom my son contracted to examine his finds," he said. There was no mistaking the slur on Michael's professional standing that he had intended. "Or should I put it this way? You were employed to verify the conclusions he had already reached."

If Van's father was determined to be as offensive as possible, it was clear that Michael was equally determined to keep his equanimity.

"I'm an expert, certainly," he said, still smiling. "As

for verifying your son's preconceived opinions, no. I'm sure that you're aware that he was too much the professional to want that."

The old man waved aside the response. "And I also believe," he went on, "that you were offered a fairly substantial amount of money to work with this—this enterprise."

"I accepted a fee," Michael said coolly. "I believe you must be aware that that is customary."

Few people spoke to Van's father in that manner. There was no hostility in Michael's voice, no insolence, but there was a certain assurance which I knew that the old man infrequently encountered. He was too accustomed to being treated as the master by disciples of Etruscan art.

"Actually," Michael went on, "I was particularly interested in your son's theories. Any archaeologist knows, as a scientist, that old theories are apt to be upset by new ones in the wake of new discoveries. I'm sure that you would agree that no effort should be made to prevent those discoveries from occurring."

"Are you insinuating that I tried to prevent new finds from coming to light?" Mr. Harcourt was sitting very erect in his chair, and I could see his eyes glitter. I saw Bernice glance at Anthony with anxious eyes. Saw him shake his head.

"I don't think that either one of us has to insinuate anything," Michael said calmly. "I came here to talk about facts, not possibilities."

"Did you indeed?" Van's father had always frightened me when he spoke in that particular thoughtful tone. He glanced at me. His eyes were like marble. Involuntarily, I shivered. "Strange," the old man continued, "I had somehow gotten it into my mind that you would probably prefer to talk about possibilities."

Michael did not look at me, but I knew what he was

thinking. And Mr. Harcourt was doing it deliberately. Deliberately making it appear that he knew more about why Michael had come than he was saying. It would put him at an advantage. He always saw to that. I wanted to interrupt. To tell Michael that it was not true, that I had said nothing.

"Perhaps," Michael said, "you won't mind my asking you a question now, sir. Have you met the man who financed your son's expedition, Mr. Winton Greene?"

"I haven't had that pleasure," the old man replied coldly, "but I've heard a good deal about him from my son, Anthony."

"I imagine that you have." It was pleasantly said. There was not an intonation that one could object to. But it was obvious that Michael could utilize sarcasm as expertly as Van's father. I saw the old man's hands clench and unclench on the chair arm. "Do you also," Michael went on, "know anything about Mr. Greene's background?"

Mr. Harcourt made a gesture that implied that it scarcely mattered. And turned to Anthony. Indicated with a nod that he should answer. I caught my breath. Never before had I seen Van's father opt out of any game. But if he had, I thought that I knew why. He was burning with rage. Rage which he would have died rather than show. His eyes were wild with it. Not for the first time I found myself wondering if he was entirely sane.

"He's a wealthy American," Anthony said briskly, rising, rubbing his plump hands. "But then I'm sure that you know that as well as I, Mr. Kyd."

Michael ignored the implied rebuke. "Are you aware of whether or not Mr. Greene had ever before demonstrated any interest in archaeological expeditions?" he went on.

"I really couldn't say," Anthony reported. "Examining Mr. Greene's past history would surely have been my brother's province. I'm certain that no one of Van's character would have accepted money from an impeachable source."

I felt my face grow hot with anger. It was one thing for them to talk to one another like that, but Van could not defend himself. I started to speak, but Michael interrupted me. His voice slashed at father and son. For a moment he was no longer detached.

"I'm aware," he said, "that certain manipulated circumstances made it impossible for Van to get money from any of the usual sources." His eyes fastened on Mr. Harcourt. "It's possible that under ordinary circumstances he would never have touched Mr. Greene's money."

The old man had recovered himself. "I thought, Mr. Kyd," he murmured, "we were here to talk about facts, not possibilities."

"*Touché*." Michael smiled again. He seemed genuinely amused. But I was still raging.

"It shouldn't be difficult to find out all that we need to find out about Mr. Greene," I said. "According to Bernice, he's here in London. According to her, he wants to meet me."

There was silence. Michael appeared surprised. And displeased. Touching two fingers, he brought them thoughtfully to his face. Bernice grew pale. And her eyes were frightened as Anthony turned slowly to stare at her. I could not see his face, but there was an animal tenseness about him that I had been aware of that afternoon when I had glanced through the office window and seen him take Bernice by the arms and shake her. Rising, she murmured something, and left the room, taking short, frantic steps, the noise of her heels on the parquet floor punctuating the silence.

"Miss Woodring seems to be upset," Van's father said in a voice that curved upward. His eyes as they fastened on Anthony were expressionless. "Perhaps," he went on, "it would be a good idea if you went after her, Amanda. To see if there's anything you can do."

I desperately did not want to leave the room. My eyes implored Michael not to let them make me leave. But he did not look at me. His fingers were still pressed to his lips, and he was staring intently into the shadows.

I left them. There was nothing else I could do. Bernice's coat was not in the closet, and I did not bother to search for her. Instead I waited in the darkness of the space under the curving stairwell. Ten minutes. Twenty. And then I heard their voices raised, and footsteps. Pressing myself against the wall, I saw the drawing-room door open. Michael was the first to appear, his face drawn and white. He passed quickly out of my line of vision, and I heard the front door slam. And Anthony and his father were left. I could see their faces very clearly, see the way the deep lines etched in the old man's expressionless face, see the look of triumph in Anthony's eyes.

Michael was the only man I had ever followed in my life, and I followed him twice—once thinking he was Van, and once because I could not bear to feel that he had left the house thinking that I had betrayed him. This time it was no chase through darkened streets. Not bothering to put on a coat over the sleeveless flowered silk dress I was wearing, I hurried past Van's father and Anthony and out of the house in time to see Michael stepping into a cab, which he must have kept waiting. I thought I heard the word "Hilton," and he was gone.

For a moment I panicked. I did not really know

where in London he had gone. He might be flying back to Italy that night, for all I knew. I could always find his address. Write to him. But somehow I knew that if I really wanted him to understand, I would have to talk to him tonight.

I did not dare stay where I was. It was a wonder Anthony had not come after me yet. As I started down the stairs, the door behind me opened and I heard Anthony's voice calling my name.

"I'm going for a walk," I said, my voice echoing in the silent night.

"I'll come with you." I did not turn to face him, but I could hear the irritation in his voice. Neither he nor Van's father wanted me to talk to Michael. Probably they guessed that that was why I had left the house. They could not order me to return. And yet I had no doubt that, whatever had been said after I had left the drawing room, they did not want me to see him again.

Anthony's feet clattered on the stone steps and his hand slid under my arm. I shook myself free.

"I want to be alone," I said.

He was puzzled. He did not want to make a scene, I'm sure. It was a dark night, but not yet particularly late, and there were a good many lights showing in the town below.

Somehow the lights accentuated the isolation of this place. Before me the park stretched itself into the darkness. Suddenly I desperately wanted people about me.

"Don't try to come with me," I said to Anthony in a low voice. And left him half running down the gravel drive. I could not be certain that he had not followed me until I reached the main street of the town. In front of the station I found a cab, told the driver to take me into London. The Hilton. I had to take a chance that that was what Michael had said.

I felt excitement build in me as we passed through the shopping district of Knightsbridge and up the hill to Hyde Park Corner. The after-theater traffic slowed us as my driver tried to turn onto Park Lane, and we sat for a long time waiting to move, the pale yellow lights of automobiles cutting the blackness.

And then we were on Park Lane, and turning right to the curb in front of a blaze of light which I knew to be the Hilton Hotel. I paid for the cab and let a tall, elaborately uniformed doorman help me out of the car. It had begun to rain again, a light mist, and he held a vast black umbrella over my head as we walked the few steps to the glass door. Above me the hotel loomed like a living monolith.

The lobby was an endurance course of shrill women and cigar-smoking men, and even at this time of night, screaming children running back and forth. The lights seemed to burn into my skull, and the sense of urgency, or rush, took my breath away. When I asked at the desk for Michael Kyd, I was not surprised to learn that he was not registered there. And yet he had told the cabdriver, "Hilton." What else could he have meant? Another place with that name in it? Unless, of course, he had come directly here to see someone, to tell someone about what had happened when he had talked to Van's father. I had simply assumed that he had come to London alone. Or that he had begun this mission to clear up the cause of my husband's death with no other contacts in England except me.

I had turned away from the desk and started to weave my way through a crowd of what appeared to be American businessmen when the idea came to me. Perhaps it was the sight of a red-faced, overweight man of fifty that made me think of Winton Greene. Because that was the mental picture I had formed of him the night before when Michael had talked about him.

Perhaps because I suddenly remembered that he, too, was American. Perhaps because Bernice had said that he was in London. Whatever the reason, I walked back to the desk and asked if he was registered.

It was only after the desk clerk told me that he was that the implications of what it might mean that Michael had come here swept over me. My first thought was of collusion. Blackmail. It was the first time that I had really doubted Michael, but the doubt must have been there, close below the surface, because the possibility that he had, in actuality, not wanted to suggest to Van's father that his son had been murdered, but that the fibula had been found, and that for a sum its existence would be supressed, came full-budded to my mind. Perhaps Michael had been disconcerted to find that he must talk to me alone the night before. Perhaps, in an attempt to cover the real purpose of his visit, he had made up the story of the suspicious circumstances of Van's death. I felt numb. A woman jostled past me and began demanding a room in a shrill voice, but I could not move. It was an absurd idea, I told myself. Far more likely that when I had said that Bernice had told me that Winton Greene was in London, it had come as a revelation to Michael. Perhaps he had come to confront the man. But if that were the case, how could he have known where Greene was staying? A lucky guess, like my own? But that would be too coincidental.

The shrill-voiced woman had disappeared, and the desk clerk was watching me curiously.

"Can you tell me the number of Mr. Greene's room?" I said.

He shook his head. He was very young and obviously impressed by his own position. "I'm not allowed to give out that information," he said. "If you would like to call him on the phone over there, he can tell you himself if he likes." There was the implication in his voice that probably Mr. Greene would prefer to do nothing of the sort.

I went to the phone. So many ideas were coming to the surface of my mind that I could not make a decision. Could Michael and Greene have actually considered blackmail? They knew how far my father-in-law was willing to go to defend his Etruscan theories. Perhaps, if the fibula existed, they had decided to let him know that the only way he could keep its existence unknown would be to buy it himself. I pressed my eyes tight shut, trying to close out the people rushing about me. I was being unfair to Michael. I had only talked to him once, but if Van had trusted him I could trust him too. And it was not Van's judgment alone. I had sensed the man's integrity. I could not possibly be wrong. But the only way to prove that would be to see him. See him now.

I picked up the phone and asked the hotel operator for Winton Greene's room. I was connected immediately. A man answered, and I could hear the sound of a good many people talking in the background. Talk blended with raucous music. I asked for Michael. The background noise was so great that the man had to ask me to repeat the name three times. Then, apparently covering the phone with his hand, he called out Michael's name. The talk continued unabated.

"Someone says Kyd's here somewhere," the man told me. "But I can't see him in this room." His voice lurched into a higher register, and I realized that he had probably been drinking. "Want to leave your number, baby?" he inquired. "I'll have him call you when I see him. Perhaps you've got a friend. . . ."

It would have been easy to have been put off. But if I did I might never see Michael again while he was in London. A letter to Milan would not be the same. I would never be able to sleep until I had talked to him.

"I'm in the lobby," I said.

"Then come on up, baby! Come on up!"

I took a deep breath. "I don't know the number of the room."

He gave me the number, stumbling over the pronunciation of the digits. Refusing to let myself consider whether what I was doing was wise or not, I hung up the receiver and went directly to the elevator.

The trip up to the twenty-eighth floor took my breath away. When I stepped out of the elevator into a corridor that seemed lined with plush, there was a strange, unreal silence, as though I alone was the occupant of the entire floor. Until, that is, I reached Winton Greene's room, and even then the party noises that I had heard on the phone were muted to a dull roar.

It was a suite rather than a single room. Looking past the man who opened the door, I saw a sitting room crowded with people. The collective accent was American. I turned to ask the man who had opened the door for Michael, but he had disappeared, and I found myself caught in a cluster of beautifully dressed middle-aged women who were urgently discussing the affairs of someone named Charlotte. It was like being plunged into another world. I turned and found myself looking into the bloodshot eyes of a freckle-faced young man wearing a loosely cut silk shirt, dungarees, and a rope of black beads.

"Can you tell me where Michael Kyd is?" I asked desperately.

"Winton! Hey, Winton!" His voice was like a foghorn. "Here's the doll who wants Kyd."

There was a momentary silence. Every eye in the room seemed to be focused on me. And then on a tall, slender man in a white jacket who was standing at the side of the room, one hand on the knob of a door. If this was Greene, he did not match my preconceived concept of him. His steel-gray hair was long and curly, and his features were finely drawn. Raising his thick eyebrows inquiringly, he started to make his way toward me. The talk began again. Slowly. Tentatively.

"You're looking for Michael?" Winton Greene was very tall. He bent over me, inclining his head like a stork. "I'm Winton Greene."

He extended his hand, and I could not avoid taking it. Strangely enough, I felt no repugnance. He was an interesting man, obviously. Handsome. Cultured. And, for the moment, I had to put my prejudices behind me. I would have a response to him in time. Trust him or not. Fear or be feared. But for the moment, despite what Michael had told me, this man roused nothing but curiosity.

"I'm sorry to break in like this," I began.

"On the contrary. I'm glad that you came. Beautiful women are never in that great a supply." His voice was soft, but clearly articulated. "Michael is here, as it happens. He dropped in only a few minutes ago. We've been discussing something of concern to us both in my bedroom. Perhaps if you could give me your name. . . ."

"I'm Amanda Harcourt," I told him.

He was startled, and for a moment, when his eyes narrowed, he reminded me of Van's father.

"My dear," he said, "I'm so glad to meet you. I had great regard for your husband, as you must realize. It was a great loss when he died. A great loss. I believe I wrote to you. . . ."

There had been a letter. I vaguely remembered it. But then there had been so many letters. And I had been so distraught for so long that I had answered all of them with a sort of formula.

"I intended to call you while I was here," he went on. Somehow he had managed to take my hand again, and he was holding it between both of his. The reaction I had expected began to come to me, and I knew that not even taking into consideration what Michael had told me, I mistrusted this man.

"Bernice Woodring told me that you were going to contact me," I said. Testing his reactions. Watching him closely. Unless I was wrong he did not want to be reminded of Bernice. He became more formal.

"Yes," he said. "Of course. Miss Woodring. I met her quite by chance—at the house of a friend. We must talk, Miss Harcourt. But not now. There's much too much noise, and I suppose Michael is waiting. But perhaps we might arrange to have dinner sometime this week."

"Perhaps," I murmured. He had, I knew, delicately suggested to me that I should leave now. He had made it clear that he was engaged in an important discussion with Michael. Under ordinary circumstances I would have left abruptly. Angrily. But my determination now would not allow for anger.

"I'll tell Michael that you're here," Winton Greene said. "While you wait, you must have a drink. Here, I'll get you one." He took my arm and steered me to a corner of the room where a beautiful woman with auburn hair reaching to her waist was putting ice in her drink. "And here's someone I know you'll enjoy talking to while you wait," Winton Greene said. "It's Iris Kyd, Michael's wife."

I felt sick. The thought that Michael might be married, that he might have brought his wife to London with him, had never crossed my mind. And even if I had imagined him married, it would never have been to a svelte creature like this. She was wearing what

70

appeared to be a leather midi skirt with a fringed hem and a soft jersey top the color of an orange. Long orange and gold earrings dangled from her ears. Tossing her long auburn hair back from her face, she stared at me uninterestedly. Now, looking at her directly, I could see that although her face was beautifully structured, there was no vitality in it. No life. For some odd reason I felt relieved. And annoyed as well. My reaction to this woman, to the knowledge that Michael had a wife, disturbed me. Perhaps I had never been convinced of the truth of what he had told me about Van's death, perhaps from the beginning I had simply been attracted to him.

"This is Mrs. Harcourt," Winton was saying. For some reason he looked pleased. Almost smug. "Her husband was an old friend of mine," he went on. "And of Michael's."

The young woman smiled and stopped smiling in the matter of a second. It was less of a smile than a grimace, as though she had had some sort of Pavlovian reaction to a set stimulus.

"Make her a drink," Winton said. It was a strange tone of voice for him to use to the wife of a friend, I thought. "Make her a drink and talk to her. I won't keep Michael long."

Keep Michael long? As though they had met here at Winton Greene's command. What a fool I had been to trust a stranger so readily. And why? Because he had claimed to be a friend of Van's. He had worked with him. I was certain of that. But friends. Why had I been so ready to believe that? Perhaps I had made a fool of myself coming here. Simply because I was so willing to mistrust Van's father and Anthony.

"What do you want to drink?"

The voice was almost inflectionless. So were the eyes. It was clear that she intended to do what Winton

Greene had asked her to do without any particular grace. I was silent, watching her mix the Scotch and water, letting the roar of the conversation roll over me, wondering if Winton had told Michael that I was out here. Wondering what Michael's reaction would be. I would stay now. Because I was here. At least I would wait a little longer. But I was no longer convinced that I had instinctively done the right thing.

"Hello, Iris baby. Who's your friend?" I recognized the voice as belonging to the man I had spoken to on the phone when I had called from the lobby. He was wearing a red dinner jacket and a ruffle-fronted silk shirt, and his blond hair was tumbled over his eyes. He stood in front of us, weaving back and forth like a metronome, attempting apparently to leer lasciviously.

Iris gave him the sort of long, cold, scornful look that would have caused a sober man to run in the other direction. "Let's get out of this mob," she said. Now that there was more life in her voice, I saw that she, too, like Winton Greene and everyone else in this room, had an American accent.

We went into what was probably another bedroom, but the furniture had been rearranged in such a way that the twin beds now served as couches, and easy chairs were set around to provide the atmosphere of another living room. There was only one dim light burning in the corner, but the curtains were drawn open and the lights of London blazed below. The sight was breathtaking, and for a long time I stood staring down at it, forgetting why I had come here, forgetting everything but the sheer beauty of the scene.

The noise from the other room brought me back to the present. Iris had not closed the door, and I could look out and see the party in progress. Someone had apparently spilled a tray of drinks, and there were wails from those who had been spattered and screams of delight from others. It was like being in the darkened orchestra of a theater, looking at a lighted stage. I wondered whether Iris had simply brought me in here to get rid of me, whether while I had been looking out the window she had returned to the party. And then I saw a movement in one of the chairs that faced the window, and saw that she was curled in it, her chin on her hand. There was a fresh round of screams from the other room, and I heard her sigh.

"Winton's friends are a bit of a bore," she said.

Her voice was still strangely lacking in feeling, but I sensed that she had decided to make conversation. I went to sit in a chair close to hers and for a few minutes we said nothing, both of us staring out over the light-specked panorama of a great city.

"Have you known Michael long?"

Suddenly I was aware that she had come into this room for a purpose. She wanted to talk to me, but for some reason she did not want to be observed. Now that I could not see her face, she seemed much more relaxed.

"Not long. Since last night. He worked with my husband on an archaeological dig, you know."

"Did he?" The voice was wary.

"Van Harcourt," I said. "You must have heard your husband mention the name."

"We weren't married last year," Iris said abruptly.

We sat in silence for another few minutes. In the other room someone had put a record on, and the aching strains of soul music blasted through the room. My head was beginning to ache too, and I was very tired. I tried to see my watch in the darkness. If Michael did not come in five minutes, I would leave. Why had I wanted to see him in the first place? To assure him that I had not told my father-in-law and Anthony what he had told me? But why shouldn't I have informed them? Even he had not asked me not to talk. I had simply assumed that he wanted to spring the suspicion that Van had been murdered on them himself. But that was my idea, not his. I lived in some sort of dream world. It had made a fool of me this time. And it would do so again unless I came to grips with reality.

I started to rise from my chair, and then realized that there was one thing I wanted to know before I left. I had to know, or be able to imagine, how Michael had come to marry this extraordinary woman.

Oddly enough, Iris did not seem to want me to go either, for she stretched out her arm as though to stop me. "Winton always does take his own good time," she said. "But you mustn't go. He'll be in a devil of a temper if you do."

She spoke as though Winton and not Michael were her husband. "Tell me," I said, sinking back on the chair, "have you been married long?"

"No." She seemed to hesitate. "Only—only a few months."

"Where did you meet Michael?" I asked casually.

"Michael?" Again she hesitated, as though there were limits to what she could tell me. "Oh, I met him in Italy."

"In Milan?"

"That's right." She sounded almost relieved. "Milan."

"What were you doing there?" I persisted. To have asked this sort of question of an Englishwoman would have been awkward, but perhaps, being American, she would see nothing unusual in it.

"Oh, I . . ." Her voice trailed off into silence. The music in the other room came to a crescendo and died. "I was acting in a movie," she went on more quickly. "Only a bit part. But they—they said it might lead to something else. Only it didn't."

For the first time there was some real emotion in her voice. "You can't believe a word they tell you," she went on resentfully. "I didn't even have enough money to get back to New York."

An out-of-work actress abroad and Michael. Somehow it seemed unlikely. And yet what did I know of his tastes, his friends? No more than I knew of his character. Iris was beautiful enough, and perhaps there was more to her personality than there seemed to be on the surface.

"You must be glad now that things worked out the way they did," I said tentatively.

I was looking at the lights of the city below, but out of the corner of my eye I saw her glance at me. She murmured something that I did not catch. Whatever it was it did not sound particularly enthusiastic. I tried again.

"Have you known Winton Greene long?" I said.

She uncurled her legs and sat up straight in the chair. "You may think you're clever, asking me all these questions," she said in a low voice. Her mood had changed to one of obvious hostility. "But you'd be smarter to stay out of this." Suddenly I knew that I had gone too far. I started to say something about simply having been making conversation, when Winton Greene's voice interrupted me.

"What are you two doing sitting here in the dark?" he said. I turned to see him and Michael standing silhouetted against the light from the living room. "Admiring the view, eh?" Greene continued. He came into the room and then, when Michael was inside the door, shut it against the sound and light. It was so dark now that both men were only shadows. There was the sound of a switch being snapped, and a table lamp bathed the room in orange light.

My eyes fastened on Michael's face. He was staring past Iris at me, and his expression was grim.

"Michael and I have finished our little business talk," Winton Greene said. There was a heartiness in his voice that had not been there before. "We're sorry to have kept two such lovely ladies waiting so long."

"How did you know I was here?"

I rose from my chair as Michael came toward me. There was no hostility in his tone, but he was not the same with me as he had been the night before. I had suspected several times in the past hour that I was playing the fool, and now I was certain of it.

"I shouldn't have come," I said. "I thought that I wanted to talk to you, but now I don't think there's anything to say."

I started past him toward the door. Winton Greene blocked my way. He was smiling—a thin, unpleasant smile. "Now that you're here, we can't let you go that easily," he said. "Why don't we all join the others? Eleven o'clock at night is really no time to be discussing business anyway. I was just telling Michael that. What we all need is a drink."

"I think," Michael said distinctly, "that Miss Harcourt and I would like an opportunity to talk together. If we can't talk here, we can—"

"I quite understand," Winton Greene said. "After all, your discussion with her father-in-law and that young man—what *was* his name? Anthony?—must have raised all sorts of interesting questions. But I think that your wife will agree that it could all be put off until another time. Tomorrow, perhaps. Yes, tomorrow would be excellent. We could all have lunch together. I have an interest in the fibula, too, of course."

When Greene mentioned her, Iris rose as though on cue and took Michael's arm. A curious expression passed over his face, and he stood very still. I felt suddenly quite ill. Michael had told Winton Greene all that he had told me, then. Or perhaps the story had been hatched between them before either of them had come to London. They seemed to know one another very well. Of course, they had associated with one another on the dig, but there was more than that. . . .

"I don't think I'll stay," I said in a clear voice. "I'm sorry to have intruded. Good night."

I opened the door and fled through a crowd that seemed, if possible, thicker than when I had come. In the far corner a group of middle-aged men in business suits were singing in what was intended to be harmony. The tousled-haired man with freckles opened the door for me, and suddenly I was standing alone in the silence of the long corridor.

I had nearly reached the elevator when Michael caught up with me. The carpet was so thick that I had not heard him, and I cried out as he touched my arm.

"I've got to talk to you tonight," he said, turning me to face him. The elevator door slid open, waited, and then slowly closed.

"You shouldn't leave the party," I said bitterly. "Mr. Greene expects you to stay, and I'm sure that your wife does too."

"My wife!" His face was so close to mine that I could not distinguish the features, but his eyes were bewildered. "Listen, Mandy," he said in a low voice. "Listen to me. I've only seen that woman once before in my life."

Chapter Four

I BELIEVED HIM. Not because it was logical or rational or even believable, but because I wanted to. We walked together through the small, quiet streets that lead into the heart of Mayfair, and went into a wine bar, a low-ceilinged relic with diamond-paned windows and dark oak tables and chairs burnished by the firelight. We were silent as we sipped port and ate the cheeses that we had chosen from a huge tray. And for the first time I think I realized that Van was really dead, and that it was possible for me to fall in love again.

"Who is she, then?" I said finally. We had not spoken since we had left the hotel, but it was accepted that I believed him when he said that Iris was not his wife.

"I don't know." His eyes met mine. "A friend of Greene's. An actress." He shrugged.

"You can't mean that when you came into that room with Greene and found her and me there that you had no idea that he had already introduced her to me as your wife."

"I didn't know that you'd already been introduced," Michael said. "I didn't even know that you were going to be there. But he had threatened me a few minutes before that. Veiled threats. I don't know the man very well, but I would imagine that that would be his technique."

"But what would he hope to accomplish by doing anything so absurd?" I demanded.

Michael shrugged. "He wants to discredit me," he said. "Look here, Mandy, I'd better tell you what I know about this and let you make your own decision about whether or not to believe me."

For a moment he did not speak again. There were small red candles on our table, and the light flickered across his face, weaving a pattern of shadows from his forehead to his chin. And I realized in that moment that for the first time in a long time I was content. That I could take the moment for what it was. And I was conscious again of my own newfound awareness to what was around me: the warmth of the fire, the muted conversations of the people at other tables, the rich taste of the wine in my mouth. I was no longer locked inside myself as I had been for so long. And whatever happened I owed that to this man, this stranger who was not a stranger.

"I first met Greene in Milan," he said. "Van took me to see him after I had agreed to be involved with the dig. I wasn't impressed by him. I think I told you that last night. Neither was your—was Van. But, as I said before, he had to have the money and the ordinary sources had been closed to him."

"By his father."

"Yes. After talking to him tonight I'm even more certain of that. Although, of course, he wouldn't admit to having prejudiced museums and antiquarian societies against Van. But the point is, I met Greene for the first time there. It was obvious that he knew very little about the scientific side of what we wanted to do. He was living in a big hotel in Milan. And he seemed to be surrounded by the kind of people you saw in his rooms tonight. I met Iris at that time, too. She's a curious sullen sort of person unless she's talking about her acting career. We had dinner with Greene once, and he brought her along. I had the impression that she was living with him."

I nodded. I, too, had had the impression that she was an intimate of Winton Greene's. She had seemed vague in her references to Michael, but her attitude toward Greene, and his toward her, from the moment he had told her to make me a drink and talk to me, had been that of two people who know one another very well.

"Iris never turned up at the dig," Michael said. "To tell the truth, I had forgotten that she existed until tonight. All right. Now, I told you last night the essential things that happened in relation to the dig. The discovery of the fibula. I don't need to go over that. Its disappearance. Reappearance."

I shook my head. I remembered everything he had told me.

"Well," he went on, "I decided to come to London. Because I was convinced that your—that Van's death was not an accident. That was my only motive. That and the desire to have him vindicated. He believed in something. The theory concerning the development of an Etruscan artistic development independent of Greek influence was his theory. The fibula proves that he was correct. And that has to be known. You understand that, don't you?"

I laughed. "You forget how long I've lived with archaeologists," I said. "I know precisely how important that is."

"All right. So I came hoping to see you. Because I thought that you should be the first person to know. And then the next day—today—I made an appointment to see your father-in-law. And just after I made that appointment, I received a call from Winton Greene. I didn't know he was in London. I'd had no contact with him since Van's death. I haven't the slightest idea how he happened to know that I was here in England. But he called me at my hotel——"

"What hotel?" I interrupted. I had almost lost sight of this man once and had felt the desperation that came of not knowing where to find him. I did not intend to let that happen again.

"Brown's. I always stay there when I'm in London. At all events, Greene said that he wanted to talk to me. He was casual about it. As though we were old friends. But we weren't old friends and I knew that he wanted something. I had no intention of talking to him until I'd talked to Mr. Harcourt."

"I want to tell you something before you go on," I said quickly. "I know that my father-in-law made it appear that I'd told him everything that you'd told me the night before—about the fibula, the way Van died. Your suspicions about that, I mean. But that was simply one of his tricks. To make you think that he had the advantage. I didn't even tell him that you'd been to see me."

Michael looked puzzled. "But he appeared to know——" he began.

"Anthony got me to admit that it was you," I said, flushing. "And Anthony found out that we'd talked about the fibula. But I didn't tell him that it had turned up again."

Michael cradled the wineglass in his hands, looking down into the port as though he saw something reflected there. "I see," he said thoughtfully. "That makes a difference."

"Did you tell them everything that you told me?" I asked him.

"Practically everything. I didn't give them any indication where the fibula was now. I'd intended to do that. But I found, after I'd actually met Van's father, that there was something—something about him that I didn't trust. No, that isn't it exactly. But he's—"

"He's obsessed," I said flatly. "Obsessed with the idea that his theories are the only correct theories. He treats Etruscan art as though he were the only expert whose opinions mattered."

Michael laughed softly. "In a sense, you know, he's right. He's considered the final judge even by his colleagues. Even by me. I've read all his books. All the articles. Until Van came along with this idea, I'd more or less taken his father's professional opinion as the final word."

"But he ought to be willing to consider new evidence," I insisted. "And the fact that he isn't indicates that his judgment can't be trusted any longer."

"I suppose that's what I meant by saying that I was reluctant to be completely frank with him," Michael said slowly. He took the bottle and poured more wine into my glass. "I told him that I thought that there was something in Van's find that ought to be considered. He took a rather condescending attitude to that, implied that my professional opinion was questionable. And then he followed up by saying that the whole thing was a moot question anyway, since the fibula had apparently been melted down in the fire."

"You didn't go on to tell him that it had been found?"

"I went only far enough to suggest that the dig that Van started ought to continue to be explored. Under competent direction. I told him that as far as I knew Greene was still in the process of finding someone to take Van's place. After all, that dig is of no use to a man like Greene unless he has experts working on it."

"How did he react to that?"

"He said that there was no evidence that that particular dig was worth continuing with. He challenged me to cite any other finds that came out of it. And, of course, I couldn't do that. The fibula was the only absolutely definite proof of Van's theory that we found. I suppose it was at that point that I realized that he was a long way from taking a detached attitude toward the place."

"So you didn't mention the fibula further at all?"

"I approached it obliquely. I asked him if he'd be willing to suspend judgment if something could be produced from that dig that indicated that his son's ideas were true. That was when he said that he understood from the Italian authorities that the dig had been closed. His face was completely expressionless when he said that. But Anthony was another matter. He was smiling like a Cheshire cat. And it occurred to me that perhaps your father-in-law hadn't been satisfied with simply seeing to it that no legitimate organization would back the dig, but that he'd been responsible for the Italian government taking the attitude that they were taking. And if the man is willing to go that far to see that his theories are unchallenged, then I'm not about to disclose the whereabouts of that fibula. I'd come to him with some idea about his seeing to it that it was purchased by a museum. All that needs happen as things stand now is that another private individual who likes to own these things for his own personal satisfaction buys it from the estate, and it could disappear again permanently."

"You think he wants that to happen?"

"He's an old man. His work is almost over. I suppose that he doesn't want to have the whole professional structure that he's created overturned. That's the kindest thing I can say for his attitude. I may be wrong, but I think that had I told him where the fibula was, he would have turned heaven and earth over for the chance of putting it out of sight forever."

I knew instinctively that he was right. The obsessiveness with which Van's father had refused to be challenged during the past few years sometimes had seemed to me to approach madness.

"Did you tell him that you suspected that Van hadn't died accidentally?" I demanded.

Michael shook his head. "It was quite clear that he'd had enough of my ideas after the first half hour. He would have laughed me out of the house if I had suggested that. As it was he implied that he thought that I was bent on blackmail. He more or less asked me to leave."

Michael flushed. Or perhaps it was the fire casting its reflection on his face. However that might be, he was tense. And worried. But whether about Mr. Harcourt's reception or Winton Greene I did not know. I hoped that he would tell me, but I had determined that if he did not do so voluntarily, I would not pry.

"Let's walk." He rose and held out his hand. "When you come to know me better you'll recognize that one of the signs that I'm under a certain amount of tension is that I can't sit still."

Then he was taking it for granted that I would know him better. Out on the cool night-gray street I walked the narrow streets with him in silence, tasting the full relief of the knowledge that Iris was nothing to him. He would explain all that soon. But whether he did or not, I believed him.

We crossed Park Lane to the park. Under a street light I glanced at my watch and saw it was nearly one. There was little traffic. A few private cars. A few speeding taxis. The lumbering red buses had long since disappeared. The park was full of parkness and the smell of flowers. His hand touched mine and our fingers intertwined. The night breeze caressed my face. And I was very happy.

"Do you want to hear about how I happened to see Winton Greene tonight?" Michael asked me. We had reached the edge of the park and the Serpentine lay glittering between the trees in the distance. There was an iron-railed fence in front of us. With a low laugh Michael offered me his arms, and I let him lift me up until I could clamber over the top. I fell to the ground on the other side, and in a moment he was beside me. For a moment we lay on our backs in the soft grass staring up through the billowing trees to a sky made milk-white by moonlight.

We walked after that, keeping to the edge of the water, past the deserted boathouse across from the Lido, turning left onto the bridge. We stood there with our elbows on the stone, looking down toward the Edgeware Road hidden from us by trees. And we were awkward with one another for the first time. We had, perhaps, gone too far too fast.

"Tell me about Winton Greene," I said softly.

"That's not much to tell, actually." His head was bowed as he looked down over the parapet at the water. "I was annoyed when I left your father-in-law. Annoyed and frustrated. I'd come to London to put a few things out in the open, and I suppose that I'd convinced myself that once he heard what I had to say, he'd take over. Demand an investigation of Van's death. Go to Italy. Examine the fibula. Use his influence. I suppose it was stupid of me to expect so much. There's no reason why he should believe me. But I had thought that he would at least have an open mind enough. . . ."

He shrugged his shoulders. Laughed. "You'll find that among other bad habits I have the tendency to demand that other people react the way I think they should in any given situation," he said. "All right. Forget your father-in-law for the moment. So I was angry, and I decided to take the stoppers all out at once and go to Greene. Demand to know how he knew I was in London. Tell him what I suspected. That I thought that he was responsible for the fibula getting into private hands. That I suspected him of financing the dig in the first place so that he could smuggle artifacts of value into private hands for large sums. I meant to tell him that I thought that he had gone to Van with this sort of proposition and that Van had said no. That that was all right until the fibula was actually found. He was content to argue with Van until then. But then it looked as though your husband was going to make sure that that thing got to a museum. And Greene couldn't afford to see that much potential profit going down the drain. I meant to tell him that I suspected that he was implicated in your husband's death."

Now he had said outright what I had suspected he believed. The only thing that he had not said was, I knew, on his mind. I was certain that he did not believe that Greene was the only person implicated.

"Do you believe," I said in a low voice, "that the reason Anthony was sent out to look around the dig was to report back to his father any finds that might have helped Van substantiate his theory."

Michael was silent for a moment. His face was very pale in the moonlight. "I've considered that possibility," he said.

"Then have you gone further than that?" I demanded. "Have you considered that Van's father might have been willing to work with Greene to get that fibula out of public view once it was found?"

Michael turned to look at me. "I suppose I have," he said.

"It would be easy for Van's father to find out who

the men are who want to collect unrecognized Etruscan remains and keep them out of public hands," I said. "Not that he has ever dealt with any of those people. I'm not implying that. But——"

"How do we know?" Michael said in a low voice. "On the surface, I'll grant you, he's a completely scrupulous type, the top-rung professional. But he's always had a good deal of money to work with. His private collection alone must be worth millions. How do we know that that money all came from grants and the compensation he gets from museums and the royalties of his books?"

"We don't," I murmured. "We don't."

"He could keep his own fingers clean in getting that fibula into private hands," Michael went on. His mouth was so close to mine that I could feel his breath on my cheek. "Particularly if he'd done this sort of thing before. I imagine that Greene's been a front man a good many times. And he has contacts, too. Together it would have been easy for them to have hidden that fibula out of the way. They were only unfortunate in that the man they sold it to happened to die too soon, that his estate had to be settled the way it was. And particularly unfortunate that I happened to be called in as I was."

"But you don't think that he had anything to do with his own son's death?"

I spoke in a whisper, but the sound carried on the night air. Seemed to echo back at me from the surface of the water below. Michael did not answer. Again he took my hand, and we crossed the bridge in silence and cut across the grass in the direction of Queen Anne's Gate.

"What did you actually say to Greene when you saw him?" I asked finally. This was the question I had not wanted to ask. I had wanted him to tell me voluntarily.

And now, although I knew that he would answer me, I was afraid that he might lie—or that I might sense, rightly or wrongly, that he was lying.

"I didn't get much of a chance to ask him anything," Michael said slowly. It was dark on the grass, with the trees overhead shutting out the sky. I looked at him, but I could not see his face. "Obviously he was surprised to see me. He tried to put me off as far as business was concerned—as he did you. But I insisted, and as soon as we were alone he took the initiative. He's very adept at that."

"Did he tell you why he was in London? Why he wanted to see you?"

"I can't repeat what he said exactly," Michael told me. "But the gist of it was that if I had come here to make any trouble for him, I'd better forget it."

"You mean that he threatened you?"

"Not at first. At first he made a point of the fact that the dig was closed and that he intended to forget the whole thing. He said that it had been a dead loss to him, and when I reminded him that he'd promised your husband that he was providing the backing for the dig with no profit in mind, he shrugged his shoulders."

"Did you tell him that the fibula had turned up?"

"Yes. I didn't see why I shouldn't. Because if what I think is true, he was responsible for selling it in the first place. He'd been in Italy until last week. He would have known that the man he sold it to had died. Known that the estate would be in the process of being settled. I didn't mention the man's name on the off chance that he'd acted through a third party and never known who the buyer actually was. That sort of thing often happens. But I did make it clear that I was interested in doing everything that I could to see that it was brought to the attention of the proper archaeological authorities."

"How did he react to that?"

"He was angry. But he didn't lose control. I don't expect he ever loses control. That was the point when he went out of the room for a minute. To get some legal papers that I might be interested in. At least that was what he said. And while he was out of the room, apparently you appeared. I think that must have thrown him for a bit of a loss. Or perhaps it didn't. God knows how much he knows about my activities since I've been in London. He may have been having me followed, for all I know. That would be the sort of thing he'd be likely to do. Obviously it's dangerous for him if I stir up any sort of police action in the matter of Van's death. I've been trying to think it out, and what I expect he'll try to do is discredit me. And not simply by insinuation. He's too heavy-handed for that. That's why I think he's about to blackmail me. That bit about Iris being my wife is a case in point."

"I don't see . . ." I began.

The lights of Knightsbridge were ahead of us. I could hear the roar of an occasional car. It occurred to me that we would have to climb out of the park as we had climbed in. But that scarcely infringed on my consciousness. What Michael was saying was too important.

"He must have seen you just before he came back in to see me," Michael went on. "Because he told me that you had come. I wanted to go straight out to see you. But he stood in front of the door. Made it clear that I'd leave the room when he wanted me to, and not before. I'm not going to try to tell you everything he said. But he was obviously sure of himself. Cocky. It was as though he'd just been given a chance to play a trump card."

We reached a gate. Beyond lay the street and beyond that the town houses and apartment buildings. White-faced. Most of the windows dark. Even in the park I had not felt as alone with him. And I realized that although I had been afraid when he began that I would not believe what he was telling me, once he had begun to describe his interview with Winton Greene I had suspended disbelief.

"He asked me, among other things," Michael said, turning to face me, "how much you knew about me. I don't think he listened to what I said. He wanted to make his point. And that seemed to be that unless I stopped prying into affairs that didn't concern me, I might find myself painted a very different color. Thinking back on it, he took a long time to say a very little. He was carrying an envelope in his hand, and he said that there were ways of making black seem white. I didn't know what he was talking about until he gave me the envelope and I saw the copy of the marriage license inside. A license with my name on it. That was when he suggested that we'd better join you and—and my wife in the other room."

Michael put his hands on my shoulders. "You do believe me, don't you?" he said in a low voice. "Greene's cooked up this thing about my being married to her to discredit me in your eyes. A man like him would find it easy enough to have papers forged to prove that it was so. He wouldn't let it get into the hands of a court, probably. But I'm pretty certain that he thinks he can scare me off. And if he can convince you . . ."

I moved toward him, and for a moment I was in his arms. And I knew that that was answer enough.

It was nearly two thirty in the morning when I got back to Kew and Grove House. After we had managed to get out of the park, Michael and I had tried to find a cab, walking arm in arm along the deserted sidewalks.

I suppose that I was tired, but I scarcely noticed. I took off my shoes and our laughter brushed the silence of the streets, until finally a cab came into sight and we hailed it with the glee of children. And in the darkness of the back seat, I had nestled in his arms.

Michael left me at the foot of the hill because I asked him to. There seemed to be no lights on in the house except for one in the hall, but I did not want to risk a possible confrontation. I let myself in with my latchkey, stealthily, feeling like a schoolgirl. In the gilt-edged mirror over the table in the hall I saw myself, hair tangled, my cheeks stained with dirt where I had fallen in my first attempt to negotiate the fence of the park. My dress was torn as well, but that did not matter. Nothing mattered except Michael. Somewhere at the back of my mind was the realization that I should somehow feel guilty. Because of Van. But surely there was nothing wrong with feeling as much alive as I did. In the morning it might seem wrong. But not now. Not now.

I had started up the stairs, still carrying my shoes, when I became aware of a movement to my right. Turning, I saw figures standing in the doorway of the drawing room. There were no lights in the room behind them, only the jagged flames of a nearly burned-out fire in the fireplace. Everything inside me seemd to freeze. I stood motionless, one hand clutching the railing, and saw that it was Anthony and his father. And another man. They moved forward together, and I saw that the third figure was that of Winton Greene.

"You're very late, Amanda." Van's father was standing at the foot of the stairs now, staring up at me. His face was drawn and haggard.

"We've been waiting for you for hours," Anthony said angrily. "Where the devil have you been?"

"Walking," I said. My voice was hoarse. All the

vitality that I had felt a moment before had drained away, and I felt curiously vulnerable. I could not bear to have anyone else intrude on my consciousness at this moment. Particularly not a stranger. Greene was still standing by the doorway to the drawing room. In the shadows. I could not see his face, but I imagined that he was smiling. "I'm going to bed," I said.

"We were worried about you, my dear," Van's father said. "Anthony has been out for over an hour searching the grounds for you. We were very much afraid that something unfortunate had happened to you."

Slowly anger rose in me. "I'm twenty years old," I said. "Not a child. I've never been in the habit of reporting my whereabouts to you. I'm sorry, but I don't want to talk about it."

"You've never behaved like this before," Anthony said.

"What I do is my affair," I cried.

"We have a certain responsibility," the old man said. "I think that Van would want—"

"Don't talk to me about what Van would have wanted," I said. "He wouldn't have wanted that man in this house. I'm certain of that."

Anthony and the old man stared at me, silent. My reaction had startled them. That was clear. They had known how to deal with me all these months since Van's death. Now my very existence constituted a problem to them.

"I think, perhaps, I was in part at fault for Amanda being so late," Winton Greene began, his voice like silk.

"Mrs. Harcourt," I said. "My name is Mrs. Van Harcourt."

It was an absurd reaction, I suppose. Never before in my life had I returned rudeness with rudeness. But the sound of my first name on his lips repulsed me. I wanted no intimacy with him, real or symbolic.

"Of course." He bowed, his hair gleaming silver in the dusk. "I must apologize. I hope that someday we can be on a first-name basis with one another, but you're quite right. It's too soon now. As I was saying . . ." He walked to the foot of the stairs and joined Van's father. He moved, I noticed, like a cat, with great economy of motion, balancing himself slightly on his toes.

"As I was saying," he went on, "I feel that I ought to apologize. Not only for being here at this time of night, but for not realizing the urgency of your—your need to see Michael. They wanted to talk alone, you see," he said, turning first to Anthony and then to Van's father. "Perhaps I told you that. They wanted to talk alone, and I suggested that business would be better done the next day. I didn't realize until Mrs. Harcourt left, obviously upset, and when Michael followed her, that I should have offered them the facilities of my rooms."

Again that thin, unpleasant smile. And I knew, suddenly, that he was threatening me by demonstrating how quickly and effectively he could respond to my having interfered. I found myself literally shaking with rage. What right had this man to intrude himself in my affairs? I had not wanted anything from him. I had gone to his hotel to find Michael. That was all. And he had not only had the audacity to lie to me about Michael's personal life, he had assumed the role of Michael's mentor. The business talk with him. All the rest of it. The implication had clearly been that he was closely involved with Michael's affairs. Whereas, I now knew, the reverse was true. And now he was trying to do the same thing to me, to insinuate himself into my life. If I did not do something right away, he would be at this house every day, talking to me, assuming privileges he had no right to assume. God only knew what excuse he had used to come here at this time of night. But I could tell from his attitude to Van's father that they had had a chance to talk to one another, and that they were already acting as compatriots, at least as far as I was concerned.

"Listen to me, Mr. Greene," I said slowly. I turned full around so that I was staring directly down at him, and began descending the stairs. "I did not come to your hotel tonight to talk to you. As far as I am concerned I would be quite delighted never to set eyes on you again."

I broke off as I saw him glance at my father-in-law. A look of understanding passed between them, almost as though they had anticipated this reaction on my part, this reaction of hostility.

"I came to find Michael," I said. "That was all. And I found him. And I've talked to him. And whatever role you had to play in my life is over."

"My dear." I was close enough to him now so that he could touch me, but when he put out his hand I drew away, pressing myself against the railing of the stairs. We were all standing in the light now, knotted together about the foot of the stairs. I could see their faces, and I realized suddenly that they could also see mine. See the dirt-stained cheeks. Worse than that, see the glow that despite my anger I still felt. Or perhaps it did not show in my eyes. Although Michael had said that it did, as we had stood in the moonlight at the foot of the hill, and he had held my face in his hands.

"My dear," Winton Greene repeated. "I realize that it must have come as a great shock to you to realize that Michael was married. Oh, don't protest. I could see the minute I introduced you to Iris, that you didn't know about her existence. It's not as though Michael hadn't pulled this sort of trick before, you know. He——"

"What's come over you, Mandy?" It was the first time Anthony had spoken since I had come into the house, and his voice was rough. "You've got a good deal of common sense. At least you used to have. And yet the first charlatan who comes along, hoping to pick up a few quick bucks with a bit of blackmail, bowls you over as though you were some sex-starved spinster."

"Shut up!" I cried. "It's not true. If there's any blackmail involved here, it's this man who's responsible, not Michael." I pointed at Greene, and in the same moment saw him smile. He was sure of himself. Too sure. I loathed him.

"What do you know about this Mr. Kyd?" Van's father said stiffly. He was tired; his face was thin, but what extra flesh there was hung in loose folds about his mouth and eyes. "What's made it so easy for him to prejudice you against Mr. Greene? Against all of us?"

"Why does it matter so much to you how I feel about Michael?" I said, keeping my voice low. I had come close to losing my self-control a moment ago, and I determined not to do it again. "What do you know about Mr. Greene, for that matter? Why did he come here tonight?"

"I think she ought to know what you've told us," Anthony said in a harsh voice. "Perhaps she'd change her mind about a few things if she'd heard what we have."

"I'm not likely to believe anything that this man says," I told him. "He's told me one lie already. I don't want to listen to any others. Besides, I'm tired. I'm going to bed."

"Wait." Some of the silk was gone from Winton Greene's voice. "Before you leave us you can at least explain what you just said. I'm not aware of having told you any lies, Mrs. Harcourt."

"You said that Michael was married," I countered. "To that woman in your hotel room."

"To Iris? But, my dear, that is the truth. There are papers. . . ."

I laughed. "Michael said that you'd go to any length to make it appear that he's something he isn't. I'm not surprised that you should claim to have papers. But I take it that a man like yourself wouldn't find it too difficult to have papers forged."

"Amanda!" Van's father stiffened. "I'm afraid that I can't have you insult our guest in that manner."

"What made you so ready to believe what he's told you?" I demanded. "Considering the fact that his only claim to introducing himself into this house lies in the fact that he financed Van in an enterprise of which you disapproved, I'm amazed to find you so ready to defend him."

"I think, perhaps," the old man said, "you ought to hear what he *has* told us, Amanda. You said a moment ago that it shouldn't matter to us what your attitude is toward this situation, but—"

"As far as I'm concerned," I interrupted him, "there *is* no situation, as you call it."

"I'm afraid that you're wrong about that," Mr. Harcourt said stiffly. "We're all about to become involved in something rather distasteful. It was not Mr. Greene who informed me of that, but rather your friend, Mr. Kyd. I think that as a family we should stand together. Under the circumstances it would be extremely unwise for you to continue to see Mr. Kyd, and for that reason, if for no other, I would like to have you hear what Mr. Greene has to say."

I could have ignored his request. Gone up the stairs. I would not sleep. I was sure of that. But at least I could avoid the unpleasantness of having to hear anything that Winton Greene had to say. I very nearly made that decision. And then it occurred to me that tomorrow, when I saw Michael, I should give him whatever information I could. It would be to his advantage to know what sort of attack Winton Greene was making on him. For that reason alone, I should hear what he had to say.

"All right," I said in a low voice. "What is it?"

"We can't talk here," Anthony said in an irritated voice. "We've made enough of a disturbance as it is. This isn't the sort of thing we want the servants to hear."

"I don't suppose it is," I said sharply. "Very well. We can go into my sitting room, if you like. No," I went on, as Anthony took my arm and started toward the drawing room. "I don't like it there. You know that."

I was aware that Anthony and his father exchanged glances as they followed me into the sitting room. And I knew that I must, in fact, be bewildering them by my show of independence. For the year that Van and I were married, and the year that had passed since his death, I had behaved like a guest in the house. When I had been alone I had made my own decisions, but when Van's father was with me I had initiated nothing. Now I knew that I could never go back to that sort of life. The best thing for me to do, no doubt, was to begin to search for a flat of my own tomorrow. It was incredible, in a sense, that I had not done so long since.

I suppose I had insisted that we sit in this room because it was my own. I was hostess here. Switching on the lights. Taking my seat in the corner. Folding my hands in my lap and waiting for them to begin. I knew that I was making it quite clear even by the way I moved that I had no intention of listening any longer than absolutely necessary.

Winton Greene lost none of his equanimity in the face of my rudeness, however. He sat on the sofa facing me, Van's father beside him. Anthony stood by the window, glowering at me.

"Very well," I said. "Why *did* you come here tonight, Mr. Greene?"

He smiled. The lights disclosed no signs of weariness on his handsome face. "I must plead guilty to coming here because of you, my dear. I intended to meet your father-in-law formally, of course. And you. But simply because I wanted to extend my sympathies on your husband's tragic death. No other reason. But I certainly would not have come at this hour of the night—as I understand, incidentally, that Michael came last night—unless I had not been concerned about you."

"What could possibly have caused you any concern?" I said sharply.

"I think, Amanda," Mr. Harcourt said, "that there is no need to challenge Mr. Greene. I suggested that you should hear what he has to say, and since you have agreed, it might be best simply to listen."

There had been a time when I could have taken that sort of rebuke with a shrug of my shoulders. My father-in-law's insistence on treating me like a child had annoyed me since Van and I had come to live in this house. When Van was alive, we had at least been able to laugh together when we were alone about the old man's oddities. But now I was aware of an intense irritation, which it was almost impossible to repress.

"No, that's quite all right," Winton Greene said. "Believe me, Mrs. Harcourt, I can understand why, under the circumstances, it is distasteful to you to think that I had the audacity to become concerned about you. The fact is, nevertheless, that I was concerned. I have a good many reasons to believe that young Kyd is not the best influence in the world. I waited an hour before I called your father-in-law to see if you had reached home safely, and when I discovered that you had not yet arrived, I suggested to him that I might come and talk to him, and he was kind enough to invite me."

With an effort, I kept myself from making any response. Instead I reached for a cigarette, not so much because I wanted one as because I knew that Van's father hated to see me smoke. Winton Greene leaned forward, flicking a silver lighter, but I ignored the gesture and struck a match.

"I can see," he went on easily, "that you're impatient that I say what I have to say and leave. I can understand that. You must be exhausted." His eyes deliberately fastened on the dirt on my dress. He smiled. "My association with your husband was a very rewarding one," he went on. "He was a fine person, and although Mr. Harcourt may feel that I was unwise to invest my money as I did, I had great faith in Van's professional opinions."

The old man's face tightened, and Winton Greene went on hurriedly. "We had the best sort of relationship," he said, "no matter what Mr. Kyd may have told you. Your brother-in-law can testify to that. But the point that I want to make is that I early on had reason to mistrust Michael's motives for involving himself in the enterprise."

"Why?" I threw the question at him.

"For a good many reasons which I cannot go into at this time. His attitude toward a young actress friend of mine from America was not good. I felt that he took advantage of her, as he took advantage of everyone."

"If you're speaking about Iris," I said, "it seems to

me that she's the sort of young woman who is perfectly able to take care of herself."

"I can see," Winton Greene said, smiling, "that you are very prone to make snap judgments, my dear. Like a good many young people, I'm afraid. Like Iris, for example, when she agreed to marry him."

"They are not married," I said defiantly.

"Because Michael said that they were not?" Winton Green shrugged his shoulders. "All right. We won't belabor that point. More important is the fact that Michael took your husband in. He encouraged him to believe what he wanted to believe, and when the fibula was found, I have good reason to think that he deliberately represented it as something that it was not."

"That's easy to say," I retorted, "now that it has disappeared."

"I don't believe that Michael has any intention of letting it 'disappear' much longer," Greene said. "That, in essence, was what I was talking about before you returned."

"Kyd is going to blackmail my father with that thing," Anthony said. He still stood by the window, shoulders slumped, his hands thrust in his pockets. His dark eyes were watchful. "Did he tell you that it was worth a quarter of a million pounds?"

Something seemed to freeze inside me. I had made the mistake of answering Anthony's questions before. I did not intend to make the same mistake again.

"Did he talk to you about that fibula, Amanda?" Van's father's voice made the question a command. "Did he—"

The shrilling of the telephone interrupted him. Muttering impatiently, Anthony went to answer it, and then turned to Winton Greene. "It's for you," he said.

The tall man rose with a murmured apology and

walked slowly across the room. He said hello and then listened. His face was turned toward us, and the suave ubanity of his expression was replaced by one of concern. "I see," he said. And then: "I'll be there right away."

Putting down the receiver, he turned toward the door leading to the hall. "I'm sorry," he said, "but I have to leave immediately. That was Michael's wife. He's with her. Threatening her. She's locked herself in my bedroom at the hotel. She says he's going to kill her."

It was so absurd that I nearly laughed. But they were taking it seriously, all of them—Mr. Harcourt rising stiffly from the sofa, his hand outstretched, Anthony going to Winton Greene and putting a hand on his arm. It was as though I had suddenly been transfered to a stage where a farce was being performed. And whether I wanted it or not, I was one of the characters.

"You'll never get a cab at this time of night in Kew," Anthony was saying. "You'd better use our car."

"I'll call down to the chauffeur," Mr. Harcourt said, starting out of the room.

"No matter what form of transportation you take," I interrupted, "it's going to be over a half hour before you get to wherever you're going, and—"

"She's at the Hilton," Winton Greene snapped. He had taken his coat out of the closet and was struggling into it. If he was acting, he was doing a good job of it. His face was ashen. "Michael must have gone directly back there after he left you."

Anthony had taken his father by the arm and was urging him not to call the chauffeur. "I'll drive him," he said. "It will save time. Come along, Greene."

"I was about to say," I went on, "that if you're really worried about—about that woman, you ought to call the Hilton desk and have them send up the hotel detective. Or, presumably, if she *is* locked in the bedroom, she can call them herself. Or perhaps you'd rather not have the authorities involved."

But they were not listening to me. Or, if they were, they did not want to hear what I was saying. The door was already open and Winton Greene and Anthony had disappeared.

"You'd do best to keep out of this, Amanda," Mr. Harcourt said harshly, shutting the door behind him. "This is Mr. Greene's affair. If he doesn't think it best to bring the hotel authorities into this, I think you ought to abide by his decision."

His shoulders slumped, he walked past me and into his office. The door shutting behind him was a rebuke. But none of that mattered to me. After my first incredulity, the truth had come to me. This had to be part of the plot to discredit Michael. Not content with the implications that he had made about Michael's motivation for involving himself with the dig, not content with his efforts to make me disbelieve Michael's personal integrity, Winton Greene had decided to go one step further and attempt to involve Michael in criminal action. And it would be so easy for him to succeed if he wanted to. Iris could have been on that phone. I had no doubt that she had been. Later she could say that Michael had tried to kill her. Together she and Greene could ruin him. And why? It had something to do with the fibula. I had no doubt of that. Something to do with the fibula and a quarter of a million pounds. Men had been willing to murder for less than that.

The silence of the house seemed to be pressing in on me. I could not simply stand here, doing nothing. I had to warn Michael. Let him know what was happening. I picked up the telephone in the hall. As long as my father-in-law was in his office, I could make the call safely, since his telephone was on another line. I fumbled through the pages of the telephone directory, and rang the number of Brown's Hotel.

The desk clerk was polite but distant. "I'm sorry, madam," he said, "but Mr. Kyd expressly requested that he not be disturbed."

"But he's there?" I demanded. "In his room?"

"He said that he was retiring for the night, madam," the clerk said stiffly, obviously reacting unfavorably to the note of panic in my voice.

I stood there clenching the receiver in my hand, aware of a sense of relief spreading over me. There would be no way that Winton Greene could involve him with the law, then, not if he was in his room at another hotel. It was a perfect alibi. And that, of course, would be what it would be considered. The relief faded. Simply because someone had told a desk clerk that he was going to his room would not prove that that was in fact what he had done. Michael could have left again. Out the back way, or, for that matter, through the lobby, without anyone noticing him. That would be what Greene would claim. I had to be able to prove that Michael had in fact been in his room at Brown's at the time that Iris was claiming that he was trying to murder her.

"Is there any message, madam?" the desk clerk said.

"No," I told him. "I must speak to Mr. Kyd personally. It's an emergency."

"I'm very sorry," he repeated. "But Mr. Kyd specifically directed that under no circumstances was he to be disturbed. He made that very clear."

"But something has happened," I began. "Listen. You can do this, at least. Ring him up yourself and tell him that Mrs. Harcourt must speak to him. He'll want to talk to me. He—"

"I'm sorry, madam," he repeated like an automaton. "If there is any message—"

I slammed down the receiver. I could not blame the man for following instructions to the letter, but I had to see Michael. See him there at the hotel. Prove his alibi beyond question. And yet how could I possibly do that? I did not know the number of his room. Even if I were to go there, the desk clerk would not give it to me. Michael was as isolated from contact as though I had no idea where he was. The only thing that I could possibly do was to prove that he was not at the Hilton. And the only way to do that was to go there. To be able to refute anything that Winton Greene and Anthony and Iris might later decide to claim.

I rifled through the pages of the telephone book again, aware suddenly of an exhaustion behind my anxiety that threatened to overcome me. Anthony had been right when he had said that it would be impossible to hail a cab in this part of town at this hour of the morning. But I could call for one. I dialed the number and gave my address. Urged them to hurry. And then I went out of the house and sat on the steps, pressing my forehead against my knees like a child. I wanted to think, but my thoughts were a jumble. There was so much about all this that I did not understand. Images rose and faded in my mind. Unrelated images. Michael's face the night before when I had called Van's name coming up these same steps and he had turned. Winton Greene coming toward me across the crowded hotel room. Smiling. Iris' laconic voice coming out of the depths of the armchair as I had sat staring out across the lights of London at night. But the recurrent image was of Michael when he had taken me in his arms by the gate in Kensington Gardens. And that was not an image, really, but a mass of sensation. Primarily that of happiness. I had felt happy when he had held

105

me close to him. Happier than I had felt in a long, long time.

Suddenly the cab was drawing up in the circular drive. I ran to open the door, suddenly afraid that Van's father would try to stop me. I did not tell the driver to hurry. Probably my tone of voice when I gave him the name of the hotel told him that. I leaned back against the seat and closed my eyes, aware of the speed which only the open country would allow. I did not open them again until I could hear the night sounds of London.

Within minutes we were rounding the corner by Marble Arch, and the hotel towered into sight. There was the same doorman, or perhaps a different one. My eyes were too blurry with weariness to notice as he opened the cab door and helped me onto the deserted pavement. There were no hordes of Americans crowding the lobby now. The clock on the wall told me that it was after four. The sofas bore the impressions of many people who had sat there during the past twenty-four hours, and there was no music coming from the adjoining bar. Everything seemed in limbo.

For a terrifying moment I did not think that I could remember the number of Winton Greene's suite. Only when I was in the elevator with the door closing in front of me did I remember. There was that terrifying moment of suspense as the elevator shot up twenty-eight floors without any real sense of motion. And then the doors were opening again soundlessly, and I was again in that plush-carpeted corridor, walking quickly, looking anxiously at the numbers on the doors, hoping that I was not too late. Although too late for what I could not have said, since not for a single moment had I believed that Iris's life was in danger.

I came to the door, and it was partially open. I did not bother to knock. The party was obviously over, the large sitting room empty except for disheveled furniture and heaped ashtrays and dirty glasses. For a moment I had the sensation that I was the only person to have survived some sort of universal disaster. And then I heard the sound of muted voices coming from behind the closed door of the room where, earlier, Michael and Winton Greene had closeted themselves.

I went toward the door with the full intention of pressing myself against it and listening, but before I had reached it, it was flung open and Winton Greene stood facing me, his eyes narrowed with suspicion. Behind him stood Anthony.

I came toward them, but they pushed me back, literally, their hands on my arms, and closed the door behind them. And for the first time I was afraid.

"What's happened?" I demanded. "What is it?"

"I'm going to call the police," Anthony said through clenched teeth. "Get out of my way. Why did you come here, Mandy? Get out before you're involved."

"Is it Iris?" I demanded. "It can't be Iris!"

"Why not? You knew that she called me?" Of the two, Winton Greene seemed least disturbed. Whatever emotions were besetting him, it was obvious to me that he was still watching me. Gauging my reactions.

"But you said that Michael—"

"He's been here and gone," Anthony said. He had picked up the telephone.

"Don't call anyone yet," I begged him. "Whatever's happened isn't Michael's fault. He's in his hotel."

"He may be now," Anthony said between clenched teeth, beginning to dial. "But he was here not too long ago. Let her go, Winton. Let her look, if that's going to be the only thing that persuades her."

I heard him dialing. It was like some kind of terrible background music as I pushed open the door. It was a bedroom, done in green and pink with a white and gilt

French provincial bureau and bedside stand and a reproduction of Gauguin's "The White Horse" over the king-sized bed. But the pink of the bedspread was stained with blood. And the green of the carpet was a vivid background for the naked body of a woman whose breasts and face were so mutilated by knife wounds that it was impossible to know whether or not it was indeed Iris.

Chapter Five

It must have been the sleeping pills that Mr. Harcourt forced me to take after Anthony had brought me back to Grove House that produced the nightmares about Iris. The sight of her mutilated body had left me cold with shock, but once I was asleep the numbness disappeared and I suffered for her as though I had cared whether she lived or died. I saw her alive and struggling. Saw the terror in her eyes as she tried to escape. Saw, as though I were the murderer, the blood pour out of one wound and then another, until her eyes becamed glazed and she sank to the floor at my feet. But suddenly it was no longer I who stood looking down at her, but Michael. I saw triumph in his face, a face that swelled until I could see only his mouth distorted in a smile, and I woke screaming.

Bernice was with me. Her face replaced Michael's as I opened my eyes to reality. She was bending over me, her thick glasses enlarging her eyes until they, too, seemed like an extension of my nightmare. Her hands were on my shoulders and she was shaking me.

"It's all right," she said impatiently. "You were only dreaming."

But it was not all right. There was no long moment of recall. I remembered instantly everything that had happened the night before.

"Go away," I said. "Go away and leave me alone."

My mouth was thick with the aftereffects of the pills I had taken, and my head ached. Worse than that was the gray mist of depression and anxiey which seemed to be pressing me down against the bed more forcibly than her hands. The curtains of my bedroom windows had been drawn back, and outside it was raining once more, a hard, steady downpour which beat against the glass.

"You're in no condition to be by yourself," Bernice snapped. "After what you apparently saw last night, your nerves are bound to be shaken."

I had pictured it all in the nightmare and that had been terrible enough, but now her words brought the image of Iris's blood-spattered body back to me with the clarity of something that was far from being a dream, something that had really happened, and nausea overcame me.

"You're as white as those sheets," Bernice said, crossing the room out of my line of vision. She had always prided herself on being the perfect secretary, and she had now, temporarily, apparently determined to be the perfect nurse. "You're in no fit condition to be by yourself," she threw back at me.

"What do you know about what happened last night?" I demanded weakly.

"As much as you do," her disembodied voice retorted. "Probably more." I heard the clatter of china. "Mr. Harcourt told me all about it. And he told me to stay with you this morning. Which is precisely what I'm going to do. He said that you weren't to get out of bed."

"I'll do as I like," I told her, pulling myself up on the pillow.

"No, you won't." Bernice appeared beside the bed carrying a silver tray covered with dishes, which she planted firmly on my lap. "Now, eat your breakfast. You'll need all the strength you can get."

She took the silver cover off one dish and I stared, revolted, at scrambled eggs and bacon. Breakfast for me was usually the meal I enjoyed most, but this morning even the idea of food revolted me.

"Take it away," I told her. "Take it away or I'll push it onto the floor. No, I'll keep the tea. But take the rest of it!"

Bernice had always known when to stop arguing. She lifted the tray and set it on the table by the window, and I waited, staring at my angry, flushed face in the mirror opposite the bed, while she poured the tea and brought it to me.

"You may not want to eat," she said. "I can't say I blame you, if you want the truth. But you're going to stay in bed."

"Only as long as I want to," I murmured. The tea was strong and very hot, and it cleared my head. I had to get rid of her as soon as possible. Call Michael. Find out what had happened. Or warn him. Perhaps it was not too late to warn him.

"If you're thinking of getting in touch with Michael Kyd, forget it," Bernice said, as though she had read my mind. She was wearing a slate-gray skirt and sagging gray sweater, and her hair was pulled untidily behind her neck. She stood looking down at me, her arms akimbo.

"Why?" It occurred to me that I could at least find out what she knew before I got rid of her. "Why shouldn't I 'get in touch' with him, as you put it, if I want to?"

"Because he's probably already in custody," she said triumphantly. "There was a story about that woman's murder on the radio this morning. They say that the police are talking to everyone who can give them any information about what happened." She sneered. "I don't imagine they'll have to go much further than Mr. Kyd."

So it had been reported on the radio already. It made me want to scream from sheer frustration. While I had been asleep a lot had happened. Things that perhaps need never have happened if I had not agreed to take those sleeping pills.

"Why shouldn't they interview a good many other people?" I demanded.

She stared at me myopically. "Because he was married to—to that woman," she said.

"A good many people are married to other people," I retorted. "They don't all necessarily commit murder."

She knew that I was mocking her, and she hated it. But because, for all her intelligence, Bernice had no sense of humor, she did not know what to do about it.

"Even supposing that Michael was really married to her," I continued, kicking the blanket and sheet off my legs.

"But they were married. There's no mistake about that."

"What makes you so certain? Is that what it said on the radio?"

"No—no," she stammered, flushing.

"Did they even mention her by name?"

"They said a young woman had been stabbed to death, but—"

"So how do you know that she was Michael's wife?"

"Because Anthony told me that she was," Bernice said triumphantly.

I laughed. It was a good thing to make her talk in this way. She was telling me things that she might possibly refuse to tell me under other circumstances. Obviously Anthony, and probably my father-in-law, wanted to keep me a temporary prisoner in this room.

Heaven only knew how uncommunicative they had cautioned her to be. Besides, the interrogation technique made me think more clearly. I swung my legs out of the bed.

"All right," I said, "even assuming that she was his wife, what makes you think that the police won't bother to go any further than to interview Michael?"

She shrugged. The gray light of the rain-filled day was cruel to her. "You know that as well as I do," she said. "You were there in the room last night when the call came from that—that girl. When she said that Michael was trying to break into the room to kill her."

"Who told you that she called?"

"Anthony," she flared.

"And did Anthony actually hear what she told Greene? Actually hear the words? Was he listening in on another phone?"

"You know that he wasn't," she shrilled.

"Then how does Anthony know that she was on the other end of the line?"

"He—he said that he took the call."

"Are you implying that Anthony knew her? Knew her well enough to identify her voice? The police might be interested in that. I must remember to mention it when I talk to them."

"You're twisting everything!" she cried. "He knew that it was her because Winton Greene said that it was her."

I laughed again, and standing, pulled my nightgown over my head. Perhaps I guessed that it would embarrass Bernice to see me naked. She flushed a deep red and turned away. I knew that she would give a good deal to leave the room. With a little persistence I might be able to make her do just that, despite her orders. It would be a good deal easier than forcing her out bodily. My wrap was lying at the foot of the bed. I did not bother to put it on.

"You've met Greene, haven't you?" I said in a low voice.

She had gone to the window, her back still toward me, and was fidgeting with the blind.

"I've met him," she said in a low voice.

"Under what circumstances?"

"At a party." She was so upset that she turned, but after one horrified look at me, pinned her eyes on the further wall. "I told you that yesterday," she said desperately.

I pretended to think for a moment. "Tell me, Bernice," I said, "did meeting Mr. Greene at that party have anything to do with your deciding subsequently to rifle my father-in-law's desk?"

All the color drained from her face. Smiling, I went into the adjoining bathroom and turned on the faucets full force. I kept them on while I took a bath, letting the extra water pour out the drain at the top. It was time to let Bernice think, to let the full implications of what I had said sink in. She had obviously decided to ally herself with Anthony and Mr. Harcourt. There had never been any question about her doing otherwise, probably. But she was my enemy. I knew that. Mine and Michael's. It would do no good to let her think that I was harmless. I got out of the bath and wrapped myself in a towel. She was still standing where I had left her, near the window, with the rain dashing against the glass behind her.

"I wasn't rifling his desk," she said in a low voice. She had had time to collect herself, and she was calm. Dangerously calm.

"I don't really care what you were doing," I said lightly. "I'm not really very interested in you at this point, Bernice." I went to the dresser and took underwear out of a drawer. Slipped it on. She was so intent on what I was saying now that she forgot to look away.

"Tell me, Bernice," I said, "how did you come to meet Winton Greene in the first place?"

"I said that I met him at a party in London," she said flatly. "A party given by a friend—someone you don't know."

"That's too coincidental," I said, keeping a smile on my lips. "I find it difficult to believe you. Tell me one other thing, Bernice. Do you know what a fibula is?"

The thick glass of her spectacles magnified the look of horror in her black eyes. "Don't bother to dress to go out," she said in a voice that seemed torn from her throat.

I straightened the thin tweed skirt around my hips and pulled a pink cashmere sweater over my head.

"I asked you," I repeated, "if you know what a fibula is."

"It's a clasp," she said in an expressionless voice, as though she were repeating a lesson. "A clasp that the Etruscans used as an ornament or a—or a pin."

I ran a brush through my hair. "You know a good deal about Etruscan artifacts, don't you, Bernice?" I said, still keeping my voice low. "And you knew a good deal about Van's dig, didn't you? Probably more than I did. Anthony must have written you about it. You and he were still very good friends then, weren't you? He wrote to you a lot, didn't he?"

I had never played this unfairly with a woman before, traded so freely on weaknesses. But this had to be done. I could see her face in the mirror. She looked as though I had struck her. But there was more than that. There was viciousness, too. She disliked me even more than I disliked her. I would do well not to forget that. I did not wait for her to respond.

"It was really Winton Greene's dig, wasn't it?" I

115

continued conversationally, leaning toward the mirror to draw eyeliner on my eyes. I had not used makeup for a year, and I had forgotten the effect. "You must have heard about Greene through Anthony," I said. "He wasn't a complete unknown when you met him the other day at a—what did you say it was?—a party in London?"

"I don't know what you're trying to prove with all these questions," Bernice said shrilly. "If you ask me, I don't think you know what you're trying to prove, either. You don't want to admit that you were taken in by someone who's in all probability a blackmailer and a murderer. You're just lashing out in any direction at all. You—"

"Didn't Anthony write you about Iris, too?" I said sharply. "I notice that ever since this conversation began, you've called her that woman or that girl, as though you didn't know her name, and yet from what Greene told me last night, I take it that Iris was a rather close friend of his there. And I don't think Anthony would have failed to mention that in his letters."

"My God, you'd blacken anyone to protect a man you scarcely know, wouldn't you?" she demanded. "Have you gone absolutely mad?"

"I asked you if you knew about Iris," I persisted, whipping her with the words.

"Yes. No. I can't remember."

"That's surprising," I said softly, starting toward the door, pulling the suit jacket over my shoulders, taking my handbag from the desk. "Presumably Greene is unmarried, and I always thought that you had a particularly good eye for sizing up the competition."

To say that to a woman as plain as Bernice was vicious. I did it deliberately. I wanted her to hate me.

Whatever happened in the immediate future, it was obvious that there were to be no halfway measures.

I think that she was numbed by the virulence of my attack. The door was locked, but when I put out my hand and demanded the key she gave it to me, walking toward me like an automaton. When I left her she was standing motionless in the middle of the bedroom, her face rigid with loathing.

The back door was locked. Standing there in the shadows of the narrow brown-walled hallway, I was suddenly overcome with a sense of humiliation. What was I doing? What had my life become that I must creep down the servants' stairs of someone else's house to pull futilely at a locked door to gain the simple privilege of walking into open countryside. I saw a flicker of white to my left, and turning, saw one of the maids watching me. I did not know her name. The young girls who worked in this silent, brooding house came and went with such frequency that it was useless to try to remember. Only the housekeeper-cook, a woman who had been with Mr. Harcourt since he was a young man, and an equally aged chauffeur were permanent, and they had been so long engulfed in the old man's life that they were like dour alter egos to him. They would do nothing for me. But this girl might.

"Who locked this door?" I demanded. "Or hasn't it been unlocked yet this morning?"

"I—I don't know, ma'am." There were no windows opening into this hall, and only a single unshaded bulb hanging from the high ceiling, and that unlit, so I could not see her face. But it was clear that she was frightened. The white of her apron seemed to be fading, and I knew that she was backing away from me toward the kitchen.

"Then where's the key?" I asked her in a softer voice. After all, this was no fault of hers.

"I—I don't know that either, ma'am."

She flitted to the left and disappeared. I forced myself to go after her. I had known this house for two years. There was no reason why its echoes should begin to frighten me now. There was nothing sinister about a locked door. My father-in-law wanted to keep me in the house. He and Anthony. It was as simple as that. And the way to deal with this locked door was simple, too. I would leave by the front. There was no way they could keep me from doing so.

I went down the narrow corridor, following it as it passed the door to the kitchen through which the maid had disappeared. No use asking questions there. The cook would tell me nothing. I forced myself to walk slowly. Danger had nothing to do with shadows. Iris had been killed in a luxurious enough light.

There was a green baize door at the end of the hall, and I pushed it open to disclose the light of the front corridor. There was the wide white door in front of me. Only a few steps and I would be outside. Outside in the rain. I had forgotten the rain. No matter, my raincoat was in the closet here to my right.

It was a mistake to have paused. When I emerged with the raincoat in hand, Anthony was standing there. His dark face was haggard, and his eyes were angry. Without speaking, he came toward me and took my arm. Before I could begin to struggle he had propelled me into his father's office and closed the door. Pushed me away from it. Positioned himself with his back against it.

It was the most claustrophobic room in the house. Empty, it would have disclosed its size, but now, full as it was with glass cases, Etruscan busts, desks, and file cabinets, it always gave me the feeling that I was in a deep pit, with the ornate Italian plastered ceiling acting as some sort of grotesque cover. The barred window through which I had looked the day before from the outside was the only window that had not been shutter-sealed. The air was close and dry, and had something in it of the smell of a not-very-well-cared-for-museum. I had always hated this room. Never before had I allowed myself to remain in it with the door closed.

"Let me go," I said to Anthony. "This is absurd. First Bernice. Now you."

"I have to ask you where you intend to go," Anthony said. His voice was breathless, as though he had been running, and he ran his hand restlessly back over his slicked down hair. "Don't play games with me, Mandy."

"I'm not playing games," I spat at him. "I want to leave this house. Where I intend to go is none of your concern."

"My father made it my concern," Anthony said. "He has to be gone for the morning and he told me that you were to stay here until he had a chance to talk to you."

"I'll be back later," I said. "He can talk to me then."

"He wants to see you before you make a fool of yourself trying to see Michael," Anthony replied. "That's where you were going, isn't it? To see him."

"What if I am?"

"It won't do you any good." Anthony's voice rose. "Kyd is probably in custody by this time."

"If he is, it's because a few people have told lies," I said, trying to hide the desperation that the thought of Michael in prison made me feel. "If I can't find Michael, I'll go to the police. I have a good many things that I want to tell them. About your friend, Mr. Greene. About your father. About you, for that matter."

I pushed past him and tried to wrench the knob out of his hand, but he flung me back. He was a little man, not much taller than I, but he had a man's strength.

"That's just what we want to keep you from doing," he said angrily. "You'll turn this into a public affair if you aren't watched. I don't know what's the matter with you, Mandy. You used to have a good deal more common sense than most women, but now . . ."

"But now you've discovered that I have a sense of justice as well," I mocked him. "How unfortunate for you."

"Listen." Anthony came toward me, his hands reaching out for my shoulders. I remembered his hands on Bernice's shoulders the day before, remembered the way his fingers had been digging into her arm. He would not touch me in that way. No man would.

"If you put your hands on me again I'll scream," I said in a low voice. "If you don't believe me, try."

He believed me. Lowering his arms, he backed toward the door. "Listen," he said again. "Try to keep from being hysterical, for God's sake. I haven't slept at all for plugging up all the loopholes. Greene helped. There's nothing, as it stands now, to connect any of us with Iris's death."

I stared at him incredulously. "Not even Winton Greene?" I said. "Considering that she was killed in his hotel room, I find that a bit difficult to believe. Or did you move the body?"

"When I said 'any of us,' I meant us as Harcourts. Greene is involved, of course, to the extent that it was his room, that he knew Iris, that she called him here to say that Michael was going to kill her."

"Here? I thought we weren't involved."

"I mean that we're not directly involved. Greene happened to be here when Iris called. If we're interviewed we can say that he received a call here. And that's the end of it."

"It's just the beginning," I said in a low voice. "Because I'm going to tell them a good many things that I imagine Winton Greene won't bother to mention. About the necessity of checking on the validity of any so-called marriage license that turns up. About investigating Winton Greene's associates when he was backing that dig in Milan. About why he really happened to come to London just now in the first place."

"You'll be a fool if you do that," Anthony said in a tight voice. He reached out for me again, and then, remembering my threat, dropped his arms. He had always been a man who touched other people. It was one of the reasons that I found him so repugnant. His hands were attached to his tongue. He found it difficult to talk without touching you. Or, at least, touching me.

"I have to make my own decisions," I said.

"Don't you feel any gratitude at all?" There was that narrow, foxy look about his face now that I hated. As long as other people reacted the way Anthony wanted them to, he was smooth as oil, but the moment they became recalcitrant he became wily, and if still thwarted, he turned nasty. We were still in the second stage, but I knew that we would soon be in the third. And I didn't want to have to go through it. There were so many things to do.

"I don't know what you're talking about," I said wearily. "You aren't suggesting, are you, that I have any reason to feel grateful to you?"

"I could." His voice rose. "I could remind you of all the things that I've done for you since Van died. But, actually, I was talking about my father. He's given you a home. He's . . ."

That was a sore point with me, and Anthony knew it. I had had no money of my own when I had married

Van. Neither, for that matter, had Van. The digs that he had worked on before the one in Italy had been his father's projects. He had received a salary like everyone else, but never very much. Money hadn't concerned Van. We had lived here because it was convenient for his father to have him close by. I had always hated it, but I had known how much his work meant to my husband. After his death—that was another matter. I should have left. Inertia had kept me here. That and the fact that the old man had wanted me to stay. And, perhaps, because there was, at least, more of Van here in this house than any other place.

"I don't know what gratitude has to do with what happened last night," I said. "A woman was murdered. You're not suggesting, are you, that your father wants to keep the police from finding out who really killed her?"

"I'm saying that there's no reason for him to be publicly involved," Anthony said angrily. He had reached the third stage now. His eyes had narrowed. The viciousness in him seemed to fill the heavy, dust-laden air. And yet he was trying to maintain his self-control. He knew from past experience that I reacted badly to him when he was in this mood.

"We need to talk, Mandy," he said in a calmer voice. "Let's at least talk before you do anything—anything you may regret later."

It could have been a threat. I did not care. Or perhaps he was sincerely eager to make me see this affair as he saw it. There was one other possibility. His father had told him to keep me in this house. Perhaps all this was simply part of a stalling process to keep me here until my father-in-law came back.

"I'm not going to talk to you now," I said steadily, spacing my words as though I were explaining something to a child. "You can't keep me here by force. If you try, there'll be more trouble than you think. Because, in the end, although you may not believe it, Anthony, I'm going to act according to my own principles. Not yours. Not those of Van's father's. So stop acting like a fool, and let me out of this room."

Something in my voice must have let him know that I was not simply mouthing words because he stood aside, but with his hand still on the knob of the closed door.

"Just one thing before you go, Mandy." He was obviously playing his last card—gentleness. Understanding. Both attitudes were foreign to him. He was like an amateur actor playing a new role. If the circumstances had been less serious, I would have laughed.

"I know how difficult this last year has been for you," he said. "With Van gone. I know how much you—you loved him. You've been lonely. It's only natural that a man like Kyd, someone who worked with Van, could touch you. Don't think I don't understand. I want to see you happy, Mandy. God knows I've tried to tell you often enough that I love you, that I want to take care of you. Let me—"

"Don't!" I said sharply, reaching out for the doorknob, tearing the back of his fingers with my nails. "Don't say it!"

There was blood on his fingers. I saw that. Saw the look on his face as he let me open the door. And for the first time I was afraid of another human being. Really afraid.

I was in the hallway when the phone rang. I took the receiver just before Anthony's hands closed over it. "Hello," I said, my heart suddenly beginning to pound. It had to be Michael! I was certain somehow that it was Michael.

And then I heard his voice, sounding strangely far away. "Amanda," he said. "I haven't much time. Can you meet me? Right away. In the Egyptian section at the British Museum. I—"

That was all I heard before Anthony took the phone away from me. But it was enough. I left him shouting "Hello's" into it and ran out the front door into the spring rain.

Michael was there before me. I found him staring down into a stone sarcophagus in which the brown, wizened remains of a mummy lay curled on its side like a child asleep. There were not many people in the long, high-ceilinged room. I had often come here in the past with Van or alone, and, particularly in winter, it had its charm, warm and dry, with hours to be lost moving from case to case, projecting oneself back into a more exotic past. But today, with the spring rain drying on my face, it smelled of dust and inertia. I had been too long among unchanging things.

"You came quickly," Michael said. He was smiling, but his face was pale. I had not forgotten the lines of his face, the intensity of his eyes, but I was aware of him with a fresh acuteness.

"I was afraid that they'd keep you from coming somehow," he said. "When your brother-in-law took the telephone away from you, I was certain that he'd managed to hear what I'd said. About wanting to meet you here."

"Did you talk to him?"

Michael shook his head. "I hung up while he was shouting 'Hello.' He didn't want you to come, did he?"

"No."

"I can understand that. They think that I killed her, you know."

"What does it matter what they think?" I demanded.

"I'm talking about the police," Michael said in a low voice.

When Bernice had told me that, I had been able to discount it. And I had only half believed Anthony. But now I felt as though everything inside me were suspended. My pulse. My breath. My thoughts. A woman came to stand beside us, bending close over the printed card that described the exhibit. Michael took my arm and led me to the corner. There was a well-preserved mummy standing upright in a case, its linen wrappings aged to a pale brown. On the bound head some long-forgotten mortuary artist had painted the face of the woman whose body had been so tightly encased. I stared at the vividly colored features, the elongated black eyes, the thick, sensuous lips, waiting for my mind to begin to work again, waiting for the shock to pass.

"I had to tell you," Michael said in a low voice, "because I may be arrested as soon as I go back to my hotel. They let me go this morning after they'd questioned me, but I have an idea that after they've talked to Winton Greene again they may decide to bring charges."

"Don't go back," I said. My mouth was dry, and it was difficult to articulate. "Don't go back to the hotel."

"Amanda." His hand was still on my arm, and he turned me toward him. "You don't believe that I killed her, do you?"

"I knew it was a lie when she called," I said. "I knew it then."

"When who called?"

"Iris. Last night when I got back to the house Winton Greene was there. He tried to—tried to convince me that you weren't to be trusted."

"But what's all this about a call?" Michael's voice was sharp with tension.

"Didn't the police tell you?"

"They don't tell you anything. They ask questions and you answer them. All I really know about it is what I heard on the radio this morning. I know that she was murdered. Stabbed. I'm not even certain where it happened. The papers said at a hotel. I assume they mean the Hilton. But I didn't go back there after I took you home, and we were away from Greene's room for a couple of hours. She might have gone to another hotel. To wherever she was staying. Unless she was staying with Greene."

It was obvious that he was so caught up in his own self-questioning that he found it a relief to say the words aloud. I knew what it must have been like, answering the questions of men who assumed that you knew more than you did. He deserved some answers now.

"Greene had been talking to me for about half an hour," I said, "when the phone rang. Anthony answered it. Said it was for Greene. And Greene told us that it was Iris. That she'd locked herself in his bedroom at the hotel. According to him, she claimed that you were trying to murder her."

Michael's eyes narrowed. "So that's what's supposed to have happened," he said in a low voice. "Greene really means business, doesn't he? He knows that I've located that fibula. And he's here to see if he can get money out of your father-in-law to keep the thing in private hands. Out of sight. With a fat commission for him. That has to be the reason he's trying to discredit me. Or perhaps its more complicated than that."

It was clear that he was scarcely aware of me for the moment. Jamming his fists into the pockets of his slacks, he walked over to a display case and stared down into it absently. Following him, I too stared at an assortment of stone scarabaeuses arching their beetle backs on the blue base of the case. "The scarabaeus," the display card announced, "was used in ancient Egypt as a talisman, ornament, and a symbol of the resurrection." Suddenly I felt as though I had spent my entire life looking at artifacts, reading signs, breathing the dead air of museums. I threw back my head and looked around me and had the sense that the glass cabinets, the sarcophaguses, the display cases, were all moving toward me.

"I've got to get out of here," I said, touching Michael's arm. "You'll think I'm mad, but I can't breathe."

He understood. That was one of the incredible things about him. We walked down the long flight of stone stairs to the central lobby, smiling. Until we saw the uniformed policeman standing at the bottom. For a moment we both stopped, suspended. But the man's eyes brushed past us, and when we reached the bottom of the stairs he did not speak.

I had intended that we go out onto the broad porch and talk. The British Museum is a depressing reminder of a Greek temple, particularly in the rain with its grimed exterior and its hoard of wet pigeons, but I have always liked to sit on one of the wooden benches that dot the interior of the porch and watch the people representing so obviously such a wealth of nationalities, listening to soft babble of scores of languages as the visitors pass into the museum. But today, for the first time in my life, I knew what it was to lose the freedom of choice as to where I would go, where sit, where stand. Obviously it was possible that by now the police might be looking for Michael for that last interview. If Winton Greene had told them all that he obviously wanted them to believe by now, they would want Michael. And that meant that until he had decided what to do, we would have to play the role of fugitives.

We ended up in the back booth of an Indian restaurant two blocks away from the museum. It was a faintly lighted place, the air thick with the smell of curry. But we were not visible from the street and we were able to sip our tea in absolute privacy, while at the other end of the table-crowded room two dark-skinned waiters sprawled in wicker-backed chairs and talked laconically as they waited for the luncheon crowd.

"I'm sorry, Michael said. "I know that I'm probably not communicating too well. But I've been trying to reason this thing out." He ran one hand through his already touseled hair. "That's why I holed up in my room at the hotel last night after I left you. That's what I did, you know. Because I had to have a chance to think. I've got to figure out exactly what Greene is trying to do to me and why. Up to last night I could believe that he was simply trying to descredit me in a mild way with your father-in-law. Now its obviously more serious. And yet I can't believe that he actually had that—that girl killed simply to implicate me with the police. There have to be a lot of things 1 don't know." He broke off, laughing wryly. "The ironic thing is that in the process of trying to think it out—to protect myself—I left myself without an alibi. I told the night clerk at the hotel that I wasn't to be disturbed for any reason, and—"

"I know," I said. "I called you—or tried to—after Greene and Anthony left the house. When they were on their way back to the Hilton."

He swore softly under his breath. "Then if I hadn't insisted that I didn't want any calls, I'd be clear," he said. "The desk clerk could testify that I was still in my room, and you—"

"I'll testify to that anyway," I said quickly. "I can tell the police that—"

I broke off, and he laughed again. "You can't testify to anything," he told me. "Even if I'd let you lie, the clerk would remember that he'd refused to ring me. It wouldn't even do any good if you said that you came to the hotel to see me. Even if you had, it wouldn't prove anything. There would have been time for me to have come back from the Hilton. It's only a few minutes' walk to Brown's. I could have killed Iris and been back there by the time you arrived. The police are going to realize that. No, the truth is, Mandy, that I haven't got an alibi for the time that really counts. The time that she was killed. And it will be easy for them to believe that I had motives. Either she was the wife who turned up and ruined my plans, or she wasn't. And that will mean to them that she was trying to blackmail me. Either way I lose, Mandy. Either way I lose.

Chapter Six

I SUPPOSE it was because he was disheartened that Michael let me convince him that he should not return to the hotel, at least not until I had had a chance to talk to the police. Somewhere, too, in the back of my mind there was the awareness that I had to convince Van's father that he was being used by Winton Greene, that unless he was careful he might find himself involved more intimately than he liked with murder. I did not mean to threaten him. I'm certain of that. I only wanted time, time for muddied water to clear. And meanwhile Michael must be free from the risk of arrest. We were not really evading the law; we didn't *know* that they actually wanted him now.

As for him, I think what he wanted most was a chance to be alone. He was uncertain about the wisdom of keeping away from the police, but for the moment he was willing to go along with my idea that he take a room at the country-house hotel near Grove House. We did not talk much during the ride out of London. When I left him there in front of the rambling brick building, shrouded in ivy, we had not made any definite plans to meet again.

It was still raining, a slow, steady rain that drew a gray veil over the front of the house. I hated to go inside. As the cab had woven its way up the narrow drive, I had seriously considered the possibility that I should go first to the police. But then there was the eventuality that they would not really be interested in anything that I could tell them. I could say that I had gone to Winton Greene's hotel the night before. That I had gone to find Michael. And that he had been there, closeted with Greene. But might not that only strengthen their suspicions that Michael was mixed up in something unsavory? I could tell them that I had met Iris, that Greene had said that she was Michael's wife, and that she had not denied it. Those were the facts. My own certainty that both she and Greene were lying would carry little weight. The police might assume that I was jealous, that I was interested in Michael myself. And that, after all, was true. But it would make them even more inclined to find my evidence worthless. They were probably not too much inclined to take into considerating a woman's intuitive convictions. And, after all, what else had I to tell them? I had seen Iris dead. But so had Anthony. So had Winton Greene. I had been present earlier when Iris had presumably made that call to Greene. But my evidence there would only be a further substantiation of what Greene wanted them to believe—that Iris had called because she was afraid that Michael was about to kill her.

Mr. Harcourt came first then, obviously. But it took effort for me to climb the stairs, to dredge the key out of my purse. I hated the thought of that heavy door swinging open and the musty museum smell that would engulf me. On rainy days the place was particularly ghostly, with that long drawing room to the right full of dead things.

But it was different that I had anticipated. For the first time it was different. The lights over the glass cases in the drawing room had not been turned on. And the door to the office on the left was open. Every light in the room was on. That was the first thing that struck me. And there was the sound of drawers slamming. And the atmosphere of immediacy.

Mr. Harcourt was there alone. He was kneeling on the floor in front of the bottom drawer of one of the file cabinets, leafing through the files with impatient fingers. The floor was strewn with papers, and the fluorescent lights, which were so rarely turned on, touched his white hair with silver.

"Did you find her?" he demanded in a harsh voice, not turning. "Was the bitch at her flat?"

I had never heard him swear before. He was always so elegant, so self-contained. I had come to hate him for that air of emotional impenetrability, but I hated this even more. I did not want to see this man lose control. Anthony was different. One expected violence. But violence was not part of this man's makeup.

He turned, still kneeling, and saw me. "So you've decided to come back," he said, pulling himself to his feet. Ordinarily he avoided circumstances in which the stiffness of his old body would become apparent. But now it was obvious that he was oblivious to his physical self. Everything in him was drawn inward. Taut. He faced me accusingly.

"Where have you been?" he demanded. "It would have seemed apparent that you shouldn't go off anywhere today without informing me. I told Bernice specifically—"

"To keep me in this house?" I demanded. "I'm not a child. Have you forgotten that?"

I would have expected, ordinarily, a sheet of ice to cover his response to my insolence. But he was obviously too disturbed for that. His face, as he came across the brightly lighted, littered room to meet me was twisted as though he had suffered a stroke.

"Where have you been?" he demanded again.

It was obvious that he had not talked either to

Anthony or Bernice about me. Obvious, too, that for some reason or other Bernice had left the house before he had returned. There was no need, therefore, to tell him anything about where I had been. No need to answer questions. For once I had the advantage.

"You thought that I was Anthony," I said calmly. "Where is he?"

The old man turned his eyes away from me and stared wearily around the littered room. "We're looking for something," he said. "Something important. Papers. Bernice knows where they are."

I watched him curiously. I had never seen him look so haggard. So much his age. Perhaps it was the strong overhead lights. Or perhaps he had suffered a shock. When had it happened? Last night he had seemed to take the news that Winton Greene had to return to his hotel to protect an unknown woman with equanimity. But I had not seen him since. Surely he could never have known Iris. Surely her death could have meant nothing to him. And certainly he was not upset because Michael was in danger of being charged. No, whatever had affected him so strongly was something else, something that had to do with his business affairs.

"Bernice was here a few hours ago," I said. "As always. Except that this time I woke up to find her in my room, serving me breakfast. I would have thought she had enough to do without playing maid."

My father-in-law's pale blue eyes sketched my face vaguely. "This morning," he said. "Oh, yes, this morning I was afraid that you would need someone with you when you woke. Anthony told me about what you saw. A murdered woman. Blood." His wrinkled face twisted in an expression of distaste. That was like him. More than that, in this particular moment it was significant. The murder itself meant little to him.

"Bernice didn't go out to try to find me, I hope," I

said sharply. "Perhaps she took your directions a little too literally." I could not prevent bitterness from creeping into my voice. "Perhaps she mistook her role for one of jailer."

He ignored the barb. "Usually," he said wearily, "she's an extremely conscientious young woman. I can't imagine where she's gone to. Without leaving any message, you know. Most unusual."

For the first time I noticed in his voice the querulousness of an old man. He was more vulnerable that I had ever seen him. And I knew that I should take advantage of that. I had not come back to this house to discuss his problems with his secretary. I had come to try to make him see that we could not jointly or separately support Winton Greene. I had to convince him of more than that. He must be as sympathetic to Michael as I. He must understand that the fibula was the key to finding out what had happened to Van—really happened—and perhaps to finding out what had happened to Iris.

I took off my raincoat and threw it over one of the chairs in the corridor. A maid appeared, the same frightened little thing I had seen that morning by the back door, and glanced into the office hesitantly.

"Bring some tea, please," I said. I had rarely given orders in this house. Perhaps it was time I gave more.

"Now," I said to Van's father, "I'll help you clean up this mess, and then I want to talk to you. I don't know what's been lost, but I'm certain that Bernice can find it for you when she comes back."

"Don't touch anything!" The old man's voice was shrill. I had bent, my hand outstretched toward a pile of letters and his involuntary movement was to put out his foot, poise it over my hand. There was so much implied violence in the move that I froze. For a moment neither of us moved. And then, rising, I went to sit down on the swivel chair by Anthony's desk. Two terra cotta masks leered down at me from the wall, but somehow the bright lights robbed them of their ominous quality.

"I don't want to interfere in your private affairs," I said quietly.

He could have said that he was sorry. Instead he simply lowered himself onto his own chair and stared past me as though he were waiting for me to go. His expression was as set as usual, as controlled. But he was breathing with some difficulty. The room was very quiet, and I could hear the sound of his breath being exhaled. Suddenly I was angry. What chance did I have of his even listening to what I had to say? His confidence had, for as long as I had known him, rested in Bernice and Anthony. He had never even trusted Van. Suddenly I wanted to destroy his trust, to prove to him that he had not judged well. It should be easy to make him wonder about Bernice now. At this moment, with important papers obviously missing, and her gone as well. I could never attack Anthony with any chance of success. Those bonds were too tight. But Bernice. . . .

"Did you know," I said, "that Bernice knew Winton Greene earlier? Before he came here?"

He stared at me under thick white eyebrows. "No, as a matter of fact I didn't know that. But, of course, Anthony did. It's probable that he introduced her."

He was interested in what I was getting at. Over his concern for what had been lost I could sense his interest. And his control was nearly completely regained. It had always been his way, ever since I had first known him, to make a point of how close Bernice and Anthony were. Obviously he wanted his younger son to marry her, although why he should I could never understand. Except that Bernice was the sort of dedicated woman who would work herself to the bone for him. Still, it was absurd to think that he wanted her for a daughter-in-law so that he could have an unpaid secretary. He had always been parsimonious except for his investment in Etruscan art, but that was carrying cheapness too far. No, there was something else about Bernice that recommended her. The old man had been increasingly cold to me ever since Anthony had begun to turn his attention from Bernice to me. Yes, it would be well worth my while to push him to a point of distrust. I searched my mind for something else that would be damaging to her. And suddenly I remembered. . . .

"I suppose," I said, "you depend a good deal on Bernice. She's been with you how many years?"

"Ten." He shot the word out, still staring at me with his head lowered. It was not like me to make small talk with him, nor like him to encourgage it from anyone. "As to depending on anyone—"

"I mean that you must trust her completely with your private affairs," I said smoothly. The little maid appeared in the doorway with a tea tray, and Mr. Harcourt told her brusquely to put it down on top of one of the file cabinets. As soon as she had hurried out of the room, he rose and shut the door. And switched off the overhead lights. And gained the advantage. I felt my confidence ebbing away. I had meant to pour the tea myself, as a gesture. Now he did it. Passed me a cup. Reminded me, as he so often had before, that I was a guest in his house. A guest surrounded by shadows.

"What are you getting at?" he said quietly. It was obvious that I could not afford to delay much longer. He was distracted, wanting to get back to his search. Perhaps after I had said what I had it say, he would not bother searching any longer.

"I mean," I said carefully, "that I realize that Bernice probably has keys to all your files, all your drawers. And so perhaps it doesn't matter. . . ."

"What doesn't matter?" His shoulders were squared now. Perhaps it was because the overhead lights were off, but he looked years younger. In a few minutes, if I were not careful, he would have completely regained the initiative.

"I saw her in this office yesterday morning," I said. "While you were still away."

"Why shouldn't you see her here? She's my secretary. You know that she's often here when I'm not. Probably she had letters to finish."

"She wasn't typing," I said, sipping my tea, hoping that, as so often in the past, my hands would not begin to shake. "She was kneeling in front of a desk. Your desk. Going through one of the drawers. The third drawer down on the right."

Involuntarily his gaze dropped to the drawer in question. His expression did not change. Like me, he brought the teacup to his lips. But he was startled. I was certain of it.

"Something about her attitude made me think that she was doing something—something she didn't want anyone else to know about," I said. "She was upset when she saw me watching her. She slammed the drawer shut and followed me out of the house. Talking about other things. Talking about Mr. Greene, in fact. How she had met him recently at a party, how he wanted to meet me. But I wondered. . . ." I took a deep breath. "I know it's probably absurd, but just now when I saw you searching for something, I wondered if perhaps Bernice might have it."

The old man leaned forward, setting his cup on the floor. It rattled noisily in its saucer. "Are you telling me the truth?" he demanded in a hoarse voice.

"What reason would I have to lie?" I said.

"You never liked her. You're like all women. Spiteful. Even if you were my son's wife I can say that. That's why you made yourself so attractive to Anthony. To spite her."

I stared at him incredulously. This was the kind of pettiness he never concerned himself with.

"I never encouraged anyone, as you put it," I said, rising. "I'm not interested in Anthony."

It was as though he had not heard me. "I don't know why you've felt you had to get back at Bernice," he said. "She's complained to me about you many times. It's rather cruel of you, you know. You have so much and she has so very little."

I wanted to cry out when he said that, I had so much! A dead husband. An existence that was like a living death in a two-thousand-year-old tomb. People around me who did not care whether I lived or died. I laughed, but it was not a real laugh.

"What I've told you about Bernice is no lie," I said stiffly. "If you don't care to believe me, that's your affair. But if you're missing a paper that was in that drawer, perhaps you ought to think twice about her— about her loyalty."

I meant to leave the room then. I had forgotten what it was I wanted from this man. He had always had the ability to upset me. But as I started past him, he reached out and touched my arm. Lightly.

"She'll turn up," he said in a low voice. Even the dim lights did not hide the lines in his face now. Outside, the rain dashed against the windows in a sudden fury.

I felt a renewal of confidence. "Are you certain," I said, "that there was nothing of yours that she could have taken to put to her own use?"

"She's been with me for ten years." It was a protest, but his voice was too weak for it to ring true.

"She knows Greene," I persisted. "Knew him before you met him last night. I don't trust that man. Neither did Van. He only allowed him to finance the dig in Italy because no one else would. But then, you know all about that. You know about that better than I."

"Van was a fool." I could scarcely hear the words. His hand fell back in his lap and he slumped forward in his chair. "A fool."

I waited. I wanted to leave this room. To open this door in front of me and be out of the musty smell of artifacts. I wanted to open the front door of the house and feel the fresh wet air against my face. But I had to stay. What this old man did, what he thought, what I could make him think, were important now.

"Who told you that Van didn't trust Greene?" he said finally. "Did he tell you that himself? You always told me that he didn't go into details about the dig in his letters to you. When I asked you, you always said . . ."

I remembered now. He and Anthony had always been after me to find out what Van had written. And I had been vague. And then Anthony had left for Italy.

"No," I said. "Van didn't tell me. But Michael Kyd did."

"Kyd!" He spat out the name. "What makes you think you can believe anything he says?"

"What makes you think you can trust Greene?" I countered.

"Kyd's a murderer," Mr. Harcourt said. Something of the old bite was back in his voice. "You ought to know that now. After last night."

"I don't know anything—" I began. And was interrupted by a knocking to the door. The young maid appeared, her face white.

"It's the police, sir," she said in a thin voice. "They want to talk to Mrs. Harcourt."

Her glance fled to me as though to safety.

"Tell them Mrs. Harcourt isn't able to talk to them now." With an obvious effort the old man pulled himself up from his chair. "Tell them she hasn't anything to say."

"Tell them I have a great deal to say," I announced, my voice clear, penetrating. Loud enough for anyone in the corridor to hear. "Tell them I want to talk to them now."

The police inspector was waiting in the drawing room. He was a squat square-headed man, wearing a black raincoat which glistened with moisture. When I offered to have someone take his coat, he shook his head and indicated the chair in which he wanted me to sit while he stood over me, fingering his plastic-covered hat restlessly.

I knew at once that I would be insane to give this man anything but the facts. He was no womanizer; his eyes never met mine, but darted about the room. He was not interested in interacting with me as a person; indeed, he was determined to prevent such interaction. But he would be interested in the quality of my mind, and he would trust me most if I showed myself as a pragmatist. There would be, I determined, no tears, no protestations. I had been crisp and blunt with my father-in-law because that was the only way I could keep control of the situation. Now I would play the same role for different reasons. What did it matter. In both cases I was interested in only one thing—turning away suspicion from Michael.

The inspector did not mention Michael directly, and for this I was glad. I had half expected him to ask me where Michael was, although I knew that since by this time he had only been gone from his hotel room for a few hours, there could have been no search for him. After all, from what he had said I gathered that the police had asked him not to leave London, but they had certainly not restricted him to his hotel.

The squat frogfaced man asked factual questions at first—my name, my address, my relationship with Mr. Harcourt. I had answered him for ten minutes before I fully realized that the other man huddled on one of the deep sofas was writing it all down. It did not make me as uneasy as I would have thought. What did upset me was the growing realization, as the interview progressed, that this man who was questioning me was a very clever man. Not the kind of man to be influenced by pure speculation. When he asked me about the events of the night before, I told him the truth in the exact factual sense. But did not add by way of intonation or implication that Greene might have lied about Iris being married to Michael.

"Mrs. Harcourt! Are you listening?"

The inspector's deep voice propelled me out of my reflections.

"Have you lived in this house long, Mrs. Harcourt?" the inspector went on in a dry voice.

"For two years. Ever since I was married."

His eyes bulged, I noticed, as he turned from me and looked around the room. The lights over the glass display cases were still off, and the static stone moldings of the Etruscan statues of warriors and dancers that stood in the corners seemed more awesome than usual. The gray velvet draperies were drawn on all of the long windows. Obviously none of the servants had been permitted in this room since the evening before. On any day it was an ominous room. Now it seemed to threaten actively. The weight of dead things . . . I heard myself sigh.

"It's a rather depressing house for a young woman like yourself to live in, isn't it?" the inspector said in a low voice. I glanced at him sharply. He had not asked that sort of question before, and I was not certain how to respond to it.

"One doesn't notice the museum atmosphere after a while," I lied. "Besides, I have my own sitting room."

As soon as I had said it, I realized that I should not have. He had, with one question, found out that, although related by marriage, I had kept myself separated from this household to some extent. And he would be persistent. He would find out that I had never been a real part of this household, and, no doubt, he would evaluate anything I told him about Van's father and Anthony and even Bernice in the light of this knowledge with the result that any evidence that I gave against them might be suspect.

He asked me about Van. Ordinary questions about where I had met him. And then, quite suddenly, he asked me about the dig. But not about Van's relationship to Greene. I had been waiting for that, determined that I would let him know that my husband had not wanted to accept money from Greene, that his association with the man did nothing to verify his or my confidence in Greene's character. Instead, he asked me about myself. Why I had not gone with Van to Italy. "You were not working," he said. "You were still recently married. Why, may I ask, did you prefer to stay here?"

I stumbled over the answer. I had not thought about that for such a long time. For a day or so the question of whether or not I should go to Italy had been a real crisis in Van's and my relationship. I was a fool, I suppose. But Etruscan artifacts seemed to preoccupy him to the extent that I was often not certain that he knew that I existed. He was not particularly fond of his father, and yet he would rather spend hours pouring over some new find with him, or a magazine article in one of the professional journals, than be with me. I had wanted to go to Italy, although I knew that I would probably not be able to contribute anything constructive to the dig. I was willing to try. Willing to work, to spend the entire day in a trench if it would bring us closer together. Because I had loved him. I loved him. And yet, in the end, he had made it clear that he wanted me to stay in London. I would be company for his father, he said. That had almost made me want to scream with laughter. I could come out to visit him after a few weeks. He was willing to say anything not to have me come, although he loved me. He loved me. But I would distract him. And he was, in many ways, as single-minded as his father. To prove his theory that a long-dead people had continued to practice their own culture after the date set by the experts! It seemed incredible to me, then and now, that he had been willing to risk what was between us for a single professional fillip.

But then Van had died, and I had put all the difficulties that had been between us out of my mind. I had tried to remember only the good times. And now in a second this little man with the froglike face had brought it all back to me.

"Van had to concentrate on his work," I said, trying to make my voice sound confident. "He wanted me to come, but I—I was afraid that I might be in the way."

I clenched my hands, suddenly aware that although I had used that as my excuse not to go to Italy with Van, that sometime I might have to face the possibility that I might simply have not wanted to be with him.

"I hope," he said, "that you understand, Mrs. Harcourt, that I am not prying into your private life merely on a whim. You are involved, to some extent, in this case, and as a consequence it is essential that I—"

He broke off as a knock sounded on the heavy oak of the door at the other end of the room. The policeman who had been taking notes unfolded himself from the depths of the sofa and went to answer it. I could not see who was on the other side, since even when he opened the door he kept it in my line of vision. I turned back to the inspector, bracing myself, waiting for the questions that I knew would come, and dreading them, now not so much because of what they might reveal to him as because of what they would reveal to me. I had never been much given to self-examination, and I did not want to begin. Particularly now.

But the inspector had lost interest in me. He waited patiently, his hands plunged into the pockets of his black raincoat, until the door was closed and the uniformed man came to speak to him. Quietly. Obviously not wanting me to hear. I stared at my fingers.

"Well, Mrs. Harcourt," the inspector said, "I think that I won't bother you anymore just at present."

"But," I protested, "I haven't had a chance to tell you—"

"I'm sure that we have a great deal more to talk about," he said, and it was as though he were talking to a child. My heart sank. I tried so hard to be businesslike, but, in the end, he had not taken me seriously.

"As it happens," he said, "someone wants urgently to speak to you. He is, it seems, quite unwilling to wait. I want to talk to your father-in-law, in any event. Perhaps afterward we can continue our little chat."

Our chat! Had he chosen such an incongruous word deliberately? I half rose.

"No," the inspector said. "Please don't leave. Why don't you talk to your friend here? I believe that Mr.

Harcourt is in his office. It might be best if I just stepped across the hall. . . ."

He billowed away from me into the shadows. I was so certain that it was Michael who had asked for me that I did not turn as the door opened. I was afraid. He should never have done this. Come here. We had agreed that he would wait for a while before deciding to make himself accessible to the police again. Coming here was a mistake. I wanted to see him, God knew, but not here. Not now.

And then I heard Anthony's voice. I turned in my chair and saw him and Bernice standing in the center of the room. Both of them wore raincoats, as the inspector had, with the water still glistening on them. Bernice's long hair had come untangled from her bun and was streaming about her thin face. She held her glasses in her hand, polishing them absently with a handkerchief.

"What do you think you're doing?" Anthony demanded. He came closer to me and I could see his eyes. Hard. Expressionless. Like his father's except that behind the hardness lay violent rage.

"I've been talking to the police," I said. My voice was hoarse and I cleared my throat. "At their request. Do you really think it was wise to interrupt us?"

Anthony did not answer for a moment. He was standing looking down at me now, and his face was grim. Why, I wondered frantically, did the fact that he wanted to talk to me carry enough weight with the inspector so that he would cut short an interview? It didn't make sense, not if I had gauged the little froglike man correctly. The Harcourts could influence a good many people, but surely not the police on a murder case.

"I've been talking to my father," Anthony said accusingly. "He told me—"

"You tried to make him think that I stole papers from him!" Bernice cried. "We want to know what you're trying to do."

There would have been a time when a confrontation like this would have made me numb inside. I would have run from the room, telling myself that I hated unpleasantness. But now I felt only an icy calm. I turned my back to them. Stared at the empty fireplace.

"You did take something, didn't you?" I said in a low voice. "Yesterday morning, when I surprised you going through his desk drawers. You're working for Winton Greene, aren't you, Bernice? Anthony knows it. I saw him with you the other morning in the office. When I was coming back to the house. I was by the window. He was angry. Threatening you. Isn't that true, Anthony? You thought you could depend on her, but you couldn't. Because, you see, she doesn't trust you anymore. None of us trusts anyone anymore."

I was not certain what I was talking about. I meant to imply that I knew more than I did. That much I am certain of. But beyond that I was not sure. I was playing all of this by ear. But the look in Anthony's face told me that somehow I had stumbled on something. He caught me by the arms. Lifted me from the chair.

"Leave her alone!" Bernice screamed. "You'll only make everything worse, you fool!"

Anthony's fingers were like steel. I had told him once that I would scream if he touched me. Scream as Bernice was screaming now. But, perhaps because she had lost control, I gritted my teeth. Let him begin to shake me as he had shaken her. Until the inspector's voice sounded from the direction of the doorway and I was suddenly released.

"Yes," he said quietly, but in a voice that carried the length of the long, shadowy room, "I think the lady is

right, Mr. Harcourt. Let her alone, or it may be worse
for all of you."

The inspector was an overwhelming man when he
wanted to be. His squat, waddling figure should have
been absurd, but it was not. He wore every vestige of
his power to advantage, but he wore it subtly. He came
to stand, legs apart, beside the cabinet that ran along
the west end of the long room. Stared at us in silence.
Turned and switched on the light over the cases. Stood
on the tips of his toes to look down at the relics under
the glass. It was as though he were tempting us to laugh
at him. But we stood waiting, like puppets. Anthony,
angry still. Bernice, sullen. But we waited. I cannot
speak for them, of course, but as for me I was in awe of
the little man, and at the same time grateful to him for
imposing some sort of order on threatening chaos.

He switched off the light over the cases finally, with a
puff of exhaled breath, and came toward us. "It is
necessary," he said, "for all of you to exercise self-control during the next few days. Perhaps the next few
months. Until this case is completely settled. And it
won't be settled until there is a conviction. Now, I
understand, of course, that you are under emotional
strains of various sorts. Murder rarely occurs in a
peaceful environment. But I have seen cases in which
one murder leads to two. And two to three." He
squinted at us quizzically. "You know the sort of thing
I mean?"

"I had no intention of hurting you, did I, Mandy?"
Anthony demanded, forcing a smile onto his sallow
face. "I'm sorry if you misunderstood what you saw, Inspector, although I can understand——"

"I don't think there is any need for us to discuss it,
Mr. Harcourt," the little man said. How he managed to
avoid sounding pompous, I don't know. But he simply

gave the impression that that was the end of the affair, that he had said what he wanted to say and that there would be no more comments. I saw Anthony open his mouth to protest and then change his mind. For a moment his eyes met those of Bernice. Or seemed to meet them, since she still had her glasses in her hand, polishing them. Her long face was expressionless.

"I would like to talk to you for a while, Mr. Harcourt," the inspector went on. "In this room, if you please. I had intended to speak to your father first. But it appears, unfortunately, that he is not feeling well at present."

"That's your doing," Bernice said under her breath. Her spectacles were on again, and she was staring at me with that particular intensity I had always associated with her.

"And so," the inspector was saying, "if you young ladies will leave us . . ." He escorted us to the door, waddling between us, his head scarcely coming to our shoulders. "Of course," he said, "I'll want to be talking to both of you again, you know. I'm terribly sorry to keep you tied up with this for so long, but it's essential you know, to talk to everyone. And it seemed most convenient to do it here. And although I know that it's thought traditionally that policeman talk to one witness and then to another and that sort of thing, I find it much more helpful to talk for a bit to one and then to another. Then back to the first and on to the third." He laughed, and I have never heard a sound that was less like real laughter. "Like putting pieces of a jigsaw puzzle together, you know," he said, beaming affably at first one of us and then the other.

We had reached the door, and he held it open for us. It was almost as though he were on the verge of clicking his heels together and bowing. If he had been an ordinary man, I would not have been able to keep myself from giggling. As it was, I felt only a twinge of anxiety. This was not the natural manner of the man. He was no fool. Why then had he insisted on chattering on so as we crossed the long room? To keep us from talking? To put us off our guard?

"Incidentally, Mrs. Harcourt." I was nearly out the door when he said it. "I wonder if you can tell me where I might find Mr. Michael Kyd this afternoon?"

Dead silence. Even though I had suspected him of using a technique, I was still not prepared. I fumbled for an answer. I had to lie, of course. But could I say that I had seen him earlier? Did they know? How much *did* they know?

"I thought perhaps you might have seen him this morning," the inspector went on pleasantly. "Did you?"

"Of course she did," Bernice sputtered. "Just look at her face. She was supposed to stay in the house this morning. Mr. Harcourt gave me distinct orders not to let her go out. And yet she insisted—"

She broke off, flushing. And then peered across the hall anxiously. But the office door was shut, and there was no one in evidence. I knew why she was upset, of course. It was not to her advantage to admit that she had collaborated with anyone to keep me in this house. Was this little man more subtle than I had thought? Had he been tricking not me, but her? I decided to answer him honestly in part.

"I saw him," I said. "At the British Museum. He told me that he had no intention of leaving London."

The little man's bulging eyes considered me. "That's good to know," he said slowly in that deep bullfrog voice. "I can assume, then, I imagine, that someone will let him know I'd like to see him here as soon as possible. Because he's part of the jigsaw, too, you know. Part of the jigsaw."

I suppose he was telling me to call Michael. But

there was nothing unpleasant about the way he did it. He was smiling as he went back into the drawing room and closed the door behind him, a broad, lipless smile. And I felt strangely reassured. If Michael was innocent—and he was—then this man would never think him guilty. There was no need for Michael to hide, to avoid the police. I would call him now and let him know. He could come here. I needed him here.

I had forgotten Bernice. But she was beside me, bending toward me, her face all but in mine. Staring at me with those repelling myopic eyes. And smiling unpleasantly.

"The little man is a fool, of course," she said. "But even he couldn't be fool enough to miss the obvious. You'd better drop Michael now, Mandy. Call him and tell him to come here, if you want to. Obviously you know where he is. But then drop him. Because even that idiot of a policeman knows he's guilty."

There was no purpose in talking to her. Anything that I said to her would be twisted and turned against me. As, I suppose, I had twisted her own actions—made them appear something which, perhaps, they were not. Perhaps she had been going through my father-in-law's desk drawers for a perfectly legitimate reason. I had obviously involved her in some sort of story. Worse than that, Anthony's anger with me had set the stage for the inspector to hear something that I was certain he was not meant to hear. He would know there was trouble in this house, now. It was something I could never have explained to him. I had no proof. Nor did he, yet. But he would have. And if the trouble here had anything to do with Iris's death, then I did not care whether or not Bernice felt that I had been unfair to her.

I started toward my sitting room and she came with me, taking two steps to my one, going on about

Michael with venom in her voice. I did not listen. My hand was on the porcelain knob. There was a telephone by my chair. I could lock the door against Bernice and Anthony and all the rest of them, and call him.

But when I opened the door I found Winton Greene sitting in my chair. I was startled. My fingers, when they touched my cheek, were cold. And beside me I heard Bernice draw her breath.

"My dear Amanda," he said, rising. "And Bernice. How good to see you both. I really should apologize, I know, Amanda, for being here. But the inspector asked me rather specifically to wait here, and I didn't want to contradict the little fellow. He *is* a perfect caricature, isn't he? Here. Do I have your chair? No. I'll move. You sit down. And I'll sit just here on the sofa with Bernice beside me."

He was so confident that I wanted to strike that smooth white face, to startle that assured expression from his pale blue eyes. He was handsome for a man in his fifties, and he knew it. He had the self-assurance of a wealthy man who is accustomed to things going his way. And there was a more immediate confidence. In this particular circumstance he felt certain that everything was going just as he wanted it to go. The last time I had seen him was when I had risen from kneeling beside the body of the girl called Iris. He had expressed concern for me then, as he had now. But he meant nothing by it. He did not care whether I was upset that he should be in my sitting room now any more than he had cared that I had seen a mutilated body.

Bernice sank down on the sofa where he had told her to, and folded her hands tightly in her lap. She stared up at him with a curious expression on her face. Whatever she was feeling, it made her features softer. Surely she could not imagine herself in love with this man? Or, even if she did, how could she believe that someone like Greene could ever care for her? Bernice had called the inspector a fool a few minutes ago. But she was the real fool, and fools are always dangerous.

"My dear," Greene was saying to me, "I understand that you find it—er, distasteful to have me here. I assure you that under ordinary circumstances I would never have intruded. Perhaps you think that I'm unsympathetic because of your—your confidence in Michael Kyd. But nothing could be further from the truth. I know what the man is, but still, I admire your—shall we call it loyalty? I intend to comment on it to the inspector. Although it's obvious that he's not a particularly sensitive man. I mean to say, I want to make him understand that simply because you chose to find Mr. Kyd more believable than myself, you are not necessarily Mr. Kyd's accomplice in murder."

I brushed past him and left the room, so furious that I did not trust myself to speak. Upstairs, locked in my bedroom, I called Michael. He had to be called to the public phone in the downstairs hall of the hotel, and while I waited for him I watched the rain toss the branches of the trees and saw the tiny fingers of fog touching the rooftops of the town below. I dreaded night. This night. Every night I had to spend alone in this house. Because I had been insane to think that I could escape so easily.

When I explained what had happened, Michael agreed to come to me. He was not as confident as I was about the inspector's virtues. But he had, he said, been thinking. And he knew that whatever happened, he could not hide for any length of time.

"Come here now," I said. "Just come. And hurry."

For a long time after I hung up the phone, I sat on the edge of my bed trying to think ahead, to plan, to make order out of the confusion that engulfed my mind. I don't know what sort of instinct finally told me to go back down to my sitting room. Perhaps it was no instinct, but simply the awareness that no matter how I disliked him, I could not avoid Winton Greene. My role in this affair was clearly to be that of catalyst or nothing. Greene was loose-tongued. Cleverly so, I was sure. But still loose-tongued. I could help Michael more by listening to what he had to say.

And that was why I went downstairs again, why I opened the door without pausing, why I found Bernice in Winton Greene's arms.

Chapter Seven

THERE WAS that moment before Winton Greene saw me. And the moment after. I swear I do not think his face changed by the shift of a single muscle. His arms were around Bernice, true, but both before and after he knew himself to be observed, he was smiling a sardonic smile. As though he were laughing at himself. Certainly he was amused by the situation. Bernice drew away from him with a little shriek, but it was clear that she was pleased that I had seen. Had she, I wondered, propelled herself into Winton Greene's reluctant arms, or had she been lured there? And if lured, why?

"It seems," the inspector's voice announced from behind me, "that you share my penchant for breaking in on awkward situations, Mrs. Harcourt. Although I'm certain that Mr. Greene and his—er, charming friend will forgive us."

It had been one thing, apparently, for Winton Greene to have realized that I had seen Bernice in his arms, and quite another to discover that the inspector had been a member of the audience as well. Greene's face turned a mottled red, and for a moment he looked his age. Beside him, her hand groping for his, Bernice tried to clutch his hand. Greene came toward the door, his mouth twisted in an ugly line.

"What you just saw," he said in a low voice, "was a result of a misunderstanding."

The inspector looked up at me, his bulging eyes wide with delight. "That sort of situation often *is* a result of a misunderstanding," he said. "Don't you agree, Mrs. Harcourt? The same might be said for marriage."

How like him. He had seemed to draw me in with him, to insinuate that it was the two of us against Greene, and then that remark about marriage. His question about why I had not joined Van in Italy for that last dig still rankled. I must not let myself forget that he was a clever man. I was glad of it. I trusted him because of his cleverness. But it would still be wise not to forget it if I did not want all the self-defense, so elaborately erected during the years, destroyed. If I did not want to risk the chance that when he was finished with me, I might have to look at myself squarely.

"Actually," the little man said, hunching his shoulders so that the collar of the black raincoat bunched around his stubby neck, "actually I was looking for the elder Mr. Harcourt. I had hoped, you see, that he would have recovered from his indisposition by now and that I could ask him some questions. There are a few little mysteries I would like to have him clear up." His eyes darted in the direction of Bernice. "For example, the mystery of the missing papers. I'd really be interested to know what they concerned. Of course, if Mr. Harcourt feels too ill to tell me, the young lady here might be able to help. I understand that you're privy to all his business transactions, Miss Woodring. Is that so?"

It was the first time that Bernice had ever received one of this man's direct shafts, and she literally winced.

"I'm afraid," she said, "that anything that concerns Mr. Harcourt's private affairs is quite confidential. If he is agreeable to my telling you something, of course—"

"Nothing is confidential after someone has been murdered." The inspector's voice was so deep that it seemed to come from his feet. He smiled that lipless, froglike smile. "That is, it seems, one of the most difficult things for people to understand. Once murder has been done, there are no more secrets."

Bernice flushed and adjusted her glasses on the bridge of her long nose. "That's all very well for you to say," she said pentulantly, "but I'm his secretary. Besides, I don't know anything about any lost papers."

"Strange." The inspector beamed at her benevolently. "That's directly contradictory to what the young Mr. Harcourt tells me. Do you realize that, my dear? He and I just had a lovely long talk, and he told me that in his opinion you might very well have borrowed some of his father's things."

"He said that!" Bernice's voice was a croak. Greene, who had been trying to reestablish his poise by leaning against the mantelpiece, straightened and threw her a look of warning. But she did not see him. Her squinting eyes were trained on the squat black figure beside me.

"Oh, he said a good many things, my dear," the inspector said. "He was particularly interested in discussing your new friendship with Mr. Greene. A bit of jealousy, I imagine, but he didn't seem to be convinced that your loyalty was as absolute as it had been once. Your loyalty as far as the Harcourt family is concerned, of course."

"If you're implying that I stole anything from Mr. Harcourt's office the other morning—" Bernice began. Then, realizing what she had said, she turned to me, her hand covering her mouth. It was incredible to see how quickly the inspector had managed to get under her skin, to throw her off. Bernice was hard. Tough. She had had to be. But there were weak links in her armor, and he had found them instantly.

"See here, Inspector," Winton Greene said. His voice

was beautifully modulated again, and that impenetrable smile was fastened on his mouth. Only his eyes disclosed the extent of his hostility. But his purpose was clear. Obviously the collapse of Bernice, had made it necessary for him to salvage the situation. "I really think that there's nothing much to be gained from your repeating to any one of us what one of the others has said. You're upsetting Miss Woodring unnecessarily by implying that she is no longer performing her duties satisfactorily. I think, don't you, that her employer is the person who should inform her of that. Perhaps you don't realize it, but this family has been Miss Woodring's life for the past ten years. She's an extremely sensitive young woman, Inspector. I felt the obligation myself, a few minutes ago, to try to reassure her. As you saw."

The grin did not fade from the little man's face, but he said nothing. Bernice threw Winton Greene a startled look and opened her mouth to speak, but he spoke over her.

"Now, as for any papers which may or may not be missing, I hope that you don't mean to imply that there's been any—er, dishonesty within this group." He was gaining confidence as he spoke. Now he was that suave, controlled being that had first presented itself to me. "And there's another point," he said. "What we are all presumably concerned with is the murder of a young woman. The Harcourts did not know Iris. Neither did Miss Woodring. It is absolutely impossible that any of them should be directly concerned in any way with her death. As far as their private matters are concerned—such things as the loss of these papers you were mentioning—I think that this is a separate matter entirely."

"Separate from what?" The inspector's bulge-eyed expression indicated that he was very interested in what

Winton Greene was saying. His hands dug even deeper into his raincoat pockets, and he was no longer smiling.

"Separate from murder." Greene said smoothly.

"And what was the motive for murder, Mr. Greene?"

The tall man shrugged. "I thought that I made that clear to you this morning, Inspector. Iris called me here to tell me that Michael Kyd—her husband—was threatening her life. A short time later she was found dead. I think that it should be obvious that—"

"And what was the motive?" the inspector repeated.

Winton Greene smiled. "That's for you to discover, of course. But you must realize that we are all of us concerned only peripherally. If you want my opinion, I think that Kyd killed her because she had come to London against his wishes, and because she threatened his standing with Mrs. Harcourt here." His eyes fastened on me, and for a moment there was a flicker of viciousness there.

"But I understood that he had only met Mrs. Harcourt the day before his—his wife, as you refer to her, was killed?"

"That's quite so," Winton Greene said patiently.

"Mrs. Harcourt is a lovely woman," the little man beside me said, "but don't you think it's stretching our believability a bit to tell us that Mr. Kyd, in a single day, fell so violently in love with her that he was willing not only to kill his wife but mutilate her body as well?"

Winton Greene's smile faded. "You're deliberately trying to make what I'm saying sound absurd," he said.

"On the contrary, Mr. Greene," the inspector said. "I'm very interested in your opinions about the lines on which this investigation should be conducted. You feel, then, if I may summarize, that the murder of your unfortunate young friend—"

"Of Michael Kyd's wife!" Greene shot the words out like bullets.

"Ah, yes—that her murder had nothing to do with, let us say, the dig which you financed in Italy?"

I watched, fascinated, as Winton Greene's self-control began to crack for the second time.

"How could it have anything to do with that dig?" he demanded. "That's been over and done with for a year. Since the death of Van Harcourt."

"Another death. Yes." The inspector shook his round, thickly thatched head sadly. "Two young people dead."

"The one had nothing to do with the other," Greene protested. "Van died in a fire. It was a terrible accident."

Abruptly the little man beside me changed the subject. While Greene had been talking he had been humming under his breath, and now he began rocking back and forth on his toes like a contented child. "Did you know the young lady who died when you were in Italy?" he asked casually.

Winton Greene's eyes narrowed. "What has that got to do with anything?" he demanded.

"I know that it's difficult for you to go along with my little idiosyncracies," the inspector said, "but I really must insist that you answer the question."

Bernice gave a little sigh and sat down abruptly on one of the Queen Anne chairs. Her bespectacled eyes had not left Winton Greene's face since he had begun to talk. I was aware of movement behind me, and turning, saw that the policeman who had been taking notes when I had been interviewed in the drawing room was still on hand, writing swiftly in a notebook. I wondered whether Winton Greene was fully aware that what he was saying was being transcribed, and whether it was purely accidental that the inspector had positioned himself in such a way as to block an easy view of the man.

"I knew her there. Certainly. I knew a great many Americans in Rome. She was an actress. Unfortunately, a part she had been promised had fallen through, and she was temporarily stranded. I was able to give her some assistance from time to time—professional contacts, that sort of thing."

Greene was more relaxed again. He took a package of ciarettes from his pocket.

"And her name?"

"Before her marriage?" Greene smiled as though he had made an important point. I began to wonder if he were as clever as I had thought him.

"Before her marriage." The inspector's froglike face wore an expression of unutterable patience.

"Iris Maddock."

"And I suppose that since the dig was the reason for your being in Italy at the time—" the inspector began.

"I have many business interests," Winton Greene said, with the air of one having succussfully avoided a trap.

"I'm sure you have," the little man beside me said benevolently. I was suddenly aware of the stiffness of my body, and realized that I had been standing motionless for a long time, much as though I were witnessing an absorbing drama on a stage. Except that I was part of the cast. I should not forget that.

"However," the inspector went on, "the point I was making was that Miss Maddock presumably heard you talking about the dig. She might, perhaps, even have gone to the site."

"That was where she met Michael Kyd," Winton Greene said triumphantly. "But you can forget trying to make any link between her and the dig. She knew nothing about archaeology and cared less."

"But she did know something about money." The inspector's voice was so low that I scarcely heard him. However, Winton Greene heard. He crossed the room and ground out his half-smoked cigarette in the silver ashtry beside my embroidery.

"What is that supposed to mean?" he demanded.

"About the dig," the inspector said, beginning to teeter on his toes again, shifting his bulk ponderously. "Were there any important finds?"

Winton Greene assumed a bland expression. "No," he said, "there were not."

"None?"

I held my breath. Would Greene fall so easily into a trap?

"There was a fibula," he said, shrugging. "Something that Van found interesting. But otherwise, nothing."

"A fibula?"

Was the little man pretending ignorance? I turned to look down at him and saw his face puckered in thick creases.

"An Etruscan clasp. They're quite common, really. I imagine that Mr. Harcourt has a large number of them in his collection. Perhaps you should ask him to show you one."

It was a deliberate attempt at condescension, but the inspector was impervious to insult. Obviously this was one of his strongest advantages.

"But you say that this lady's husband found it interesting?" He did not look at me. It was obvious that no one was to interrupt this dialogue. "Does that mean that his father would have been interested, too?"

Winton Greene paused before answering. He was tense now. He was too clever to think that he had been led all this conversational way for nothing.

"Perhaps," he said. "I really couldn't tell you."

"You were not acquainted with the elder Mr. Har

court? I would have thought that professionally— But I'm forgetting, of course, that you are not an archaeologist, are you, Mr. Greene? Do I understand correctly that you financed this Italian venture purely as a matter of business?"

"There's nothing to be made from that sort of thing," Winton Greene said harshly. I felt the skin at the nape of my neck begin to tingle.

"I thought you were a businessman, Mr. Greene," the inspector said softly.

"I was interested in her husband's theory," Greene snapped, and then broke off the words with his teeth.

"Theory?" I could scarcely hear the inspector again. Although his voice was thick and gutteral, he used it as though it were a musical instrument—for effect.

"It's rather complicated," Winton Greene said quickly. "Something about independent Etruscan artistic development."

"And would the fibula have proved the point he was trying to make?"

"No!" Bernice blurted out the word. "The only so-called expert to look at it was Michael Kyd. He told Van what he wanted to hear. Besides, it's gone. It was melted down in the fire. I know all about this. Mr. Harcourt—"

"Shut up!" Winton Greene muttered.

"No, on the contrary. This is very interesting." The inspector looked up at me. "You remember," he said proudly, as though his pupils had performed well, "what I said about the jigsaw puzzle? The pieces fit. In the end, they all fit. So Mr. Harcourt was interested in his son's dig even though he apparently did very little to assist him?"

"Van had a crazy idea," Bernice shrilled. "Ask anyone who knows anything about Etruscan art. That was why Mr. Harcourt sent Anthony to Italy. To try to

keep Van from making a fool of himself professionally!"

Winton Greene did not speak again, but the look he
threw Bernice made it all too clear what he wanted to say.

"Thank you, Miss Woodring!" the inspector crowed.
"I think you've put it very well. There was a certain bad
feeling between Mr. Harcourt and his son. Mr. Anthony Harcourt was well acquainted with Mr. Greene
here. A fibula which Mr. Van Harcourt considered to
be extremely valuable is missing. You yourself, Miss
Woodring, have strong feelings about the entire affair,
and apparently a considerable interest in Mr. Greene
personally, if what I observed when I came in this door
was any indication. Mr. Greene, a man of business,
backed a venture which ordinarily would reap him no
profit. You *do* see what I meant about a jigsaw puzzle,
don't you? Oh, yes, and one more thing. Mr. Greene
insists that all of this has nothing whatsoever to do with
the death of Iris Maddock."

No one spoke. Not even Winton Greene. The little
man in the black raincoat held the center of the stage.
Behind me the policeman scribbled frantically in his
notebook.

"One more thing," the inspector said conversationally. "Would you say, Mr. Greene, that you were a
good friend of Van Harcourt?"

"That's an absurd question," Winton Greene replied.
In some inexplicable way his poise was gone. He was
still the same man, his expensive suit still hung as
smoothly from his shoulders. He had reassumed his
pose with one arm on the mantelpiece. But one knew,
somehow, that his confidence was gone.

"Would you," the inspector continued blandly, "say
that you were an even better friend of Anthony Harcourt? I mean, were you sympathetic with him on the
subject of the value of the fibula?"

"I know nothing about archaeology," Winton Greene muttered.

"And yet you invested a sizable sum of money in the enterprise?"

"I suppose so, yes."

"And there were no regrets when you abandoned the dig?"

"It was pouring good money after bad, if you want the truth," Winton Greene said in a loud voice. "Van Harcourt sold me a bill of goods. When I found out that other eminent Etruscan experts discredited what he was trying to do—"

"Other eminent archaeologists like his father?"

"Yes." Now it was Winton Greene's turn to speak in such a low voice that I could scarcely hear.

"And in gratitude to him for putting you 'straight,' as I believe you Americans say, you made a point of coming to see him when you came to London. When was the first time that you saw the elder Mr. Harcourt, Mr. Greene?"

"Last night."

"At what time?"

"I'm not certain. At about one, I suppose."

"A rather unusual time to pay a visit. But let that pass." The inspector was not smiling now. It was obvious that he was about to make his final point. "And you met Miss Woodring here, when?"

Greene glanced at Bernice as though willing her to keep quiet. "About a week ago," he said. "When I first came to London. At a party."

"You imply that it was an accidental encounter?"

"It was a party at his hotel suite," Bernice said. Her face was very white, and behind her glasses her eyes were wide with something like horror. "He invited me and Anthony. Both of us."

"And not the elder Mr. Harcourt?"

"No!" Bernice rose. "I don't know why it matters. I don't know—"

"Did the elder Mr. Harcourt know that you had met Mr. Greene? Did you tell him about the party?"

"I can't remember. You're making it sound like something it wasn't."

"Perhaps Mr. Harcourt's memory will be better on that point," the inspector said, suddenly turning toward the door. The policeman moved rapidly out of the way as though he expected his superior to break into a run, stumbled, and dropped both pencil and notebook. Behind him Anthony appeared, his dark face grim.

"No one is going to talk to my father until he's seen a doctor," he said. "I've been with him. All of this upset has been too much. He's a sick man. I think he may have had a heart attack." Short as he was, he was taller than the inspector. His eyes challenged him. "I'm calling the doctor," he said.

"The family doctor, I assume," the inspector said thoughtfully. "A loyal friend. To speak absolutely frankly, Mr. Harcourt, there is a bit too much loyalty around here to suit me. I'm afraid that I'll have to insist that a police doctor be in attendance as well. Because, although I hate to disagree with such an able businessman as Mr. Greene, I'm afraid that this affair is not as simple as it seems. In fact, I think that it is a very tangled web indeed. As far as I can see, it's perfectly possible that nearly everyone in this room might have had a reason for wanting Iris Maddock dead. And I might add to the list Mr. Michael Kyd, who seems to have decided not to put in an appearance here after all."

He turned to me. "In fact," he said, "you might be interested, Mrs. Harcourt, in knowing that Mr. Kyd was intercepted just now at Heathow Airport. He was, apparently, trying to leave the country."

Chapter Eight

SOMEONE LAUGHED. I think that it was Winton Greene, but for the moment I was nearly oblivious of the others. It had to be a mistake. Michael would never try to leave the country. Only a guilty man would try to leave like that—with no warning. And he was not guilty. *He was not guilty!*

The inspector was still staring at me. Smiling. But I knew now how much his smiles meant. I had seen what he had done to Winton Greene. To Bernice. He would be perfectly willing to do that to me as well, if he thought that in so doing he could find out something that would help him solve this case. That was all he cared about. This case. His own reputation. The violence of my reaction against him was absurd, but I was in no mood to be reasonable.

"I don't believe you," I said. My lips were numb. "It's a lie."

"I assure you that it is not a lie, Mrs. Harcourt," the inspector said happily. "He was reported as having tried to a buy a ticket to Milan. The airport was given a list of names, you see. We try to be very thorough. Your name was on that list. So were all of your names."

He turned theatrically, waving his short arms at the group of people around him. The policeman in attendance still wrote steadily. Bernice was standing beside the sofa, peering at us in her usual myopic way. Winton Greene was wearing a satisfied expression, as though an opinion had been vindicated. And Anthony was smiling.

"Where is Michael now?" I demanded.

The inspector shrugged his thick shoulders. "Unfortunately," he told me, "we are not certain. He, shall I say, eluded his pursuers. That sometimes happens, you know. We do not make a great point of it, naturally, but it sometimes happens."

I felt a wave of relief. The one thing that I could not bear at this point was to be completely out of touch with Michael. His guilt or lack of guilt was, strangely enough, of secondary importance. Because I was willing to accept the possibility now that he might be guilty. Why else would he have tried to fly to Milan? He had told me that he would come here. Had he, then, deliberately lied? Had I been made to play the fool? I swept my hair back out of my eyes with one hand. That didn't matter. The important thing was that I see him.

They were all watching me. And then, suddenly, I heard the door of the office open and Mr. Harcourt appeared in the doorway of the sitting room. His face was gray. Ashen. Even his arrogance seemed to have deserted him. I had never liked him, but it was a shock now to see him looking so totally exhausted. With his appearance, the little group of which I was a part, shattered. Anthony, muttering something under his breath, went to the telephone. Bernice went to stand beside the old man. I heard her urge him to go back into his office and sit down.

"The doctor is coming," I heard her say. And I vaguely realized that I had never heard that much gentleness in her voice. Winton Greene was talking to the inspector, saying something to the effect that it was intolerable that Mr. Harcourt be put through this. As for me, I was not concerned with any of them—not even Van's father. Slowly I turned and hurried up the stairs, glancing back over my shoulder to make certain that no one noticed. Then, without stopping at my room, I ran down the back stairway. This time the door was unlocked. I had made my escape. Escape! I breathed deeply of the rain-chilled air as I ran through the alley between the house and the stables, bending down as I came level, for a brief moment, with the window that opened into Mr. Harcourt's office.

There was no question in my mind as to where I should go. Michael would either return to the country-house hotel, not two miles away, or he would not. If he was guilty, he would not. I kept saying that over and over to myself as I ran down the footpath, like a child reciting a charm. If he was innocent ... If he was innocent ...

The old woman who greeted me in the gloomy, oak-paneled hall stared at me curiously, but gave me the number of his room. He was there. I ran up the stairs and pushed open the door and found him sitting on the side of the bed, staring at some papers in his hands. The little room, which must once have been a dressing room, was thick with cigarette smoke.

"Why did you do it?" I demanded breathlessly.

"Do what?" He looked up at me, his eyes dull with weariness. His graying hair was touseled and his face seemed somehow to have thickened. But just the look of him made me feel the same way inside. Or was my heart only pounding because I had run so frantically up the stairs?

I closed the door and leaned against it. Eyes closed. Waiting. He would not lie to me about having tried to leave the country? He had no way of knowing that I would know. He could tell me anything he wanted to about his activities since I had left him. But let him tell the truth! God, let him tell the truth!

"You mean, why did I go to the airport?" He laughed shortly. "How did you know about that? I suppose the inspector got a call from one of his men. All right. I admit that was a stupid thing to do. But I was desperate."

"Desperate?" I opened my eyes and stared at him.

"Desperate to get back there and talk to the executor of the Paduolo estate. I've got to find out who the man was who acted for Paduolo last year when he came to us with an offer for the fibula. He's the key to this thing, don't you realize that? Whoever he dealt with—whoever he paid the quarter of a million pounds to—must be the murderer."

It seemed, suddenly, as though the last few days had been nothing more than a continuing alternation between fear and relief. I wanted to break into laughter, but I was afraid that if I began I would never stop. He had not tried to leave because he was guilty, then. I should have known that there had to be another answer.

"I was a fool not to have thought of trying to find out who the agent that came to Van was," Michael said. It was as though he were talking to himself. "I should have done that as soon as I talked to the executor. When I first found out that the fibula was still in existence." He shrugged. "I guess it was because I didn't realize the seriousness of all of this. Theft is one thing. But murder . . ."

"But you believed that Van was murdered," I protested. "You told me that the first night."

"I know." Still he did not look at me. The rain dashed against the windows. It was cold in this little, sparsely furnished room. Cold and damp and unlived in. I hated it. Hated the thought that for the present it was the only place that we could feel safe. Not even here, perhaps. I had no way of knowing that the inspector had not had me followed. I crossed the room. Went to the window and stared down at the street. A man walked along the road. A black umbrella bobbed. Why hadn't Michael answered me?

"I'm not certain," he said slowly, "whether I really believed that Van had been deliberately killed. I thought that someone had set the fire. Yes. I thought that someone wanted it to appear that the fibula had been destroyed. And the effect had been the same. He died. It was murder. But perhaps not deliberate. Then, when Iris was killed, anything became possible. Do you understand what I'm trying to say?"

I watched him rub his forehead with one hand, as though thinking exhausted him. I knew that in a subtle way he was asking for my help. He wanted to reason this thing out. And it helped to talk. But I must ask the right questions.

"When you talked to the executor of the Paduolo estate before you came here," I said, "didn't you question him about how Paduolo came by the fibula?"

"Yes." He took out a cigarette and lit it. "I did, but he claimed not to know, and I didn't press. Obviously he wasn't aware that the purchase had been illigitimate."

"But you knew. Why didn't you go to the police?"

"The Italian police?" Michael laughed. "Foreigners who imply that men as wealthy and important as Paduolo have been guilty of crimes are given short shrift. I wanted to be sure of my facts. I've made a pretty mess of everything, haven't I, Mandy? I came over here so damned cocksure. . . ."

He butted out the cigarette in the already full ashtray on the table beside the bed and rose heavily. I was still standing by the window. The light was dim. Rain-reflected.

"I feel most sorry about involving you in all of this," he said in a low voice. "I think you ought to leave me to take care of this in the best way I can. Someone is obviously willing to kill to protect himself. I don't want you in danger."

"No."

"No, what?"

"No, I won't leave you."

"Why?"

I did not answer. In the road a passing car's tires screamed.

"All right." He took a deep breath. "Then what do you think that I should do? Go to the police? Let them take over?"

"They've taken over," I said gently. And then I told him about the inspector. About the way he stripped people bare of pretense. About the way he manipulated them. About his cleverness and total unscrupulousness.

"And who does he think is guilty?" Michael said when I had finished.

"I don't know," I told him. "I honestly think that he hasn't made up his mind. I mean, I don't think that he formed an opinion in advance and then tried to twist the facts—twist people—to prove it."

"But if enough evidence presents itself against one of these people, he'll have to make an arrest."

"I suppose he will," I said.

"And if I go to him, it will be a gamble. There's enough supposed evidence against me now to satisfy a good many courts of law. You know that, don't you?"

"I'm not trying to tell you what to do," I countered. "You have to make that decision."

"There's another thing." Suddenly his voice was crisp. Businesslike. "Until this morning I assumed that I knew the answer to all the questions. Greene had manipulated the deal with the fibula. Sold it to Paduolo for a quarter of a million and no one the wiser. Then Paduolo dies, and by a stroke of bad luck I'm called in as an expert to evaluate the very fibula which I had been led to think had been destroyed. Greene hears about it, and knows that I may very well make trouble. He has an eye kept on me. I make plans to come to London. He comes to London. He guesses that I'll go to Harcourt *père,* so he arranges to discredit me. Brings Iris here. Provides her with a fake marriage license. This is an important thing to him. If the truth about the fibula gets out, not only has a serious theft been committed, but there's the question of Van's death. A man like Greene likes to keep his hands clean. He'd take every precaution. Hence the license. But I've got that license. He gave it to me that night at his hotel. A copy, at least. That was part of his threat. I didn't really examine it until today. It was a fake and that was that. But I did look finally. Just a few minutes before you came in here. And it was dated a year ago last April. Before we found the fibula. Before your husband died."

I stared at him, puzzled. Crossing the room, he came to stand beside me at the window. Our arms touched, and then our hands. My mind grappled with the problem, but my body relaxed. Side by side we stared down onto the rain-drenched lawn.

"There are a lot of holes in my precious theory, Mandy," Michael went on in a low voice. "The police didn't tell me anything when I talked to them. It wasn't that inspector of yours who interviewed me. Although at one point a little man wearing a black raincoat came in and listened for a while. A little man with a face like a frog."

"That's him." Our hands tightened. I glanced at him and saw that for a moment he was smiling.

"The point is," Michael went on, "that although the police didn't tell me anything, the newspapers did. I bought one on the way to the airport this afternoon. They say that Iris had been dead about two hours when the police doctor arrived at a little after four in the morning. That would mean that Greene couldn't have done it. From what you told me, he was with you and Anthony and Mr. Harcourt for some time when you got back to Grove House at two-thirty."

I hated the desperation in his voice. I didn't want it to be like this with us. I wanted us to laugh together. I hated Iris for having been killed. Hated the rain. Hated Kew.

"I only talked to him for about a half hour before the phone call came," I said wearily. "But you're right. He'd been there longer. For well over an hour. All of them made a point of that when I came in."

"All of them?" Michael's hand was pressing mine so tightly now that a streak of pain ran up my wrist.

"Someone said that he'd been waiting for a long time. That he called to see if I'd returned home all right, shortly after you and I left his suite. He came over there directly on hearing that I hadn't returned. Someone made that clear, although I can't remember whether it was Mr. Harcourt or Anthony."

"Or Greene himself?" Michael's voice was low-pitched. Calculating. His eyes were fastened on the window. And suddenly he stiffened. Dropped my hand. Pointed. Following the line of his finger, I saw Bernice below, standing in the shelter of a gnarled oak tree, her hands dug deep in her raincoat pockets and her long hair plastered close to her narrow head with rain. And she was looking directly up at the window in which Michael and I were standing together.

174

"She knows we're here," Michael said, dropping my hand. "Well, that's one solution ready provided, then. I might as well go to the police now."

"No." I turned to him. His face was pale. Drawn. I had never felt so close to him. "She may know that I'm here," I said. "She may have followed me. She must have done. But she doesn't necessarily know that you—"

"She was looking directly at this window," Michael argued. We had both stepped back into the center of the room, but I knew that he, like me, felt as though she were still staring at us.

"She's shortsighted," I argued. "She can scarcely see something ten feet away from her, even with her glasses on. I'm going down to talk to her. No, don't try to stop me. I know her. She's a foolish woman in many ways, but she's not completely irresponsible. I can make her see. . . ."

He was going to stop me. I darted past him and ran out of the room. Down the stairs, one hand brushing the wall. Through the dank, deserted hall and out into the rain.

She was still there. Still staring at the window. She did not even know that I was there until I touched her arm. She turned to me, and looking at her wet face I became aware that the rain was running down my own face like a torrent of tears.

"I saw you from the window," I said, pulling her back under the overhanging branches of the trees. "What do you want? Who told you to follow me?"

Now was the time for her to tell me that she had seen Michael, to say that she was going to call the police. I glanced up at the window and saw his outline dimly. Or what I thought was his outline. Even I could not be certain. The rain had brought an early dusk. If I could not see him with any certainty, how could she?

"You have to come with me," she said. Her eyes behind the thick glass did not meet mine directly.

"Who sent you?" It was not a question but a demand. If Bernice sensed any hesitation in my response, she would take advantage of it. But I had had proof before that when I chose to assert myself I was the stronger personality.

"Anthony. You shouldn't have left us the way you did, Mandy." Her voice was petulant. "You're needed back there at Grove House. Poor Mr. Harcourt—"

"Van's father will be well taken care of," I said crisply. "Why did Anthony send you?"

"He has to see you. There are some things he has to talk to you about."

"I can't imagine what they would be," I snapped. "Why didn't he come after me himself?"

"Because he couldn't get away when you left," Bernice said, taking my arm. Her fingers were like claws. "You know what it was like just then. Mr. Harcourt ill, and everyone upset. So Anthony told me to—to keep an eye on you. To go after you and tell you that he had to see you."

I shook her hand away. "I thought," I said deliberately, "that you were taking orders from Winton Greene now."

She flushed, and her mouth twisted in an ugly line. "That's not fair," she said in a shrill voice. "Mr. Greene's been kind to me. He saw that I was upset this afternoon and tried to comfort me. And then everyone tried to make something out of it that wasn't there. That terrible man from the police. . . ."

She controlled herself with an effort. "You've got to talk to Anthony," she went on. "If you won't come—if you won't come, I'll tell the inspector that you went to see Michael Kyd this afternoon—that's he's in this hotel."

The virulence in her voice surprised me. I had seen her as a bitter, overly sensitive woman. But I had not thought she had the capacity to hate. And yet her voice had just given her away in a way those vague myopic eyes could never do. She hated me. Nothing would give her more pleasure than to place Michael in jeopardy. Because she hated me.

"I'll see him," I said. "But not at Grove House. I don't want to go back there now. I don't want to see his father. I—"

"Anthony thought you might say that," she replied sharply. "He'll meet us in the stables. We can be alone there. You know that Mr. Harcourt never goes out there to work with those statues when it's damp. Come along. Anthony said he'd leave the house as soon as the doctor came to attend to his father."

I followed her. I had no choice. Neither of us spoke as we made our way to the foot of the hill and then turned onto the footpath through the rain-drenched meadow. One day, I promised myself, I would leave this place. One day I would leave and never again walk through these iron gates. One day I would look for the last time at this ghostly, gray-turreted house looming above me, this house that had been my prison.

Bernice seemed as eager as I to be certain that no one saw us approach the stables. We did not stay on the gravel drive, but zigzagged across the lawn under the dripping poplar trees until we reached the door at the side of the converted stables farthest from the house. Bernice tried the door, and gave a sigh of relief when it opened.

"He's here," I heard her mutter to herself. "Anthony's here."

We stepped into a dark gray world lit only by thin rays of pale light which managed to force their way through dirt-stained windows at the further end of the long, crowded room. The first impression was that this place was full of motionless people, but as my eyes accustomed themselves to the gloom the nightmare quality faded, and I saw that I was facing, not a silent crowd of people, but at least fifty Etruscan statues, their blank, slanted eyes staring indefinitely into time. Slowly I began to breathe again. I had always hated these things, because they were static and colorless and grotesque in their awkwardness. I wanted to rush in among them and fling out my arms right and left, knocking them to the floor.

"Where's Anthony?" I demanded.

"I don't know." Bernice's voice trembled. "The door was unlocked. He should be here." Her voice rose. "He said that he'd be here. Anthony! *Anthony!*"

Her voice reverberated in fifty pairs of stone ears. Fifty pairs of blank eyes stared at her enigmatically.

The flesh on my back began to crawl. I hated it here. It was absurd for him to have made this a place to meet. We could have talked at any cafe in Kew over tea if he wanted to talk to me. If Bernice was not lying. Suddenly, for no reason, I remembered that earlier I had seen her in Winton Greene's arms.

"Obviously he isn't here," I said briskly. "That being the case, how do you explain the unlocked door?"

Bernice was standing very close to the door, her hand still on the knob as though at any moment she expected to flee. "I don't know," she muttered. "Unless we forgot to lock it the last time we were here."

"We?"

"Anthony and I." Her glasses glittered briefly in the thick gray light as she turned her head away from me. "We came here to check the inventory before Mr. Harcourt started work. That's customary, you know. Part of my job."

"You have a fascinating job," I said in a low voice.

"There doesn't seem to be any end to what you're expected to do."

I was baiting her, as the inspector had baited us all earlier. I was willing to spend a few more minutes here if she would talk to me. Because I guessed that Bernice knew more than she thought she knew. If I could get the truth out of her, Michael and I would be better able to gauge what had really happened. Whether Anthony came or not, I should do that. But I had always hated this place, peopled with men and women of stone. I groped for the light switch, flicked it, and found that nothing happened.

"It must have burned out," I heard Bernice murmur. "It worked when Anthony and I were here."

"What does he want to talk to me about?" I said casually.

Bernice backed even closer to the door, as though my questions somehow frightened her. She was uneasy here. Perhaps it was the statues crowding about us. Perhaps it was something else. "I don't know," she said. "You'll have to ask him that yourself. But it's important."

I moved a way into the room, although it took an act of will to force myself among those hulking objects. I found myself close to a warrior, his sharp-nosed face turned in profile, his body twisted into an impossible pose. I did not like Bernice's insistence on staying close to the door. It was quite possible that were I to decide to leave she would keep me from it. I could force myself to stay here, but if I thought that there was no way out I knew that I would feel terror. The important thing, then, was to keep her talking in the hope that she might tell me something that I wanted to know, and at the same time urge her, by my own movement about the room, to follow me.

"Don't expect me to believe that you don't know

everything that's going on," I said lightly. "You always do. Anthony and his father depend on you. You're the only person with whom they would be perfectly frank."

She responded obliquely to flattery. I could not see her face distinctly, but her voice was petulant. "It's odd that you should say that," she said, "considering that not too long ago you accused me of stealing papers from Mr. Harcourt."

"Did you?" I moved back two steps, wedging myself between two statues. The stone was cold against my hands. Cold and dead.

"What did you say?" Bernice moved toward me, separating herself from the door by a few feet.

"Did you?" I demanded in a louder voice. "Did you take anything from him?"

"I did not." Her tone was one of outrage. "I found the papers he was looking for for him today. Just before the inspector talked to me. They had simply been misplaced."

"I thought perhaps you might have taken something to Winton Greene for him to see," I said in a low voice. I could see her straining to hear me. "I didn't think that you stole anything. Not really. But you could have borrowed—"

"You're guessing," she shrilled. "You don't know anything about Greene."

"And you do?"

"I know that he's a reputable businessman."

I laughed. She had forgotten about the door now. Not only did she have to be able to hear me, apparently, but she had to see me as well. I wound my way around stiffly molded forms and she followed me. Once fingers touched me, and I nearly cried out. But it was only the hand of an Etruscan maiden. When I turned, her face was very close to me. Her smile was enigmatic.

"Odd," I said, "that given two men—Winton Greene

and Michael, two relative strangers—you would chose to believe the so-called businessman. You've had far more contact with people like Michael. Academics. Experts. That's what Mr. Harcourt is. Perhaps that's why you chose to believe Greene."

"It's Michael Kyd who's caused all the trouble about the fibula," Bernice blurted out. "He won't make it clear exactly where it is right now, will he? Not to us, he won't. We don't have anyone else's word except his that it's as significant as Van believed it is. I can't understand why you keep insisting—"

"So you know about the fibula," I said in a low voice.

Bernice's hand was at her mouth. I could see the glitter of a ring on her finger as she moved her hand back and forth as though she could rub the words away.

"I shouldn't talk about it," Bernice said. "If Anthony wants to say something, that's another matter."

"Why do you think Michael came to London?" I demanded.

I could sense that she was struggling with herself. She did not think that she should talk to me about this, but she felt strongly about Michael. She feared him. We were near the windows now, and through the grime a last streak of light illuminated her face. There were dirt stains on her cheeks where she had touched the statues with rain-dampened hands. I knew that I looked as bedraggled as she. What were we doing here, two wet, dirt-stained women roaming through a crowd of stone figures?

"He came to blackmail Mr. Harcourt," Bernice told me in a shrill voice. "That's obvious, isn't it? If I hadn't believed that do you think I would have agreed to call—"

She broke off in total confusion.

"Don't ask me any more questions!" she cried, her voice ricocheting off the stone figures until it seemed that each one of them echoed her. "I'm too tired to think straight. I don't know what to believe anymore."

She backed away from me and disappeared behind the figure of the cylindrical robed figure.

"You're trying to trick me!" Her voice rose straight upward out of the shadows. "I won't let you do that. When Anthony gets here you'll understand! Then you'll understand everything!"

There was a sound of running feet and then silence. I realized suddenly that I had let her get back to the door before me. And I knew, too, that I had been a fool to come here. Perhaps she would let the police know where Michael was. Or rather where he had been. By the time the police came, both he and I would be gone. That was what we should have done in the first place.

I started pushing my way back through the crowd of statues, aware of a nightmarish sensation that they were trying to hold me back. I could almost feel their stone fingers pulling at my coat. I pushed them aside and toppled one of them to the floor. It was too dark now to see, but I heard the splintering of stone. And then a cry of agony, as though a stone mouth had opened.

I had reached the door. But Bernice was not there. Had she left the room? But surely, if she had, I would have heard the door close. I pulled on the knob, twisted it with fingers damp with fear. And found it locked.

"Bernice!" I cried. "Bernice, where are you?"

There was no answer, but I was certain that I was not alone in that crowded room. Or had I simply become so aware of the massed statues, now only dim shapes in the dusk, that their presence was a living thing? I twisted the knob again with no result and felt panic rising in me.

"Bernice!" I cried.

Something moved! To my right! And then moved again, just to the right of a sharp stone profile which stood out against the little light from the window.

"Bernice!"

No answer. Why would she play this sort of game with me? To frighten me? To repay me for imagined hurts? Or was she insane? Had she lured me here for reasons of her own? What evidence did I have that Anthony actually wanted to see me? None. She had followed me. She had brought me here. She had claimed not to have the key. But she could have had it. Could have locked the door, unnoticed, before she followed me across the room. But then who had cried out? Or had I imagined that?

I was afraid now, my heart throbbing against my throat. I had to get away. I could break that dingy window. I did not want to go back into that mass of stone figures again. But I had to! I had to!

I did not give myself time to think. To anticipate. I pushed myself against them, and it seemed that I could feel their breath hot on my face. And then, halfway to the window, I slipped on something. Fell, striking my shoulder against a stone leg. For a moment the pain canceled out everything else. And then I became aware that my right hand was palm down in something warm. Something thick but liquid. A scream seemed to be locking my throat against itself. I could not breathe. I pulled my hand back toward me, and felt something else. A small, smooth-edged object. Scarcely aware of what I was doing, I traced its outline with my finger. Steel. And broken glass. Bernice's glasses. And then I knew that somewhere close beside me Bernice was lying dead.

Suddenly there was light. A tiny flicker of light. Someone had lit a match. I looked into the heart of the flame and then beyond it into Michael's eyes. Neither of us spoke. The flame died. I heard him strike another match.

"No," I heard myself say in a choking voice. "Not you, Michael! Not you!"

The flame flared again. This time his eyes slid past me, and I turned my head and saw Bernice. She was face down on the floor, and the back of her head was a crushed mass of blood and hair. And there was a pool of blood around her.

I gagged as the match went out again. Michael had done this, then? I pushed myself to my feet, slipping in the blood, clutching out for the support of one of the stone figures, groping my way behind one of them, feeling the folds of marble drapes under my wet fingers. And then the flicker of another match, making hooded shadows rise around me. I crouched down, and then, because my legs would not support me, dropped to the floor.

"Amanda!" Michael's voice was low but imperative. "Where are you?"

I wanted to answer him. I wanted everything to be the way it had been before he had killed Bernice. I did not want to feel this growing fear of him.

"My God!" I heard him say, "you don't think that I did this, do you?"

The light went out again and we were in total darkness. I heard him move. But I could do nothing. Silently, I bent double and buried my face in my hands.

"Amanda!" He was closer now. So close that if he struck another match he would see me. "I followed you and Bernice here," he whispered. "I was worried about you. I stood outside and heard you talking. The door was open and I slipped inside. I heard it all."

I pressed my fingers hard against my skull. Everything in me wanted to believe him. I had trusted him before, because I loved him. I had to trust him now. I might be wrong. He might kill me. But if he was the murderer, I would want to die.

"Do you believe me, Amanda?"

"Yes," I said in a loud, clear voice, raising my head from my hands. "I believe you."

His hand reached out for me, following the sound of my voice with his fingers. I felt him touch my cheek. My throat. And I was not afraid.

And then the darkness was split by the light of a powerful flashlight. It blinded me. I stared up into it, paralyzed by the blaze. Someone was holding it. I could see the faint outline of a man. It was not Michael. Michael was on his knees beside me, holding me.

"You always were a fool, Mandy," Anthony's voice said. "It's a pity that you didn't choose to believe that Kyd killed Bernice. Then he could have gone to prison for murdering her and Iris. And you would have been quite safe. As it is now, something will have to be done about both of you."

Michael's arms tightened about my shoulder. And I began to laugh. I threw back my head and laughed and knew I could not stop. I was weeping at the same time. Soon, I knew, I would begin to scream.

"Keep her quiet!" Anthony hissed at Michael. "If you don't, I'll have to take care of her here and now."

Beyond the light of the flashlight, I could see his right hand. His left hung at his side. There was a hammer in it. He raised it into the light threateningly, and I saw that the end of it was covered with blood and hair. I stopped laughing. The tears dried on my cheeks.

"Why did you do it, Harcourt?" I heard Michael say. "My God, why did you have to kill her?"

"Because she was a fool," Anthony said. His voice seemed to vibrate with its own tautness. I could not look at the light any longer. I closed my eyes. Pressed my face against Michael's shoulder.

"All women are fools," Anthony went on. "Iris, too. More of a fool than Bernice, because she tried to blackmail me. Bernice couldn't keep her mouth shut. But she will now."

He had to be mad. No sane person would talk this way. Mad or desperate. And we could do nothing. He must have been in this storeroom all along, hidden among the statues. He could not have heard Michael come in. He had crouched somewhere, listening to me and Bernice. And discovered, if he had not known it before, that he could not trust her. She had said something about making a call just before she had cried out. He must have struck her in the back of the head, at the moment when I had knocked the statue over. To keep her from saying more. But what call had she been talking about?

Michael was talking now, his voice moderate, reasonable. I did not need to listen to the words to know that he was trying to calm Anthony, to take him off guard. And at the same time I had a terrible awareness that he would not be able to do it. That Anthony would beat us both to death.

"I think," Michael was saying "you must be wrong about Iris trying to blackmail you. Don't forget, I knew her, too. She quite literally wasn't interested in anything except acting. I can't believe—"

My head was pressed against Michael's chest, and I realized that although he sounded calm and even argumentative, his heart was pounding as hard as mine. What in God's name was he trying to do? Why risk making Anthony even wilder than he was by arguing with him?

"Shut up!" Anthony rasped. I opened my eyes and saw that he had come a step closer. The hammer was clearly visible now. I was thankful for the blazing light of the flashlight only because it prevented me from seeing his face.

"You don't know anything about Iris," he went on scornfully. "I tell you that she was blackmailing me. Who do you think was the middleman in the sale of that fibula?"

"You don't mean that she—"

"It wasn't her idea," Anthony shouted. "She didn't have the brains for that. She did what I told her to do. Because she understood what a quarter of a million pounds meant. She wanted her share."

"Are you trying to tell me that she acted for Winton Greene in that transaction?" Michael said. His voice was almost casual, but his arm tightened around my shoulder.

"Greene!" Anthony spat out the words. The flashlight wavered, and for a moment I saw his eyes. I turned my face and buried it again in Michael's sweater. I did not want to see madness face to face.

"Greene didn't have anything to do with it!" Anthony went on. "It was my idea. All my father wanted was for me to find out what was happening and report to him. That's all I've ever been to him—an errand boy. Oh, he took Van seriously enough. But I was supposed to be a bloody errand boy!"

He laughed. The sound made me want to block my ears. "Van was naive in some ways, but he may have guessed I was after something because he sent some of his record books back here. Didn't he, Mandy? He should have known you'd hand them over to father if he asked for them. So the old man got his hands on some of Van's data by himself. No need of me. But I fooled him," he said. "I fooled all of you. It wasn't hard to get my hands on that fibula."

"You set that fire?" Michael's voice was low.

"Yes, damn you, I set the fire. But I didn't expect Van to die in it. I was in his room with him when it started. You didn't know that, did you? None of you knew that! I soaked a few rags in oil and set the fire in the kitchen. And then I went into his bedroom and told him that I smelled smoke. He left the fibula behind him on the table when he went to try to put it out."

"And you took it and went out and left him?"

"I didn't think he'd let himself be trapped in there!" Anthony shouted. "If you're trying to insinuate that I deliberately killed him, you're wrong. It wasn't my fault that he died. Do you hear! It wasn't my fault!"

I forced myself to look up at him. He was standing almost directly over us now. The glare of the flashlight threw the face above into grotesque relief. The hammer was raised. Why didn't Michael do something? We couldn't just let him kill us. And he meant to kill us!

"I got the money," I heard Anthony say in a low voice, as though he were talking to himself. "I got the money. I didn't spend any of it. Gave Iris her cut. Gave her enough to be satisfied with. Everything would have been all right if Paduolo hadn't died. Iris read about it in one of the Milan papers and let me know."

"She couldn't have known that I had been called in to evaluate it," Michael said.

"She didn't. All the little fool knew was that she could make a little more money. She said that Greene was bringing her to London and that she was going to contact my father unless I came up with five thousand pounds for her. Five thousand pounds! Even the money wasn't as important as the fact that she thought she could make a fool of me!"

"What about Greene?" Michael shot the question out, and I realized that he was aware of the urgency of keeping Anthony talking. At the moment Anthony was willing to brag about his ingenuity, albeit in a desperate voice. But when the talking stopped, the hammer would descend. Michael was a strong man. Larger than Anthony. But he was at a great disadvantage, situated as he was on the floor. I knew that I should move away from him. Give him, at least, the freedom of both his arms. But I was afraid to move, afraid that any change might precipitate Anthony into what he so obviously meant to do. He was mad. Guilty of two murders. Guilty of theft. We had known too much about everything to be let off, even before he began to talk. He had nothing to lose by killing us. With any luck he could blame everything on Greene. Or could he? I did not know where Greene was now. Perhaps he was with the inspector at Grove House still. But all that did not matter. Anthony had a great deal of money hidden away. And he was clever in his madness. Perhaps he could elude the police. Whatever happened he would be better off with Michael and me dead. And it was clear that he did not mean to answer many more questions. When Michael had asked him about Greene, he had not answered. My face was still pressed against Michael. I could see nothing, but I could hear a deadly silence.

"He's a fool!" I heard Anthony hiss. "That slut Iris convinced him that he could edge in on the deal. Oh, she didn't tell him about me. But he knows that the fibula has turned up. He came here to discredit you. That was why he faked the marriage license. He was going to ask my father for money to keep the fibula out of sight. Iris put him up to that. She thought she could play both ends against the middle. But I took care of that. Just as I'm going to take care of you."

189

I knew in that moment that he was about to strike. And I knew that I could not let Michael bear the burden of his attention. He would kill Michael first. But if I could only distract him. . . .

I threw myself away from where I was sitting and forced myself to my feet. My legs and skirt were wet with Bernice's blood. I heard Michael call out a warning and saw Anthony turn toward me, his arm raised. The light of the flashlight searched for me and found me.

"I won't say anything to the police, Anthony," I gasped. "Believe me. I know that you had to do what you did. I've known since this morning. Bernice told me that she destroyed those papers of your father's— the reports that you sent back to him from the dig. She didn't know why you wanted them, but I guessed from the start. I saw you and her that day in your father's office. She'd seen Greene. Talked to him privately, hadn't she? You didn't trust her anymore. You couldn't trust anyone. You had to make sure that there was nothing in those letters that would mean something to the police if they looked at them. You told her to get Van's letters away from me, too, didn't you? But she failed. She was always failing, wasn't she? Even when she agreed to call Greene at the house last night and pretend to be Iris, so that no one would realize that Iris had been killed when you were presumably out hunting for me. When Bernice called, Iris was already dead, wasn't she? And Bernice couldn't even keep it a secret that she was the woman who called. She started to tell me that. That's why you killed her. But I'm not Bernice, Anthony. I can keep secrets. I could have told the inspector all I knew about you today. But I didn't, did I? Can't you guess why I protected you, Anthony? I've—I've always been attracted to you. I pretended not to be because of Van. Even after he was dead it didn't seem right. But I was a fool to hide the way I feel, Anthony. You and I can take the money and go away. We can—"

For a moment he hesitated, the hammer still raised.

"I mean it, Anthony," I said in a low voice, fear clutching at my throat.

"No! You're lying!"

He struck out, and I threw myself to one side, pressing desperately against one of the statues.

"You can't get away!" Again the hammer was raised. In the light of the lowered flashlight I saw his twisted face. Saw those terrible eyes.

"Michael won't go to the police if you and I leave now," I cried, begging for time. "Please, Anthony! Please!"

He struck out again. The hammer barely missed me and struck stone. He lost his balance then. And as he fell, Michael threw himself against him, pushing Anthony away from me. I heard the crack of his head as it struck the base of one of the statues. And I saw his body limp on the floor.

Michael was bending over him now. "He's unconscious," he said, turning toward me. "Are you all right, Mandy? For God's sake, are you all right?"

I felt his arms go around me, felt his lips against my hair. I knew that we would not be able to stay long like this. The door would have to be unlocked, and locked again. The police must be called. In a little while lights would burn away the shadows and men's voices would break the tomblike silence. But for one moment I wanted only to press myself against him and hear his voice whispering my name over and over again.

Other SIGNET Gothics You'll Enjoy

Big Bestsellers from SIGNET

- [ ] **THE SHINING** by Stephen King. (#E7872—$2.50)
- [ ] **CARRIE** by Stephen King. (#J7280—$1.95)
- [ ] **'SALEM'S LOT** by Stephen King. (#E8000—$2.25)
- [ ] **OAKHURST** by Walter Reed Johnson. (#J7874—$1.95)
- [ ] **FRENCH KISS** by Mark Logan. (#J7876—$1.95)
- [ ] **COMA** by Robin Cook. (#E7881—$2.50)
- [ ] **THE YEAR OF THE INTERN** by Robin Cook.
  (#E7674—$1.75)
- [ ] **SOHO SQUARE** by Clare Rayner. (#J7783—$1.95)
- [ ] **MISTRESS OF DARKNESS** by Christopher Nicole.
  (#J7782—$1.95)
- [ ] **CARIBEE** by Christopher Nicole. (#J7945—$1.95)
- [ ] **THE DEVIL'S OWN** by Christopher Nicole.
  (#J7256—$1.95)
- [ ] **CALDO LARGO** by Earl Thompson. (#E7737—$2.25)
- [ ] **TATTOO** by Earl Thompson. (#E8038—$2.50)
- [ ] **A GARDEN OF SAND** by Earl Thompson.
  (#E8039—$2.50)
- [ ] **DESIRES OF THY HEART** by Joan Carroll Cruz.
  (#J7738—$1.95)

THE NEW AMERICAN LIBRARY, INC.,
P.O. Box 999, Bergenfield, New Jersey 07621

Please send me the SIGNET BOOKS I have checked above. I am
enclosing $_____(check or money order—no currency
or C.O.D.'s). Please include the list price plus 35¢ a copy to cover
handling and mailing costs. (Prices and numbers are subject to
change without notice.)

Name_____

Address_____

City_____State_____Zip Code_____
Allow at least 4 weeks for delivery